Saving Eden

Book Three of the Eden's Court Saga

by

Michelle Picard

Dedication

SAVING EDEN is the culminating novel of my first published storyworld, and its launch has been a long time coming. I started writing the Eden series in 2005, before my youngest son was even a year old. Now, he's twelve. Life is amazing, although it also likes to smack you in the face once in a while.

I'm dedicating this book to Eli, Jacob, Jill, Peggy, and Jason. You all touched these pages in your own unique ways. Thank you.

Saving Eden
Michelle Picard

ISBN: 978-0-9987835-4-3

This book is a work of fiction. The names, characters, places and incidents are products of the writer's imagination or have been used fictitiously and are not to be construed as real. Any resemblance to persons, living or dead, actual events, locale or organizations is entirely coincidental.

Printed in the United States of America

www.michellepicard.com
michellepicardwrites@gmail.com

Table of Contents

Chapter One

Saving the world on a deadline messes with a gal's circadian rhythms. The voices outside my bedroom definitely didn't help.

"My lady."

Bang, bang, bang.

"My lady, let us in."

Noise. All that damn noise. Sleep. I need more sleep. "Go away," my groggy voice slurred out from amid my gigantic bed. I sunk down further into the quilt, back into the fog of my dream.

I dreamt of my necklace, the gold and silver, copper and pewter wires unraveling from their mesh and growing into gigantic twisting vertical snakes. Twining around one another like spiral staircases before untwisting and recombining again into long, endless ladders disappearing into the sky. Me trying to catch the ends as I climbed them like some diminutive Jack and the beanstalk, to wrangle them into place in a pattern I knew as well as I knew my own name.

The burning vibration of my anger stiffened my muscles as I strained. The angrier I got at my lack of progress, the more I slipped down the stalks of the metal, farther from my goal. I thought I'd conquered my temper since coming to Eden, but not in this dream.

Desperation hammered at my spine and sweat trickled down my back as I climbed. Endlessly.

In waking life, the necklace and I existed in an uneasy truce. I'd inherited it upon taking the throne of Eden's Court. The thing pulsed at my throat with enigmatic warnings in reaction to my thoughts as I navigated the crazy corridors of this place. It also channeled the intense pain that came from using my magic. Granted, the pain happened less often now, and, when it did, it supposedly grew my power. That didn't make it any more pleasant.

Yeah, the jewelry and I maintained a love-hate relationship ever since I'd inherited it three months ago, though I'd never dreamed about it before. Never fought snaking ladders up into the unseeable ether.

"Rachel, wake up," an insistent male commanded again, barking the order. Loud. Scaring away the snakes and jerking me fully awake into the reality of my dimly lit palatial bedroom. Only seconds must have passed, although as is the way of dreams, it felt like hours.

My hand shot to my neck to feel the mesh of the necklace in its usual place and shape. I never took it off. The memory of the pattern I struggled to create in the dream slipped away into nothingness, like the last bit of morning mist upon a lake, dissolving as the sun burned into fiery life.

I rubbed sleep from my eyes, stared over at the empty space next to me on the mattress and sighed out against the heavy feeling in my chest. I fought the same surprise and heartache each time I woke and rediscovered my former guardsman and lover Gabriel's absence. Universe, it was hard. No. This was his choice to make. I kept up that mantra each time my thoughts slipped sideways into plans to convince him to return.

The dark of predawn in the Garden of Eden squatted outside my window and I groaned at the hour. A quick glance to the corner confirmed the lack of the baku. A supernatural being from Japan, the baku tended to show up after every nightmare. He liked to munch on them to leave my day free of the frightening beasties lurking when I slept, the bad dreams a much too frequent occurrence. But this dream hadn't exactly been nightmarish, just... I pushed away the unsettled feeling the giant strands brewed and shoved aside my bedspread.

"Coming," I yelled, annoyed with the demanding racket as the banging continued on my door.

My half-brother, Christian, was out there. I recognized his voice along with the more polite tones of my guards, Tarn and Sebastian, faerie and shapeshifter respectively. The guys better have a damn good reason to disturb me this early. I got little sleep as it was. Though, with the way disaster after disaster haunted me since I took up the throne of Eden's Court, nothing surprised me anymore.

I belted on my white terry cloth robe over my sweats and tee, ever in defiance of my seneschal Morven's opinion that I dress the part of royalty. Tearing down the shields I erected nightly on my bedroom door, I sent a tendril of magic into the outer room ahead of me, checking. No threat there.

For Tarn and Sebastian to wake me when I knew they worried about my constant exhaustion, the situation had to be bad.

"The null has escaped," Christian said the moment I stepped into the outer room. "Her cell is empty except for the corpse of a demon and a bloodied knife."

"What?" My lungs squeezed tight and I rubbed my forehead hard against the immediate pain behind my temple. Way to start the day. "What in the hell was a demon doing in there and who brought a weapon into the containment area?"

Tarn opened his mouth to answer and I held him off with a gesture. "Strike that, just tell me if anyone's spotted her."

"No," Sebastian answered, looking grim.

"How long since she escaped?"

"I found the two guards outside her prison knocked unconscious," Christian said, jamming his fingers through his hair. "They came on shift about midnight. It's four now, about twenty minutes since I discovered them."

"What in the universe were you doing in there at this time in the morning?" My voice edged up into an irritated growl. I stopped myself. We didn't have time for this. Christian's bizarre reactions to our prisoner had left me perplexed for weeks. He was a vampire, and she was a vampire hunter. Or at least assisted them.

I continued before any chance for his reply. "Okay, where would she head?"

"The garden," Tarn said, gripping the hilt of his jeweled fae sword.

My face went cold. "Near the portal gates? No, she doesn't know about them. She was unconscious when we brought her through."

Christian blushed. "Actually... She knows."

I threw him my best scowl. "You told her. How much time are you spending with this woman?" I loved my vampire brother, usually the soul of gentlemanly calm and kindness, but recently he was getting under my skin.

Tarn turned to him. "Would she try one?"

"Pray to Lillith she doesn't," Christian replied.

I twisted my lips at the sour taste in my mouth. "Sorry, stopped that nasty habit a while back."

Lillith was the goddess responsible for creating Earth and everything on it. This included mortals and the Kesayim, the term for the seven magical races of angels, demons, faeries, vampires, dragons, shapeshifters, and witches, the whole crew of which I ostensibly led. Lillith did not inspire my prayer or devotion. This may have had to do with her constant threats against those I loved, the spells she'd cast over me which changed my personality from time to time into a cold-hearted psychopath, or her refusal to tell me how to save the world despite her insistence I do just that. Oh, yeah, the small details like an escaped null prisoner were nothing to the fact the world rested on the edge of oblivion.

Mortal humankind usually replenished the source of magic through the natural decay of their bodies after death. They supplied the raw material of the power. Unfortunately, current bodies didn't provide the force they used to, hence an imbalance because the Kesayim kept drawing heavily on the magic. I wasn't sure why the mortal bodies held less oomph, but it meant the planet had about four months left of life. Then, kaboom. Unless I found the solution first. And, shhhhhh, don't tell. Nobody was supposed to know all this. These were secrets laid on me by Lillith, with threats to destroy me and mine if I broke them. You'd think the goddess didn't really want the planet saved. Although to be fair, which I preferred not to be with our creator, her fellow alien species had placed tough restrictions on her that prevented much disclosure.

For the moment, though, I had the problem of the null and a dead demon.

"Rachel, if she tries to go through a portal to get home—"

My mouth went dry as an arid desert. "I know, Christian. She's a null. She'd cancel out the freaking magic and maybe collapse the whole damn thing." My stomach dropped. What happened when a portal gate collapsed? Nothing good.

I carried the title of Mother Heir, and as the ruler of the Kesayim, I embodied all of the powers of the seven magical species rolled into one complete package. You'd think that meant I'd rock any battle in front of me. It usually turned out to be more complicated.

Sebastian held out a pistol to me. More practical than a sword and my magic wouldn't work much at all around the woman we needed to hunt. I took the gun. Ever planning ahead, my shapeshifter guard. Maybe he'd taken it from Gabriel's store of weapons.

"Come on," he said. "Let's go."

We ran.

Chapter Two

I'd say we ran like the devil was at our heels, but that sounds too cliché and, besides, I knew Satan personally. The son-of-a-bitch was scary, but not someone I'd run from. It would bring him too much pleasure.

We hurried down the corridor of my private wing of Eden's Court and out into the garden. The vine-covered walls of the interior gave way to the rich, verdant multitude of life that was the center of all creation. Eden wasn't anywhere on twenty-first century mortal maps of Earth; more like a parallel realm snapped out of normal space, disconnected long ago by the goddess, Lillith, yet still attached somehow to the planet. Each of the home realms of the seven Kesayim people were attached similarly and accessible through portals.

Tarn threw up bright glowing fae balls of light around us to help us see under the night sky, and I copied his actions with a dozen of my own. My fae guardsman easily kept pace with his long legs and graceful stride. His braided, waist-length white-gold hair trailed after him with our speed.

Tiny nocturnal creatures scurried under our feet as we started our search, excited into movement by our passing. Tarn told me Morven, prim and proper and always on detail, had already called out the regular guards as part of her seneschal duties, placing them to the task of searching for the missing prisoner. The garden's size infinite, I doubted our ability to find this needle in the haystack. At least I did until receiving unexpected aid.

A dozen steps into the garden under the tepid glow of a crescent moon, Eden's strange sentience came to life. It twittered in my ear, gasping out words in its awful excitement. It pushed at my mind with the disturbing words I'd come to expect. *"Yes, find the gardener, feed us, gardener, feed us. Yes, she's the one. Quick, quick. Make haste."*

The words traveled up and down in scales, hundreds of tiny tinkling glasses clinking together to form the sounds, bouncing off my skin and drawing me forward. The voices led me, like a compass gyrating around inside my head, bobbing its needle between the halves of my brain.

It was then that I spotted it. I'd found her trail, marked by withered vegetation, her touch killing it as she fled.

"This way." I pointed down the rightmost path, a direction I rarely explored. I'd already found myself developing preferences on my visits: the merkaz, my throne room at the very center of the garden; the cactus-ringed pond, a location of considerable bloodshed in the past both inside and out of my dreams, as well as being the nearest landmark to the portal to Faerie; and the hilltop and grassy glade from where I'd spotted the unicorn. For the most part, I'd neglected this new direction. At least it was away from known portals.

"Hurry." The garden kept up its racket.

"Okay, okay, I'm going," I answered. My pulse started a sprinting race. The garden's urgency ate away at my stomach.

The guys sent me strange looks as they followed the jogging pace I set. Sebastian sped faster, forging ahead in the direction I pointed.

Christian jogged at my side, our speed diminished by the dampening of our magic, a sign we were on the right track. "How do you know which direction to go?" he asked.

"The garden told me. Plus, you see the browned plants? The null did that. Hurry."

He pulled up short. "It speaks to you?"

I slowed to answer. "Unfortunately. And too often. Keep going."

The Garden of Eden harbored a deep-seated death wish worrying about this null. But I was in no mood to care about its melodrama. Not with the threat of that woman on the loose sucking magic from my home. Her name was actually Leslie, but I preferred not thinking of her at all. Now, I had no choice.

The bitch had been part of the movement that hunted the vampires. And when we'd finally found the location of her group and infiltrated their headquarters, her mysterious ability to cancel out the magic of the Kesayim in her direct proximity meant more of my team died in that showdown. Including Colin, a witch I had started dating and, despite my misgivings about doing so, a sweet and lovely man.

"Rachel, over here," Sebastian called, his voice on edge.

Tarn and Christian sprinted toward his call. I tore my robe free of the brambles and ran like hell, farther into the wood that cropped up in the garden as the security crew sought the null prisoner responsible for the death of so many vampires.

My chest tightened a fierce squeeze as Colin's auburn hair and welcoming smile flashed through my memory. Guilt settled in next. *Not now, Rachel. Get off your self-pity trip. You aren't that important.*

"Hurt, she hurts. Help her. Help the gardener," the garden screeched in my ear, refusing to shut up.

Three male bodies crowded the base of a tree as I rushed into the clearing. Withered grass encircled the trunk, and a line of crumbling dead bark ran up the side of the gnarled oak.

Sebastian and Tarn grabbed onto Christian, holding my brother back from climbing the tree. He strained against their grip. "Let me go," Christian said.

Tarn's grip tightened. His fae face was beautiful, but with no glow of his usual magic. "You can't hurt her and we don't want you injured."

All of us were mortal weak near the null. The concept wasn't so strange to me as I'd lived almost all twenty-five of my years with none of the power my recent inheritance brought me as ruler of the supernatural world.

"I'm not going to hurt her," Christian growled. "She's the one hurt. She needs help."

"Get the fuck away from me, Christian." The woman's voice shook, bouncing down from the branch above.

She'd climbed about fifty feet to the first most solid branch available. The leaves were not plentiful around her perch, or maybe they'd fallen away with her magic death touch. I made out a pale glimpse of her gold hair in the pre-dawn air. The moon was our only light as the glow globes fizzled near her null power.

How much time was Christian spending around her cell to be on a first name basis with her? I moved close to the base of the oak.

Christian struggled again against my guardsmen's grip. "Get off me and guard my sister as you should."

I rested my fingers on Christian's forearm, feeling the tense muscle and tendon. "He won't climb the tree."

He turned at my words, imploring. "She needs help."

What was it I saw on his face? The last I knew he'd hated her guts. I nodded. "Let me speak to her."

Christian relaxed, shoulders dropping a hair.

I pitched my voice louder and tilted my head. "Leslie, come down and no one will hurt you."

"Liar," she called. "You're trying to kill me."

"No decision has been made about that. The council is considering options." And wasn't I a bitch saying this.

"Then why did someone come into my cell and stab me while I slept?"

What?! "When?"

"Earlier tonight."

"We found a dead demon in your cell."

"I don't know about that. I didn't kill him. He tried to kill me, but he was alive when I ran."

My blood froze and simultaneously boiled like mad. Just then, a drop of red fell through the evening air, landing on the exposed skin of my foot above the edge of the sandals I'd thrown on earlier.

She was hurt. "You need medical attention, Leslie. I won't hurt you and I will personally make sure you are unharmed by anyone else here in Eden."

"Why trust my executioners?"

In her place, I'd think the same.

"Because as tempting as it is for everyone to kill you, we want to understand you and your power more. We are about magic. You cancel out magic."

"So I trust you because you want me as a guinea pig?" Her disbelieving laugh made complete sense.

I paused. Brutal honesty or else I'd lose her. "Yes."

Her bitter exhale spat into the night air. "If I come down, then what?"

"I escort you to my quarters."

"What?" Sebastian said.

"No!" Tarn added.

All of these protests peppered the air as my guards reacted.

My palm rose. "Hey, supreme ruler speaking, guys. Shut it and let me finish." I refocused up the tree. "We get you healed and then assign you a single twenty-four-hour guard, plus additional guards. Get you your own quarters to isolate who can come and go. No more prison cell."

Silence. Maybe she was thinking it over. Her options were poor.

"Please, Leslie," Christian said. "You won't come to harm. I guarantee it."

Why was my brother acting this way? He hated the null with a passion. She'd caused the deaths of five hundred of his kind. Or maybe it was the lure mortals had on a vampire soul. She wasn't exactly mortal, but she was closer than any of the Kesayim.

The branch shifted, bobbing as she readjusted. "I can't," came her answer, muffled on a sob.

The garden moaned again. *"She comes,"* it sighed.

And with that briefest warning, the bushes behind us shifted and through them a different female walked. I stopped breathing for a long moment to take in her beauty.

The unicorn.

She'd returned.

Her sea foam coat lit the waning night with its glow. The black tipped spiral of her horn contrasted with the pearly opalescence of its base. The unicorn had become my personal touchstone -- my childhood dreams come true -- the force which had united Gabriel with me months ago when I first arrived.

The pain squeezed my heart as it always did. *Not now. Don't think about him now.*

The majestic creature came closer, her piercing robin blue eyes holding unknown wisdom. She blinked. I reached out a hand, unable to stop myself, and grasped her spiraled horn.

Gasps from behind me erupted as Tarn and Sebastian reached for me as if to keep me from throwing myself off a cliff. Their rough hands grabbed my shoulders, one from each side. And that's when it happened.

Our magic connected--mine, Tarn's fae energy, Sebastian's shapeshifter force, and the unicorn's. Weaving. The null's static, which had shut away our power, sputtered and winked out. Our combined force spilled down into the reservoir of magic within the earth. A tidal wave force erupted back at us, snapping into place. A firecord of light. And I saw the vision...

A girl. Maybe eight? Lying on the bottom bunk of a tight box of a room. Best I could tell in the dim light, she had gold-tousled hair. Eyes open wide with worry. Jaw clenched. Silent crying, shoulders shaking as she sucked in the noise of those sobs. Her pain forced a small gasp from me and the child turned her head toward my noise, as if she heard it although I was not really in the room.

"Miss Laura?" she said, voice small and unsure.

Hearing the voice, I wanted more than anything to save this girl. Because I knew, somehow, she needed saving.

My magic stirred, the telltale press of heat and vacuum, reaching into the reserves of the earth and drawing up its energy. Gently wrapping a coil of power around the girl and pulling her toward me. The vision blurred, room darkening further, misting and dissolving as I latched onto the girl...

Until we landed, me hard on my butt, in the same place I'd stood all along in the garden. This time cradling a small girl in my lap. My necklace sent me a jagged pulse of pain, but it soon calmed back down.

What the...?

The girl opened her gray eyes, took one look at me, and screamed.

A whirlwind of motion hit next as Leslie cried out, and clamored full speed down the oak. "Anna?" She landed, stumbled, and threw herself at me and the girl. "Get your hands off her! Don't you dare hurt her."

She grabbed as my guard moved to keep her from me.

"Let her do it!" I ordered, handing her the girl, trying not to fumble her as I transferred the small body. My muscles were milk toast. The magic had taken its toll.

The unicorn made a soft snuffling sound, drawing my attention. Her gaze lingered on me, delivering a gimlet-eyed stare. If only I knew what it meant. She had a purpose, my unicorn. She always did. She blew out another whuff of sound, turned, and departed as quietly as a whisper on the air.

The little girl whimpered and my gut somersaulted a few times. Somehow, this child was Leslie's.

"Baby, sweetie, I have you," she crooned, backing her away from our crowd toward the tree. "Mommy is here." Her wide eyes caught mine over his shoulder. "How is she here?"

"I don't know." And Universe, I didn't. I didn't even know Leslie had a kid.

"What will you do to her? She's an innocent." Mother ferocity painted Leslie's voice, while blood painted her right shoulder, smearing down to her hand wrapped protectively around her daughter.

The situation became more convoluted by the moment. "The offer of a room still stands. You can both rest there."

"You won't touch her."

"No." She needed to believe me. Something about watching the woman's intense love and protection of her daughter softened my bitterness toward her. I had to get us out of the garden and back to bed. Even my tired was tired, and the fact that new magic just overtook me, even in the presence of a null, left me scared.

"Yes," she answered. Her gaze caressed her daughter, eyes pained. "Give us the room."

"You heard her, Tarn, Sebastian. Let's get us all back to my suite."

Maybe then we could solve the mystery of Christian's fascination with the null, my magical vision which teleported her child, the fact I even pulled off potent magic in her presence, the assassination attempt on the woman, and the dead demon in her cell.

My life never stopped imitating a thrill ride. Poor Rachel. Let's hope the night ended better than it began.

Chapter Three

I heard the voices before we reached the front door of the suite.

"No, dear cousin, I will not allow you entrance." This from a sweetly pitched feminine tone. One I didn't know.

"Get out of my way, Delta. The doorway recognizes me and I will enter."

Hearing that hot chocolate voice, male and naturally seductive in his worst moments, brought me to a stumbling halt. *Gabriel.* It couldn't be. What was he doing here?

Christian heard it too and raised a questioning eyebrow. His arms were full of a girl. Leslie's injury prevented her from carrying her daughter, although she limped as close to Christian's side as she could.

A pulse of longing shuddered through me. It had been too long. *Don't jump to conclusions, Rachel. You're going to get skewered on the spikes underneath when your jump falls short.* He couldn't be here to return to me.

Instead, I pasted on my Mother Heir face and started walking again, around the last bend to the ornately carved wooden front door of my suite. To face the man I loved and had hurt so much that he'd chosen to leave. Of course, that was right after I'd magically banished him from court for his own good. My stupidity knew no bounds.

His back was to us when we approached. A woman faced him. Her eyes glowed red, with power sluicing off her in waves as she held her dagger raised. Even without seeing his face I knew Gabriel was similarly ready for battle. His normally pine-green eyes would match her glowing red as his demon magic rose to meet hers.

The petite woman, with short black hair cut close to her head, lost her bizarrely gleeful smile as her power shut down at Leslie's approach. I watched the bright red of her irises dim to a normal subdued red and confusion furrow her brow.

Yet neither she nor Gabriel dropped their stances.

"Can someone tell me what the hell is going on here? Who is this woman, Gabriel?" I took pride in my voice's lack of waiver. In its regal demand. Yay me.

"This," Gabriel bit out, his back still to me, "is the newest member of your personal guard. Or at least Satan's candidate whom Morven ostensibly approved." He kept his eyes riveted to the petite demoness as he spoke, his voice vibrating.

A new guard? When did Morven plan to share this tidbit? And a demon? Demons weren't appropriate material for that kind of job. They lived to create chaos, Gabriel being the notable exception as his half-angel heritage changed the whole deal. But he wasn't my guard any longer.

I watched his fingers tighten further around the hilt of his dagger. The man was angry, although I didn't understand the threat. This usually calm man was unusually agitated and allowing it to show. "Although soon she will be a bloody heap if she does not put down her blade and step away from your door," he said.

"Delta, my lady," the sprite-like demoness offered me an introduction with a mock dip of courtesy. The effort fell flat as she still gripped her dagger.

"I accompanied her here as a favor to Satan which I regret to no end." Gabriel switched beats with barely a breath. "Tell me why you have the null here with you. Trouble?"

The fact that he hadn't yet turned to glance at our party, yet knew the events at court, including the implications of the magic drain from the null despite being absent during all of them, did not surprise me. Nothing got past Gabriel. Except the secrets I'd kept from him purposefully. Those had driven the wedge between us for which I still suffered. Was he suffering, or glad to be rid of me?

I was way too tired for this. "Delta, could you tell me why you are blocking Gabriel from my rooms?"

"He desired entrance, but I have no reason to believe you would approve it as the two of you are no longer knocking boots. And especially as the faerie queen now employs him. A conscientious guard should refuse to allow a potential spy for that psychopath into your suite."

"You're working for Solinthe?" Universe, I hated the squeak to my voice that came with that nasty surprise. My anger rumbled low and loud, but my newly found control kept it more or less placid.

Christian stepped forward with an armful of his young charge. "Can we talk about this inside? The priority needs to be Leslie and her daughter."

I nodded. "Delta, although I thank you for your vigilance, time to drop the dagger and let us get inside. I give official permission for the alleged spy to enter with us. I promise to keep a close eye on him so he doesn't lift any important Mother Heir documents or secret information. But if we catch him doing it, I promise I'll let you beat him."

"Don't encourage her, Rachel," Gabriel growled.

"Then don't show up at my doorstep in the middle of the freaking night."

I marched up to the door, the magic spell in the wood recognizing me despite the null's presence. The wooden door dissolved and I led the way into my home, turning to usher in the crowd. Christian followed with Leslie close behind. Then Sebastian and Tarn, both giving Delta an appreciative once over. Men!

When neither Gabriel nor Delta moved from their stalemate, I reached my limit. "You get in here now, or I close the door and you can both spend the night in the hall."

Gabriel entered, all smooth glide, skirting both Delta and myself. Which only hurt like a thousand-pound anvil.

Delta followed, a pleased smile on her face. A cat eating the canary smile.

"What kind of demon are you? I asked. The flavors were many and the whole break-down of their species confused me.

"Her sub-type, the Scaevus, thrives on the perverse and takes in its energy," Gabriel answered.

Great. At least she wasn't another succubus.

Time to get down to business. "Christian, take Leslie into my bedroom. There is gauze and antiseptic in my drawer in the bathroom. Clean off her wound. See if she needs stitches. Magic healing isn't an option for her. She's immune to it on top of draining everyone's power. You can put her daughter in my bed. I'll be in shortly to talk to you."

They left the room, and I turned to my team to figure out our next steps. Delta was busy assessing my wastefully large apartment. She'd even taken off her shoes and was digging her toes into the deep plush of the layered Persian rugs.

I cleared my throat to gain their attention.

"Sebastian," Gabriel interrupted. "I need to speak to you. It's one of the other reasons I'm here. It is urgent."

Sebastian straightened. "What?"

"It's about your brother, Felix." He paused and I didn't like it one bit. "I am sorry to tell you, but Samuel took him and your sister-in-law, Cindy, hostage yesterday. Samuel has challenged Aubrey for leadership of the shapeshifters. Fight to the death."

"No!" Sebastian closed in on Gabriel within seconds, his anger filling the room. "The asshole, I knew he'd make trouble."

"Samuel is calling for Cindy's execution. He believes the shapeshifters should quit marrying humans. He says this is one of the reasons their political position has been weak among the Kesayim."

"He's a power hungry asshole, that's the real reason. Where did he take them? No way I'll let that fucker get away with this." Sebastian rarely swore. He was my gentle-souled guardsman. This time, the situation certainly called for it. Samuel was Sebastian's clan leader, but there'd been no love lost between them.

I was glad Leslie's proximity kept a lid on the accidental triggering of my own magic. Perhaps my anger wasn't quite as controlled as I liked to think.

"I don't know where he took them," Gabriel said. "But Samuel is spending time in Faerie. Solinthe is offering him training for the challenge. He'll make the official announcement of his intentions in two days from Faerie's doorstep. The actual challenge will happen at the court-sponsored combat games in two weeks."

"Solinthe is supporting him because she agrees with his agenda," I said. It made sense. She wanted the human race, which the Kesayim derisively referred to as Achras, made into the slaves of the magical races. "So who did she assign to train her newfound ally?"

Gabriel turned to me, aiming a pointed stare my way.

And I knew.

"You." It came out as a whisper.

"Delta is correct. I work for her now. My employment opportunities are limited."

I leaned heavily on one of the leather armchairs, trying to absorb the cool of the smooth hide to steady my threatening shakes. "You decided better a known evil than a new one? Don't fool yourself. She's evil. Crazy, maybe even insane, but definitely evil. How could you do this Gabriel?"

"We all make difficult choices, Rachel. You are well aware." The not so subtle sarcasm in his voice twisted the familiar knife in my gut.

"Don't drag our past into this."

Tarn placed a hand on Sebastian's shoulder, ignoring our argument. "We'll free them."

Sebastian's shoulders fell at the contact, as if the reassurance from his closest friend was the lifesaver he desperately needed.

Poor Sebastian. *Don't be the selfish bitch, Rachel.*

I stood straight and stepped toward my large shapeshifter guardsman. "Tarn is right. We'll get them free. First thing is to talk to Aubrey and Morven. Find out how other players are positioning themselves and collect information. Find out if we would put them in more danger by arranging a rescue or we'd have better luck with a political solution."

My hand strayed to Sebastian's forearm, gave it a squeeze, paralleling Tarn's actions. "I need to focus on the null situation tonight. You won't be offended if I do some crisis management before I call Aubrey? None of us are safe until we can figure out what is happening with her."

"Of course I'm not offended, Rachel. I'm fine. Really."

Like I believed he was 'fine.' Damn noble fool.

I swung to Gabriel. "You can leave. Your special deliveries have lightened all our days."

"I do not savor the news I brought, Rachel."

"Great. Kudos to you. But I'm busy now. If you need another appointment with me, contact Morven." After months of pining for him, with guilt over my actions filling my days, I was done. The familiar wash of my anger helped me cope in this moment. Old habits die hard. Yeah, I wasn't finished with my anger at all.

I refused to look at him as I walked into my bedroom, scraping my fingers over the backs of each stuffed camel couch and chair-top to ground myself in the rasp of their fabric. The real world. Not the world of my dreams. Not Gabriel.

* * * * *

I found the little girl, Anna, tucked under the cream-colored silk duvet and in the far corner of my oversized king bed. Pillows were mounded on either side of her as if to keep her from falling off. The girl needed all the security she could get. I knew how she must have felt. Seeing her small body lying there with her chest rising and falling reminded me of what was important. Keeping us all alive. Saving lives. Saving all of my people, which I interpreted literally as everyone on our planet Earth.

Low voices emptied out from my bathroom where I found Leslie sitting on the closed toilet seat, Christian kneeling in front of her, spreading cleanser on her shoulder. Her torn shirt, pushed low on her arm, was stained with blood. The make-shift surgery looked strange framed by the decadence of my sunken tub, kitted out with marble.

"I have no family. Your people killed them," she was saying. "You know that. They must have had Anna in a foster home. You've kept me here for two months now and she had no one else."

As Leslie spoke, neither noticed my presence in the doorway. Christian's total absorption convinced me of what I had already suspected. He was falling in love with this woman. This null. His enemy. Was it the allure that all mortals posed for vampires?

Christian shook his head, a gesture seemingly tinged with gentle exasperation. "I have told you time and time again, vampires did not kill your husband and parents. They are biologically incapable of it. Our creator, Lillith, the Goddess Mother of all, programmed vampires to be unable to kill humans."

"They were drained of all of their blood, Christian. Explain that."

"I cannot. Just like you know nothing about your power as a null."

"I'm no creature. Just a human. If some freaky twist makes me able to hurt you guys more, then good. Call it whatever you want."

Enough with my eavesdropping. I stepped forward. "Do you need stitches?"

"She does," my brother answered, leaning back into a squat.

Leslie's head snapped in my direction. "What happens next? To my daughter? We need to get her out of here."

"Are you sure you want that? To send her away from you?"

Leslie sucked in a hiccupped breath, but made no response for a long count. "No, but this is no place for her."

"Neither is foster care. I know that well. I grew up in that system." Abandoned there because of a stupid accident leaving me without my Kesayim family and no knowledge of my origins for twenty-five years. Without my real mother. "I promise you she won't be harmed."

"And what happens to her once you kill me?"

I owed her honesty, not another denial of her fate. I wanted to hate her. I had hated her. But now, seeing her with her daughter... Besides, the unicorn wanted her here. There had to be a reason. "I will protect her. No matter what." My necklace heated at my throat, registering my vow.

Her gaze bore into me, searching for the truth, as if she could wring a guarantee of it with her eyes alone. "Like how you protected me in my cell?"

The dead demon. Damn. "You need to tell me about the attack."

"The plexiglass cell wall opened. He came inside with a knife. Good thing I'm a light sleeper or I'd be dead."

"You got past him?"

"After he slashed me I was able to push him away. He seemed surprised. Like his body was awkward, not moving right. I ran out of the cell and no one was there to stop me."

My brother gripped the gauze he'd use to clean the wound tighter. "I doubt he expected the nullifying effect on his power. Even long practiced combat moves change without the underlying magic we take for granted. But there was no reason for all of the other guards to be absent from the prison."

The blood on the gauze he held caught my attention under the bright lights. I smelled the copper tang and then examined the red ragged tear along the skin of Leslie's arm.

My magic stirred. The buzz of it returned in a surge and streamed up from the earth into me with a breath-stealing pulse. Up and out into the room in a quick jolt.

Leslie gasped with surprise, and her other hand grabbed her injured arm. She blinked long and slow. "What did you do to me?"

Christian lifted her hand away from her limb. "She healed you. The skin is unmarred. Magic."

Leslie scowled. "Don't do that again."

I shook away the stupor from the jolt. "I hadn't planned on it this time." She was supposed to be immune to magic. There had to be a pattern to the break in her null effects. Dammit, I had to figure it out.

"I have extra nightwear in my bedroom drawers," I said. "Take what you want. Sleep close to your daughter. Tomorrow we'll find you your own quarters and assign guards. For tonight, you share mine." I shrugged my brother over. "Come on, Christian. Let's give her privacy."

"Will you be alright?" he asked her.

"Don't ask that," she whispered, turning her head away. Her bangs hung low over her eyes, as if she hid from him. All of her defiant warrior nature dissolved. Sitting on the toilet seat, Leslie's shoulders hunched, shrinking her into herself.

Christian hesitated.

"Give her space, brother. Let's go." Some moments you had to get through on your own. This was one of Leslie's.

And my time to face Aubrey, Satan, and, unfortunately, Solinthe, the faerie queen. The players were trying to shuffle the deck on me. My only hope was to throw out the old deck and start brand new. New rules. My rules.

Chapter Four

"The fondness between the three of you is apparent," Delta's amused voice echoed from the main room behind my bedroom door.

The soft exhalations of the sleeping child drifted behind me. I'd sent Christian out earlier after we left the bathroom, returning to hand Leslie a nightshirt and leaving her to clean up in the bathroom. And here I was, eavesdropping again with one hand on the knob and about to turn it. Way to go, Rachel.

"She's worth your loyalty?" the demoness asked.

"More than you can imagine," Sebastian said.

"So fierce, shapeshifter," she chuckled. "And when you are not protecting our Mother Heir, what do you both do for fun?"

"There is not much time for it, other than amusing ourselves as we work," Tarn added.

"Yes, regular life is often more absurd and more fun," Delta agreed.

Although I admired the attitude, I reserved judgement about this woman. How could I not after the situation with Jet, and before him Gabriel? Not a good track record with my guards. I turned the knob and entered, looking around the room.

No Christian.

No Gabriel.

I'd known he would be gone, but my throat tightened for a split second.

"My lady," Sebastian greeted me. "Is the null settled?"

"Yes. And how have the three of you been getting along?"

"I like them, my lady," the demoness smiled. "I understand this post does not come with much free time." She was standing against a wall, at ease, ankles crossed. And of all things, strumming a dark wooden mandolin. The simple chords softened the barest edge of my mood.

"It doesn't," I agreed. "And I work my guards hard. Are you sure it's the job for you?"

"The right co-workers and boss make all the difference," she beamed, punctuating her amusement with a thrum of the strings.

I flicked my fingers with agreement. "Fine. We'll figure it out as we go."

To her credit, she switched modes, placing the mandolin to the side on a table and standing away from the wall with a semblance of guard-like attention.

Now for my hurting friend. "Sebastian, what can I do?"

His jaw flexed. "Aside from using your magic to blow Samuel into fine bits? I need to figure out if my nephew is safe. My brother has a son. About ten. Gabriel did not know if Samuel had taken him as well."

"If he's safe, do you want to bring him here?" I asked.

"I don't know if Eden's Court is the place for a child."

"We seem to be collecting them. Not only Anna in my bed, but I promised Jasper he could send Peter here starting tomorrow for a month." My precocious nephew, the son of my witchly eldest half-brother, had quickly snagged my heart.

"Then I accept the offer," Sebastian said.

I turned to my blond-haired fae guardsman. "Tarn, can you get a message to Morven about—"

A regal knock sounded at the door of my suite. I gave myself one lucky guess as to my visitor. "Come."

The door dissolved and my guess was confirmed. Morven. My seneschal, looking as prim and proper in her navy suit as can be for Universe-knows what ghastly time of night. Or morning. She glanced at Delta, acknowledging her addition with a glance.

"My lady," she nodded to me. "I understand you have the null and her daughter here in your quarters. This is unacceptable. I will arrange a separate apartment for them immediately, take security measures to keep them contained, and move them now."

She amazed me with her ability to know every move in this place. But I was in no mood to deal with her dictatorial nature, even if we'd recently hit a new level of closeness.

"Tomorrow morning's soon enough, Morven. The little girl is asleep. Just post a few extra guards outside and we'll call it good."

She shook her well-coiffed head.

"Too dangerous."

"Too bad," I quipped. "She survived an assassination attempt and her daughter was magically transported with no warning from her foster home in the middle of the night. If you feel driven to arrange things right this moment, tell Satan and Aubrey that I want to meet ASAP."

Her lips pursed. "Satan is not currently in Eden's Court. He will take longer."

The ostensible leader of the demons was not what his name had led me to expect having lived most of my life on mortal Earth, prey to standard Judeo-Christian mythology. No horns for Satan, or for any of the demons. No grotesque pumped bodies. He was attractive instead, and possessing the fashion sense of an Italian runway model. Also just as catty, with a generous dose of lethality in the mix. Plus a twisted sense of humor.

The woven metal strands of my necklace tingled against my skin. My necklace acted as a messenger, portending a big bad, or just important information to which I needed to pay attention. But I questioned its reliability with the rising and falling strength of my magic in Leslie's presence.

Time to rely on Team Rachel's brainpower, even if the players on it kept shifting. Gabriel replaced by Jet, replaced by Delta. "Any ideas about why my power is coming and going in the null's presence? The garden withered away as Leslie passed, but with the unicorn I did some pretty big magic bringing her daughter from the mundane world. Maybe her effect is weakening. In the bathroom a moment ago, I healed her injury with no effort."

Morven raised an eyebrow in her ever-constant understated manner. "Her effect was not uneven while she sat in the prison cell these weeks. Everyone's magic sputtered when near her. But reports from the garden state that the withered path she traveled tonight has regrown to be more lush than before."

A rebound effect?

Universe, my neck hurt. I placed a hand at the base of my skull and tried to massage the tight muscle. "The council still insists there are no myths about nulls from Kesayim history. I've asked repeatedly. They're the most unhelpful lot of politicos I know." My voice sounded pouty. I hated pouty. I needed sleep. My couch was looking pretty appealing.

"Power brokers hoard their power selfishly," Morven said. "Knowledge is power. Until it is worth the council's while, they will not offer up information."

"Then I'll go directly to the big guns of each of the Kesayim races. Cut deals or threaten their asses." That meant trips to see the leaders of the seven magical races.

"Crudely put, but necessary," she agreed.

I had already planned on speaking with Aubrey, the current leader of the shapeshifters, and Satan, the same for the demons. That left Kemuel of the angels, Gwen of the witches, Natalya of the vampires, Solinthe the queen of Faerie, and my not so loving grandmother, the Eemah of the dragons.

I'd survive visits with all but the last two. Solinthe's madness knew no bounds, and her allegiance to the upstart shapeshifter Samuel came with untold machinations that would take untangling.

The Eemah, matriarch of the dragons, just hated me, blaming me for the death of her son, my father, before I was even born. Not to mention the fact that she didn't believe in the Kesayim's future or simply didn't care. The last I knew she was considering ordering the suicide of her entire people, and had the power to force all of the dragons into a mass grave. That my youngest brother, Qest, her other grandchild, was a dragon did not enamor me to the Eemah. I loved him. I wanted him alive. He was my only full brother, the son of my dragon father, Rom, my mother's third and final consort, and the love of her life.

"My lady," Tarn said. "You look like death reheated. It is time for bed."

Ever the charmer was my fae guardsman. Without outsiders present, namely Morven who insisted on formality, the guys called me Rachel. But my seneschal's formidable witchly power made her scary to defy.

"I'll collapse on the couch when we're done. Sebastian, could you be a sweetie and grab some sheets from the closet?" I turned to Morven. "Which reminds me, Sebastian's nephew may stay here at court if we locate him."

She nodded. "I understand his parents are Samuel's unwilling guests."

How did she do that? I nodded. "Peter will be arriving too, so they can stay together in the bedroom you prepared for him."

Sebastian's shoulders tightened, but he went to retrieve the sheets. Tarn followed. Retrieving sheets did not require two grown men, but Sebastian needed the support. And Tarn was his best friend.

Thankfully, they were back to normal after a shaky period when Sebastian discovered Tarn was in love with him. Fae were often bisexual, but Sebastian had considered himself firmly in the hetero camp. Any future between the two would take a miracle, but I was all about miracles. As Tarn and Sebastian made up the couch, and Delta added unnecessary commentary to their effort, I realized bed needed to wait for one more issue. The dead demon.

I scrubbed at my eyes and took a deep breath to try to stay awake. "Not to make tonight longer, but what is the status of the demon who attacked Leslie?"

"I imagine that he's still dead, my lady," Delta chirped in response.

She and Tarn would get along marvelously.

Morven sent her a frigid look, but ignored her. "His body has been removed from the cell."

"A lot of people wanted Leslie dead for what her group did to the vampires and for the numbers of Kesayim they killed during the raid, but why sooner than her likely execution?"

The demoness cocked her head. "Perhaps others felt threatened by her null status, too afraid of losing their magic. Although a demon would be less likely to dwell in that fear. A better bet is greed motivating the assassin. Like the last unlucky one of my people who got swept up in the angels' conspiracy." She chuckled unexpectedly. "Perhaps working for you will be dangerous to my health, my lady. The inner plottings of Eden's Court seem deadly for demons."

"I'll try to keep you alive, Delta. I promise." I walked to the sheet-covered couch and sat. My bones creaked. Age twenty-five was a little early for creaking bones, if you asked me.

I looked up at Morven and blinked to stay awake on the soft cushions. "How did the demon die?"

"His body was drained of blood. Completely emptied, but with no wounds. By magic."

Like Leslie's family? I sat forward, instantly awake. "What does that mean? Who can do that?"

To my left, Tarn stood straighter. His jaw twitched. "The fae."

Shit! Solinthe! The faerie queen was a very busy lady, not to mention the first fae ever created. That made her scary powerful, and as old as dirt.

My visit to Faerie was shaping up to be one fun fest after another. I only hoped the fun didn't kill me. I had a sneaking suspicion that if anyone succeeded, it would be the mad queen.

Chapter Five

Our footsteps reverberated through my aching head, painful enough to make me think I'd been out all night drinking instead of chasing nulls in the garden and dealing with dead demons and shapeshifter politics. We were up early because I'd insisted we visit Mother's Rest before the late morning gathering in Faerie. What had I been thinking? Oy!

"What exactly is Mother's Rest?" asked Delta, sharing rear guard with Tarn behind my clodding footsteps.

In an interesting development, it had been she, not Sebastian, who presented me with a piping hot morning coffee at dawn. My shapeshifter friend typically provided the goods. It was our routine.

He'd frowned as she handed the drink to me, to which she responded by blowing him a kiss. Followed closely by his blush. What was that about?

Tarn spared a glance to his right to answer the demon. "Mother's Rest is Rachel's private, royal subterranean retreat where she mixes up her Mother Heir voodoo and keeps her big bad secrets."

Delta chuckled. "Sounds intriguing and mysterious."

"Annoying is more like it," I grouched.

I turned to glance at Delta's progress next to my other incorrigible guard. She seemed at home.

Her mandolin was strapped in a case swung on her back and she'd adopted my guards' uniform quick enough--tight leather pants and a leather vest--though buttoned closed instead of hanging open as it did on the men. Her leather color of choice was a rich red to Tarn's blue and Sebastian's brown. And her forearms sported the same matching gold bracers engraved with etchings of the garden and my throne. Her dagger set was strapped to one thigh and one upper arm respectively, and her hip carried a short sword.

There was more steel on the demoness than my other guys. Competition? Even now she hummed a lively upbeat tune, adding more incongruity to her person.

My feet did a quick skip in stride, responding to her music with a little dance jig in personal revolt to the rest of me which had no plans to start dancing. "You're cheery for such an early hour."

"Making the most of the day, my lady. It should prove to be interesting."

I slowed down as we approached the dreaded cherrywood door. Mother's Rest. We stopped in front of it and the wood loomed, mocking me.

"Don't look so excited, Rachel," Tarn quipped.

"She's upset that Samuel moved up his official challenge of Aubrey and we have to go to Faerie today," Sebastian answered.

"I am not upset." My necklace pulsed around my neck, sending me an unpleasant shock.

He shook his head. "Liar. Your face gave you away when Morven came this morning with her moving crew for Leslie and she told you of the revised schedule."

"I'm allowed to be surprised, Sebastian."

My shapeshifter's face softened. "Gabriel's the problem."

"What?"

"His role training Samuel. It's bothering you."

"That's his business," I said. My throat squeezed too damn tight.

"It's not him." Sebastian sounded confident.

"What do you mean?"

"You know Gabriel well. Would he train a cutthroat like Samuel, with no qualms, for profit only? He's my friend. I know him."

Would he? I hoped not.

"You aren't pissed at him for doing that to you?" I needed to know. How could Sebastian be so calm in the face of this disaster?

The frown lingered only a moment on his face. "I trust him. I may not know his motivation or plan, but I trust him."

Trust.

Weeks ago, the last time I'd seen Gabriel, I promised myself I'd trust those I loved to make their own choices. To give up my foolish attempts at controlling them to keep them safe. Even if it ripped my heart apart. Those attempts at control, and the secrets they'd necessitated, drove Gabriel away. Yet here I was, judging him on the basis of a crumb of information. Throwing away all I knew of his nobility and integrity as I let my anger have its head. I needed to trust his choices. Trust *him*.

But Tarn interrupted just as I gathered the courage to agree with Sebastian out loud. "Gabriel knows how much you hate Samuel. He also knows what your family means to you. I do not care what his secret plan entails,

I intend to thrash him within an inch of his substantially long life for helping Solinthe."

"Tarn, chill, will you?" Sebastian answered. "No need to defend my honor."

"I care, Seb. I am allowed."

"I can't stop you from caring, but I'm no princess in a tower for you to come charging to the rescue."

"Would you stop me caring if you could?" Tarn's voice rivaled frozen tundra in its bitter hurt.

The tension between them was palpable. I'd thought they'd reached a return to normal.

Sebastian's silence flooded the hallway. For a long count.

"Tarn, as delicious as this little spat in your relationship is, I think you are being unfair to Sebastian talking about this here." Delta stepped in front and a little to the side of my shapeshifter guard, as if to shield him. "I fancy myself a relationship expert, so if you'd like a consultation later I would be more than pleased." She winked at the fae. "But for now, our lady needs to do her stuff down in this Mother's Rest place. Make nice so we can send her on her way without a need to worry about the two of you. She's frowning up a storm and it will leave her with nasty lines on her face. She's too young for those."

I was not frowning! Okay, I probably was. My face ached. Wow, the balls on this demoness. A little excessive for having only met us all last night.

Tarn stepped in toward Delta, blowing away her personal space. "Watch out or I will take you up on your offer, lovely one. I am just desperate enough."

"Tarn," I barked. I'd had enough. "Put it back in your pants and leave everyone alone. No thrashing Gabriel when we get to Faerie later either. I need your help today. So does Sebastian. And our newest Dr. Phil guardswoman needs to take a minute before setting up her therapeutic shingle, Universe knows what she's offering."

Delta smiled her perky smile at that.

I needed to get on with my day. Faerie beckoned. But first I had unavoidable business with Lillith and a map.

"Try to have normal discussion while I'm below. All three of you behave. Please."

The odds they would were depressingly low.

* * * * *

I descended the spiral staircase behind the wooden door to Mother's Rest. Rock closed in on both sides of the steps, narrowing the path. The cramped conditions caused me a twinge of claustrophobia despite no predisposition to the condition.

Specks of silver freckled the stone walls, gleaming in and out of view as I entered the austere stone room which was the heart of my subterranean retreat. The chamber's eerie sentience plucked at my nerves every time, even though I'd visited the place almost daily since arriving in Eden three months ago. Each time the power centered in this room scanned me, tasting and assessing. Screw it if it found me wanting.

I pushed aside the sensation and focused on the large, round table in the center of the room. A topical map of

Earth's surface was laid into its top, the map surrounded by a lip jutting from the edges of the table.

Lapping mist drifted over the map, gray with roiling black spirals making me dizzy with constant movement. The color of the eddies acted as clues to the status of Earth's stability. As more black crept into the mist, the world marched closer to the destruction I was working so hard to prevent. The magic core of our planet shrunk daily. When it finally dissolved...boom!

Magic was dissipating, and the problem was somehow linked to the Kesayim's failing mission to nurture and protect the Achra—otherwise known as mortals. On top of it, I had a null--maybe considered mortal, maybe not--who cancelled out the magic surrounding her, but strange moments when that effect weakened. Her blood withered the magical plant life of the Garden of Eden, but the plants grew back more lush after the culling. And finally, a demon who'd attacked her drained of all his blood.

Blood.

Memories of one of my meetings with Lillith, the goddess creator of our planet and both Achra and Kesayim, surfaced. I pictured her that night, strolling through the garden after my coronation, laying out more of her cryptic puzzles for me to unravel.

Lillith wanted me to save the world. I'd seen enough of her story to understand her investment in her creation. Her love for the Achra was potent, though more akin to lust. Yet, she refused to tell me how to accomplish her ends.

Her words from that evening filtered through my mind as the gray-black mist floated over the map.

"But blood is exactly the question," she had said....."Where it flows and how it mixes with magic. How it is balanced...Where I planned to go, you may walk in my stead. My creation is still unfolding...Trust your instincts..."

My gaze returned to the map, to the tendrils even now forming new shapes. Weaving into tiny ladders, the strands twisting like the spiral staircase I'd just descended. Like the ones in my dreams from the night before. Like my woven metal necklace. Like miniature strands of DNA. DNA! Blood!

"Very good," a cold voice said from behind me.

Lillith.

I would wonder if I'd said that last bit about DNA aloud, but the goddess easily read my mind without me speaking a word.

I dug in my heels and refused to spin in response, despite my heart spiking in tempo.

Remember, Rachel, you hoped she'd show.

With a slow count to ten, I pivoted toward the entity, blinking as I adjusted to her chosen form.

Me.

Or more specifically, a close likeness of me I understood to be the exact double of my mother, Eva. Long, black hair. Emerald green eyes. Tall. I never met my mother. She was dead. Would she be glad I looked so much like her?

My stomach burned. Lillith wore her image to unsettle me, damn her.

"Hello, Lillith. Here to make my day cheery?"

The goddess quirked a brow and smiled an alien and uncaring greeting.

I never learned to tone back the sarcasm with her and it usually bit me on the ass. My internal sigh made Lillith's eyes glint with pleasure. Bitch.

My fear settled down for a nice long visit.

"Hello, daughter. Your map is not reflecting much progress on your part. What do I do about that?"

Her threat sucked the air from my lungs. In a blink, she could decimate everyone I loved. She'd said as much before. Not to mention her prior use of goddess voodoo to spell me into a frigid monster much like herself.

My fear of that trumped even the threat of death to those I loved. *Courage is acting despite fear, not without it.*

I closed my eyes, centered myself in this moment to welcome the tight mess of tension in my body, and kept going.

"I'll tell you what you should do about my lack of progress." I opened my eyes and circled the map table around to where she stood. *This was what you came here for, girl. Just do it.* "Show me something from your past. Show me something of your people. If I'm detective Rachel with the job to stop the decimation of humanity, then I need clues. Give me some. Your kind saw Earth and its population as a failure after the creation, but why?"

Lillith's smile evaporated. "You dare demand?"

"Yes."

The stone of Mother's Rest held its sentient breath around us. Ticking silence.

"You would not understand what I show you. Your insignificant language does not mesh with my species' communication."

"I understand you well enough."

"It's taken eons of interacting with your limited minds to translate my speech to an equivalent you understand."

I shrugged. "Can't hurt. The worst is I am overwhelmed and humbled by your incredible complexity."

Silly me, the knot of my apprehension loosened as she nodded in acknowledgement.

And then--her hand moved with a blur--to a painful grip around my neck. My body lifted into the air. Viselike agony ringed my throat. No air. *Fuck. Help.*

"Life is fragile, my dear." The goddess's voice broke through my desperate panic; with red and black spots swirling in my vision.

I reached for power, diving into the earth to draw on it. Nothing!

"You play a game with me I do not appreciate. Yes, I want something from you. But even if you do not deliver, I will survive. It is you who will not. Nor those you love."

Please. Not long. Air. Gabriel.

Thoughts broke apart. Fractured. Losing. More black. Then...

Free falling.

Oomph! My bones screamed at landing.

Air, glorious air. I gulped buckets of it.

She'd dropped me. Wracking coughs shook my frame. Lillith was so not getting a holiday card from me this December. The stone floor cooled my pain-filled, flushed body. After Lillith's embrace, its cradle was downright cushiony.

"You asked for a memory of my past after the creation." Lillith swept her hand. "I give you one as you remember how tenuous your place."

In a blink, we were at the center of the Garden of Eden. This was the merkaz, the location from which creation took place on Earth. The place my throne sat.

It looked different. Expansive as always, but this time...connected. An Eden not cut off into its own realm with a tether to mortal Earth as it now existed. This version was part of the planet--contiguous. A version from the distant past.

Lillith strolled across the grass, gazing into the wilds of her creation. "This 'conversation' I show you happened after my people judged that Earth could continue even though they found it flawed. After I created the Kesayim as my last effort to impress them and protect the Achras. The other individual you will see in the memory is one akin to my father, for lack of a better comparison."

No way would I remain on the ground longer, vulnerable to this creature. I stood, pushing past the weakness, legs shaky, dragging myself over to the Japanese Maple that even now existed in the current merkaz.

I leaned against its trunk for support. My throat still throbbed and I didn't trust my voice to answer. Words curdled in my stomach anyway.

Lillith cocked her head and examined me. "Perhaps you will make more sense of his meaning than I was able."

A pea soup fog dropped over the area between one breath and the next. A film of wet covered my skin. My fingernails dug into the bark as cutting shards of bright light pierced the fog in front of me.

Lillith disappeared. Instead, the light carved out the features of two larger bodies. Their lines appeared to shift in constant jarring motion.

Even squinting, there were no clear shapes. Just those lines, raveling and unraveling, twisting over themselves again and again. And their conversation came in a blare of noise--volume, rhythm and harmonies taking time to settle into intelligible patterns.

"You will not destroy my world." The first of the shapes dipped toward the other. Lillith 'speaking', I imagined.

The second of them, wider in form and with a deeper, raspier 'voice', answered. "The Gathering decides to stay their hand for now, but it is sick, your creation. If it lasts, it must on its own merits. Your people acting of their own free will to make it survive," said the other. He, It, whatever, gazed around the merkaz. "It is beauteous your world, even in its sickness. I see shadings of your talent, daughter, despite your failings. But your weave falls short."

"My power runs dry for now, although the future will replenish it. Then, I may weave further." Lillith zagged in place with agitated movements.

"No, young one. We disallow it. I repeat, it must survive as is on its merits. Disobey and we will wipe it from existence ourselves. But even if we allowed your weaving, you will fail. You do not possess the quality most vital to success."

"Of course I do."

"You never learned. Never understood, little one. And I am sorry."

"And what pray tell do I lack?"

"Joining. Healing. Connection. Love. All are one and the same."

"I love! Though what that has to do with creation I do not follow."

"And that is the problem, sweetling."

"Sweetling! You mock me."

"Why would I do such? You are part of my creation. The Gathering loves you as you are. But we cry at your empty soul. It tries to weave, and fails. The strands come apart in the end. The glue is missing."

"You are wrong. And my creation will stand. Will thrive."

The wider form dipped and rose. *"You create with separation, with competition in your heart. You do not picture the whole. Only in the whole is strength. So, we watch. Even if it be simply to witness the end of this new place you built. Patience. There exists love from us even through the failure."*

The She who was Lillith paused. The pattern of what passed for her face grew still with contemplation. Calculation. Then, the pause turned to rigid lines, a tightening of her form. Anger returning. *"I need no Gathering. Leave me to my children. They care if you do not. I will not return to you. This is my home."*

"They will never understand you, but I leave you to them. My wishes for your contentment, sweetling."

The lines blurred. The bodies fell apart into the fog, light dimming to extinction.

And back to Mother's Rest we popped. I stumbled and my hip hit with a thump against the map table in the relocation. *Ow!*

"You see, there is nothing to be learned from my people," Lillith intoned. "The exercise is foolishness."

As her words drew my attention to the goddess, I saw her not as I usually did, as the image of my mother, but the same outline of a body made up of small twisting strands of black. Little ladders of DNA writhing throughout her skeleton.

My gaze jumped back to the table and the tiny DNA shapes skimming over the top. But this time they were unraveling in clumps, blocking the flow of mist and clogging the surface. Our world falling apart one molecule at a time.

"Time is short, daughter. Do not waste it," the goddess warned.

"I have four more months, Lillith."

Four months and *finally* a direction.

Chapter Six

I opened the door from Mother's Rest to find Sebastian waiting with a worried frown. "Jack's been here and gone. We have an emergency."

Jack was Morven's poodle familiar. Funny dog. Much put upon, according to his own report. And the little comic relief available in my life. Talking dog. Imagine?

"He reports that Samuel, the upstart, has cornered Aubrey in Faerie and they're facing each other down," Delta said. "Morven's afraid the battle will be now."

What happened to the plan for them to fight at the combat games in several weeks? My mind sidestepped into this next crisis. "Let's get a portal to Faerie."

*****

We ran, but we'd never make it if Samuel intended violence. The hall was a straight shot down my private corridors to the garden.

As we hit the garden, I started down the path to the Fae portal, but stopped short. "I need to create a new gate to Faerie."

"You'll drain yourself," Tarn warned. "You need your wits to face Solinthe's whims on the other end. And a battle."

"I did it before to Hunter headquarters and survived."

He wisely said nothing. Particularly after he glanced toward Sebastian's fists clenching and unclenching with impatience.

Now or never, Rachel.

My guards stood in a circle around me as I kindled my power, dropping awareness deep into the earth as I reached to coax magic up and into my body. My necklace pulsed and I recalled the pattern I'd used to forge the last portal gate, the terror spiking through my body remembering the disaster at the other end.

My energy ran high this time, too. Fear licked through me on so many levels. Could I do this again so soon? Would I damage something inside of me in the attempt? But Samuel could unleash destabilizing change on our world if he disturbed the balance of power. And put Solinthe in too much control.

Pressure built and storms of magic fought to be released as they funneled into my muscle and sinew. I needed to build this force high to reach the level needed for a gate.

Last time the garden eagerly assisted, wishing for another link to mortal Earth. This time, the destination was Faerie. Any sane life form, apparently including the garden, was loathe to forge a new tether to that place.

The energy lit my body with fire, but it wasn't enough. Not only did building portals defy the natural order of reality, but the garden put up more barriers. My skull ached with the force. It hurt. I needed to get this done. Tendrils of awareness snaked out of me and they pictured the warping of space, reaching, reaching...a barrier I couldn't breach. Please, help.

The tendrils warbled in desperation out to my guards encircling me. The fae, the shifter, the demon, all protecting me. Their life force stood strong. And their own magic reverberated from them, overlapping auras flowing out and circling around one another. Combining, weaving, forging a strong, rich source. The garden noticed and crowed with joy even though it still hated my destination.

My power grabbed at this resource, gobbling it up and weaving it into my own supply, recently lifted from the earth's core.

The energy pulsed with new strength and reached again to warp the universe. I pictured Faerie, specifically a location in Solinthe's Greek-themed gardens, the center of her court, and where I imagined the drama was located. This was the goal for the location of my newest gate.

Snap. The barrier broke. Success, as the magic twisted and pulled the needed shape for a portal gate. The fog settled into place in a whirling vortex of linkage. Yes!

My limbs trembled after the effort. A spike of payback pain radiated from my necklace to grip my neck but faded fast. Time to shake it off and step through. Tarn surged forward, seemingly determined to go through first as my advance guard into the treacherous landscape he knew so well. The headache Faerie usually kindled started squeezing my temples early. Nothing to do about it.

I took a deep breath and walked into the mist.

* * * * *

The mist of the portal skittered over my body as usual, disturbing me with its visceral intrusion. I hated using the gates. Their sentience reminded me of both my experience in Mother's Rest as well as of the garden's life force.

I hurried through the misty vortex and stepped out into Faerie. Into blaring Doctor Seussesque colors. Solinthe, Faerie's queen, might be seriously deranged, but she was potent as all get out. And her influence showed in this place.

We exited into the middle of a shouting match, the elegant Greek revival columns of her courtyard at odds with the claws-out business of the current threat. The picturesque purple-tinged, sunset-hued skies contrasted with the bizarre threat of Faerie.

To our right, about a half a dozen yards away, stalked Aubrey and Samuel. They circled one another with shapeshifter energy pouring from their bodies. They both teetered on the edge of shifting, my sight showing the superimposed animals they would choose. Tiger for Aubrey. Polar bear for Samuel.

Shifters chose whatever form they wanted. Or more accurately, they borrowed the blueprint from the animal patterns resting in the earth. The larger the shift in body weight from their humanoid form, the more painful the process.

"Then fight me now, Aubrey," Samuel shouted. He was shorter and bulkier than everyone in the space, but his aura was one hundred percent Alpha. His stance said it all. Listen to me or suffer.

"I have told you before. We fight at the court games," the shapeshifter leader answered. But his energy stayed on high alert. "You want to lead our people, then you have to learn that sometimes protocol pays off. You have to do it smart, Samuel. Though I doubt smart is in your vocabulary."

"You are a coward," Samuel said.

"I am a leader. You are a bully," Aubrey answered.

"Shift, and we'll see which of us stands at the end."

Sebastian pushed past me and into Samuel's personal space. "You want someone to fight? Fight me. You goddamn asshole, you took my brother and his wife and you will pay."

I followed Sebastian, my stomach dropping at the risk he took with the hairpin temper of these men.

Aubrey spared a quick glance my way but shook his head hard in the negative. He didn't want my interference. I bit my tongue and watched. We'd see.

Sebastian kept going. "Before you win leadership, you have to face and defeat Aubrey in your human form. You shift and kill him before that battle and you can't get what you want. And your human form fights piss poor."

Samuel finally turned to the disruption.

"Looking out for my interests, Sebastian?" His sneer said it all.

"No, just making it clear how stupid you really are."

"I agree," Aubrey added, growl in voice. "And you assume a hell of a lot about this fight. I can choose any other shifter to be my proxy in the challenge. In fact, I think I'll choose Sebastian here. Perfect timing for me, thank you, Sebastian. You are, after all, the reigning champion in the court games for ten years straight."

Dammit! The stakes grew every minute.

Samuel smiled wide and cruel. "You think to escape me, Aubrey. You are mistaken. After I kill your 'proxy' I'll still rip your throat out."

My shapeshifter guard stepped even closer toward Samuel. "I accept, Aubrey. I promise to fracture every bone in this asshole's body and deliver them in a neat pile to you."

A rolling female voice broke the impasse. Solinthe strolled right into the fray between the men, chuckling and looking damn demure with her blond, Aphrodite-like appearance. But I'd be a fool twice over to believe the guise covered anything beside a poison, crazy interior.

"Gentlemen," she purred, "let's not get away from ourselves." She paused dramatically and pivoted toward me. "Welcome, Rachel. We are blessed to have you witness our drama. And what a lovely opportunity it will be for Samuel to fight your guardsman. Are not he and *our* Gabriel close friends? Perfect poetry to have Gabriel responsible for training Samuel. He can provide him with insider knowledge of Sebastian's weakness and fighting style. True, Gabriel?"

Only then did I see him. His calm, silent strength tucked into a corner to the side of the crowd. After his pine green gaze caught mine, he closed those eyes for an overlong moment before gliding toward Solinthe.

"My position as trainer has been established, Solinthe."

Universe, Gabriel, what are you doing here? You can't be her minion. You hate her. Trust him, Rachel. Just do it.

The glittering queen bowed her head toward my former lover and then blew him a kiss. He did not react.

"You will formally witness the nomination of Sebastian as proxy for Aubrey in the challenge to his leadership," the fae leader pronounced in my former lover's direction.

'Our' Gabriel, she'd called him. My mind caught up to that earlier word choice. He did not belong to her. He didn't even belong to me I was finally starting to realize.

I cleared my throat to catch her attention again. "Solinthe, I am witness plenty for this challenge. Why you are involved hosting the shapeshifter challenger has me confused. You hate the shapeshifter people. You were on the verge of war with them months back."

Okay, the confused part was a lie. I knew why she backed Samuel. Solinthe could read minds sporadically, but not mine, thankfully.

Behind me, Tarn stirred. Everything about this situation must be setting him on edge. Sebastian at risk; Gabriel's involvement; and Tarn's constant unease over his fae queen popping a gasket and destroying us with her infamous, unpredictable temper.

Solinthe's face reddened. "Samuel knows better than to lead his people into assimilation with Achras."

There was the separatist dogma I'd come to expect. My anger started poking at my skin, scraping my insides and trying hard to force its way out. "I know, I know. The only good mortal is an enslaved mortal. Your philosophy leads us to the most glorious dead end imaginable."

Solinthe's magic undulated up, winding tighter than a funnel cloud, meeting my own growing anger-laced power. I petted the anger back while keeping up the energy. My anger would *not* be in charge of this battle. And I didn't doubt a battle threatened.

The fae queen's faced twisted and she barked an epitaph.

She raised both arms, her left hand gripping a silver funnel-shaped object. A sharp knife of magic shot out of her hands, arcing over to me.

I reached for a source, letting the vacuum sensation of my power sweep over me, braiding the air into a shield. But instead, her magic engulfed everything, including my shield and scooped me up...and to some destination unknown.

* * * *

My body folded in on itself in space, wherever she'd taken me. More. More. Pressure condensed it into a painful miniature. Until I was shoved through a tiny hole.

Agony.

Then...

Poof! Out the other side.

Landing jarred me down to my cells. I panted hard, stunned. Heat began to form beads of perspiration on my skin. Wherever I'd landed was sweltering. The rocky terrain started singing my palms.

Solinthe stood over me and offered a hand. Her other still held the silver funnel. She'd built a miniature portal. And portable. Universe help us!

Her scowl was replaced by a wide grin. "You owe me an apprenticeship. I have not forgotten." The fae's power included a gift for forging magical objects. Like that mini-portal. And like my necklace. Solinthe sought a protégé for her craftsmanship.

The toasty ground was incentive enough to take her hand for help to stand.

I'd bargained to become her 'student' to get her assistance with stopping the vampire hunters. Apparently I'd put off that 'honor' as long as I was able.

Was that why Gabriel was working for her? Was she collecting on a past debt?

Focus, Rachel. Not the time.

"Dammit, Solinthe. We have business back in your courtyard."

She shrugged away my concern. "The boys will be fine. Samuel knows I will be displeased if he kills before it is time."

The hairs on my neck stood on edge as hissing, popping, and roaring noises forced a quick observation of the area. We were at the base of an active volcano!

"You see our future," she said. "Earth is tearing itself apart. Tectonic plate activity has skyrocketed in the last few months. Look below us with your vision to see the crisis."

Morbidly curious despite my better judgement, I took a breath and sent my sight down into the ground below the crust of the volcano. As I passed through earth, the molecules around me crumbled in the wake.

Lower. Lower.

Searching, I found a well of power, but with its reservoir almost empty.

Magic sparks flickered, so few in number. They branched out from the well and burrowed a tepid path through the rock, spreading out in thinning veins.

The further the surrounding rock was from these weakening veins, the faster the molecules crumbled. The magic was a glue keeping Earth together. As the glue disappeared, everything fell apart.

I wanted to run from the problem. Far and long from the heavy brick of this burden. But, no. I chose to stand. This was my job. My destiny. I refused the desperate wish to give it up, though part of me wished nothing but.

I surfaced from my vision and settled into my body.

My throat grew unpleasantly hot breathing the molten air. "I know Earth is dying, Solinthe. This is no newsflash." The rumble above sent my heart skittering as I watched the slow roll of lava streaming down the mountainside. Toward us.

Solinthe never flinched. "Then join with me and we will remake the world to end this threat. Our magic together can capture the minds of the Achra. We will direct their behavior and prevent them from the self-destructive ways which are causing our planet's death."

We'd been over this territory. She was so sure this was the path to saving the world. If she thought she was powerful enough, she would have already taken direct steps. But I'd also bargained to allow her the chance to convince me of her vision.

I swallowed small sips of air to keep the heat from scorching my windpipe more. Lillith's mandate prevented me from subverting free will with my magic on promise of dire pain. Lucky me. But Solinthe didn't need to know that. Only my personal choice on the matter. And it was damn personal.

"Even if I agreed with you, which I don't, I'm not strong enough to do it," I replied.

Her eyes lit with excitement. "But I can teach you."

The lava kept coming and the soles of my feet began to burn as my shoes disintegrated.

"Can we talk about this elsewhere?" I gestured toward the mountaintop.

She rolled her eyes and casually threw up her arm holding the funnel.

Aaah!

The magic came faster this time. Pressure and pain. I was twisted through her portal and out before I could find the words to curse her.

This time, I landed on my singed feet back in Faerie. The ground here always felt insubstantial, like it was made of paper mache and any step might send you crashing through into the below.

We stood in an outdoor workshop. A fire burned in a stone fireplace built into the ground and the tang of metal punctuated the air. A bellow was propped nearby. A forge!

Smoke rose from the fireplace, mixing with the scent of the wildly blooming flowers in the empty field beyond us. The color of this carpet of petals shifted every few moments. Red then blue then purple then yellow then back to red. Solinthe's mood must be careening all over the place since the poppies usually reflected her emotional state. My temples pounded harder with my Faerie-induced headache.

"Come, Rachel. I will teach you to forge a fae blade. With one I helped to split the Janii into angel and demon. With such a template, you can split the will of an Achra from his spirit."

"If you are going to teach me creation of magical items, how about something that helps, not harms."

She tsked up a storm. "My dear, it is all in how the object is used. Like the spindle of a spinning-wheel. One woman's weapon is another's tool for creation. Each can prick along the way, but the intention of the user makes the difference."

Wow, a nugget of wisdom from this creature.

"Your necklace, for instance. I made it. It has great potential to lead you to helpful information. It can funnel power, which can be used for good or ill, and it can deliver pain to its wearer as warning. There is no value judgement on whether such a tool is benevolent or evil. That is an Achra mistake. We Kesayim are outside morality."

Wise, but still nuts.

Solinthe busied herself near the fireplace, blowing the flames hotter with the bellows. She turned to a table sitting to the right of the hearth. "Come here, Rachel. I will not bite."

Maybe not this second.

As I neared, she slid a thick leather glove upon her hand and lifted an oblong bar of metal about a foot in length with a pair of tongs, gesturing to a second glove and bar of metal for me to use.

Solinthe tilted her head. "You can help, dear. Tap into the earth and draw up some of that lovely energy that comes to your calling. Wrap it around my hand and arm.

Yours as well. For protection. These are the habits of a wise craftswoman. Taking care of herself while forming the treasure."

I resisted rolling my eyes so as not to poke the bear. The sooner I cooperated, the sooner I left.

Instead, I imagined reaching below the insubstantial ground of Faerie and siphoning up some of the dwindling source of power.

After taking up the glove and steel, I wrapped my arm and hers in the protective coating of power. Solinthe threw her own additional energy at the flame, turning up the heat without using the bellows or worrying about the amount of fuel a blacksmith usually needed to control. Metallurgy 101 in my high school shop days. Gotta love it.

We placed our metal in the flame, watching the steel turn pretty shades of red.

Solinthe's dulcet tones kept us company as she instructed. "This next part is key, my dear. As we finish heating the workpiece, we must scoop the smallest amount of magic up from the earth. Delicacy and accuracy are the issues. Most fae are unable to control fine amounts."

She hummed an annoying tune as I dove down through the ground again to retrieve the smallest amount of energy I'd attempted. Funny how most of the time I'd relied on brute strength of plentiful magic. What had I missed by scooping up such indiscriminate amounts of power?

I held the modest amount inside of me while Solinthe continued. "We will take our projects over to the anvils and begin to hammer. See how I arranged twins of all of

the equipment? How fun having a work companion."
She tossed her golden hair. "The key will not be how you
strike with the hammer to forge the shape, but setting
your mind to the task of imagining and feeling the
pattern of a knife. Use the magic to shape as the
hammer strikes. It will press the steel into the correct
form if you handle your will correctly."

After which she began to merrily take up the hammer
and strike with glee. The woman enjoyed her work. The
humming continued. Universe, help me.

I tapped into my demon power to scan her. This
allowed me to see the patterns of another's use of magic
to learn. In the past, I'd needed to touch the person I
'observed' with this other set of eyes. Now I did not. A
fact for which I was thankful in this circumstance.
Observing her technique, I copied it with my own metal
piece.

Time chugged along as sweat dripped from my
forehead. I lost track of it with the repeated clang and
reverberation of contact up my body. Slowly, the
daggers took shape. Hers appeared longer with wicked
twists up its shaft unlike the straight and relatively
modest weapon I created.

"Before we move it to the slack tub to cool, we hit the
most difficult maneuver." She smiled and her Aphrodite
glow twisted my stomach.

The glow was not her soul. Solinthe had no soul,
admitting to me she had sacrificed it for the power to
split the Janii race millennia ago.

"Take that thumbnail full of magic," she said.
"Handle one particle at a time." Her brow furrowed as
she stopped her hammering. "You need to pass them

through your blood. Coat each with your fae power running through the liquid. The magic loves to wallow in our blood. Like a pig enjoying the mud."

Blood.

The subject screamed at me for attention.

"Once the particles are coated, it is time for the artistry. Few fae do this well. None have reached my talent level of course."

Modest much?

"We superimpose one particle of magic upon each molecule of the dagger. Cradle one on top of the other. The blood will bond them. And at this juncture, your will is again crucial."

The scholarly tone almost had me forgetting her madness. I scanned her magic again as she practiced her skills.

"The purpose of your creation," she said, "must be impressed upon the item." Solinthe raised her eyes from the dagger and gripped her tongs. "Do this carefully. Insist to the magic. Insist to the molecules. Call this dagger to its work."

I inhaled a breath and returned to focusing on the blade. If this knife was to be a killing weapon, it wouldn't be unleashed without purpose. I battled against death as a rule, but I saw the time it might need to be welcomed. The picture formed in my mind and I set to work manipulating the smallest of particles.

Later, as my attention surfaced back to my surroundings I watched Solinthe studying her own dagger, admiring the finished product as she dropped it into the slack tub for the water to cool and harden the metal.

I did the same while rolling my shoulders to release the knots.

"It is strong enough to cleave the will from an Achra," Solinthe said proudly of her dagger. The poppies pulsed a steady blood red. Solinthe was happy.

"Without even touching them?" I asked.

She chuckled. "Good girl. Yes, with a strong enough weapon and talented enough wielder, you do not need physical contact to use a fae tool. Your will is key, just like in its creation. It will meet its purpose if the purpose has been implanted well."

"Like the knife you used to kill the demon who attacked the null yesterday," I said. "Drained of his blood with no cut on his body."

The fire popped into the silence, flames burning on with no fuel to feed them.

"Yes," she finally replied.

"Why kill him after you had him try to kill her?"

"He failed. And I do not reward failure."

"You admit this so calmly to me."

"And before you ask, the null offends me. That's why I intended to have her killed. Nulls are the most degraded of all Achra. This is why she sucks out our magic. The council will execute her eventually, but I am sick of waiting." Her eyes narrowed. "And you keep me waiting more than any other."

"Suck it up." I was tired of tiptoeing around the faerie queen. My heart beat a fierce race in my ears.

"Will you join me taking control of the Achra?" she asked.

And there it was.

"No."

Her face turned hard as diamond.

Solinthe lifted the tongs from the water and unclamped the handle of the dagger. She placed it on the table and calmly removed the leather glove from her arm. She placed it and the tongs next to the blade before lifting the weapon again.

The scent of the flowers and smoke irritated my nostrils. Prickles skittered up and down my back. Danger.

I jerked out my tongs and dagger from the water and ripped off my glove, dropping it all to the ground, but diving for the dagger.

Got it!

Just in time

She struck.

Solinthe charged with her blade with a screech of rage that stabbed my ears.

I threw up my arm as I dodged to the side.

She followed, knocking me down. The air swooshed from my lungs as I slammed into the ground. I grasped her upraised arm as she pressed down with immense force, the point of the dagger inches away from my heart.

"I'll test the dagger now," she screamed. "Will it cleave your will from you?" Madness loomed in her eyes.

The fae blade shone supernova bright. The light bit into my pupils. I shut my eyes against it. But even without my eyesight, her knife was a column of fire coming close with its searing edge, threatening to burn my mind from my body. Threatening to take away my identity. To cut away my will.

My magic spiraled through me to pump strength into my arms. I grit my teeth through the strain.

Fire threatened. But fire did not have to threaten. I craved it. My dragon craved it. Kyn magic bloomed inside me, welcoming the fire. Swallowing it down as I imagined scales and wings stretching out, bathing in heat. The dragons' natural immunity to outside magic helped me deflect the fae weapon's power. The knife dulled and my identity sang clear and whole.

The dragon roared, pushing up, wanting to grow. I embraced her, whispering my love and her need for patience. Later she would grow. Later I'd let her play.

With another roar and a thrust of fire and muscle, I threw the faerie queen off of me. Full power. She landed with a crunch yards away, and lay deathly still. But I couldn't care about her survival. Not with my dragon battling to take me over.

My beast resisted the petting and promises. She wanted to feel the smoke billowing from her nostrils, hear the world of song that unfurled with dragon form. She ached to fly and taste the freedom of the winds. Dragon form was intoxicating and more potent than any mundane drug. I'd almost been lost to this Kyn form when I'd transformed before; wanting to run away and forget that I usually lived in a smaller, human body.

But I had obligations. More mounted every second. And people I loved who could not share the skies with me.

"Rachel," the voice came from a distance to draw my hazy attention.

I lifted to my knees, resting hands on the ground, panting. *Control, girl.*

In the next blink, Gabriel was there, urging me to turn over again and sit back on the ground. Running his hands over my body to check for damage. I craved the touch even in my confusion.

Tarn, Sebastian, and Delta crouched next to us.

"You disappeared," Gabriel told me. "And I could not sense you for a long while. Then I knew you were back in Faerie. I am sorry it took us so long to find you. Are you hurt?"

And by that, he did not just mean physical harm. Yes, I was, in so many ways. It was not the time for that conversation. It might never be the time for that conversation.

"She tried to kill me." Or next to the same thing. No one seemed surprised.

I glanced at Tarn. "Go check on your queen."

His fists tightened. "She is not dead. I would know. Although I wish she were. I do not care to check."

"You need to leave before she wakes," Gabriel said.

I snorted. "How practical."

He shrugged.

Leaving him to face her wrath when she woke.

I shook off the heartache. "She tried to have Leslie killed and then killed the demon assassin for the failure."

"I know," he said.

His hand still rested on my thigh. The warmth tingled out and stirred all of my nooks and crannies.

I paused and put aside my lust and love, hurt and fear, enough to look at him. His true aura. And there, I saw his pain, longing and disgust for what he did. Along with dark corners of hidden intentions. Finally, I accepted it all and my body loosened.

I sighed. "It's okay, Gabriel."

He raised an eyebrow.

"You being here. Not wanting me. But understand you can always come home to Eden's Court. You will always have a place there. No strings and not about you and me. Just a home. I trust you. Any choice you make." I swallowed hard, amazed I got out the words around the lump in my throat.

Saying those words helped because with each day I survived, I accepted the loss that much more. And in some way the words were true. I trusted him. I did.

I pretended not to notice his small shudder. He removed his hand from my thigh. "She will wake soon. Leave now." He backed away and stood. Distant again.

So, I did what I had to do. I packed up my guard, and I left.

Chapter Seven

"How is your nephew, Sebastian? His name's Gregor, right?" I asked.

My guard marched me down the private corridor of Eden's Court toward the more public hallway housing council business. I was on my way to meet with those politically infuriating lovelies this morning. At least I'd gotten a good night's sleep, crashing hard after returning from Faerie.

"As good as he can be. Thanks for asking. He's hanging out in my apartment for now. Morven found him a sitter. It's a lot for him to understand. All shifter-Achra children are born Achra, and their shifter parent's identity is hidden from them. He's learning about the Kesayim world and magic for the first time as his parents have been ripped from him."

The edge to his voice had me turning my head to check on him. Sebastian was not okay.

"Peter's arriving today. He'll have a friend while he's here to distract him. And they can stay together in Peter's room while you're working." My nephew's easy going personality regularly soothed my nerves. He'd be a good playmate for Gregor.

I wished there were a similar distraction for Sebastian. Instead, there was only threat.

My mouth opened without thought. "I'm not sure I like the plan for you as Aubrey's proxy. He should be fighting this battle." *Shut up, Rachel. It's his choice.*

"I am a stronger fighter than he in human form."

But what about animal form?

"Sebastian is talented. We will spar with him and make sure he is ready," Tarn added.

"We will?" Sebastian asked, dry doubt and an edge of hostility in his voice.

"Delta and I."

"Yes, Delta and you seem to be settling in nicely. I did return to Rachel's suite last night after Gregor was settled. You guys were oblivious. Was it strip poker the two of you were playing while guarding Rachel? I'm sure any intruders would have waited patiently to attack while you put on some clothes."

"She was safe and asleep. Are you jealous, Seb?" Tarn asked.

I sighed. "Is this deja vu to yesterday? We are going to council now, children. Please, I know you're stressed, Sebastian. The priority needs to be you and your brother's safety. Samuel cannot win this fight."

Delta chirped in from behind. "You sound testy, my lady. I have every faith in Sebastian."

That's it. Enough. "Listen, Delta. I appreciate your readiness to join in the spirit of our team. And I'm very glad you and Tarn are such fast friends, but what you don't know about the situation could fill volumes. I don't need added drama right now. I have a psychotic faerie queen and her rabid attack shifter ready to destabilize the Kesayim and pretty much the whole world. If you guys need to play dating games and get your jealousy groove on, can it wait until a more private moment? Plus, Morven wants me to deal with Satan's shit before the council meeting when we arrive. You know his schtick, Delta, and I need at least a few seconds to catch my breath before I spar with him."

I paused and noticed a tremor to my clenched fists. My whole body felt hot and my magic stirred. Damn!

The guard and I walked forward in silence.

"I'm sorry," I said.

Sebastian stopped the group. We were almost out of my private wing. "Is there something we don't know, Rachel? I get the worry about Samuel, my brother and me. I appreciate that. I get the stress over Gabriel. But I've been feeling more and more like there's something else going on."

He used way too much intuition for my comfort.

Tarn circled to join in the confrontation. "I feel it too. If you do not want to tell us, I understand. And I apologize for my behavior. Throwing the conflict between Sebastian and me in your face is not mature and I often forget there should be some lines between our group. You are like a sister to me, but there is too much on your plate. Obviously more than we know."

Delta held her tongue. I so didn't want to answer this challenge.

Just like with Gabriel, I'd kept the truth from my team thanks to Lillith's rules and her warning of consequences. And my fear. But maybe it was time to take a risk. I needed help putting the newest information together and forming a plan, despite the peril. Because a larger peril loomed.

"I have more to share, but it'll need to wait until later. And you sign on to new threats from Lillith if you decide you want to know."

Tarn nodded. "Fair enough."

Sebastian agreed.

Delta cocked her head. "I will think on it."

"Okay, then. Get me to council."

* * * * *

My private corridor with its vine covered walls and shaker benches gave way to the circular promenade on the outside of the court complex. We followed the promenade around to the corridor housing council business. The energy and crowds of the public contrasted sharply with my empty wing.

Walking among the bright costumes of the Kesayim and their various sizes and varieties reminded me of the vitality I'd grown to love in my new home. The leather, silk and jewels blended with shining wings, stalking cats and hints of fang. Auras and the scent of magic tickled my nose along with the cascading smells of earth and vanilla, copper and burnt sugar, musk and coffee. With so many more I could not catalog.

My insides gurgled with contentment as my people smiled at me. A number dipped their heads in a mini-bow which I considered completely unnecessary. Old habits die hard for the Kesayim. I didn't need the recognition, but the acceptance let my soul breathe out in peace.

Months ago, when I arrived, the Kesayim looked at me first with curiosity, then doubt and finally fear.

Since then I'd worked hard to show them strength balanced with candor and accessibility. I'd uncovered an angel conspiracy to start a war, and stopped the mortal vampire hunters from their plot to annihilate the species. Plus, Morven had planned a kick-ass coronation for me where the community partied until all hours. All people appreciate a good party. That and a few appearances in my regal attire of jeans and tee had broken down a few of the Kesayim's misconceptions about me. I'd bite if I had to, but I'd rather purr and snort.

Council's corridor came up on us fast and we shot down that hallway. Our walk was close to a jog. I was late, yet Sebastian stopped short yards from the main council meeting room. Looming in front of him was the red-eyed devil himself. Satan. Leader of the demons and self-proclaimed wit. He'd kill as soon as kiss, but liked to do either with a sparkling smile.

His Armani suit contrasted with the bright emerald high-tops he wore. The button on his lapel read "Smile if you want a spanking." His collection must be gigantic. Last time I was treated to "Demons need love too." And before that, "You call me a bitch like that's a bad thing."

Despite today's button, his smile was nowhere to be seen.

"Rachel, we need to talk," he said around a pout.

"Where's Kemuel?" I asked just to piss him off. It worked.

"That's what I want to discuss, and don't be a bitch. The small side conference room is open." He gestured to the left, pivoted and marched to the room.

"My guard comes with me," I called to his retreating back.

"Coward," he responded.

"Sticks and stones," I answered, and entered the room after him.

He took a seat at the petite conference table and crossed his arms. "Well?" he asked after I stood around debating whether to take the chair near him.

I sat.

My guard stood fanned out at my back. Sebastian and Tarn glared. Delta kept a neutral face. Satan spared her a quick look, grunted at her, and finally got down to business.

"I offer a deal. I'll provide you full backing on the consort issue, the entire matter with this shapeshifter coup, and anything else that's top of your agenda as long as you stop this ridiculous angel-demon buddy program."

Ahhhh. Now I got it.

"Are you and Kemuel having a difficult time?" Push buttons much, Rachel?

His pout grew. "No. And that's the problem. I am loathe to admit it, but I actually...like him sometimes." He squirmed in his seat.

"Really?" I leaned forward. Couldn't help it.

He scowled. "Don't look so happy about it. I'm not. It's highly unnatural and it must stop. Not to mention that Morrea and Celendine are bumping uglies. It's disgusting. Angels and demons should not be buggering one another."

"Does Kemuel know?" The hairs on my skin stood at attention. Shit!

"No. Don't go all cross-eyed, Rachel. I will not tell him...yet. The man would only execute Celendine in punishment. Angels lend a new meaning to the word uptight. Like demons sully them so terribly they need to cut out the disease if they touch one of us. If you would end the pairing between our peoples this would become a non-issue. I will not tell as long as it serves my purpose."

That was as good as I would get from him. And I would have to live with the risk.

I'd forced a good portion of the angel and demon contingent to Eden's Court to pair up and teach each other the finer points of their different fighting styles, with their cooperation mandatory on pain of death, or worse--being permanently chained to one another. The two races had been mortal enemies since Solinthe did her magic and split their common ancestor, the Janii, into their two peoples.

Celendine was the most recent political appointment from the angel camp to council. Morrea was a succubus demon who'd also been staffed to council recently. And Kemuel, of course, was the supreme leader of the angels, as Satan was to the demons. The two men could have been twins if not for their opposite coloring, Kemuel's wings, and very disparate clothing choices.

But Satan's newfound relationship with Kemuel pushed his buttons.

It's working! Their rivalry as mortal enemies needed to stop. My plan was step one.

I crossed my legs and leaned back in my chair. "As to a deal, I'm not sure how you can help me, Satan. I'm not actively pursuing a consort."

He rolled his eyes. "Please. Gabriel is bound to come sniffing around. His detour with Solinthe means nothing. Your honey is too sweet to resist."

"Gee, is that supposed to be a compliment?"

"You can use my help and I will barter for it."

"Give me time to consider your generous offer." Gag me now!

"You will want my assistance with the shapeshifters. And the null issue."

"You don't know my position on either."

"Rachel, you are predictable. Of course I know. The null holed up comfy in your rooms? Your beloved shifter guard the proxy for defending Aubrey's leadership?"

"You don't have the demons' interests to consider?"

"Escaping the tether to the angels is my interest. The rest is window dressing."

"But what if that tether was meant to be? The Janii are your origins."

I held my breath expecting his explosion at my statement. Satan was a Morte Noir demon which meant he thrived on violence. That left little incentive for self-control when provoked.

He cocked his head, examining me through slitted eyes. "You say that to justify Gabriel's existence."

"I say that because in the time I've been here, I see how the divisions between all of the races do not work. We need to try addition. Multiplication."

"Cute."

"I don't value status quo for its own sake," I said.

"You want us holding hands and singing Kumbaya together."

"I want you all alive and building something."

"Self-actualization for the Kesayim?"

I nodded. "Works for me."

"You are not in touch with reality."

I held up two fingers twined together. "Reality and I are close, personal friends. Close brutal friends. She's taught me many lessons."

His lips pursed. "Consider my offer."

"Maybe."

Time. I needed to buy it.

* * * * *

Council met in a larger conference room behind another set of majestic wooden doors. Hard-backed chairs surrounded an oval wooden table dominating the room. Sparse and uncomfortable. I hated this place.

The usual suspects sat around the table with a few substitutions. Satan sat in for the demon diplomat Kazar, and a new vampire named Frederick attended for my brother, Christian, who apparently was self-appointed as Leslie's new guard. Finally, Gwen McKinnon, the head of the witches' assembly, had dropped by to stand in for Stuart LeMonde.

Stuart was like my step-father before the fact, having been my mother's first consort before she met my father. Out of that initial relationship came my oldest half-brother Jasper. It was Jasper's son Peter who arrived later today for a visit. Stuart was the usual witch diplomat assigned to council. Gwen was another story.

"So, what you're saying, Ivryind," Gwen spoke, interrupting the fae representative's bullshit politico-speak, "is that the fae want the null executed immediately."

Ivryind, said fae representative, tossed back his long lavender tresses and struck that ridiculous pose of studied elegance. "As you are so kind to clarify, that is exactly our position."

Aubrey, jeans clad, blond, and looking recovered from his tete a tete with Samuel yesterday, leaned into the conversation. "Your timing is obnoxious, Ivryind. The null can wait. I have a fight for leadership on my hands at the court games."

"Your internal matters are not my concern, shifter," the fae said. "We have been kept waiting for a long time since the null's capture, and it is time to act."

"If my 'internal matters' aren't your business, then why is your queen sponsoring Samuel? Two of my people are being held hostage by that asshole."

"The fae are not holding them hostage. Samuel is acting on his own and is following the rules of your people in this challenge. If my queen likes the fellow and gives him a place to rest his head while he prepares, then it is a matter of personal friendship."

"You are splitting hairs, Ivryind."

"You suggest that the council beat their breast and launch a campaign to stop Samuel's challenge of your leadership? For what reason? Our personal feelings for our fellow councilman? If this body sets a precedent for handling matters internal to the Kesayim races, then we all risk losing control and self-determination. I for one remember how unhappy you were when our lady insisted we attend the memorial service for your fallen shifter." The fae turned to Satan. "It is not pretty when the Mother Heir interferes, is it demon lord? You must feel similarly, Celendine."

Amazingly, Satan kept his mouth shut. He wasn't stupid enough to risk the hope I'd capitulate to his request on Ivryind's desire to stir the caldron.

The room remained quiet. No one wanted to go down that slippery slope. Guess it was my turn.

"The null issue is an issue for a central authority. But none of you have rushed to share any inside intel on interactions with her like over your long histories. And I don't buy that you've had no run-ins with others. Ivryind, your race is the longest lived and I'm confused at how Solinthe of everyone has no broader understanding of the null mechanism."

"That is why we need to execute her and dissect her brain. You are a champion for Achra institutions such as their sciences, my lady. That plan must strike your sensibilities nicely."

Like a damn lab animal. Right now, I wanted to slice Ivryind into little pieces and examine him under the microscope.

Frederick, sitting quietly until this time, threw his hat into the ring. "I propose her execution in one week, before the challenge, so that it doesn't affect Aubrey's concentration."

Christian would have done better to skip babysitting Leslie and come to the meeting as the regular vampire rep instead of letting Frederick take his place.

My necklace shot a warning with a constricting pulse. It didn't like the direction of the discussion any more than I did. My fist hit the table. "No!"

"She must pay for killing my people," Frederick said.

"Yesterday, her blood withered the garden, but it rebounded tenfold. Her effect has been erratic with me. I need to understand it, which won't happen by dissecting her. The experiments need to be live."

Gwen, in her short lycra mini-skirt, with bright red hair shining, and her Irish brogue in place, cleared her throat. "Three weeks, then? Enough time for more live experiments directed by our lady. But the woman is accountable for Colin's death. She needs to suffer consequences. As the witch responsible for Colin's presence at the hunter battle, it's my responsibility to see him avenged. Yet I can wait until after the court games."

Shit. Gwen was one of the more reasonable of the Kesayim leaders.

"A vote then," Ivryind called.

When did this become a democracy?

Ivryind voted yes on the execution in three weeks.

Frederick, yes also.

Celendine, yes.

Gwen, yes.

Aubrey, yes, although with little interest. He couldn't work up much concern about any event happening after the challenge.

Satan...abstained.

And my youngest brother? Qest, representative of the Kyn, the Kesayim name for the dragon race, had been the only council voice quiet the entire discussion. Qest's troubled silence broke my heart. His dark midnight hair and emerald eyes mirrored my own coloring, although his eyes reflected the vertical pupil of a dragon. Qest and I shared a father, making him my only full brother. He'd grown dear to me quickly. Maybe because he reminded me so much of myself.

Qest. Voted no.

Ivryind tried to poke him into explaining his choice. Qest turned cool eyes upon the fae.

The subject was dropped. The majority had spoken. And what little political smarts I owned warned me not to push right now. But I was Mother Heir, and I ruled the Kesayim. *Wait, Rachel. Your moment will come.*

Christian would not like the news. Not to mention Leslie. And what did I do about her daughter? I feared mentioning Anna lest the council decide to kill her too. I'd seen the look on Leslie's face as she described her anguish over her family's murder. I'd seen her cradle her daughter with ferocious love. And it changed my perspective on her actions. Despite Colin. What would Colin say? I knew. Enough death. He had been a warrior for life.

The council had decided. I had three weeks to get out of this mess. Because I knew one thing. I would not let Leslie die.

Chapter Eight

I invited Gwen back to my suite for drinks. She asked for a meeting and I liked the woman. Four of the seven Kesayim races were led by females. One hated me; my dragon grandmother. One was borderline sane; Natalya the vampire queen. One was patently insane and had just tried to kill me; Solinthe. That left Gwen as my go-to girl for powerhouse female companionship.

I left Sebastian, Tarn, and Delta outside my doors this time. Maybe they would work out more of their conflict. Or not. It was one of the many issues tickling the back of my brain, but now wasn't the moment. Instead, I focused on my guest.

"Morven told me you brought Peter." I'd uncorked the Malbec and scrounged up a few glasses as Gwen made herself comfortable in one of the armchairs.

"Jasper knew I was headed this way and asked if I could drop him," Gwen said. "He is the sweetest boy."

I finished pouring the wine and handed Gwen a glass before flopping down with my own on the couch. "I checked in with him before you came. He's out in the garden with Sebastian's nephew. They're competing to see who can climb the tallest tree."

"Does size matter?" she asked.

"Size always matters." I winked and clanked glasses with the witch.

"You're in fair form after council's decision," she said.

The wine made a smooth track down my throat. I needed it, even though my magic quickly squashed the potential buzz. "Good enough." Hedging bets never hurt.

"I know you didn't like the outcome, my lady."

"It's Rachel. And I didn't."

"I admit Colin is a sore subject for me." Her warm brogue took a melancholy turn. "I'm sure your wish to keep the null alive is part of a grander political perspective, but I'm not up to that level of maturity."

"You miss him. I do, too."

"Aye. He was a fine one." She closed her eyes for a brief moment, then sat up straighter. Her sea-green gaze focused with more intent. "But enough of this. I came to discuss another matter."

I took a swallow of wine. "And that would be?"

"Gabriel."

My immediate jerk sloshed a lot of the vino from my glass.

"I met with your lover three days ago."

"He's not my lover."

She ignored the protest. "I'm here in the role of messenger. Gabriel is playing a different game than you imagine."

"I imagined no games. Just..." But I didn't really know, did I? In fact, my goal was to be okay not knowing. I pulled at a strand of my hair, twirling it around a finger, and tried to slow myself down. "Why did he call you?"

"I've had my share of interactions with him. His work for your mother put him out and about. I imagine I was familiar and as trustworthy as he could find."

Relax, Rachel. It's just a conversation. Universe, I kept thinking I was farther along than this.

The witch sat straighter. "Gabriel claims he visited Lillith a month back."

"He visited *her*?!!!"

"So, it's true. The goddess is back."

Maybe it was unfair, but my anger started a spiky dance in my gut. He'd said nothing about this to me yesterday. I managed a terse, "Yes."

How dare he put himself at more risk. I'd done the wrong thing shielding him for his own good, but did he have to run directly into oncoming traffic?

Gwen leaned back, took a sip of her own wine, and looked to be considering me. "Lillith strongly suggested he present himself to Solinthe and position himself to collect intel from Faerie. To pass on to you. The goddess seems to fancy herself his patroness, although I don't know Gabriel thinks of it that way. What he wants is to help you any way he can."

"I can think of better ways." I swallowed the last dregs of the wine.

"Nevertheless, I'm here to pass on the fruits of his spying."

I grunted, put down my now empty glass, and crossed my arms. *Defensive much, Rachel?*

"Gabriel tells me Solinthe is up to something with the nulls," she continued.

"I know. She tried to have our captive killed."

"Beyond that. He suspects she's targeting a known list of nulls on the Achra world. Murdering them."

"No one on council claimed to know jack shit about identifying nulls. Have you held back on me, Gwen?"

"Not really. Witches knew about oddities among Achra, but not definitive information. Colin came closest to finding some patterns in his research now that I look back on it."

I needed to review the information Colin had collected on his drive and presented me. To sift the research for clues. He'd tracked the increase of environmental degradation, viral activity and mutated diseases among mortals, and compared them to the witch community's decreased fertility. He measured levels of magic in himself and others. He'd believed something was wrong with Earth's magic, and he'd been right. But maybe he caught patterns of which he wasn't even aware. Something reflecting nulls.

Solinthe's interest in killing the nulls was telling. I needed that list and to understand how she was finding them. They needed protection. That meant I needed Gabriel's help in Faerie, dammit.

"Can he get me a list of names and locations?"

"I will ask."

"Tell him I said to be careful."

"That may be difficult," Gwen said. "He asked that he be an anonymous source. That I come to you with what was to be information the witches accumulated through connections."

"You promised not to tell me?"

"I never made the promise when he asked, but he assumes it."

"No." I shook my head. "He never assumed. Gabriel knows you'll tell me. He notices everything, including what you left unsaid."

It was another message to me that he let Gwen go ahead and make contact. There was no way Solinthe really trusted him. This was a deeper game for her. Stay alive, Gabriel!

"Just tell him what I need." I hesitated. "And tell him I know he can do it. That I trust him."

"He loves you."

I closed my eyes to fight the flash of pain. "That's not the issue that matters."

"It's the only issue that matters."

Not really. Not if Gabriel needed to find his own way and I needed to respect that path. Not if the basic question of our survival was at stake. I clamped down on my urge to jump up and start pacing the floor, and wished like hell I still had wine left in my glass.

Knock.

The rough rapping at my door vibrated the room. Magic enhanced.

My power wisped out into the hall to check. Along with the signatures of my guard was another distinctive aura signature. Qest. Fire and earth, flexible and soft. Greens, oranges and streaks of black. My brother wanted urgently to see me.

I rose. "Qest's here. Do you mind?"

She shook her head and I waved open my door and went to meet him.

He came in a storm, narrowing in on me and embracing me in a tight hug. Strong emotion pulsed off of him. As he pulled away, I read the desperation in his face.

Gwen made a distinctive noise behind us, maybe to cue him he wasn't alone with me.

It drew his attention. "Gwen. I didn't realize you were here."

"Qest." She nodded.

"I can come back," he said.

"Of course not," she answered.

"Stay. What's wrong?" I spoke to his mind. As Kyn, we could talk in each other's heads.

"The Eemah wants your presence tomorrow. She's doing it. Announcing the Kyn's mass suicide. A week from now at the most."

"No!" That was out loud. "Over my dead body."

"I don't think she'd mind that," he said.

"Not that I understand what's happened, but can I help?" Gwen asked.

The secrets had to go. Keeping quiet helped nothing at this point. "The Eemah plans to force all of the Kyn to commit species suicide. She's making the announcement tomorrow."

Gwen's face contorted in response. "That's madness."

"Yes." My insides twisted so hard I wanted to tear open my stomach to make it end. "We'll stop her, Qest. I promise you. This will not happen."

"I don't see how." The black streaks of his aura widened.

I rested my hand on his biceps. "I promise you."

Now I had to figure out how to make good on that promise.

* * * * *

Restless in bed, I punched and fluffed pillows while struggling to sleep. The king plus mattress was a vast desert, empty and endless. I should be exhausted. Between starting the day with council, settling in Peter for his visit, my tete a tete with Gwen followed by Qest's announcement, and then a sparring session with Delta, good old fashioned fatigue was due to kick in at any moment.

Yet, my mind stewed over the details of my day. After promising to meet Qest at the Kyn's portal first thing tomorrow, I found my guard in the hall with frowns aplenty. That's when I decided to grab Delta for a sparring session to give Tarn and Sebastian alone time to talk it out. I know the demoness meant well, but her nature and her sexy saunter stirred the pot between them.

Plus, I wanted to fill her in on Solinthe's ability to hear everything Tarn said and thought, not to mention everything said around him. A magical fae book we'd found together some time ago had bonded itself to him and left him vulnerable, because the faerie queen owned said magical book. It was a dangerous oversight that Delta had spent the last days with us not knowing this tidbit.

Even now I needed to remember to be careful what I said around my loyal fae guard, especially with Solinthe's investment in the null issue and any discovery of clues about saving the world. I'd promised to share information with my guard earlier. Now I wasn't sure that was advisable with Tarn. Maybe I could share select details. He understood his vulnerability and had agreed to be excluded whenever I felt it necessary. But that doesn't mean it wouldn't hurt both of us to make that choice.

I reviewed the conversations and activities of the last few days to remember what Solinthe knew via Tarn. Nothing she didn't already understand.

I'd throw Tarn out of the conversations if they strayed into difficult territory. Solinthe's spy network was formidable on its own, so there was little she didn't know.

The upside to bringing Delta to spar in the gymnasium of my wing was the look on her face when she saw its living mural for the first time. No matter who you were, the first glance at the gym was startling.

The court games happened here every year, and my private wing was opened up just for the event. I was not looking forward to the games for many reasons.

The enormous gymnasium held mad amounts of weaponry, but the vividly detailed mural covered every bit of the high ceilings and walls not filled with the weapons. It depicted the garden, including hosts of magical beasts that populated it. Unicorns, baku, centaurs, spider monsters, and harpies popped out of the pictures; literally. Their eyes followed all visitors, tracking their every move. Hundreds of species were depicted. They were as close to 3D as possible without walking out into the room. Even the trees, vines, and greenery of the garden grew out of the surfaces, texturing the walls.

Once Delta got over her shock, she gave me a decent workout. We focused on the close knife-work since that was the demon specialty. A girl never knew when she had to wield a mean dagger. Solinthe came to mind.

Now, despite that workout, I was still awake. I fluffed more pillows. As I flipped to my other side for the millionth time, a tugging sensation wrapped my skull. I shook it off and pressed my head harder into the pillow.

Tug.

There it was again.

One moment I was wide awake, the next my lids drooped with leaden weight. I struggled against the intruding force. Magic.

"Rachel," a strumming call skated inside my head.

Oh!

I stopped fighting the weight of my eyelids. And let it happen.

Sleep. And dreams...

Swirling grey enveloped me.

I walked toward the pulling sensation until I emerged out into a starlit night. The shimmer of the moon reflected off a dark lake. Shadowed green field, broken up by stands of trees, sloped down to rocky ground trailing into the water.

He was standing on the rocks, as still as the flat surface of the lake. Watching me with those thick, dark lashes and pine-green eyes.

I walked toward him. Gabriel had called me here. Called me through dreams. He was half-incubus and he surfed the dreamscape with little effort. I could do it too, and had in the past when desperate to find Gabriel. But I'd resisted recently.

Summer sounds punctuated the air. Cicadas and nipping barks of the wild forest animals. Gentle breeze combed through branches of the trees.

My body wound tighter the closer I got to him. I couldn't help it. The connection between us pulsed as strongly as ever. I'd noticed it from moment one of meeting him when I spotted the ghostlike chain snaking out from the center of my body below the ribs into his. The invisible chain was not imprisoning. It was centering, grounding. With it came safety and the balance I craved. Did he still feel it too?

I stopped a few feet from him, afraid to get too close.

"Why do you trust me?" he said with no introduction.

The question startled me, but the answer sprang to my lips. "Because you're you. A good man with integrity, valor and compassion."

"You did not trust me when you threw me out of Eden."

Cut to the chase why don't you.

"No." I shook my head. "I threw you out because I didn't trust myself. I threw you out because I was afraid of losing control and of losing you. Ironic, because I never had control to begin with, and I lost you anyway with that stupid choice."

He continued to watch me. Silent. Digesting what I said. The silence pressed on me to keep my promise to myself. I spoke. "Lillith demands secrecy about a number of things. Her price for sharing those secrets runs steep. But it's time to tell you."

"You don't have to."

"I do."

So I told him. About the time bomb set to go off in four months destroying Earth. About the link between mortals and the source of magic. And about the need to unite the Kesayim to fix this crazy mess. I shared how I was starting to make sense of what that meant. And about my gut that the nulls were important, along with blood. DNA. The DNA of every species, Kesayim, mortal, and null. I described my vision of Lillith and the father figure of her species. I filled Gabriel in on the impending disaster with the Kyn and Satan's attempt to bargain. Just about everything I could think of I shared.

It came out as a whirlwind and I exhausted myself in the effort as we stood placidly by the lake. After I was done, I shut up again and waited.

He never blinked.

"You have carried this burden alone. I hate that," he said. *His fists tightened.*

"And I hate the danger you face involving yourself with Lillith, even if it means she may not consider it such an offense for me to tell you about my plans if she's chosen you too. Not to mention the threat to you from Solinthe. She knows you're a spy."

"She does not seem to care."

"And that fact makes her more dangerous. She must believe any opposition is irrelevant. Or maybe it's because she's been obsessed with you forever." *I dragged in a breath.* "Either way, I'll live with my fear. You can still send information I need."

"Thank you." *A man of few words was my Gabriel.*

My Gabriel?

He would always be mine, even if he never returned to me. Just like he'd always be his own at the same time.

"Where do we go from here?" *I asked.*

My helplessness marbled my bones, weakening them so much I wondered why they didn't disintegrate to dust right here. I wished I could rest in his arms. Close my eyes for a few moments and feel safe. I hadn't felt safe in so long.

"I do not know," he answered. "But I wanted to see you. My love for you remains, Rachel."

My heart stuttered near to stopping.

"It is only my wisdom and decisions I doubt," he said. "And you do not have room at your side for someone with such doubt. That is too dangerous."

I pressed my lips tight to keep from protesting, and decided carefully on my next words. "I love you, too. That won't change. And if I disagree with you about the danger you pose to me, it's not my choice to make." Amidst the pain, a perverse humor forced its way out to relieve the tension. "But I suppose you wouldn't consider being simply fuck buddies? Friends with benefits? I'm lonely in that ocean-size bed of mine."

His eyes flared, even in the dream. "You joke, but I am crawling out of my skin standing so near you."

I sobered fast. "Is that a yes?"

"I would be using you."

"We would be using each other. But really, it's not using. We're two consenting adults. And to tell you the truth, I need something to stay afloat in this."

"Justification."

"Maybe. But it's what I would choose now."

Pause.

I held my breath as he moved forward. Hesitant steps. For a man whose seductive qualities oozed from him, he looked like an unsure virgin approaching me.

Gabriel lifted a hand to stroke a single finger down my cheek. My breath caught with a hiccup. This was not a gesture from a man preparing for a quick fuck.

I stepped into him, arms grasping at his waist, my mouth pressed up against his neck. A gentle kiss and lick. He shuddered and I felt it in the center of my body.

Power stirred between us, even in this dreamscape. Growing, buzzing around us.

Gabriel tangled both hands in my hair, keeping me steady as I licked his throat, adding teeth. My desire grew and he hardened against my belly. I loved the steel of him. The promise.

Around our feet, magic changed the previously rocky earth. The ground softened, transmuted by Gabriel's power over the dream. He pulled me down to the now spongy surface.

I pawed at his clothes and he backed away to peel off the layers with a blink. Disappearing them into the ether, mine as well. Leaving us exposed to one another just like I wanted. He whispered soft promises, driving me wild as he bent over me to lick at my nipples, suck, and worship my body. The lake next to us began a slow boil, bubbles rising to the surface.

I wanted this. For so long. Universe, I had missed these strong arms and the roll of his essence against my skin. The feather light tickle of his wings.

His wings were not now manifest on my angel-demon lover. This was only a dream and Gabriel rarely imagined himself with them, being such a new development in his life. But they were part of him and his aura wings had always been real to me. My fingers stroked them, rubbing my tips over the feathers. The effect brought a growl to Gabriel's throat.

The buzz of magic strengthened, becoming nipping eddies, pricks of pleasurable pain on and inside my skin. My breasts full and my body wet, I ached for more.

I cried out as his hand found the sexual nub above my entrance and he copied the same rub of my own fingers at his wings. Pressure grew as we tangled together, grasping, groping, ravenous for the hard and the sweet. Drunk as magic soared.

The softened dream of the landscape enveloped us like quicksand. It sucked us down and into the grey stuff of the mind's sleepy wanderings.

We dropped together deep into the earth, diving downward as we gasped at each touch. Colors sped past me and I grabbed for Gabriel, enclosing his hard length in my fist to center myself while blurs of gold and orange, greens, blues, magentas, and silver surrounded us. We traveled through the veins of the earth, their life blood still tepidly pumping with magic.

We bathed in that energy, slippery like our bodies as they rubbed together.

We spiraled down faster. But I counted on his supple and sinewy muscle to contain me, hold us together in this dive.

Until finally, we reached the end, dropping into the core, the center of Earth's dream of itself. The mostly empty chamber cradled us as I refocused on the man holding me close.

I crawled down his body to take him into my mouth. He called out, a hoarse gasp of need, and rocked up into my suction.

"Rachel, please." The begging words echoed in the earth's core.

I lifted my head and smiled at his tight features. "Feel good?"

"An understatement, sweet. I want you." He caressed the side of one breast and tapped on its hardening tip.

"You only had to ask." I returned to his mouth and found myself flipped to my back in the process.

He rested just outside of me, the tip of him teasing with its pointed brush. I squirmed and grabbed at his hips to get what I wanted.

"Patience," he goaded.

Now it was my turn to growl. "Inside. Now."

"Ever the authoritative leader," he said. Gabriel leaned into my mouth and brushed my lips with the gentlest movement. "I love you, Rachel."

And with that, he positioned his hips, realigned my own, and thrust inside. Sweet fullness.

Universe, yes!

Together. Thrust and pull back. I met his stride, wrapping my legs around him. The chamber pulsed as if tied to our arousal. He was silk rubbing against my body. Gorgeous.

Heat flickered up and down me with the rhythm. The magic played through us as channels of my powers came alive. Witch patterns flitted through as vampire strength fired my bones. Fae enchantments wisped off my fingertips and shifter animal spirits roared their attention inside of me. Mischievous demon chaos stirred my blood and the angel music joined it to demand pattern. My dragon blinked awake and added her yearning.

Gabriel leaned into it, his own demon-angel magic feeding into this cauldron of power. Building strength. Knitting into longer chains of energy.

The heat of it all coiled tight in my middle. Growing more taut. More friction. Faster movements.

The beautiful sounds of slapping bodies and wet sliding contact grew the wildness of this magic and the approaching orgasm to the teetering edge.

Rocking.

Tilting.

Almost there.

Thrust.

And...starburst. Climax. He pushed me over that knife edge. Gabriel fell right behind me, screaming release. Gorgeous deathlike pleasure exploded through me.

And the well we had created of our power spilled over and out around us. Our magic flooded the core, finding the offshoots of the earth's veins and roaring down those canyons to filter out into our planet. Or at least the planet's dream of itself.

A replenishment. Minuscule given the greater need, but Earth's satisfaction screamed around us as our own screams of orgasm receded. A final dream drifted over me as I lay panting in my lover's arms. The same vision that followed our first lovemaking. A sprite-like little girl with raven locks, a boy with emerald green eyes flying high above me on angel wings. Our children. Or their promise at least.

If I lay here quietly, maybe this moment wouldn't end. Maybe the dream wouldn't dissolve.

The sweat on my body began to dry although the dreamscape kept me from the chill. I pulled tighter into Gabriel's body. The glow of the core sifted around us.

"Did you see them?" he said finally.

"Yeah."

Just like the last time, the vision of those children came to both of us.

He shifted, cradling my head against his shoulder.

I breathed in the storm scent of him to still my shakes. "It makes me scared."

"That you would bear my children?"

"That they may not happen. That they're only a possibility of the future. I know that. Too much is on the line to be sure of anything."

I felt his nod against the top of my head. "True. Now is the time for other work. We put that dream aside."

Dammit, he was right, but the tears floated beneath the surface anyway. More stupid longing refusing to stay tucked away while I did what I had to do. Compartmentalization, where were you when I needed you?

Gabriel always knew what was happening inside of me. Maybe because he read my near tears, or maybe because he needed it himself, he squeezed tighter and stroked a hand firmly down my spine to ground me. To make it okay as I struggled to put away the longing.

He kept his voice even and matter of fact. Exactly what I needed. "What are your plans now? If the blood of the Kesayim needs combining to replenish magic, there must be a way."

"I know when I'm with you my magic is stronger. It's why we filled up the core a moment ago. Although, I doubt that large scale interspecies sex is the answer to the crisis."

Gabriel chuckled. "Perhaps magic grows for you because your blood already combines all the needed DNA."

"But I don't. Or I'm not sure I have mortal DNA although I've suspected. Or null DNA if it's different."

"Your mixture is enough to be a partial solution."

"My blood isn't enough to tip the balance for the entire world, even when I'm with you. The garden likes it, though. It's embarrassing when it moans like it's in heat when I'm doing magic there."

"It makes sense if your power replenishes the garden when everyone else's drains the earth. Of course the garden likes you."

Facts clicked into place for me as I sorted all I'd learned. "Leslie's blood originally wilted the garden. But it grew back more lush. So her blood saps magic, but does what then? And sometimes her null power drains me, but a handful of times I've had a sudden burst of strength near her."

"Like she provided a culling to make way for new growth."

"Or she's a fertilizer maybe."

"Or a platform."

"Done with the farming metaphors, are you?"

He feathered a kiss on my head in response.

I blew away a strand of my hair that had fallen into my eyes. "My high school science teacher would call her a growth medium. But this is just guesswork. I need to put on my big girl mad scientist goggles and do experiments."

"No matter what combinations of blood or how you combine them, the solution involves applying the phenomenon across the billions on the planet."

"Yeah. A big roadblock even if I figure out how this works."

"You will do it."

Too bad he couldn't see the roll of my eyes from his position. "Your confidence and fifty cents will buy me a gum ball from some crappy machine."

"You won't do it because I believe in you. You will do it because you won't give yourself any other option." He kissed the top of my head again. "I will get you your null list so we can identify these growth mediums before Solinthe kills them off."

"Thank you."

"Anything for my fuck buddy," he answered deadpan.

I elbowed him as an expression of my love.

He chuckled once more.

The sound danced around in my soul and painted shades of joy inside me. Sappy, but so true. I sighed. I never wanted our dream to end tonight.

But it would.

Dreams always did.

Chapter Nine

"How can you let them kill her? You are the leader. Forbid it!" Christian was on the verge of bursting an internal organ. He was beyond invading my personal space and about to perform a dental exam he was so close.

I'd left Tarn, Sebastian, and Delta outside Leslie's apartments with the guards assigned to her. None were fae, thank Morven's foresight. The null and her daughter stayed inside their bedroom after I asked to meet Christian alone in the common area of the apartment.

By this point, I wanted to wrap my fingers around my brother's neck. "Listen to me. I have a plan. But you're going to have to trust me and help me. We have to set up a series of experiments with Leslie."

"She's not a lab animal, Rachel."

I'd had the exact same thought at the council meeting.

He'd backed up a few steps, but still fought his anger with fists clenching and unclenching every few seconds.

"When did you fall in love with her?"

He spun to me. "What are you talking about?"

"It's not hard to see, big brother. Although you've set yourself up big time choosing a woman responsible for killing so many of your people."

"Don't talk to me about poor choice of lovers."

I swallowed down the arrowed words I wanted to shoot him after that comment. "I need detailed information about how she affects the different Kesayim peoples. Her effects have been erratic. We need to parade in one individual at a time and then do planned combinations. Set up different variables. Times of day. Type of place the exposure happens. Stimulate certain moods in Leslie to see if they cause changed effects. Maybe whether she's in proximity to her daughter at the time."

"You are not involving Anna in this."

Count to ten, Rachel. He's only acting like a bastard because he's scared.

"Do you want me to try to save her life or not? And its only time before Ivryind will remember Anna and petition to execute her as well. Especially if she's like her mother. Solinthe is on the war path wanting to destroy all nulls. We need to know if Anna is one. You'll have to separate her and perform the same experiments."

"Leslie would never allow it."

"Leslie's living situation may have been upgraded, but she's still a prisoner here. She has no choice. Anna won't be harmed. Maybe we can try exposing her to Peter and Sebastian's nephew, Gregor. It'll be less threatening involving other kids."

His grunt was as close as I would get to assent.

I forged ahead. "Leslie must give us blood samples. Gwen agreed to send one of her witches here who also trained in the sciences. We need to do some tests combining Leslie's blood with that of other Kesayim."

He stalked to the windows of the apartment which looked out into the garden, crossed his arms and stared intently at nothing from what I could tell. His face paraded a series of emotions, mostly dark. Time ticked a slow count and the air in the room hung still and heavy.

"Am I crazy?" he asked.

I sighed and my shoulders dropped. "No, Christian. You love who you love. I'm sorry this is happening." Even sorrier I couldn't explain the entire thing to him.

"She's strong, Rachel. Intelligent. If she chose to attack my people, it was because she believed she and her daughter were at risk. She was attacked. Drugged and raped. Her husband and parents were killed and as far as she could tell, the signs lead her to believe vampires did it."

"But you and I know that's impossible. Vampires are incapable of killing mortals. Not even raping them."

"With her family drained of all of their blood, she had no other mythology to explain it."

"Fae magic. The demon who attacked Leslie died the same way. Did she say whether there were puncture wounds on her family's bodies?"

"No."

"Solinthe has hunted nulls before." I paused and watched the light play over the blond highlights in Christian's brown hair. His Mediterranean features were starkly handsome in profile. "She's mortal enough for you to love her. At least there's one of my answers. Nulls are not an entirely separate species."

"I have not loved anyone in centuries. It is uncomfortable and possibly more doomed than ever. I am aware I have cursed myself with my choice."

I came closer and rested a hand on his shoulder. "Don't beat yourself up. Time may well do it for you, but let's not hit that moment sooner than we need." Maybe not as comforting a statement as I could make, but it was the truth.

He turned to me. "I owe you an apology."

He must have read the confusion on my face.

"For Jet," he said.

Jet. My breath caught.

The pain was still there. I'd lost a friend to his own darkness. Jet, my vampire guard who had betrayed his people by colluding with the hunters. With Leslie's people.

"You don't owe me an apology. Jet made his choices. And in the end, he wanted his execution. It hurt him too much to live."

Christian's face lit with anger. "With Leslie, I learned that explanations and motivations are never that easy. I didn't care why he betrayed us and I should have. He mattered to you and I refused to stop and wonder about that."

"Christian, it's done. I don't blame you or anyone else. We need to move on to the future. Leslie's story isn't Jet's. I want to save her. I barely know her, but I see the hint of what you see. Can you help me?"

I waited, forcing myself to sit still and let him play through all of the conflict tearing him up inside.

He blew out a long breath. "Yes. Explain what you need again. And how to find Kesayim who will cooperate in these experiments."

Relief.

"We already have willing bodies. Between my guard and yourself that's half of what we need. Although finding fae might be problematic as Solinthe is able to track all they know. We can't use Tarn unless we do it without his knowledge. I'll think about how we can handle it. Gwen will lend us someone if only her scientist. I'm thinking Celendine might be willing to send us an angel if not volunteer himself. I have some inside information about his recent antics with Morrea which may persuade him."

"Blackmail?"

"I'm not above it. Plus, no one who volunteers is sacrificing much."

"What about Kyn?"

"I'm seeing Qest soon. He's our only option now that the Eemah closed off her people from Eden's Court. He's been partially immune to Leslie's effects from the beginning. His help is crucial in understanding this."

"He stopped by earlier. Qest is worse than ever. His sadness sits over him like a dark cloud. Has he said anything more to you about his troubles?"

I hated not being able to share with Christian. But if there was any way to turn around the Eemah's decision, I did not want to jeopardize it by talking outside of school before it was time, Gwen's knowledge notwithstanding. I needed to get out of here to meet Qest at the portal, and I had a stop to make on the way.

"It's a terrible burden the Eemah places on him," I said.

Christian nodded, taking my vague response as a no. He sat with me and I reviewed the parameters of the experiments again. My older brother was no dummy. We came up with a plan in short time. Or at least a place to start.

I promised to send Delta and Sebastian over after my Kyn visit to start this process. I'd also speak with Gwen and Celendine when I returned.

Now I had to convince the Eemah to keep her people alive. Or she'd drag us down with her.

* * * * *

"What are you doing here?" I stopped short after finishing my mad dash to the Kyn portal which sat next to a granite bench in a wildflower-filled glade of the garden. A funky rock formation shaped strangely like an elephant loomed to its side. Appropriate.

I'd ran late because I'd immersed myself in the Mother Heirs' journals in Mother's Rest to dig up as much information about Kyn history and culture as possible. I needed the big guns for the confrontation with my grandmother. With what I found, I was loaded for elephant. Too bad dragons towered over simple pachyderms.

Tarn, Sebastian, and Delta had humored me with my many stops this morning. I'd asked them to go low key on our trip to the Kyn realm. So far, they were behaving with lips zipped shut.

Qest stood next to Gwen, who'd seated herself demurely on the bench. My brother's emerald eyes flashed irritation, likely due to the witch's presence. Although he had plenty of reasons to be on edge.

"She tells me she is an interested party," Qest said with over-articulation.

"Gwen." I turned to the witch. "We appreciate your support, but your presence will rock the already unstable life raft about to nosedive off the cliff into rapids. The dragons aren't planning a warm welcome."

She'd dressed conservatively for her. No mini skirt, just tight jeans and a V-neck sweater. Maybe this was her look for solemn occasions.

She stood and her demeanor flashed from casual to eerily potent. She'd had centuries to discover her power and she was not afraid to use it. "The Eemah's decision is too important. This last crisis has opened my eyes. I have a right as the leader of one of the Kesayim races to be included at such an announcement. I'm beginning to think Colin was correct. Something bigger is out of balance. A challenge to shifter leadership, vampire hunters, our dipping fertility, nulls, and now a Kyn mass suicide. How your boat could become rockier with my presence I've no clue."

I heard a swallowed cough behind me from my guard and spared a guilty second realizing this was the first they were learning of the true situation. I'd guarded Qest's secret well.

I licked my lips and continued. "I need to convince the Eemah to back away from her decision. Another person will piss her off and make it less likely."

Gwen raised an eyebrow. "How long have you known she's considered this suicide?"

Damn intuitive witch. My face heated.

"You've not been able to convince her so far. How likely is it you'll do it today?" She smirked. "Rhetorical question by the way."

My lips twisted. "I got that, thanks."

"Besides, I know a thing or two about dragons. Your father was a good friend of mine and provided all sorts of insider intel."

Qest's face lost its scowl and his eyes widened. "You spent time with Rom?"

"Quite a bit, actually. He came to stay with me for a stretch. His natural Kyn immunity to my magic intrigued the bejeezus out of me. Kinda sexy in a twisted kinky way." She winked and chuckled. "But he was in love with your mother already and was solely interested in Kesayim integration with Achra. Even back then he talked about our racial separations leading to problems. I laughed it off at the time. Witches live next to Achra, but we stop at that. Shapeshifters take it farther. Rom wanted to understand both models."

I ate up her words and Qest looked like he wanted to bring out spotlights and begin an interrogation. Hearing about my father brought up a bittersweet pain.

Still, we were late.

"I want to know more, but we don't have time. Come with us. I suppose we need all the help we can get."

"Gladly."

We turned to step through the portal.

* * * * *

The mist of the gateway grabbed at me with countless tiny fingers, and icy alien awareness scanned me as usual. But this time, unlike all others, I refused to let it creep me out. Instead, I surrendered to the sensations and grounded myself in the importance of my travel.

Lillith would capture me or not. Change me into the ice bitch or not. But I knew my work was crucial. What I could not control was not mine to control. I gave it up to the Universe and its twisted pathways.

And arrived quickly on the other side of the portal, unharmed.

I took a moment for a small personal cheer at the leaps and bounds of my maturity, and promptly laughed at myself.

The winds whipped over the rocky outcropping where the portal dumped us, drawing me back to the present situation. The highest peaks of a mountain range, purple and majestic, loomed in the distance, but the hundreds of bejeweled caverns cut into the closest mountainside straight ahead drew an observer's attention first. The openings were decorated with what I described as geodes on steroids. They made for gorgeous, multi-hued entrances.

Each cavern entrance was a dragon's home. Most lived full-time in second, more distant homes, solitary and secret. Only the Eemah's call or rare ritual occasions called Gatherings brought the Kyn back to this cliffside location.

In the past, there'd been no more than a half-dozen other dragons in residence when I'd visited. My chest tightened as I spotted what must be one hundred Kyn surrounding us. They were all that were left of the race.

The Eemah perched above a crowded field of dragons, many hanging from the entrances to their caverns to be close enough to her.

The size of them stole my breath. The hues of their scales rivaled most gemstones. My dragon, curled inside of me, started her usual rumblings; stretching and sniffing the air of her home realm. Eager to fly the skies above. I shoved her back down and turned to Qest.

His face held the hungry expression of his own beast. In the past, he fought the urge to transform when we visited together. Today he returned my gaze, his reptilian eyes resigned. "It's better for me to hear her out as dragon."

"I understand," I said.

He nodded to Gwen and my guard and jogged toward the Gathering, power swirling around him as he moved his graceful muscled body and gave up the will to remain in human form. Energy unfurled from him, tendrils of steam trailing from his skin, and he stretched into his true self.

Shimmering copper and emerald green adorned the scales of his body. A hundred feet tip to tail, his wingspan was easily twice that. Obsidian razor spikes protruded from his tail. Wicked. Gorgeous. Envy rolled through me as my dragon complained.

Gwen's eyes popped drinking in Qest in his Kyn form. I heard Delta's gasp. Not many Kesayim spent time with dragons. They were the most solitary of the races. Plus, they'd been withdrawing from court life for centuries now. I was sure Rom spent time with Gwen while only in human form.

Qest settled next to his fellow Kyn surrounding the Eemah. I dragged my crew toward the crowd. "Come on. She looks like she's about to speak."

My grandmother was ignoring me. She knew I was here, but in this moment she found me inconsequential. I'd finally learned how to protect my thoughts from her substantial telepathic power, but nothing would keep her from registering my presence.

We stopped next to a large flat boulder and climbed on top to gain a clearer view.

Gwen yelled to me over the whipping wind. "Goddess, they're friggin' big, aren't they?"

"The bigger they are the harder they fall."

"That confident, are you?"

"No, not at all. Just trying to forget how scary the Eemah can be."

"You're a dragon too, Rachel."

"I know," I said. And left it at that.

My grandmother started emitting a humming noise, which turned into a hypnotic chant.

The volume rose, weaving magic with the sound. My ears began to burn and the dragon nestling inside me vibrated in response to the music. Still, it grew louder and louder. I blocked my ears with my hands.

Just as I thought my ear drums would rupture, she finished the build up with a soul shattering roar.

The pain of it burrowed deep into my individual cells.

My dragon clawed at me in desperation. I snarled back at her and bore down with all my strength to keep her contained.

The only sound left at the Gathering was the whistling of the wind. No one dared speak after that force.

"My children," the Eemah called. "Myself and the elders call you together today to hear our decision. We are dying. There have been no Kyn young born in over five hundred years. The magic of our world is weakening. Soon it will sputter out and we will be empty."

Shit! Did everyone know? Why bother keeping secrets for Lillith?

"There is no more place for Kyn in this world. Achra stopped believing in us centuries ago. It is time for us to leave. To fade. I call you here to give you a week to celebrate and mourn and make goodbyes to one another. After that, we will assemble and I will destroy the mother pearl. We will fly into the welcoming wind and allow it to eat us."

My necklace scratched at my throat, sending protest at the mention of destroyed pearls.

Still no sound from the crowd. No dragon protested. They would all fly meekly to their deaths, no questions asked. Their reaction pissed me off almost as much as my grandmother's audacity in making the decision.

Finally, I allowed my dragon her voice and erupted in a roar of my own. Large. Loud. Ragged with a corner of my rage.

"Eemah," I called.

The stately necks of the large dragons spun in my direction. Good. I had their attention.

"Granddaughter. You have heard my decision. You may tell the rest of the Kesayim. I see you have already brought a witch friend to spread the news along with your guardsmen." Smoke curled from her nostrils. "Despite the fact that I demanded you to keep this to yourself until the correct moment."

"I won't accept the decision, Grandmother."

She snorted a dragon laugh. Disdainful. Our use of family titles was a joke. I had never been more than her son's death to her. I didn't expect anything different now.

"You have no say in the matter, Mother Heir. You were told as a courtesy."

"My job is to keep Lillith's mandate and preserve the health of mortals, Kesayim and our world. Your suicide does none of this. It threatens my job, my people, and my planet."

"It will all end soon, regardless."

"You see, that's the kind of pessimistic bullshit that brings me down. I'm a woman with a plan, Eemah. And while your fade might be convenient for you, it doesn't work for my plan. So it will not happen."

"You cannot stop me."

"Yes. I. Can. I challenge your leadership. I will battle you in the Freil Sorcha. To take your pearl and become the new matriarch of the Kyn."

I felt a buzzing warmth at my neck. That idea my necklace liked.

The dragons screamed. Steam plumed from flared nostrils of the crowd. Their screeching was nails down chalkboard in my ears.

My research in Mother's Rest had paid off.

"Impossible," the Eemah barked. "You are not Kyn."

"My father was Kyn. And I have parts of all of the Kesayim inside me."

Her eyes burned with fire.

"My lady, watch it!" Delta yelled.

The Eemah pulled back, inhaled a deep breath, and shot out literal fire in a stream. Red, orange, and blue spikes. Speeding.

Gwen wove her hands in a spell.

I grabbed for energy beneath the rock and threw up a frantic shield around the five of us. Heat shimmered the air as flames wrapped the outside of the shield, but the fire never made it through.

I coughed as the heat seared my lungs. "Don't be a coward, Eemah. Take my challenge."

She spat a final flame in irritation. "You will die."

"Maybe. But I don't think so. Your people need a new matriarch because you doom them with your hopelessness. I don't mind changing the rules. Not if it means my people live. I will be back in one week at your ridiculous deadline. Why don't you take the time to make *your own* goodbyes."

In for a penny, in for a rock. This week was a two for one special on leadership challenges among the Kesayim. And lucky me, I was getting in on the deal at the ground floor.

Chapter Ten

"What in the world were you thinking?" Fuming, Qest marched up and down my living room, smoke trailing from his skin. I was becoming tired of the constant steam bath this morning.

Tarn and Sebastian were pinning up a world map on my wall. They'd taken down the Matisse oils and stored them in the bedroom at my request.

Tarn reached to pin the left corner of the map. "He's right, Rachel. The council will never accept your interference with the Kyn."

Gwen sat on the couch watching Qest's pacing path with a frown on her face. "Given the struggle you had with them just yesterday about the fate of one null, taking over leadership of an entire race may be a bit hard for the council to swallow."

I'd heard this refrain for the last hour and was ready to kick the entire crew out of my suite. "Thanks for your support, one and all." I tried to ignore them while sitting at the computer on my desk reviewing Colin's data. Nothing jumped out at me yet.

Qest approached and slammed his palm on the surface next to my keyboard. "Are you even listening? The Freil Sorcha is brutal. The pearl is protected in her chest cavity, sister. You must cut it from her body. And that's after you've killed her. How do you think you'll do that?"

I closed my eyes and tried to block out my brother's fear. I tried to block my own, but that worked just as well. Not. "You'd rather I let you die in one week?"

He said nothing. I played to an echo.

I spun in my chair to face down some of the very people I loved most. "The Kyn is a matriarchy. A hundred dragons survive. Only two of them aside from the Eemah are female, and both are almost as old as she. I don't see either motivated to do anything about the situation even if I tried to convince them. Not to mention I don't have time for a PR campaign. That leaves me."

My brother's face fell into sadness. "I would fight her myself if the lock around the pearl didn't require female energy to unravel."

"I know."

It was Sebastian who asked the question I really didn't want to answer. My shapeshifter guard had finished hanging the map and had his full attention on me. "What did the Eemah mean when she said the magic of our world was weakening and about to sputter out?"

Damn!

Delta chimed in from the corner where she'd been strumming her mandolin quietly. "Our lady looks like she'd rather swallow knives than answer your question, Seb."

If I thought that was an option, I'd take it.

"I promised to share information with you, but warned it came with danger." I gestured to the witch.

"Though you were never included in my promise. I don't know where you stand, Gwen, and whether you will oppose my choice with the Kyn at council."

"Does that influence whether I learn what you know about the magic?"

Did it? And what about Qest? They'd both be at risk from Lillith if I told them.

Delta started singing in a melodic tune along with her strumming. "You just call on me, brother, when you need a hand. We all need somebody to lean on. I just might have a problem that you'll understand. We all need somebody to lean on."

She kept up the strumming. "Don't make me launch into the refrain, my lady. Some of the biggest mistakes I've made were when I underestimated others. I thought about it and I'll take the risk. I think the others would be fools not to do the same."

I noticed Tarn smiling at her advice. She was right. I kept having to learn the same lesson again and again.

Last night with Gabriel was my dry run explaining the situation, so this would be easier. Or so I hoped. I dragged in a breath and told them.

Definitely not everything. I stopped after the bad news because I wasn't about to share my plan to solve the problem in front of Tarn. Solinthe didn't need to know.

Next on my agenda was a search for a way to cut Tarn off from the fae artifact.

I watched Qest, Gwen, Tarn, Sebastian, and Delta digest the information. Their faces had funny turned-inward looks as they struggled to understand something not made to be understood. The end of the world.

"How long have you known about this?" Qest asked.

"A few months."

He threw up his hands in exasperation.

"You have a plan, right?" Sebastian asked.

Universe, they trusted in me. I had to do this. Shit, how could I do this? *Eyes on the prize, Rachel.*

My gaze jumped to Tarn before I thought better of it.

But he caught my mistake. "I will check on Peter and Gregor. I think Jack had them running through the labyrinth earlier." He started to leave.

I opened my mouth to stop him, but promptly shut it and bit down hard on my lip.

Sebastian frowned and moved to follow the fae. "Rachel, if it's okay I think I'll go with Tarn. Delta and Qest are enough to keep you safe. And Gwen's no slouch. I'm sure she'd help in a pinch."

Tarn rolled his eyes. "You need to hear the discussion. Do not be an idiot."

"I trust Rachel. I'll find out things as needed. I want to keep you company."

Tarn paused, examining his friend. His thumb and forefinger rubbed together in a nervous habit. "I'd like that."

Sebastian smiled with a hint of the devil in his grin. "I'm sure you would." He began to whistle and proceeded to stroll out of the room ahead of Tarn, who looked as if he'd been sucker punched. Tarn shook himself from his stall and followed.

Delta called after them. "Don't have too much fun without me."

Tarn stuck his head back in the doorway. "I cannot promise that at all." He winked and left.

Interesting. My heart lightened by a measure. I needed that.

Gwen curled further into the couch. Apparently she wasn't leaving anytime soon. "Cozy arrangement you have with your guards, Rachel."

I shrugged. "It works."

"About your plan," Qest reminded, sounding exasperated.

Ah, real life intruding again.

"It's less of a plan and more of a strong lead."

I explained the rest. Lillith's demands of me. The clues about blood and DNA. My suspicions about nulls. The need to blend the Kesayim and mortals to save our magic. And the tests I'd arranged with Christian.

I asked Delta and Qest to participate and they easily agreed. Gwen already knew I'd wanted one of her scientists to do blood work on Leslie, just not the importance of it until now. When I suggested that Gwen's scientist could also participate with his or her own blood and proximity to the null, Gwen surprised me.

"I'll do it myself. The scientist can still examine the blood samples, but I'll lend my own sample and work with Christian to test the null's influence on witches."

"Why?" Qest asked.

"Because what else would be more important to do with my time than save the planet? What I've heard is dire, and it all fits. We need to tell the others on council. They deserve to understand."

"They may deserve it," Qest answered, "but I doubt they'll believe it. And even if they do, the arguments it will breed would shake the court. If Solinthe knows

Earth is dying, as powerful as she is, yet refuses to listen to Rachel, others will easily be as recalcitrant. They will get in the way of what she is trying to do."

"That's why I want to line up the puzzle pieces first before telling them. I'm starting with Colin's research. Christian will have results in the next days. I intend to bring them proof and a firm proposal."

Gwen mulled it over and agreed to wait before sharing with others.

A sick knot in my middle loosened. I wasn't alone. *Yeah, but you're damned selfish.* I risked exposing them to Lillith. One bad risk versus another--an automatic set-up.

There was no waiting on the news about the Kyn and my own role in that drama. Tarn had overheard my challenge and I expected Ivryind to call a council meeting any moment to bitch about it.

Time to meet with Morven and fill her in. She deserved as much. Plus, my seneschal's brains rivaled most others and I needed her help. She wasn't warm and fuzzy, but her approval meant a lot.

"I'm safe with Delta if you two need to get going."

Qest shot me a doubtful look.

I crossed my heart. "Really. I promise to stay put until Tarn and Sebastian return."

The witch straightened and stood. "Can I buy you a drink then, Qest? My brother and his band are playing at the Grotto." She named their band, a favorite of the subterranean bar of Eden's Court.

"That's your brother?" I said. "He plays with shapeshifters." I'd seen them jam the evening of the vampire hunter raid.

She smiled. "My family is an untraditional lot. Come on, dragon boy. I'll tell you about Rom."

Qest laughed. "Dragon boy? Although I am much younger than you ma'am."

Gwen's mouth quirked and she tsk'd him with a finger wag. "Respect your elders or I'll send you to your room."

He laughed again. I loved the sound. My brother needed to do more of it.

The offer enticed me as well, although I had other work. Qest needed TLC. Gwen seemed willing to provide attention now that she was determined to settle into a long visit at Eden's Court. Right now, stories about my father were luxuries for which I didn't have time.

Qest gave into Gwen's demand, but wouldn't leave without a last word to me. "We're not done discussing your challenge."

"Do me a favor and go get drunk. We'll talk later and you can give me pointers about killing Grandmother."

"You are a laugh a minute, sister."

"That's me. I'm putting my stand-up routine together and hitting the road the moment we finish saving the world."

"If you're not dead before then."

"Don't catch Grandmother's pessimism. I'm all about the positive. Carpe Diem."

"Carpe pearl, you mean."

"Yeah, that too."

They left, and I called Morven.

* * * * *

Jack paraded in my door first, tail drooping, his cream-colored hair matted with leaves and twigs. I stopped him before the standard poodle could launch into his newest complaint.

"Jack, I appreciate all your work with the boys. I know babysitting is above and beyond the duties of a familiar. You are a lifesaver keeping them entertained in the garden so much."

Morven followed him in, a frown on her lips as I placated her dog.

The dog woofed agreement. "Let me tell ya, Rache, it was cute singing the alphabet song for Sebastian's nephew. It cracks him up since he still can't get over my ability to talk. Or the fact of magic at all. But after twenty, and definitely before two hundred times, the humor wears off."

Jack plopped his rump down on my oriental and sighed, tongue lolling.

Morven was looking as prim and proper as ever in a Donna Karan olive suit. The leather satchel she carried was a new addition. She eyed the main room of my suite and frowned at the map. "Are you redecorating?"

"My latest research project. I'm tracking geological and population trends. Illness, natural disasters, and unusual activity. Did Christian check in with you as I asked?"

"Yes. We've cordoned off parts of the garden for his experiments with the null."

"Thanks." I found myself wanting to move and went over to the bar to pour myself juice and grab another half of a bagel from breakfast hours earlier. I sliced the bagel and slid it into the toaster oven.

The juice was sweet and full of pulp, just how I liked it. But after three sips and Morven's calm, silent observation of me as I delayed, I knew it was time to speak.

"Okay, so here's the deal. I challenged the Eemah for a leadership fight. In one week, we battle to the death. It's the only way to keep her from her intention to have the Kyn fade as a people. And Gabriel is spying for me with Solinthe. She's murdering nulls around the world using some sort of list of them. He's trying to get me the list. She wants to kill me, too, I'm pretty sure. And either I need to kick Tarn off my team or find a way to cut off Solinthe's access to him. Too much is happening too quickly for her to have access to the information. Christian is in doomed love with Leslie. Qest's probably clinically depressed. Delta's plotting to form a love triangle with Sebastian and Tarn, who still don't have their relationship shit settled. Satan will do anything short of selling his soul to get me to drop the angel/demon project, and we have about four months till everything goes boom."

I ran out of steam and stared at the ticking toaster as my bagel burned. I didn't have any energy to pull out the blackening disc.

Silence. Even from Jack, amazingly.

The bing of the timer filled the empty air.

"I have a gift for you."

I jumped at Morven's words. She stood two feet from me at the bar counter. *Nice attention skills, Rachel.*

She had the leather satchel and was resting it on the countertop and opening the flap. She dipped in both hands, and pulled out...a puppy. Chocolate, curly-haired, madly licking her fingers as she deposited it on the surface.

"She's yours. A familiar. Labradoodle breed, although I do not think her poodle parent was as large as my Jack."

"No she wasn't. I know the bitch," Jack added, eyeing the puppy with doggy fondness. "Her dam's pedigree is sparkling. I think the Labrador sire was no slouch either. This little one will come into her powers in about six months, about the time she learns to talk."

The pup wobbled on her feet and spun twice in a circle, stopping to face me. She whined and woofed a greeting, following it with a sneeze. Her tail wagged in continuous movement.

Hands down, she was the cutest ball of fur I'd seen.

My eyes started to tear. "Thank you, Morven."

My seneschal reached out to stroke the little one. I already had my hands scratching under her chin and belly.

"You are welcome. As your litany made clear, the awful challenges are mounting. You need hope in your life. Two months after you keep the world from destruction, your familiar will meet her full potential."

It was definitely uncool to melt into a complete puddle of goo, but I came close as the pup licked at my thumb. "She'll need a name. But the right name."

"It will be clear when the time is right," Morven said.

"Do you think we'll be here when she speaks?"

"I would like to say yes, my dear."

I was about to start bawling. I hated being brave. I hated the constant ache for Gabriel. I hated walking the line between honesty and strategy.

"You will do everything you need to do, Rachel. It is all we ever do."

"Am I making the right choices?"

"Witches may work spells to see into the future, but we never see the full picture. We take what we see and make our own meaning. Much like everyone interprets and makes meaning from moment to moment. I cannot predict if your choices are right."

"You could lie and just say yes."

She smiled a soft smile. The gooey puddle softened more. "You are fine, child."

I sniffled and refused the tears. "Did you take a hit of something, Morven? I love the new you. And if it's good stuff, can you share?" The puppy whined for attention. "Are you hungry, sweetie?"

Jack chimed in. "Just share your bagel, she'll love it."

"Here is her sling to keep her with you." Morven took out a soft black leather sling from the satchel. "Its magic allows it to disappear into a separate realm when you wear it, removing the puppy's weight and keeping her safe from the normal wear and tear of your life, also leaving your body unimpeded."

Keeping her out of danger sounded vitally necessary knowing what I faced daily.

"How do you train a familiar?"

Jack jumped onto my couch, circled, and settled down into the cushions. The pup gave a yap, and before I knew it, had leaped down the several feet from the counter, bounding on small legs across the living room and up onto the couch. She pushed her way against Jack's side and nestled. She yawned and crossed her two front paws over her small nose, closing her eyes and falling instantly asleep.

The older dog licked her head. "No need to train her. She'll train herself. Just keep talking to her. Tell her your stories and fill her in on your activities. We familiars are wicked intelligent, although frequently we are underutilized and play messenger, or retriever, or nursemaid. It's quite humbling."

Jack's predictable put-upon tone comforted me. The world stopped standing on its head for this quiet moment.

Morven walked behind the bar, took out a glass, and poured herself some of my juice. She topped off my glass with the rest of the pitcher. Okay, maybe the world was still standing on its head. My reserved and disapproving seneschal was acting downright homey and kind. Even motherly.

"You will stand strong against council, the Eemah and Solinthe. Christian, Qest, Sebastian, Tarn, and even Satan will survive. Gabriel... You will both make your choices. And make the best of them. I will be there to help you organize. A tidy desk can carry you through rough waters."

Maybe it was that simple. Keep doing what I was doing and get by. Clean up my desk from time to time and take a breath. The seemingly endless balls I juggled in my head clamored for attention, but sometimes a gal just had to crawl into a bed of clean sheets with her puppy and snuggle down.

I was not as alone as I made myself out to be. Morven helped remind me of that.

"Call a meeting with council for tomorrow. I'll pre-empt Ivryind. I'm taking the rest of the day off. Disaster will have to wait."

Chapter Eleven

"Ow! Dammit, that hurt." I shook my hand furiously to rid it of the burning sensation. Unfortunately, the fingers started going numb instead. Soon, the whole hand went dead.

"You asked me to drip my blood on you, I did. Don't complain." Leslie wrapped her own bleeding fingertip with gauze and secured the end.

I grabbed more gauze and rubbed away the excess blood on my skin, but the hand stayed numb. How long was the effect going to last?

I blinked when a green tendril of vine erupted out of the grass and snaked up to my hand that held the cloth. It wrapped around the fabric and dragged it back down to the ground, pulling the entire thing under the soil.

Freaky.

We'd sat on a knoll in the garden together for the past hour trying different ideas. A small forest of cacti covered with crimson-globuled fruit lay behind us encircling a small pond. The intense aroma of the fruit made my lip curl. I hated this part of the garden. The shapeshifter, Victor, had been murdered here. But the smell routinely kept others distant from this part of the garden, so we'd chosen it for our experiments. Taking Leslie from her suite was a risk with the edgy mood at Eden's Court and the ill-will born toward the null.

I'd sent Delta and Sebastian away three-quarters of an hour ago, and Christian twenty minutes after that, to much protest over my safety. But I suspected Leslie's powers were affected by who was around her and we needed to understand fully. My guard only agreed after Sebastian pushed a gun and holster on me. Then, when Christian was leaving, he insisted on giving me a dagger. I was more aware of the danger from Leslie if she tried to jump me and get her hands on either. Christian sent her a funny look while handing the blade to me. As if he was silently insisting it was protection against others and not from Leslie herself.

His intensity over Leslie and the experiments had grown since I'd filled him in on the full threat to our world earlier. I loved my brother, and now that I'd made the decision to be honest he deserved to know the stakes as much as anyone else. Way to go Rachel. Spreading the joy of the ticking time bomb.

None of my magic had worked since Christian left the two of us alone, compared to a fluctuating amount when he was here. Strangely, more had worked with Delta and Sebastian in the mix, but in less powerful bursts than with Christian, Leslie, and myself alone.

"Does it feel different when you are near Christian versus others? Any internal twitch you feel if you know he's trying his magic that's unlike when I try mine?"

Her brow scrunched. "I don't know. No. Maybe."

I struggled to jot down notes as my writing hand still wasn't functioning. "Christian changes the formula with you. Gwen said her magic dried up when she had you alone, but came back on partially when Christian reappeared. And he told me each day he spends with you he gets closer to full power, no drain at all."

"So?"

"What's your guess about why?"

"He's becoming immune to me."

I watched her face. She turned her eyes to the grass, as if she found something there highly interesting.

"I think it's because he cares for you." I wouldn't spook her by using the word love.

As I watched her play of emotions, my magic sputtered alive. I scooped up energy from the earth and used it to heal my hand. The fingers tingled as they returned to life, and I sighed in relief, flexing the joints.

Christian wasn't here, but her thoughts were clearly of my vampire brother.

"Or more importantly," I continued, "that you have some feelings for and about him."

"Never," she spat.

"Has he explained to you why vampires couldn't have killed your family, or hurt you in any way?"

Her head straightened and her gaze burned into me. "If you were me, would you be able to believe anything that was told to you? Anything at all? I lived forty years with reality being one thing, and the last year and a half of my life finding out that none of it was true. The last few weeks particularly have been a bizarre twisted fairy tale of the Grimm variety. So, what do you expect?"

She had a point. But since two months ago, I could say the same. My twenty-fifth birthday brought magic and mayhem. Literally. My choice had been simple. Assume I was on one long psychotic hallucinatory trip, or accept the fact that my eyes, ears, and sense of touch worked fine. And that life as I knew it was something different than I'd imagined.

"My brother is a good man. I don't know if I can save your life. I'll try. Not just for him, although it helps that he wants you alive desperately. I'm scared to death you'll break his heart. But that's his business. His choice."

I stretched my fingers, ran them through the grass and savored the earth, the power, and connection. My hand brushed the thigh holster strapped to the outside of my jeans.

"But if you live, and whether you accept or reject him, you are going to have to face that not all you assumed is true, and find some good in it. Evil might exist, but the quality of our lives depends on how we choose to make sense of it and how much we let it weigh down our hearts."

"Thanks for the life lecture. Now can we get on with this?"

She was scared, hurting, and vulnerable. I couldn't expect more. I suspected she'd digested some of what I said and I wouldn't push.

"Okay. If you could remove the bandage again, I'd like for you to drop a bit more of your blood on the earth here. I want to see if---"

Thwack.

Thwack, thwack.

Arrows!

Three stuck from the ground a hairs breath from us.

My blood started a pounding race. Adrenalin spiked. "Leslie, run but stay low. Get behind the cactus."

We scrambled up from the ground and behind the nearest group of spiky plants.

I called for a shield but her null affect was back in full force. No magic. Shit!

Thwack, thwack, thwack.

Three more arrows in the body of the cactus we hid behind.

Fae arrows.

Three fae ran closer to us, bows out as they'd shot on the run, faerie spells improving the accuracy from an impossible distance.

I yanked the pistol out from the holster and took off the safety. Universe, I was a terrible shot. Especially without magic. At least the fae warriors would also be down their magic when they got close enough to Leslie.

I peeked around the cactus and squeezed out a round.

The first of the fae hesitated a moment, then kept running.

I fired off a few more bullets. I'd need the extras in the pouch on my belt.

"Qest! Being attacked in the garden near the cactus pond!" I screamed to my brother in my head, not sure if the call would make it through."

"Leslie, call for Christian in your head. Vampires can hear the mortals they love. Telepathic thing. You don't block his magic anymore."

She looked at me funny, but the panic was bubbling on her face.

"Just call him."

She closed her eyes and scrunched her face.

I squeezed off another couple bullets. Her eyes popped open. "He's coming."

Shit. They were almost here. I tossed Leslie the gun and ammo pouch. "Reload. Do your best." I unsheathed the dagger.

Leslie fumbled to reload.

Dagger to fae swords. Not good.

"Reloaded," Leslie yelled.

"Shoot."

She leaned out from her crouch and fired.

She fired again.

One of the fae stumbled, went down holding his arm. Good.

The other ones kept coming. Leslie fired again but missed.

I shifted into a fighting stance. Almost here.

She fired more shots.

"*Qest!*"

Rachel, on my way!" he answered.

"Out of bullets," Leslie yelled.

I saw Christian then, flying through the air, literally, approaching the back of one of the two running fae. He rammed into the warrior's spine and they went tumbling to the ground. Grappling.

Gwen was in the distance, sprinting toward the fae Leslie had wounded. He'd managed to stand before Gwen got there and he'd notched another arrow to launch our direction. Gwen stopped in her tracks and raised her own gun. Shot. He went down and she started running toward him again.

Thwack. Another arrow from the third fae.

And then he was there. On me.

I blocked his first thrust with the dagger. The jar of contact vibrated through me. My teeth ached from it.

I pushed him off. He came at me again.

I leapt to the side. He swung and missed. Aim was off without magic.

He turned and lunged again. I barely had time to block. Our steel clashed. He pushed me back using purchase from where our blades crossed. I fell to my knees and the edge of his sword nicked me on the shoulder as I went down.

A tiny growl filled the air. Magic stirred against my body and a sling materialized against my chest.

My puppy yapped and growled again, eerily deep and loud this time, launching out of the sling and biting the sword arm of the fae. Latching on.

He stumbled back from me. "Damn beast." The fae tried to pull the brown ball off his arm but wasn't able.

Leslie jumped on his back, wrapping legs around his middle. He fell with a bellow.

I grabbed up my dagger again from where it had dropped and lunged for the writhing pile. I had to watch out for the sword still tangled in this mess and had to get Leslie and the puppy away from the fae.

The warrior rolled us and sharp elbows slammed my side. I grabbed at his fist still wrapped around his blade and tried to pry it from him. He used his abdominal strength to raise his back and then slammed Leslie down against the earth.

He kneed me hard in the stomach. The air whooshed from my lungs. I let go, seeing spots and gasping desperately for breath.

The fae had my dagger. Raised it to slash me. I couldn't move. Couldn't do anything but wait for it to fall.

And that was when Qest, Gwen, Christian, Sebastian, and Delta charged onto the scene. Or so I later realized.

A dragon roar erupted, and a strong arm, not sure whose, grabbed the warrior's wrist and wrenched it away from me. They pulled us apart.

I heard a grunting struggle in the background.

Someone lifted me to soft, green grass. I lay there finally able to pant and recover. Sebastian knelt beside me. "You okay, Rache?"

I nodded.

"I knew we shouldn't have left you."

"Following orders," I managed.

"Stupid orders."

"Thanks a lot."

"My pleasure. You're cut." He touched my shoulder where it bled.

I raised my fingers to the injury and came away with blood. "Flesh wound. No problem at all."

"You're nuts. You couldn't even use magic with that null around."

I felt my lips stretch into what must look like a crazy-assed grin. "Just plain old female power. Me, my puppy, and Leslie. The dynamic trio."

"If Tarn were here, he'd heal it."

"Get Gwen. On second thought, neither of their magic would help near Leslie. Gwen can heal it when I'm back at my suite."

He turned to the crowd to the side of us. "Rachel's hurt. Someone get me a cloth so I can staunch the blood till we can get her healed."

Qest was there pulling off his shirt, kneeling down and pressing it to my skin. "Sister, I leave you alone for a brief moment and you get into trouble. Always picking fights. Do you have a death wish?"

"Nah, just incorrigible." I winced as he pressed the cloth harder. "Is Leslie okay? Where's the puppy?" My mind kicked in and an intense streak of worry zipped through my nerves.

"Christian's attending to Leslie. Looks like she escaped with simple cuts and bruises. Delta and Gwen have the fae. Additional guardsmen followed us here and did clean-up with the other two attackers Gwen and Christian brought down."

"You need to get them out of here. I don't want them witnessing any more than they have for Solinthe's intel."

Sebastian nodded. "Done." He went over to Gwen and Delta. They conferred and the women dragged the secured fae up to his feet and started walking him toward the complex. Sebastian returned to me.

"Who has the puppy?" I asked, realizing I hadn't gotten an answer before.

As the words left my mouth, a squirming eager dog bounded on top of me. The pup let out a whine and bounced up to my neck, almost on top of the injury.

"Apparently, you do," Qest said.

"Hey sweetie," I said. Thank the Universe she was alright. "You did great."

She licked my face and whined again. Squirmed closer and sat on my chest.

"You flew out of that sling just like an arrow, sweets. My fierce little hunter. Prowess and beauty all in one package."

Artemis.

The name came to me as she yipped with pleasure. "How about calling you Artemis? The goddess of the hunt. She was wicked with a bow and arrow." I reached up with my non-injured arm and shoulder and stroked her fur. I much preferred her as an arrow to the ones launched at us by Solinthe's men.

And there was no doubt the faerie queen had sent them. To murder me or Leslie? Solinthe would consider it a bonus to get both of us. She was smart waiting for a moment when my magic was out of commission. How had she known?

Christian carried Leslie over to me and placed her on the grass by my side. She glared up at him. "Carrying me is unnecessary, I can walk."

"But it makes me happy. Humor me."

The null rolled her eyes at him, then turned to me. "Are you okay?"

"Fine. And thank you. You did well under fire. You saved my butt jumping on the fae's back."

"I think the puppy saved you."

I smiled down at Artemis. "She came through at a tough moment, yes."

"You could have let them kill me."

"Why would I have done that?"

"They're gunning for me. It's an easy solution to your problem."

"Not to burst your bubble, but I was equally a target. I'm not on the bad guy's BFF list. And you forget I promised to keep you alive."

"If you can."

"If I can."

"Then I owe you thanks." She held out her hand to shake, awkward from our positions on the ground.

Why not? I reached to take the offered hand. We touched, and it was then I noticed the blood on her fingers and remembered the blood on mine.

I dragged in a deep breath and---

The magic burst around us. Rainbow color, buzzing, beauty, painful intensity rocketing through my body. My muscles seized. The power riffled through my cells, through sinew, muscle and bone. Magic snaked into my body, and was sucked out again, in a continuous circuit. Again. Again.

I arched my back off the ground, my screams mixing with the garden's moans of pleasure.

Until finally...

The power evaporated and I slammed back to the ground.

"Rachel," Qest was over me, holding my arms.

I sighed and rolled to my side, resting. Within seconds, a sense of complete wellbeing settled over me. My body pulsed with strength and vitality. I pushed myself up and stood, brushing off grass from my clothes. "Well that was unexpected."

Although the men had that pained look of the sexual side effect that happened after I did big magic in their proximity, they powered through it, coughed a few times, and were able to stand straight. Mostly.

I looked down at Leslie, still on her back, who lie there blinking but saying nothing. Christian hovered over her. Her bruises and lacerations had vanished.

"Was that as good for you as it was for me?" I asked her.

Leslie's gaze focused and she stared at me. "What was that?"

"Magic. Getting its groove on with no particular place to go but our bodies. I'm completely healed. Even parts of me that weren't broken. I think it erased all current wear and tear."

"I do feel strangely good."

"And that is why I need to keep up the experiments. My blood is different than everyone else's. Yours too. We need to see this under a microscope, that's if it doesn't blow up the equipment."

She quirked a brow. "Inquiring minds want to know."

I chuckled. "Yeah." I turned to the guys. "Don't look so worried. We're fine."

Qest put on his familiar look of irritation. "Stop scaring us like this and maybe we'll be able to breathe."

Then I remembered. "Artemis?"

Behind me, a low bark met my call. I turned and met my puppy, swimming around in the air and wriggling with pleasure. Her coat glowed. And her eyes had turned emerald green. The color of my own. Interesting.

I opened my arms and she floated into them. "Let's get back to the complex. I have more pieces to connect to the puzzle."

"Detective Rachel has her fedora securely in place," Sebastian teased. "Adrenalin junkie puzzle master extraordinaire."

I prayed this health euphoria lasted through my next challenge for sake of its killer energy boost. I had a couple hours before I was due at council. And this latest adventure had nothing on dealing with that crew.

Chapter Twelve

Sebastian handed me a cup of piping hot coffee. "Here."

"It's not morning."

"I know. But I wasn't here to give it to you then. Tarn did the overnight shift. If you're going to council, you need all the reinvigoration you can get."

I still felt pretty darn good after the mingled blood incident with Leslie in the garden, but Sebastian looked like he wanted an excuse to talk, so I nodded and accepted the mug.

He stood there and watched me take a sip. Hot, black, strong. Just how I liked it. Sebastian provided the best goods.

I walked over to the couch, sat, and placed the mug on a coaster at the side table. I tapped the seat cushion next to me. "Sit. You look like you need some girl talk."

He twisted his lips at me, but sighed and trudged over to sit.

"So?" I said.

He grunted. "Tarn always takes the night shift guarding you now. He says it's the only safe way to work for you. I think he's going to resign." Sebastian ran his hand through his hair and sat back hard against the couch cushion.

I knew this was coming. I hadn't worked to find a solution fast enough.

"Rache, you have to keep him from quitting."

"I can't force him to stay."

"You want him to go?"

"I didn't say that. I'm trying to figure out how to cut him off from that fae book and Solinthe, but nothing is clicking."

"He blames himself for the attack in the garden today."

"He wasn't even there."

"I know. But Delta and I saw him just after you sent us away. Then Christian showed up after that. None of us said a word about what was happening, but he figures Solinthe made the appropriate deductions."

"Shit."

"Yeah. And the worst part is, he's probably right. We barely talk anymore because he's worried he'll hear something that harms you. Instead, he's throwing Delta and me together at every opportunity and going out on his own."

"I thought he was cozying up to her." My cheeks heated at my comment.

Sebastian's grew just as red. "He was. At times. And it pissed me off. But part of me was happy because it brought him relief. From, you know, the issue between us."

Elephant. Room. Never works out leaving it alone. Better to be plain spoken, no matter how it embarrassed both of us. "He loves you. Maybe Delta was an attempt to make you jealous."

"I figured. But there's something about her..." He looked off into the nothing of the room.

"You like her."

He blinked. "She's refreshing. And as much as she feeds off the perverse, she seems to care. It's a strange and alluring combination. She doesn't see anything...weird about Tarn and my situation."

He stood up, but hesitated. As if he wanted to run away but had no idea where to go. "If Tarn comes to you, don't let him resign. Please."

"You know what would get him to stay."

The shifter's eyes widened. He opened his mouth. Closed it. "Trade my body to get what I want."

"Give something you want to give to get something else you also want."

"I can't do it."

"You won't do it. There's a difference. You are brave enough to risk your life fighting Samuel, but not to freely explore your heart? I don't think so."

He was almost sputtering. "Dammit, Rachel, just tell him no."

"Sebastian, just tell him yes."

He spun to leave. "We'll be outside when you're ready to go to council."

Of course they would.

I was being too pushy. Too controlling as was my nasty habit. I couldn't judge if this relationship was right for Sebastian. Or maybe love needed a nudge at times. You have to jump off the cliff first if you are ever going to spread your wings and soar.

* * * * *

Council again. Ugh.

Sitting in that hard-backed chair made to breed discomfort. Seven representatives of seven races staring me down. The regular crowd. Two of them were friends in this new battle. The rest foes. Or so went my best guess.

Tarn, Sebastian, and Delta stood at my back. My fae guard attended me because there was nothing more to lose. Ivryind would witness it all as Solinthe's eyes and ears.

Time to start this rodeo from a position of strength and hope it didn't degenerate into violence.

I sat straighter in my chair and took the leap. "As you may have heard, I have officially challenged the Eemah to a battle for leadership of the Kyn. My father was a dragon; the Eemah's own son in fact. A case exists for my right to the position. The leadership of the Kyn typically overturns with a fight to the death between females of the race, so this is not unusual. I witnessed the Eemah's announcement to lead her people into mass suicide and destroy all of the Kyn through a fade in one week. That is unacceptable to me, as I am sure it is unacceptable to all of you. Hence, my leadership challenge. I am here to listen to your comments, but the decision has been made."

The pregnant silence filled with prickly energy. Mounting pressure swirled the air as my words punched through their shock and pushed buttons galore.

"How dare you interfere with Kesayim self-determination," Celendine huffed with his fists pounding the table. His wings fluttered out behind his backless seat.

The angels were sticklers for rules and propriety. As well as full of their own self-importance. Celendine was no exception. Or was he given his tryst with the demoness Morrea?

Ivryind sat back in his chair, his lips turned up just a hint, watching the beginning of the fireworks and letting the natural bent of the council do the work for him. Biding his time, the asshole.

Satan laced his hands together on the table. "And what pray tell you will happen to the Kesayim if you lose this battle, my lady? I fear for your safety. Plus, we would be without a leader and you have clearly been negligent providing an heir. I note a lack of consort. I am sure you know where babies come from by this age."

Satan would lose maybe a millisecond of sleep over my death. I saw the calculation cross his face. If I set precedent further for interference with internal Kesayim matters, he'd never win the struggle to end my angel/demon intervention.

"You cannot fight her," Aubrey insisted. His blue eyes bubbled with emotion and his hands opened and closed in constant motion. I imagined the claws they sometimes became. "The Kyn are dead already in all the ways that matter. They haven't participated in court for centuries. If the Eemah wants to end her people, you have no right preventing her."

I predicted the shapeshifter's sensitivity to talk of overthrowing current leadership. Our uneasy truce from the past would go quickly South.

"Qest sits on the council," I answered. "He participates."

Aubrey snorted. "A joke. The Eemah doesn't care what he does. She allows him to sit here to humor him."

All eyes turned to Qest for his reaction. He hid well, using a blank face to keep his emotions to himself. But I saw through the mask. My brother's turmoil, guilt, and grief continued.

"I support the Mother Heir's choice. I do not want to die. I suspect many of my Kyn brethren feel the same, but see no other way out of the Eemah's decision. Our lady offers that way. I would battle for the leadership myself if I were female. There are few females left among my people."

"If your fertility fails then this challenge is pointless," Celendine added. "The goddess favors you no longer."

Gwen came to attention at that comment and I watched her feathers ruffle. "If a problem exists with Kyn fertility, perhaps finding a cure rather than killing the patient is the better path," she said. "The goddess has nothing to do with it."

The witches' fertility was a sore subject. They'd experienced a drop in conception rates for some time, although they'd avoided advertising that fact outside of making me aware. If the other races tracked their fertility with such thoroughness, I suspected they would find something similar.

"You support the Mother Heir's audacity?" Frederick asked, speaking up for the first time.

There went the hope my past assistance with the vampire hunters won me points with the vampires on this issue.

Gwen's fiery eyes lit with passion. "If the alternative is a fade, then why argue over our lady's intervention with private Kyn matters? There will be no people left whose rights of self-determination we must respect."

Ivryind's voice took on a lazy drawl. "And if the council votes and we forbid this leadership challenge, my lady, what will you do?"

Careful, Rachel.

The power in the room continued to swirl. My own magic stirred, vital and questing and looking for a target. My anger danced around it, stirring the pot. If my strength had grown since the blood incident in the garden with Leslie, my control had as well, and I whispered to the anger to settle. Pouting, it followed my direction and curled up in a corner, waiting.

"I lead Eden's Court. Countless women before me have held this position for a reason. I am charged with preserving the Kesayim and Lillith's mandate to care for Earth and its mortal children. I cannot do that without exercising my power in ways I believe are legitimate. If the Kyn self-destruct, it undermines the very mandate Lillith created. I will fight the Eemah in one week whether or not you approve."

Their voices raised in protest. Aubrey looked on the verge of tearing apart the room. Spiky reds and oranges, black and greens painted the auras of the council.

Ivryind leaned forward in a quick motion. "And if the council votes to remove you, what then?"

The room went silent.

"How would they do that?" Threat laced my words.

"Without our presence you have no court to rule. If the Kesayim races remove their people form Eden's Court, we leave you with nothing."

"And when I travel to your realms, go out into the world and make myself known..."

"You would not be welcomed."

"Who would stop me?"

"I think my queen would have something to say about it. Her power matches yours, my lady. And her interests are nothing to dismiss. You make this unpleasant."

"No, Ivryind, you make this unpleasant. Solinthe makes this unpleasant and I am tired of her threat. I have told this council before that I am not to be underestimated. I'm feeling particularly ungenerous toward many in this room. However, the Kesayim are not the council. I care about what happens to all of the Kesayim. When I recover my temper after this meeting, I might even find I care about what happens to you again. Stranger things have happened."

"We vote," Ivryind insisted. "I say no, you shall not be allowed to challenge the Eemah."

"I vote no as well," Celendine added.

Aubrey, looking uncomfortable, mumbled, "No."

Frederick, "No."

Satan paused, sending me a speculative look. Then, "No." He always did like a bet, and I'd put him off too long about the angel/demon program.

Gwen, "Yes, she may battle."

Qest, "Yes."

Ivryind sat back again. "You have been outvoted. The next move is yours, my lady."

The anger stretched out from its corner, no longer able to wait. Snarly and ready for action. I embraced it, welcoming it to me and molding it to my needs. Ivryind thought he could bully me into submission. The rest counted on his momentum to carry them through. Not gonna happen.

Solinthe would only keep trying to kill me and Leslie. I refused to host a viper in my home.

I rose from my seat, gathering the power, sucking in what swirled in the room including a small draw from each of those present. Their eyes widened and gasps erupted around the table.

I knew what needed to happen. I'd done it before with Gabriel, although this time I wouldn't act out of fear or arrogance, even if the choice was imperfect and came with consequences.

My power grew. I dove into the earth and harvested the energy I needed. I began to weave the spell, painting the colorful lines and patterns in the air with witchly intent, humming a quiet tune of angel magic to strengthen the force of it. I swallowed the chaotic reactions from the witnesses and layered the song with demonic chaos energy, punctuating the twists of the spell with the hypnotic allure of the vampires, which made it so beautiful no one would care to avoid its pull.

I lifted the pattern of a wolf from the earth and wrapped the spell with its form. The lines, dots, and swirls became a tiny picture of the beast, howling to the non-existent moon, panting and eager to take effect. Next, I absorbed that magic wolf inside my body for brief moments, coating it in my blood and my focused intent as Solinthe had taught. It burst out of my center, charging back up into the air over the table. Howling still.

Finally, I nurtured my own dragon, calling her awake, asking her to breathe her fire onto the spell and harden it into impenetrable strength. She did, and the howl morphed into the roar of the Kyn. Magic from all of the races of the Kesayim woven into this weapon.

I scooped up the spell and held it in my palm. "Gentlemen and ladies. I am all Kesayim and my will decides upon this matter. Ivryind, as you and your queen seek to influence the council to your agenda, and are bent on destroying me in the process, you will no longer be welcomed in my court.

"In four hours, this spell takes effect and banishes all fae from Eden. You will all return to Faerie and keep your queen company. The portals will not welcome you back, nor to any other Kesayim realm. Enjoy, Ivryind."

With that, I blew the tiny wolf spell off my hand and it shot toward the fae. It hit him square in the chest.

He jerked back and light burst out of him and spread across the room, into Tarn, then out the door, hunting down every last fae now at court.

Universe, I prayed the choice was right. I braced for the pain from working the magic.

One, two, th....

It struck like lightning, coursing through my veins with a fierce burn. It circled through my vessels once, then twice, sputtering out quickly, but leaving me panting. Okay. Over now. I leaned, resting elbows on knees.

"Rachel," Sebastian called in warning.

I jerked up in time to see Ivryind, recovered and launching a charge over the table toward me, fae sword gleaming. A menacing blur.

I threw up a shield, braiding air and power.

In a breath, Tarn was shoving me to the side and colliding mid-air with his kinsman. Their swords clanged and they fell onto the table grappling. Blades dropped to the floor as bodies thudded together when fists met flesh. Fae enchantments spun between them as they battled.

Sebastian handed me to Delta and climbed up onto the table trying to pull the fae apart. The ghostly image of an ape floated over his body as he called on the power of partial shift.

Qest and Gwen joined the melee, Gwen preparing a spell of binding in the air, red and orange, purple and brown, curves and slashes the designs of this charm. Qest waded in to separate the two, dodging elbows and punches while wielding dragon magic to dampen their power.

He pulled Ivryind away. Sebastian held back Tarn as my fae guardsman tried for one last lunge at the council representative.

Gwen finished her spell and restrained Ivryind in a binding, wrapping the lines of her magic around his torso and limbs. Qest coated her charm with the Kyn's energy which was proof against most magic, preventing Ivryind from breaking apart the witch's work. She and my brother functioned together seamlessly.

Qest forced Ivryind to his feet and dragged him in front of me. Another success at council. Not!

I straightened my tangled clothes. "Gwen, call Morven. I want Ivryind escorted to the fae portal now. He's forfeited his four hours."

"You will pay for this, Rachel," the lavender-haired fae warned.

"Don't sound like such a cliché, Ivryind. You and your boss have forgotten that the fae are only part of our world, not its center. Maybe you'll both do a little soul searching back in Faerie. Oh, I forgot. Solinthe no longer has a soul. Too bad for her."

I tamped down hard on the lingering anger goading me to lash out at the councilman. *Bad girl, Rachel. Don't poke at the restrained fae.*

Gwen and Qest forced a growling Ivryind out of the room to retrieve Morven and get the extra guards outside the doors in on the action. Thankfully, shifters were on duty, not fae.

Tarn wiped his mouth where a cut from Ivryind's fists trailed a path of red. "Are you okay?" he asked me.

"Better than you."

"Good." He nodded.

The rest of the council, done playing spectator, made their escape, probably to stew on the events and continue plotting. They were smart enough to avoid me after my big voodoo.

Tarn re-sheathed his sword which had dropped to the floor when the attack had turned into a match of muscle and enchantment. The intricately designed scrollwork blade slid into its scabbard. "You made the right choice. I am glad."

No! Tarn!

In four hours, the spell would suck my guardsman back to Faerie. He knew it, and embraced that escape despite the danger of being subject to Solinthe's tender mercies. He carefully avoided looking at Sebastian and Delta.

Sebastian, on the other hand, glared at me hard. Delta refused to meet my gaze.

They escorted me back to my suite that way, with the three of them silent and hoarding their thoughts. And me with my heart a bruised mess. I'd banished my friend. History repeating itself.

Making hard choices rarely left a glow of satisfaction. More often, it left a stain of sorrow, tasting like ashes and tears.

Chapter Thirteen

The garden stopped wailing after we switched from cutting away the vines with swords to using our hands. Not that anyone in my party heard its caterwauling except me. But with news that a category five hurricane hit New England this morning, simultaneous to a typhoon in South Central Asia, and a volcanic eruption in the Mediterranean, my tolerance was low.

Pain everywhere I turned. My threshold kept being stretched farther, waiting for me to snap.

I'd insisted we switch strategies and put away the blades. A pleased satisfaction vibrated from the garden once we started using hands and fingers to weed our path, yet the densely-packed vegetation crowded in as if it wanted to delay our arrival.

"Jack brought the kids through here? You're sure?" I asked Christian again. Artemis perched on my shoulder, nipping at occasional vines and brushing my neck and shoulders with her tail. Listening. Always listening to my conversations.

Christian pulled down another vine before it smacked him in the face.

"Yes. Jack was quite clear when he came for Anna this morning."

The path to the desert section of the garden lay on the far side of a tropical rainforest. Apparently, the kiddies were romping around that desiccated tundra for fun today.

Leslie grunted, struggling to rip the vines but holding her own. "Christian convinced me she needed play time with kids. Maybe Peter and Gregor are fine, but I was stupid to let her go out when you've told me about the increased tension in this place. A dog is not enough protection." She swiped Christian an accusatory look.

I couldn't blame her. Time out of their guarded suite was risky for both mortals. Still, it couldn't be good for Anna to feel like a prisoner. Our progress through the forest was slowed by Leslie's presence, but she deserved to retrieve her daughter if she wanted.

Ahead of me, Sebastian and Delta struggled to clear our path. Gwen worked to our right. Her interest in coming along for the ride piqued my curiosity. When I'd asked about it, she gave some excuse about checking up on Peter.

"Although mostly," she'd said, "I'm in the mood."

The witch was her own woman, and I'd be foolish to try to understand her motivations. Frankly, I didn't have the time to attempt it.

I ripped another vine from my path and cursed the slow progress. No way would I allow the memories of my last time fighting a rain forest to leaden my chest.

That other jungle magically grew inside a suite of rooms belonging to a long-ago fae lord here at court. Tarn and I had hacked through its vegetation to retrieve the magical book to which he became tied, and so an unwilling spy for Solinthe.

Useless memories. Tarn was gone. He left last night, although he'd chosen to walk through the portal to

Faerie on his own instead of waiting for my spell to force him through. Like Gabriel had done.

Battling vines trumped walking the halls of Eden's Court now that I'd banished the fae. My people were back to looking at me through suspicious eyes. Gwen had been meeting with other Kesayim leaders to argue our position and do damage control. Maybe she needed a break too and considered our garden adventure a respite.

My attention drifted. I listened to Delta and Sebastian's comments to one another as they worked. Their faces shifted with animated expression, small barks of laughter erupting from one or the other in moments. They looked good together, with his bulky strength, her lithe, subtle frame. Rugged at the side of sleek. Somehow it irritated me. The balance was off. Like they were missing a middle.

Sebastian glanced back and caught me watching them. His face lost its animation and he averted his gaze.

It hurt. He had a right. I'd torn away his best friend. I hadn't been able to adjust the banishment spell, although I'd tried.

A voice buzzed in my ear.

I dragged my attention to Christian. "What?" I barked. *Damn, Rachel. Chill.*

Christian's aura pulsed intensely these days. His whole self was invested in our race against time. I loved him. This mess needed to turn out. For him. For everyone. I needed to make it happen.

Gwen wagged her eyes at my flare of temper. Universe, even she'd become dear to me.

My brother snorted at my barked response. "I was telling you we need another approach. The blood is not combining to any particular effect. None of the catalysts the scientist has added make a difference. The only time blood combining worked was between you and Leslie after the attack."

"Great. Best news ever."

"You don't have to bite the head off of the messenger. I thought you wanted updates."

"Sorry. So that means our bodies must be the living test tube we need. Something beside the blood alone makes a difference." I wiped away sweat from my forehead as Artemis licked my neck. "You know I think it's an emotional trigger. Leslie's effect changes when she's feeling things about you."

The null woman harrumphed hearing my familiar argument. "I think you see what you want."

His eyes flicked to Leslie. "We can talk about this later."

"You brought it up. The evidence is there. She's stopped draining your power."

His face tightened when I refused to drop the subject, but he answered. "Except when Anna's around. I am convinced she is also a null. So possibly Anna is doing the draining." He motioned in Leslie's direction. "Although you won't let me alone with her to confirm."

"Don't start that again, Christian," Leslie warned.

Gwen piped in with a timely distraction from the potential quicksand of that conversation. "It's suspicious that Ivryind never mentioned the girl before you booted him, Rachel."

"I know."

And it worried me. Really worried me. I'd tried to reach Gabriel in my dreams last night and came up with empty air. What was happening in Faerie? My necklace squeezed around my neck with the thought.

The witch kept speculating. "Or maybe the fae considered the child's existence moot given his queen's focus on taking you down."

Gwen had a way with cheery words. Not.

She forged on without missing a beat. "Qest is meeting with Aubrey, Celendine, Frederick, and Satan now to sway their opinions over your battle with the Eemah. Not that they listened to me when I tried, but perhaps because he is of the Kyn they'll lend his words weight." Gwen stopped mid-pull and cocked her head. "I think I hear voices ahead."

"Anna?" Leslie asked. "Thank god."

Gwen laughed. "God has little to do with the situation. More a matter of sweat and persistence on our part. The garden does like to make things interesting."

Said garden started humming a children's tune in my ears. I wondered if I could find a therapist for a sprawling stand of vegetation with a perverse sense of humor and a multiple personality disorder.

Sebastian pulled a last vine. "I've broken through."

The group pushed apart the last of the greens and left behind the shaded humidity. Dry heat blasted our faces. I swallowed a mouthful of sand as wind curved over reddish cliffs and sloping hills. I coughed out the debris and rubbed my grit-filled eyes, opening them wide. Blinking to make sure I wasn't imagining what I saw.

Three unicorns flying, with our errant children on their backs. Unicorns can't fly. I said it again out loud just to make sure.

"No, they cannot," Christian agreed.

"Anna, my god," Leslie cried.

Peter, Gregor, and Anna galloped through the air mounted on three of the gorgeous beasts. Anna rode my personal touchstone, her black tipped horn in view as she glided through the air in lazy loops while the girl giggled nonstop. A My Little Pony experience come to life. My nephew urged on his mount, kicking her withers with his heels, grasping her horn for security, and whooping up a storm.

Jack trotted over from the low sandstone hill on which he watched the kids. "Hiya, Rache."

"Jack, the kids are flying. Did you think maybe you shouldn't let them do this?"

"The unicorns just appeared. The kids jumped on their backs. The unicorns thought that was dandy. I don't argue with unicorns. Do you know what happens to guys who argue with unicorns? Shish Kabob. Those horns are serious weapons and they're not afraid to use them."

"But unicorns can't fly."

"I know. We've already covered that ground. You feeling all right, Rache?"

"Peter is doing it," Gwen offered. "You can see the colored remnants of his spell floating over him."

"He's strong enough for that magic?"

She shook her head, a dazed look to her gaze. "No, Peter is not strong enough for that magic."

"But how?"

"Absolutely no friggin' idea, Rachel."

Leslie's voice turned cold. "Get them down."

Gwen shrugged. "I can try a spell, but it would be safer if Peter landed them." Her hands moved in poetry, twisting the air in knots of color to create her magic. "This will amplify our voices so we can speak to the little troublemaker."

"Peter," she called, the sound traveling loud and clear through the air. "Land the beasts and let us talk to you three."

He waved down to me. "Isn't this cool?" he called back, his voice amplified to us. "You didn't tell me Gregor and Anna would make my magic bigger, auntie. I kick ass."

I hadn't thought about Leslie's and Anna's effects. Peter obviously wasn't blocked by Anna before we arrived. And Gwen's spell worked fine.

"No foul language, Peter. Your father will skewer my hide if I send you back with a gutter mouth. The only ass that might be kicked will be your own."

"Watch what I can do," he said. The boy proceeded to wave up another spell, a glowing corded lasso forming in his hands.

My belly started a ruckus. *Remember, Rachel. You do not believe in corporeal punishment.*

Artemis yipped in my ear as my necklace tightened...and Peter threw the lasso. Score. Directly around the horn of the beast Gregor rode. Peter smiled wide.

What would the animal do? I saw it pull up short, surprised, hoofs digging into the atmosphere.

I watched the slack part of the rope tauten in Peter's hands. His fists tightened around it, the material caught around his wrists. His body began to be pulled.

He had seconds.

In reflex, I dove for my power, jerked it up from the sandy earth and flung a snapping electric line of energy at the cord.

Thwack.

The sharp tool severed the rope. Peter teetered.

Almost.

Universe, please.

Peter's gasp and yelp chimed clear, his body tipping. Until a gust of wind pushed him upright on the unicorn. Gwen lowered her arms, her woven spell knot short, sweet, and tight.

The sob caught in my throat. "Thank you." My anger burst in fast and furious after the fear. "Land! Now!"

Peter struggled to get himself together. But the smart kid grasped the horn in one hand and lifted his other to start drawing his spell. His hands shook but he managed. The unicorns rode the magic, hooves skipping over air as they lowered to the ground, as if they'd flown all their lives.

Sebastian lay his hand on my shoulder. "Calm down, Rachel. He's safe. He's a good kid. That was fast magic. Faster than I've ever seen you do."

His kindness softened me and I swayed as the fear trickled away. When they touched down, Peter jumped off but loitered near his ride, petting her and whispering in her ear. Delaying and probably rebuilding his courage.

Gregor slid off his unicorn and went over to Anna, helping her off her beast.

Jack's tongue lolled. "He's been crushing on her since he met her this morning. He's a polite tyke."

"Yeah," Sebastian said. "My brother raised him well."

My unicorn left Anna behind and approached me. I froze, amazed as always with her nearness. She lowered her horn toward me. I stopped breathing. The tip caressed my necklace. She nickered, soft breath blowing against my throat. A warm wave of comfort engulfed me, like a warm bath cradling my body, washing away the fear and anger. She sent me confidence and love, and I drank it down, welcoming every molecule.

The unicorn lifted her horn and gave me a slow blink. She turned and her two beastly friends followed her out of the desert back into the forest.

Anna took that cue to run to her mother's arms. Gregor walked our way with hands stuffed in his jeans pockets. He was a handsome kid, with the potential for all the rugged good looks of his uncle.

Peter gazed after the disappearing unicorns. I knew how he felt.

With an apologetic grimace already on his face, he made his way to us. Or to Christian I might say. Guess he was calculating odds on who would be least upset with him.

"Hey, Uncle Christian. Sorry about that last bit."

Christian enveloped him in a hug, then grabbed his arms and pulled him back to send a good glaring warning. "Whether the stunt gets edited out of the message to your father isn't decided. But you owe your aunt and Gwen a thank you for saving you from that mess."

Peter turned on his charming sparkle of a smile and went to me for his own hug. "Thank you, Aunt Rachel. I'm sorry."

Aside from the mellow my unicorn left me with, I could never stay mad at this kid. "Just don't do it again." My heart couldn't take it.

He laughed with mischief. "I promise that next time three unicorns wander along to give me, Gregor, and Anna a ride, we absolutely won't go flying with them." He turned to Gwen. "Thanks also, Ms. Gwen."

She pursed her lips, gave him a once over, but ended in a smile. "I'll take an explanation of the power you demonstrated, young man."

My thoughts exactly.

"Epic, huh?" Peter cracked his knuckles and wiggled his fingers.

"What's happening to your magic?" I asked. "You said bigger."

"When Gregor showed up, it was like he made my spells clearer, cleaner. Like I could throw them straight and they'd hit bullseye every time. But that doesn't make sense because he's Achra and Achra shapeshifter kids don't have special skills."

True. So, what the heck was going on with Sebastian's nephew?

Gregor stiffened. "Hey, magician, I can whup your butt anytime. That's skill enough."

"Gregor," Sebastian warned.

Peter shrugged. "No offense, Greg."

"What happened when Anna arrived this morning?" I asked.

"That's when it got really awesome. Now the spells are clearer and revved up a gazillion percent."

"Everywhere or just in the garden?"

"Dunno about with Anna. I didn't try magic before we came here. But I can also do these sweet aerial flips without the unicorns. You should have seen me."

"What about the effect with Gregor?"

"Oh, that's the same in the court complex, too."

I sighed. "You'd think someone would have noticed this before."

Sebastian answered. "We don't mingle our kids with the other Kesayim. Even those born to two shifters."

Damn Kesayim racial isolationism. Nothing good had come of it.

Anna pulled away from her mom. "It feels good, though. Is that wrong?"

Leslie froze. "What feels good?"

"When Peter uses his magic."

Every hair on my body stood at attention. "What does it feel like exactly?"

Anna looked at her mother as if for approval to answer the question. Leslie's lips tightened, but she gave a nod. The girl looked down at the earth, as if she were trying to concentrate. "Like a full-up feeling after eating a big meal. First, he starts to do his stuff. Then this really warm, happy food pours into me. It, like, bubbles inside. Then it goes down."

"Down where?" A churn of carbonated excitement went through me.

"To the ground. Like one of those bouncy balls. It drops, but kinda below the ground. Then it hits somewhere under there and bounces up. I didn't think I could catch it since it moves real fast. But I can. Then I bounce it back to Peter. He really likes that. His eyes light up and he starts to do, like, magic stuff."

"Can you see what happens with Gregor?"

She scrunched her face again. "Maybe like it streams through him when I bounce it back and he takes out bumpy, rocky parts and sends it on really pure. Cleaner, Peter said. Like that. It even smells cleaner."

"Do you see and smell everyone's magic?" Christian asked.

She looked at her mom again, then back at Christian, and down to the ground. "Um, I guess I've kinda felt a little warm and full around folks here and all. But it never bounced down to the ground, just kinda gets stuck and made me feel stuffed. And not so good. My ears always feel clogged when people visit our rooms here. Nose too. You know when you have a bad head cold." Anna smiled at Peter. "But I feel better now. Can we hang out in the garden every day?"

"Don't worry. Aunt Rachel's cool. I'm sure she'd say yes. And since she's the big boss, she decides."

"Hate to break it to you kid, but Anna's mom is her big boss. And her word goes."

Leslie's surprised eyes flew to me, but she mouthed a thank you. The faces of my friends and family grew sharp in that moment. I didn't feel like the big boss, more a stumbling kid trying to figure out some secret code that would let me take care of them. But I'd gone and lost the decoder ring that came in the cereal box. I desperately wanted to find that ring. I didn't want to lose them. Not now.

I was so close. My eyes started burning and filled with liquid. Frickin' inconvenient. *Stop it, Rachel! Silly rabbit, tricks are for kids.* I blinked hard and rubbed my hands together. "Okay, team. Back to the complex. Christian, you and I have strategy to plan. Gwen, can you--"

A clap of sonic noise. The pain forced me to cover my ears.

A jagged bolt of electricity sizzled the air. Then, darkness flickered over the sandstone red desert. After a handful of seconds, light returned.

She stood on the nearest rolling dune.

Lillith.

Shit!

The stunned looks from Christian, Gwen, Sebastian, Peter, and Delta gave way to their sudden lurch to their knees. Even Jack crouched on doggy fours. Bad habits of Millennia spent worshipping her illusionary awesomeness. Even after I'd told them about her true colors.

"Goddess," Delta gasped.

The others echoed her.

Only Leslie, Gregor, and Anna remained standing, clueless and confused over the identity of this visitor. If I thought she'd leave right away, I'd hit my knees, too.

I could never be so lucky. Lillith's smirk nauseated me.

"At least some of my people know how to show their respect, daughter." The goddess paraded down the hill toward us.

Stand your ground, girl. "Quite an entrance. Have you been studying theatre, Lillith?"

"If you would pause a moment before offering your bravado, daughter, you might learn something important." Hands on hips, with nitrogen cold seeping from her and turning the desert icy, she surveyed my group. "I came to warn you your timetable is incorrect."

"What?!"

"Earth will be dead in four months. But long before that, humanity will have perished." She cocked her head. "I'd say within a month. Yes, the shock waves of the crumbling core puts it at about that."

No!

I grit my teeth, held in the sob, and let out my anger. "You didn't think I'd need to know before now? You sound damn pleased for a creator who wants it all saved."

The desert grew colder. A layer of frost coated my arms. Anna burrowed into her mother, muffling the girl's whimpers.

"One month. You were so pleased with your imagined clues to saving it all. And so certain that my rules do not count any longer. That will end. Now!" Her familiar body dissipated, replaced by the jarring lines and loud, unnameable colors. Danger.

This time, she couldn't keep me from magic. I pulled every bit possible, grabbing the power of Sebastian, Delta, Gwen, Christian, and Peter--hungry, gulping sweeps as they offered it to me. My awareness of our blend grew crisp. My will to gather more power detoured, attracted to Leslie and Anna, sifting through them and out before the deep dive and scoop of energy from the core. Up again, through the two nulls, and back to my hands and body. My will.

Lillith struck.

I fireballed out my power.

The blast of contact between our force threw me backward. Skin skidded over rock and sand. Scraping burn.

The goddess's power was a maelstrom, lashing out again a moment later toward my kneeling people.

I couldn't stop it again. Not fast enough.

"No!"

Hit!

Christian cried out, a deep agony. His back arched as he fell to the ground.

Jack gave a keening yelp and his body was thrown up in the air, crashing down in a limp heap. I smelled his burning hair.

I lunged back standing, drew magic again. I wanted to hurt her. My will formed, deadly. *Not my people.*

My power flew. Contact. The swirling chaos of her form caved inward. The colors faded out for long seconds.

"One month," her screech sounded. "Do not risk it all by breaking the rules." She pulsed once more, and blinked away. Leaving an empty, awful quiet punctuated by my loud sawing breaths. It filled further with Anna's sobbing tears.

I ran to Christian. Leslie cradled him where he lay still on the ground. Peter crouched next to Jack, his tears the silent swallow of a boy trying not to seem unmanly.

Gwen was checking both. "Alive," she confirmed.

Sebastian knelt near Christian, fingers to his pulse. "Barely."

Gregor stood over him, shell-shocked. Delta had her knives out, as if there was anything left to attack.

I wanted to destroy all over again. Why did Lillith do this?

I tried calling magic. Blocked again. Not now. "Leslie, Anna, don't stop my power. Let it drop to the earth. Focus, or something. Whatever you freaking do. I need to heal them."

Peter looked at me with pleading eyes. Then over to Anna, sitting near her mother crying. He left Jack and went to Anna, whispered in her ear, earnest, with lips moving relentlessly over his words. She nodded between tears.

Leslie swallowed and squeezed her eyes shut tight. Touched Christian's face, holding his cheeks between her palms. Silent tears squeezed out from beneath her lids.

I reached again for the power. Nothing. Nothing. Then...

The flow opened. The circuit connected. I milked the energy from the core and spread it over Christian and Jack. Healing brightness, mending balm. My own body shook with it, I pumped it so fast over their broken frames.

Christian's eyes opened. He coughed and gasped in a breath.

"Thank god," Leslie said.

Jack raised his doggy head, wobbled to his feet and almost collapsed again. He got himself straightened, raised a paw to lick at it, and let out a woof. For once, he had no words.

I closed my eyes. Artemis, perched on my shoulder, having hung on to me through the battle, now licked my cheek as if to reassure me everything was fine. Universe, if only that were true.

Not four months. One month. And the goddess was willing to kill those I loved as sure as the impending disaster would in the end.

Dragons to battle and save, a shapeshifter nation to defend, and the stealth of a mad faerie queen to guard against. Nulls to find and protect, and the blood of races to combine to keep our world alive.

"O, that way madness lies; let me shun that; No more of that." King Lear had it right. I couldn't slip.

No freaking way would you win, Lillith. Or lose. Or whatever it is you want. Are you listening, Lillith?

No one answered.

Chapter Fourteen

O mania, thou art my friend. Pretty sure Shakespeare never penned that one. Eleven p.m. and I kept the fire molten hot to melt the steel. Who knew the Mother Heir had a private workshop including kiln? The kiln needed magic to burn hot enough for my purposes since it wasn't the right type of furnace, but that was easy enough.

Pots, bowls, mugs and vases of various designs dotted the shelves around me. My mother, Eva, had created these. Morven told me about it when she'd indulged my whim an hour earlier and directed me to this room.

Why was I so full of energy? I would do this. I kept seeing images of chains and ropes tying souls together. Gabriel and mine. Peter's lasso tie to the unicorn. Tarn chained to that damn book.

I never wanted to sever the first, had used my magic to sever the second, and indulged a fantasy about finally dealing with the third.

Pacing my bedroom after Lillith's attack worked me into a hyper state. The vision of those chains kept popping into my head. How did I think of it when I cut Peter's lasso? That my magic acted like a sharp tool? A tool. And then Solinthe's tutelage hit me. The solution for Tarn. I made Delta call for Morven. Here was a problem I might be able to solve, as well as a distraction from the image of Christian almost dead on the desert floor.

And here I was, having coated the smallest particles of my magic in my blood, and about to pour the molten steel into the mold for a scissors, both blades and the screw to connect them. My intent as the liquid expanded into the shape gave the magic a home as I lay each particle of my energy down upon the molecules of steel. My magic carved the grooves and head of the screw as well as any machine. My will brought the scissors' purpose to life.

I created the tool to cut the cord between Tarn and that book. A fae tool to affect a fae artifact. Now all I was missing was the man upon whom to use the tool. Timing was everything, and mine sucked.

I pushed my goggles back on my head, placed the casting ladle on the workbench, and dissolved the magical protection keeping my hands from burning.

I stared at the pieces of scissors, wishing they were cool. So I could do what with them? I needed to reach Gabriel and figure out what was happening in Faerie.

* * * * *

The Grotto was packed. Gwen's brother and his band were playing again, but this time she'd dragged me along to listen, insisting I needed a break from conferencing with Christian. The group's strange fusion mix of Cajun, hip-hop, and Indian influences drifted up as soon as we opened the iron door to the subterranean bar. Sebastian and Delta proceeded Gwen and I down the stone steps.

As we made our way over the dirt-packed floors, weaving among stone tabletops, I spotted Qest already seated in a prime position near the stage. He smiled as he listened, tapping his fingers on the table to the hypnotic beat.

Five men rocked the stage, lights strobing around their performance. I still couldn't believe the shaven-headed, multi-pierced, tattoo-faced vocalist was Gwen's brother. Non-traditional must run in the family.

Qest leaned over to give me a kiss on the cheek as we sat. Then gave the same to Gwen.

"My rooms tonight?" she asked him.

"Of course," he answered.

Interesting.

He moved his chair to make room for our party of four. "Your brother amazes me. This is a completely different set from the other night, but the music is mesmerizing."

Gwen's attention to the stage hinted of a deep fondness for her brother. "Raphael was born with a musical soul. He sang before he spoke it seemed."

Delta watched Raphael as well--fascinated. "He sings like honey."

A waitress came over to take our order. "Nothing for me," Sebastian said, and frowned Delta's way.

I worried over his growing number of frowns, although at least he'd stopped glaring at me since yesterday with Lillith.

An impulse hit. "Why don't you and Delta dance?"

He didn't like the impulse. "Our job is to guard you, which clearly you need."

"Your job is to follow my orders. Now dance. Gwen and Qest have my back."

My shapeshifter guard glanced around. "This place is crowded. Crowds mean danger."

"Everyone is steering clear of me since I banished the fae, so no worries."

I swallowed past the truth to my bravado and stared Sebastian down. A glare returned. I stuck out my tongue at him. He slit his eyes at me. I wagged my eyebrows. Sebastian gave up the battle and sighed.

Delta, watching us closely, grinned. "That settles it." She pulled him onto the dance floor. A party girl was our demoness. Her hands wrapped possessively around his backside, drawing him close and using her hips to lead the dance. Although I'd like to chalk it up to simple sexual chemistry, I could see how Delta might be good for Seb. A stab of sadness hit me again over Tarn. Delta and Sebastian's mutual consolation brought them closer, leaving my fae friend behind. Of course I was the one sending them up to the dance floor. I needed to stay out of the entire thing.

The waitress cleared her throat. She'd waited patiently for us. I ordered red wine, Qest a dark ale, and Gwen a straight shot of whiskey.

The alcohol arrived and Gwen lifted her glass to us. "May you have warm words on a cold evening, a full moon on a dark night, and a smooth road all the way to your door."

I clinked her glass. "Amen."

"A smooth road would be nice," Qest agreed. He took a swallow of ale. "But the crap I'm getting back from council is more like one riddled with pot holes." He placed the glass down on the table with precision.

I didn't like the look he flashed me. Here it comes. Brace for it.

"You can't fight Grandmother," he announced. "Aubrey and Celendine plan to have you arrested if you go through with it."

"Let them try. I'll deal with them if it happens."

Fire glinted his eyes. "I've thought about this. Let me fight her instead."

"You know why I have to be the one to do it. Even if you succeed, the rest of the Kyn would tear the meat from your bones afterward. They won't accept a male leader. It's against their code."

"Said the woman who flaunts all Kesayim traditions. Pot, kettle, sister."

"I'll take the risk."

"So, it's fine for you, but too risky for everyone else. I can't decide if you have a Jesus complex or are just that blind."

"I'm not blind."

"You need help," he answered.

"I'm taking help. Lots of people are helping me. You, Gwen, Christian. Christian's proof I'm letting folks help even if it kills them. Literally. I'm not some lone cowboy." Dammit, how dare he accuse me. I'd worked hard to change.

"I think you believe that." He sat back and crossed his arms.

Gwen leaned into the conversation. "Your brother's only worried for you, Rachel. You're on edge, running from challenge to challenge, disaster to disaster."

"You did hear Lillith yesterday? One month, Gwen. You suggesting I sit back and give myself a manicure?"

"I heard."

"Yet you drag me down here to give me a lecture."

"No one can survive twenty-four seven on a diet of work. If the task kills you before you accomplish it, no one will be better off."

My nails dug hard pricks into my palms. "You tell me that a month from now. Or maybe don't. Hard to lecture more when you're dead."

Gwen sent pleading eyes to Qest. "We might find another option. Some combination of our magics and gender to battle the Eemah."

Burning, scratching irritation stretched inside me. "We don't have time to figure out new strategy. I don't have time. Sometimes an old-fashioned battle is the way to go. Leave it, Gwen. Leave it or just leave."

"Don't be an idiot, Rachel," the witch answered.

My fists started to ache.

A new voice, male and amused, broke up the argument. I hadn't noticed that the music had stopped until he spoke. "Sorry to disturb the joyful conversation, but I thought I might interrupt before you obliterate my dearest sister." He gestured down to my clenched fists. "Gwen gets a might bossy at times so I understand your feeling. Perhaps I can help."

Rafael pulled up another chair and sat between me and his sister. He offered his hand. "Raphael, my lady."

"It's Rachel. And I'm sorry to meet you while in this pissy mood. It's not Gwen's fault, although she'd do better to stay out of my disagreement with my brother."

The singer chuckled. "I try to honor the long-standing tradition of sibling squabbles. They are a cornerstone of the meaning behind family."

Raphael's facial tattoos distracted me. The dark ink and colors of a peacock covered most of one side of his face. The other cheek had multiple smaller designs, mostly animals, jockeying for prominence. Maybe it was tribute to his band of shapeshifters.

"Raphael, don't be a jackass," Gwen griped. "Don't you have more music to play?"

"I pride myself in my jackassery, Gwennyth." He blew her a kiss. "And I'm on break. Have to rest the pipes sometime." He turned away from his sister to face me. "I've been wanting to meet you."

Within a blink, Sebastian was there standing over me, with Delta at his side. "Any problem, my lady?"

"No. I'm just getting cozy making new friends and sharing laughs. Sit down you two, my neck hurts."

They sat and shook hands with Raphael. Delta used amazing willpower to keep herself from asking for an autograph. Fangirl by her eager look at the singer.

The waitress came by and Gwen's brother ordered a seltzer and lime. He leaned back and rested intertwined fingers upon his flat belly. "You've been causing quite a stir here at court. Lots of new speculation about your hunger for power since you banished the fae."

"Really?" I drawled. "Do tell."

"Rumors run from your intention to enslave all Kesayim races, to killing us off as part of a horrid Achra conspiracy from your previous life, to the tragic story of how you're suffering brain damage from a childhood injury as an orphan. Very unpredictable behavior from brain damage you know. You're delusional."

"Where's the money rest?" I asked.

"Conspiracy with the Achras."

I tsked. "I'd have thought enslavement."

"The logistics of that plot are too complicated for the average Kesayim to imagine. No creativity in this bunch."

"You could bottle-feed them an enslavement scenario, start whispers. Or roll all three plots into one. Makes for better drama. Maybe even an HBO series."

Gwen rolled her eyes. "I'm not sure which one of the two of you are more incorrigible. You're both insane."

The singer grinned wide at his sister. "I like her." He tossed his head at me. "You remind me of your da."

"You knew my father, too?"

"Raphael lived with me the period Rom visited," Gwen said.

Raphael laughed. "I almost got your father to join my band. He played a mean bass guitar."

I slapped the top of Qest's hand. "You never told me that."

"Ouch. I never knew that."

Raphael's drink arrived and he indulged. "Rom wouldn't do it. He was fascinated with Achra. I remember him sitting and writing for hours about his research and musings over the darlings. He must have filled up twenty journals in a month."

Journals? I caught Qest's eyes. "Where are they?"

Raphael shrugged.

Qest shook his head. "Not sure. We need to find them."

My necklace tingled around my throat. "Yes, we do."

I trusted my father, but I'd never met him. He'd been murdered and I couldn't shake the idea Rom had known something about the nulls. Maybe something that would help me save our world.

"I feel I owe you and Qest my thanks, actually," the witch continued, stirring the lime in his glass with a swizzle stick.

"For what?"

"Your father did me a great service. One I never got the chance to repay. Helping his children is the closest I'll come."

I leaned forward, Qest the same, as if we could lean closer to our father with Raphael's words.

"He guarded something very important to me once," the tattooed man continued.

Gwen harrumphed. "It's not like the family was going to devour Jaida if we'd known about her."

Qest sent Gwen a quizzical look.

Gwen answered. "Raphael's wife. She's a shapeshifter. But back then he'd not shared the fact with us he loved the woman. Hadn't married her yet. Witches do not marry shifters. Rom knew and kept Raphe's plans a secret."

"Your da guarded the engagement ring for me as well," Raphael added. "And when Gwen and the family threw a fit upon the news of my marriage plans, he made the case for us and argued sense into them."

I swallowed hard. He'd guarded something precious for Raphael. Perhaps this was a Kyn trait. Even the Eemah had guarded my necklace for me all of the years Eden went without a Mother Heir.

"Rom was a good man," Gwen added. "And I'm ashamed to say I needed him to knock our heads together over Jaida." She turned to her brother. "I'm glad she's our family, Raphe. You know that, yes?"

Now the shapeshifter band made sense. This man had forged connection between Kesayim for years. Just like my father wanted.

Raphael smiled. "Maybe you and Qest can come to our place for dinner one evening. It's a wee space, but we're cozy."

"We'd love it," Qest said.

I blinked back the tears that arrived with no warning.

Gwen flicked Raphael on his cheek to get his attention. "You'll invite your sister as well, yes?"

"Wouldn't dare not, dearest sis."

She grunted. "Good. We'll be over a month and a day from now, Raphael." Gwen glanced my way and tipped her head. "Will that work for you, my lady?"

Very sly, my witch friend. Sure. A month and a day. Why not?

Chapter Fifteen

"Rachel, Rachel!"

Mist. Gray. Winding pathways.

"Rachel!"

Dreamscape. Gabriel. He'd found me.

"I'm here." *I sat up in the gray, swimming to consciousness.*

He was with me. Safe. His precious face, and sexy punch. Even a few days away from him was too much. I pushed the thin braid hanging from the side of his face back behind his ear. "I love you. How are you? What's going on in Faerie? Have you seen Tarn?"

He grabbed me by the arms, pulling me close. "Hush. You are speeding, love. I only have a few moments." *His lips came down, crushing mine. Warm. Melting. Strong.*

Gabriel broke the kiss and sighed in frustration. "Find Sebastian. Solinthe is incensed with what you did banishing the fae. She is executing Cindy and Felix tomorrow. Samuel brought them to her as a gift."

"No!" *We'd been struggling with a plan to find and save Sebastian's family, but so far hadn't located them.*

"Retribution," *he said.* "She knows I will tell you, but I will do what I can. Inform Aubrey and Sebastian."

"I have to get them out. Tonight."

"No. This is a trap. She wants you to come. Trust me to take care of it."

Trust. Yeah. But I refused to let the faerie queen kill Sebastian's family.

"One more thing," he said. Gabriel opened his palm and concentrated. Magic stirred and rippled up from his skin. A small scroll materialized. "The list of nulls and their locations."

"You found it."

"It took...some doing."

Even in a dream, my skin felt clammy imagining his meaning. I'd force the story of that 'doing' from him later.

"Concentrate, taking the scroll into your body," he said. "It can survive the transition back to waking if you absorb it and weave the information into your blood."

My hands grasped the paper. Gabriel layered his fingers over mine. The pulse of our connection throbbed deep. He strengthened me. Perfected me.

Diving for power, I pictured the particles of the scroll seeping into mine, and I tasted the names of each of the listed nulls, their faces and homes bubbling up through my mind. I took the last of it into my blood. The information settled and I was left to feel the soft caress of Gabriel's fingers on mine. I shuddered, needing this.

Gabriel closed his eyes and took in a deep breath. "Solinthe comes. I must leave."

"Solinthe knows you're here?"

"I said so. Now go, love."

"I'll be there soon. Where is she holding Felix and Cindy?"

"I forbid you to come."

I snorted. *"Like that ever had a chance of working."*

"Do not, Rachel!"

I wiggled my fingers at him. *"Goodbye. See you on the dark side."* And willed myself awake.

"Rachel, dammit, they're in the Public Forum!" he shouted as everything faded.

Gasping, I sat up in bed. A scroll lie clutched in my hands. Artemis crouched on my pillow, watching me with curious eyes.

I threw the scroll to the mattress and jumped into sweats and a t-shirt, tucking the pup in her invisible sling. Turning to leave the bedroom, I thought better of it, and went back for the dagger I'd crafted in Faerie. And Tarn's scissors. Along with two holsters for them.

Delta stood guard duty in the hall. If I planned to sneak into Faerie, bringing her or anyone at all put them at risk. Solinthe expected me, so none of my companions had a chance. That meant going solo. Which meant weaving the air into a shield to become invisible so I didn't have to argue with my friends. A few motions later, I had my invisibility and an illusion ready so Delta wouldn't notice the door opening to my suite.

The demoness stood leaning against the wall outside the door, humming a tune, her red eyes scanning the hall. Vigilant, but with her usual carefree spirit. Underneath it, she hid much more. She was a complex recipe with so many hints of sweet and savory spices. I looked forward to discovering all of them, and if we stayed alive, I'd get my wish.

My invisibility worked and after turning the corner away from the suite, I ran. To the newly created portal to Faerie since it was closer than the usual one. I'd hidden it with my magic and hoped like hell that meant Solinthe didn't know about it. When I'd arrived in Faerie using it last time, she'd been distracted by the showdown between Aubrey and Samuel and may not have been paying attention to Tarn's observations.

The garden chanted as I jogged. *"Mother Heir. Mother Heir. Mother Heir."* The racket would wake all of court if I wasn't the only one that heard it.

The invisibility spell unwound as I moved. I had no one to hide from here in the middle of the night. I'd need another spell like it when I entered Faerie. The scent of pine, spruce, and fir clogged my nostrils. Christmas themed extraction mission? The garden's humor boggled.

Almost there.

I spied shapes in the distance. Shit!

I jogged the last bit and stopped at the portal. Sebastian obviously remembered where I'd hidden it.

"What are you doing here?" I demanded of Sebastian and Qest.

"Gabriel. Funky dream magic," my guard answered.

"He tattled. Well, you can't stop me. I'm going tonight."

"Not trying to. We're going with you. This is my brother and sister-in-law, as well as my job to protect you. Don't make trouble."

"My proof against magic will come in handy among the fae," my brother added. "Gabriel is afraid for you. He loves you, obstinate sister. I feel the same but might be more willing than he to wring your neck."

"I'm surprised you didn't drag everyone."

Sebastian checked his sword and gun on scabbard and holster. "No time. Gabriel told me to get my ass here fast. Do you have a plan?"

"No."

"Which is why Gabriel tattled," Qest said. "He knew you would be idiotic enough to go alone and without any forethought."

"Isn't he Mr. Omniscient. I do have some resources of my own."

Qest straightened. "Now you have more."

"This is Solinthe we're talking about."

"Yes, it is," he said.

If they got killed tonight, by the Universe, I'd kill them dead a second time.

"Fine. Give me a moment to throw up invisibility and soundproofing around us and we'll go."

"That's almost like a plan," Sebastian teased.

At least his frown was gone. It only took a dangerous, life risking secret mission to jolly his mood. Or maybe he hoped to see Tarn there. I know I did.

"Shut up."

"She's grumpy in the middle of the night," Qest added.

I promised him retribution with my stare. He ignored me.

So I worked my power and made us invisible and silent. This time, I reached for my dragon, borrowing Kyn energy to instill my woven screen with a taste of anti-magic to protect it from Solinthe's immediate detection. Qest was right. Kyn power was a strong tool for dealing with her Most Poison Eminence.

I gulped up greedy amounts of power from the earth, storing it within myself to go in guns blazing if needed. Ready as I'd ever be.

We stepped through the portal to Faerie.

Chapter Sixteen

The lack of immediate ambush kept my gut churning full speed while creeping through the viper pit of Faerie. Where was Gabriel? Knowing him, he was distracting Solinthe. But with my scent up her nostrils, and the personal nature of our battle, even my talented incubus would be hard put to do much. Universe, keep him safe from her.

Our destination wasn't far from the new portal. The Public Forum, like every other part of this realm, was a type of manipulation and lie. The open-aired building going by the name, its roof held high by four stately Greek columns, gave visitors a clear view of a dais, twelve foot by twelve foot, at its center. Like a stage erected for use by the community. For deadly use.

A full moon, its magenta color flickering in odd on-again-off-again patterns in the sky, cast bloody shadows on Faerie. The light was plenty to show us our goal. On the center of the dais stood two wooden structures, crosses by the looks of them, with Felix and Cindy unconscious and manacled to their highest point. Red welts, contusions, and bruises covered their skin. No guards stood watch. The place was empty but for the prisoners. The entire set-up smelled of a trap. Steel and poison.

"Let's go," Sebastian whispered, his body tensed and ready to run to his brother.

"Wait," Qest said, restraining him with his arm. "It's an illusion."

"They're not there? Sure the hell looks like it. I'm getting them out."

"This is Faerie. Nothing is as it seems," I said. "What do you think?" I asked my brother.

"I see what is supposed to be Felix and Cindy, but I also see the faint outlines of a maze. Mirrored walls twisting in paths through almost the entire space of the Public Forum's interior. I can't tell if they're actually at the center or not. If we run straight at them, we'll hit the mirrors."

My magic expanded and the foggy outline of the maze appeared to me. The trap.

"Can you smell them?" I asked Sebastian. "Use other senses, not vision."

He closed his eyes and his nostrils flared. "Yes. It's them. Even over the stink of Faerie, I smell their blood and their fear. We have to get them out."

I wanted that too, but we couldn't be stupid about it. Stupid got everyone dead. "It's what the invisible maze conceals that I'm worried about."

"Then you or Qest turn into your dragons. That will shatter the whole thing."

Qest snorted. "As well as anyone inside. Kyn size and power are not subtle. The idea is to get your brother and his wife out alive."

I nodded. "Baby with the bathwater. Yeah, that's a no go. I'll throw a little bit of energy at the outside of the maze and see what happens. A pebble size since we still need to try to keep a low profile."

"Can your magic go out through our shield?" Qest asked.

"It never blocks what I purposefully send outside of it. And our senses aren't blocked from what happens out there, only what others perceive of us from the outside."

The pebble arched out and clinked the mirror.

The ripple started small, swirling over the surface of the mirrors. Faster.

Shifted. Hurricane quick. A spout of power erupted and roared back toward me as I threw up a second layer of shield.

"Incoming," Qest yelled.

Instinct had me crouched with arms over my face. The backlash ate across the outside of our protection, demanding entrance. The heat permeated and perspiration beaded my skin. The flame lasted a long minute then died away. The barrier held. Yes!

Sebastian stood and wiped his hand across his forehead. "I can see the maze now." Eight feet of tall mirrored walls blocked the view of the dais. The entrance to this labyrinth lay across from us.

I sighed. "No question Solinthe knows we're here now, and blasting the thing down with power seems like a bad idea."

Qest pulled out his sword. "Time to run the maze. As much as Kyn presence neutralizes other magics, at the heart of Faerie in Solinthe's seat of power, I doubt it will have much effect."

"Understood. We stay together. I suspect it will be tight quarters. No guns, Seb. Ricochet bad. Go boom.

And don't be surprised if you can't shift inside it. Walking the interior of fae magic is a killjoy. My shields will fall."

My shifter pulled out his sword, too. "I'm ready for old-fashioned bloodletting."

I bounced on my toes and pulled my dagger. "Let's find the center of this thing."

We approached the entrance, weapons raised. I kept my power ready, but in super small increments for careful targeting. No hitting the mirrors. We risked being trapped inside, but I prayed Solinthe's gigantic ego drove her to want a face to face confrontation and not simply locking us inside this oversized mouse trap. And wasn't that a twisted wish indeed.

Qest took point, me next, and Seb at the rear. We entered. Mirror images of us bounced back, distracting our progress. My green eyes looked too wide for comfort. Who was this woman I'd become these last few months? Every time I thought I knew, my knees were knocked out from under me.

Possible paths through the maze branched out fast. The corridor measured about three bodies wide, surprisingly roomy. Fae enchantment affected size and distance in here, so more space could exist than looked possible.

"Which way?" Qest asked.

Magical tracking didn't work, but enhanced senses did. "Smell it out for us, Sebastian."

He moved to the front of our group. I turned 'on' my shapeshifter nose and we both forged forward, following the path. The way smelled of acrid power and inky malice. A trace of sour fear and the metallic scent of blood from the captives drew me forward. Then, new scents of linen, horses, sage, and leather. We had guests.

"Ahead, coming up fast," the shifter yelled.

Sebastian raised his sword as a fae warrior turned the corner. Clash. Metal raked metal. Engagement.

Another warrior followed behind the first and Qest jumped in front of me to block the strike.

I threw tiny energy missiles at Sebastian's opponent, demon chaos magic to cause the fae to stumble. But the magic sputtered out before it reached the warrior. Dammit. The mirrors absorbed the magic, their fae enchantment greedily eating up my power.

I tried a witch spell to bind the warriors' feet. Nothing. Vampire persuasion. Fail. I couldn't shift to animal form. None of my magics worked.

Sebastian battled hard with Solinthe's warrior, his natural skill at full press to counter the warrior's sword magic. Fae enchantment honed their skill.

Fae enchantment! The key.

Fight fae with fae.

I morphed nuggets of magic into mind-twisting fae illusions of mini-daggers, clouds of them like a tiny swarm of bees, and flew them through the air at the attackers. Solinthe's men cried out, their concentration broken, allowing Qest and Sebastian through their guard to make killing strikes. The tang of the new blood clogged my nose, gagging me.

More death.

We stepped over the bodies to move forward. I swallowed hard against the bile, but urgency prodded me. What was Solinthe doing to Felix and Cindy? To Gabriel?

Sebastian kept the trail, striding forward, before he stopped short. Swish. The mirrors shifted, swinging their position, like doors opening and closing. Changing the maze. Our path was blocked. He growled, sniffed the air again and corrected to a new direction.

A few steps forward and, swish, the mirrors shifted again.

"Someone doesn't want us to get through," Seb muttered.

"Ya think?" I groused.

Within the next five minutes, the mirrors shifted a half-dozen times.

"This is lunacy," Qest muttered.

I willed a fae enchantment of a "freezing potion", and scattered the cloud of it out around me to the structure of the maze, coating the mirror frames to lock them in place.

"It's cold in here," Seb muttered.

I hugged myself and rubbed hands up and down my arms. "Cold, but we can continue."

We tentatively proceeded, although my muscles bunched, wanting to explode forward, to hurry. After five excruciatingly slow minutes, still no shifting glass. The maze absorbed most noise as we crept through. Too quiet. Too easy.

A clank sounded from ahead.

I tensed as we turned another corner and hit more warriors, three this time. Sebastian and Qest engaged two. The last came straight at me.

Instincts kicked in. I barely managed to block with my dagger. He pushed me back and I slammed into a mirror.

Crunch. Needling pain.

I fought my instincts to throw up the same kind of shield as earlier. I gritted my teeth and searched for a fae version. My strength expanded with my magic and I pushed back to heave him off. With the space between us, I threw up the protection of an enchanted invisible domed glass a la fae.

He lunged and crashed into it. Bounced back. Let out a strangled roar of frustration and ran at me again.

We had to get to the center of this maze before all my resources were drained. Wet dripped down my back.

Defenses down with my exhaustion, my anger reared its opportunistic head and snapped sharp teeth at its bars, wanting to lunge at the fae warrior and hurt him. The anger wielded tiny jaws of malicious pointed pain. The thought molded a small magic from my store, sent those miniature jaws spiraling inside the body of my foe.

Penetration. Into his heart. Its terrible teeth bit into the meat of the organ. Severed aortas. Hemorrhage.

He cried out and clutched his chest, crumbled.

The anger chortled in triumph.

My necklace laced lightning bolt pain through me in retribution and my glass dome fell as I dropped to my knees.

"Rachel," Sebastian yelled, running to me from his finally fallen opponent. He helped me stand.

Qest stumbled over, too. Three bodies littered the small space.

"I'm fine," I said, panting.

My back was on fire. Soul too. Not fine. But just deal. Just get to the center.

I forced myself to stand and reholster my dagger. I would not throw up. "Come on. Keep going." More shifting mirrors and I checked my freeze spell, which had slowly dissolved. I sent another cloud of cold to keep the mirrors in place.

We hit a stretch of floor that started as sand and morphed to sucking muck, trapping each footstep so it was a struggle to walk.

"Sinking," Qest called as the muck began to engulf more than his foot, instead pulling his body under. Quicksand.

Sebastian began to flounder as well. I reached down and mixed fae magic with the earth molecules, making them light and buoyant. Both men pulled themselves out of the ground.

Sebastian took point again. "This is getting old. She's keeping us from them. How do we face her at the end?"

The anger had never gone back to sleep. Instead, it buzzed through my head, whispering threats and promising payback. "We don't face her. I do."

"Rachel," Qest warned.

"Just keep going."

We made it about a minute before Sebastian halted suddenly. Nothing came at us. His eyes lit up, smile spreading, before it morphed into a frown.

"What's wrong?" I asked.

"Tarn."

And that's when more bodies ran around the corner with a blur, Tarn in their number, his eyes clouded with enchantment, and full of fury. He ran at Sebastian and I barely had a second to notice my shapeshifter raise his sword in time to block the attack.

Then I was busy with my own battle, a warrior running at me. I threw up another glass shield and refused the urge to use those jaws of death again, instead constructing a miniature coil to squeeze off his air passage for long enough to send the attacking fae unconscious. He collapsed.

Squeeze. Squeeze. My coil kept constricting.

Let go, Rachel, or he's dead! My muscles fought me to release the grip, my anger whispering at them with a hissing intent. Finally, I let go. My breath whooshed out in a rush. Relief.

Qest grunted as he fought two fae at once, beaten back to the mirror with blood running down his arm. Sebastian barely held Tarn at bay, but there were two men fighting Qest and he was injured. I lassoed out the coil again, sending both of my brother's attackers to the floor unconscious in quick succession. This time it was easier to stop myself from hurting them further. Little mercies.

Sebastian still battled Tarn. Usually, my shifter was the stronger swordsman of the two, but this time he worked overtime to avoid injuring his friend, while Tarn tried his best to kill Sebastian. The struggle undermined Seb's skill. Tarn broke through and sliced Sebastian's side before Seb battered him back. If I put Tarn to sleep, we wouldn't be able to carry him with us, leaving him unprotected in the maze. Decide now, Rachel!

The scissors. Would they break the spell on him along with his other magical ties to Solinthe? Time to try. I pulled the shears from my holster. "Tarn," I called. "It's me you want." I was Solinthe's preferred target and I hoped her desires permeated her enchantment.

His attention left Sebastian long enough for Sebastian and Qest to move at him, knocking away his sword and wrapping him in restraint. Tarn bucked in their hold as I approached him, my full concentration on sensing the cord tie to Solinthe. It shimmered into clarity, snaking back through the maze around winding corners.

I concentrated on my intent to break that bond. "Hold him." The blades of the scissors closed around the cord, finding resistance, like sawing at the muscle of a live tentacle of a monstrous sea creature. I strengthened the magic. More pressure.

The blades sliced through. Tarn's body spasmed into a stiff board then slumped forward. Sebastian caught the slack weight. Qest released his hold and my shapeshifter repositioned his fae friend to rest the both of them against a mirror.

Tarn coughed and blinked a dozen times, fighting the fog of his enchantment to reorient. His gaze caught on me. "Rachel." He coughed again. "Thank you."

"My pleasure." I slumped back against my own mirror. "Just try not to pick up dusty magical books lying around anymore, okay?"

"So noted." He smiled and closed his eyes. "This is nice," he said, settling into Seb's arms.

"Full service for all my friends who try to kill me." The relief relaxed Sebastian's words.

Tarn chuckled. "I'll make it up to you later."

Sebastian's amused grunt loosened another knot inside me. "Sure you will," he answered.

I re-holstered the scissors and checked my dagger. "You're both hurt."

"Superficial," Qest answered.

Damned stoic brother.

Sebastian glanced down at the blood on his side. "Same here."

I opened my mouth to call them on this, but jumped in place as a roar whipped through the halls.

"RACHEL, DEAREST. YOUR LOVE AWAITS." Solinthe, her voice riding the air, promising she waited somewhere ahead.

A deep, male scream of pain followed her taunt.

Gabriel!

My knees turned to water and I leaned harder into the mirror.

Weakness. Fear. Anger. Yes, anger.

"Gabriel," I yelled, and pounded the glass again and again with the palms of my hands.

Fear of Solinthe. Fear for my lover. Fear for the everything of my world. It battled the anger that was so eager to rend and destroy.

"YOUR LOVER IS EAGER, RACHEL. COME AND FIND HIM."

I snarled, while the red heat inside me whirled fast and furious.

"Wait," Qest warned. "We still need caution."

"While she kills him?"

"She's planned this," Tarn said, finally standing on his own.

"I know." *Slow down, Rachel.*

My terror for Gabriel reminded me of the black moments when Lillith had blasted him to the verge of death in the dreamscape. Reminded me of the helplessness I had felt. Unlike Lillith, Solinthe had no shared goals with me encouraging her to stay her hand.

She was no goddess, but the faerie queen had existed since the beginnings of the Kesayim. And like Lillith, she could easily kill me and those I love.

I wasn't ready to face her. Not in her territory. This mission was last minute, with all the planning behind it of an impulsive toddler. Not the kind of time investment needed to defeat a mad, powerful, super-genius magic user.

Think, Rachel. Do this right. What you need is something quick and unexpected. Avoid a battle and sweep everyone out of Faerie.

An idea trickled awake. My anger hated the idea. It wanted vengeance. No matter what, I needed to get out of this power absorbing maze and be able to use all of my magic. I would never win against her using fae energy. Or at least not only fae energy.

I explained the plan to the guys. This one wasn't up for conference or debate. Tarn's grin put the steady back in my knees. I reached for the lines of the fae banishment spell hanging over Eden's Court and made a quick adjustment to allow Tarn alone to return. I'd finally figured it out. The alteration could be made once the original triggering occurred.

Qest grew quiet at my plan. "I am not sure it's possible. The timing must be perfect, along with my control. Make sure you watch your distance from me."

"It's not your control I'm worried about," I admitted.

Sebastian frowned. "Even if Felix is in condition to shift, Cindy can't. This will depend on the two of you."

"Get them off the crosses. I'll distract Solinthe."

"And Gabriel?" Tarn asked.

"I don't know." The admission was the scrape of asphalt against skin. The skin of my heart. I folded away the ache and inhaled. "Let's do this."

I dove for an ocean of magic, streaming it up like endless waves rolling into me, running the flow through my body, coating it in my essence and creating countless miniature pestles to swarm over the glass of the maze and grind. The pestles flew to their task and pounded on the molecules of the mirrors to wear them to nothing.

In long moments, the glass dissolved into its component sand, the grains falling to the ground in mounds with whistling speed.

Like the wax of a candle caught dripping in fast forward motion by a camera, our surroundings melted to unveil the stage of the Public Forum ahead. With Solinthe and a dozen armed warriors encircling both crosses, and Gabriel bound wrist to ankle, head bowed, at the Queen's feet. Too still.

Solinthe's smile was wide and welcoming, showing her ready for conversation and threat as was our pattern. I counted on her wanting to gloat. Bitch.

I smiled back, noted that my full magic strummed through my limbs.

And struck.

Missiles of air-constricting coil sailed out and targeted her men, their bodies falling to the ground in a domino effect while Sebastian, Qest, and Tarn ran forward to the crosses.

With no warning and another stream of power, I blasted Solinthe yards through the air, to tumble off the Forum.

"Hurry," I called to the guys as Tarn and Sebastian finished cutting Felix and Cindy from the crosses and carrying them away from the stage.

Qest backed away from the center. "Give me twenty seconds before you lift them on."

I didn't think we had twenty seconds, with Solinthe already stirring and running toward me with literal daggers flying through the air by her side.

I threw up my usual shield as they thunked into the woven protection.

Qest let out his dragon. He began to grow, unnaturally slower than the usual unfurling, the strain of the effort tinging his growing aura with red and rust stain. At twenty feet in length, Sebastian and Tarn hoisted the limp forms of the shifter couple onto Qest's back, jumping up behind them.

My vampire energy sluiced out toward Gabriel and levitated his bound form toward the dragon while I scrambled up. My brother grew longer, larger, and I wedged my heels into his scales to give myself purchase. Gabriel's body landed next to me and I grabbed him, trying to cut the magical binds with my dagger and keep him steady. His skin slid slick under my hands and I struggled to keep him in my grip.

My shield extended to all of the riders as Qest kept growing, letting loose the full force of Kyn shape to become the glorious creature locked inside, destroying dais and columns as the building began to collapse.

Solinthe skidded to his side and threw enchantment after enchantment at him, the spells bouncing off his magic-proof hide.

He turned his giant head in her direction and released a sonic roar in her face, throwing her back again as she screamed in rage and pain, hands covering her ears.

"Fly," I screamed, knowing she needed only moments to pull out more deadly magics. I finished cutting Gabriel's ties and he struggled to get himself upright and secure on the dragon. A quick glance and I noticed his bruised eyes, his exhaustion, a thin edge where he existed in this moment. Only holding on.

Qest lifted up and the shield held as he annihilated the roof of the Forum with his Kyn form, rubble cascading down through the air. Steam blew from his nostrils.

His powerful wings pumped and soared us over the decimated building. Wind buffeted the shield and our bodies clung to his back, all of us grasping to keep the rescued passengers steady. The rush of power thrilled through me. Qest's power. My own. Not far to travel. Just to the portal.

The landing was quick and nasty, Qest ignoring the time needed for gentle decent. We knocked against the inside of my shield, but it kept us on his back. Solid ground again. Jumping down, Sebastian held out arms for Tarn to hand down Cindy and Felix. Before I could help, Gabriel climbed down on his own, turning to catch me as I leaped. Strong arms steadied me, only a slight tremor giving lie to the mask he wore to get through this moment. I hated the weariness and bruises lingering in his eyes. My gut curdled imagining Solinthe torturing him.

Our eyes locked. Relief, regret, pain, sorrow, anger, and a mind-blowing love. Love, deep and tattooed into the fabric of our DNA. Incontrovertible. No matter the shit we survived.

"You came," he scolded.

"You knew I would."

"Yes." He whispered out the answer and let me finally hear the relief and anguish in that simple word.

I swallowed my tears. "Let's go home."

My magic unlocked my newest portal. We escaped Faerie.

Chapter Seventeen

Lips feathered my neck as sure hands pushed back the drape of my hair, finding the spot just below my hairline that brought a purr to my lips.

My father's journal forgotten, I closed my eyes falling into that perfect touch.

"Good morning, lovely."

"Good morning, Gabriel."

"Your place on the mattress was cold. How early did you wake?"

"I don't know. A couple of hours ago maybe."

More like since we'd gotten into bed. I'd never fallen asleep after we returned from Faerie and took care of our basic healing, then finding solace in each other's bodies. No talk. Neither of us had been ready last night.

Gabriel came around to join me on the couch, his warmth curled next to me a nourishing spring rain. Universe, thank you. The hollow in his eyes still cut me, but he was here, safe.

He eyed the stacks of journals and open laptop discarded at my feet, and nudged the pile with his toe. "More than a couple hours I would imagine."

Why did I even bother keeping things from him? "Colin's records and my father's journals."

"Did you discover anything?"

"Let me read you this." I reached for the laptop and woke the screen. "Colin's speculations after he'd studied the witch fertility problem for several years. He wrote... *The pace of the mutations to our DNA are inexplicable. They occur over the course of a witch's life, not as to be expected in each subsequent generation. My experiments have caught a shift over a thirty-year span for at least one hundred different witches.*

"Mutations among Achra are increasing as I noted before, but not DNA mutations within a single individual's lifespan. I have been unable to compare the state of our people's genetic code farther back in history as modern science only now provides us the language and tools to examine it.

"Given that, what stands out most notably is what looks to be a rejection of certain genes in our code. The genetic "proofreaders" in our cells are identifying these genes as aberrations and cutting them out. Unfortunately, these segments are needed for successful reproduction. It is like something has shifted the mindset of the proofreader to decide our strands of DNA are incorrect. Although my sample has been understandably small due to a shortage of volunteers, three of the other Kesayim races show similar evidence of new deletions in their code on comparable locations on the DNA strands. These somewhat similar genes making proteins for reproduction are being identified as incorrect and removed. Most notable, deletions on the demons' code are happening at a faster rate. Discussions with my contacts among their people have provided anecdotal evidence that their birth rate has

dropped even more significantly than for the witch population.

"I have been unable to collect fae, angel, and Kyn specimens. Extrapolation from demon samples lead me to believe angel DNA would show a comparable problem given their shared origins. Contradictory to the above, one Achra specimen of the several hundred I tested did show a similar deletion in his DNA. I cannot assume this is more than an anomaly with such a small sample.

"Although it is difficult to measure, I notice an overlapping trend between the drops to potency of witch magic previously noted, their decreased fertility, and the intra-lifespan DNA mutations."

Gabriel's brow wrinkled. "Did he draw additional conclusions about the shifts in the genetic code?"

"Drum roll, please. He says... *Lining up comparable pieces of genetic code between witch, shapeshifter, demon, and vampire samples, there are other trends in deletions across the strands with comparably placed genes. The proteins these genes are meant to code for are similar in shape to one another between the races, with differences in design less than ten percent. Nevertheless, I do not know their function. They are not related to reproduction as in the other cases. This similarity in shape and placement leads me to believe that these other proteins play similar roles within each of our peoples.*

"Speculation about the higher number of demon deletions lead me to wonder if these gene segments are being targeted because they are incomplete. Demons and angels were created to be one people, and when

Riva split the race, the changes made in their genetic codes could be read as mistakes by the genetic "proofreading" mechanisms within our cells. The genes are seen as incomplete. If other races' genes, comparable in function, are being deleted then they may also be seen as incomplete. Perhaps the demons' genes are more incomplete given Riva's manipulation, so are being deleted at a faster pace. Images of the representative DNA are attached."

Gabriel pressed closer to me. "Reading between the lines, he believes the DNA of our peoples were meant to complete one another, and the fact it does not is leading to serious consequences."

"Yes."

"Neatly matching your belief that the Kesayim are meant to unite in blood to save the world."

"Yes. The question is, what would the unification create? But wait, there's more." I grabbed an earlier volume of my father's journals and began to read out loud. *"Although my family and many friends have ridiculed me for my fascination with the Achra, the experiences from my travels lead me to the same conclusions over and over. There is a second type of Achra in our world, and they exhibit a strange effect on me when I am in their presence. I am in part drained of my power. But the few of these strange Achra changelings whom I have befriended and with whom I have become intimate slowly lose this effect over me. Now I feel more powerful in their presence and my magic multiplies in strength. And if there is a second type of Achra, may there be even more? How arrogant we Kesayim are to think the Goddess imbued only us with special power."*

I wiggled against Gabriel's side. "Sound familiar?"

"Nulls," he answered.

"Yep. And Gregor may be another kind of blend. He did something with Peter and Anna."

I returned to reading. *"I am convinced more than ever that Achra are meant to be in the lives of Kesayim. To be beloved of Kesayim. I have surreptitiously introduced a few of these peculiar changelings to other Kesayim friends and seen those friends temporarily lose power, much to their confusion. But none have established long relationships with this new type of Achra for me to observe the later effect. I wonder if the changelings store our magic in their blood. And only later return it to us enriched if we deserve it. Are they a yardstick of our worth or some piece of our destiny we need to uncover? Regardless, they are beautiful souls I have come to value when I take the time with them.*

"How the Kesayim can meet Lillith's mandate without knowing Achra in the intimate ways I have come to these many years is beyond my understanding. The contempt I have heard from my compatriots toward Achra saddens me. Even the witches who live so close to them keep their distance. And the shapeshifters wise enough to marry Achra refuse to share their secret identities with them. I consider that torture unimaginable. To never share your most core self with the one you love. When next I return to Eden's Court, I will continue my petition of council to reveal ourselves to the Achra community. Perhaps my

experiences with the changelings will convince them it is worth their while."

I looked up to gauge Gabriel's reaction. His eyes were half lidded, as if he considered the information in a trance.

"Rom had always fascinated me. Your mother hated when he traveled, although he did so often. I wish I had spent more time with him."

"These journals bring me the closest I'll come to knowing him. Every word is a gift. But even more so because what he believed and tried to accomplish is the heart of my struggle right now. It's like he wrote this stuff just for me."

Gabriel reached to caress my cheek. "He did."

Both my eyes and heart welled up with his simple reassurance. I rubbed at a traitorous tear. Later I would cry.

"One more entry." This time, I picked up the last of his journals, the one I'd been reading when Gabriel joined me. It was written five years after the previous passage. *"Eva's recent message tells me that council again rejected my proposal. My individual meetings with Kesayim leaders have led to similar dead ends. Solinthe of them all seemed most responsive, but soon after she shut me down, refusing further discussion. Her sudden about face confuses me, although she has never been a reliable character.*

"I have carefully catalogued my changeling Achra contacts. We need a record of these people. I know it deep in my gut. Eva insists we cannot overstep council rule and make official introductions ourselves. Her hesitancies madden me, although I understand the

terrible bind of her position. And since she is pregnant, I will not tax her now by pushing on this matter. Someday, I hope my people will reach out to these Achra, changeling and otherwise, and offer friendship. May that day come soon."

I closed the journal. "He was assassinated a week after that entry. His last."

"He created Solinthe's list of nulls," Gabriel said.

"She had him murdered. Took it."

He nodded. "It makes sense. Rom's ideas threatened her sense of order. Plus, she believes the nulls can be harvested for their blood. In that blood, she thinks she can collect the magic they have supposedly absorbed from others. That much I learned in her keeping."

"I hate her. I want her dead." The depth of truth in my words scared me. But not enough to wish them away. "I need to protect the nulls on that list. If I meet with council and tell them the full story of our threat, maybe I can get guards sent out."

"Rachel, you cannot protect everyone."

My jaw ached as I clenched teeth to hold back a scream. "I am well aware. The map behind me is proof. Hundreds of natural disasters on Earth with thousands of people dead already in the last week. The map in Mother's Rest is also boiling black. Another dead demon, dead fae in the maze. And those men I killed. Felix and Cindy tortured for fun, and you. What Solinthe did to you..." I couldn't look at him.

He grabbed me, but this time, I didn't want the touch. "No. Let go."

"Shhh, Rachel, love, enough."

"What if I'm not up to it? I thought I was brought here for a purpose, but now I suspect there is none. Just random, awful shit and no guarantee it'll turn out. Lillith and her species playing games with us. I can't do this."

"You have me to help."

"You think I don't trust you again because I didn't listen to you and instead came to Faerie last night. But I can't tolerate sitting by. I won't!"

His hands tightened further on my arms. "Just listen, will you?"

The pain centered me and I nodded, a slight dip of my chin all I could manage.

"I know you trust me. I have come to believe that. But you are not Lillith. Not a god, and certainly not one who must prove her goodness by saving all in order to be worthy. You are already worthy simply because of who you are. You love. And you try. That is all anyone may ask of you."

"But I'm failing."

"Cindy and Felix are alive because you did not fail. This is not all or nothing. It is a middle path. The best one you can find."

"Total destruction of our planet is all or nothing. Dead is all or nothing."

"Yet here you are in this moment. Focus on this moment, love."

"I'm scared. And the anger won't quit."

"You have a right to be both."

"My head's spinning with it."

"Breathe."

"Don't go all zen shit on me."

"How can I help then?"

"I don't know." I shook my head. "You can't. Or just, just be here. Be with me. I need that."

"That I promise."

The nagging question kept at me. The question I dreaded asking, but knew I must. "Gabriel. In Faerie, when Solinthe knew you'd warned me. What did she do to you?"

His eyes glazed over. "Nothing that left marks. It is unimportant."

No, it wasn't. He wanted to retreat, shut away the pictures in his head.

"I understand you need to protect me, but not from yourself. We've had enough secrets between us. You tell me not to shoulder burdens alone, so I guess I'm turning your words back on you."

He looked away and I grabbed his chin to drag his gaze back to mine.

"I'm worthy? Walk the walk yourself. I love you. You refuse to tell me and I'm left believing it's because you are back taking the blame for darkness that isn't yours. If anyone is bad or evil, it's Solinthe. She bears the responsibility."

He shook off my fingers. "Why talk about something that is past?"

"If I thought it was over for you, that would be fine. But all you'll do is store it away in that childhood closet of horrors. Time to open up the door, let in the light, and share. Sharing helps. You know it does. You don't need more ghosts. I don't need them. I haven't even learned to banish the ones I already have."

He sighed, and a chuckle escaped him. "Letting you care for me brings out all the wisdom I try again and again to hammer into your stubborn head."

"Uh huh. So?" I waited.

He waited.

Impatient, I pushed the books off the couch and pushed him back onto its cushions, straddling him. The intimacy of it wasn't about sex. The power of our connection riffled over both of us.

He closed his eyes, struggling still, but I read his acceptance of my demand.

The door inside him cracked open.

My fingers brushed his tiny braid back behind his ear. Touch. Light. The texture of his smooth skin tingled up my fingertips. He relaxed into the touch.

Then, he began to speak. Low whispers. Words in fits and starts with jagged places between. Maybe five minutes worth, although it felt an eternity.

I listened. Until it was over.

And I wept silent tears. For the both of us.

Chapter Eighteen

We caught Tarn, head thrown back, letting loose a throaty laugh, apparently at something Delta said.

I stepped farther from the door of my suite. "Someone took a happy pill this morning."

He made a courtly bow in my direction. "Simply pleased to be home, my lady."

Delta tossed her head at him. "Sebastian's post-escape solicitousness did not hurt either."

Was that a blush on my fair fae guardsman's face?

Tarn coughed. "Sebastian is still basking in the reunion with his family. I am only happy for him. There is much to be thankful for. For one, that you saved me from my queen. I am in your debt, Rachel. My apology is overdue for attacking you in the maze while under her spell."

"Considering it's my fault you were back with the bitch, I'd say we're even."

Delta took the mandolin from its sling upon her back and started strumming a few notes. "I believe I'm owed an apology as well, my lady." She eyed me pointedly. "Sneaking off without me was cruel and unusual. Morven wished to ram a hot poker up my backside she was so livid."

Gabriel stepped out from next to me and addressed the demoness. "Your job is to protect the Mother Heir. If you neglected your duty and allowed her to get past you, then it is you who were at fault."

I shoved his shoulder with my own. "Cut it out, Gabriel. If I didn't know you better, I'd think you sounded jealous. Why that would be I couldn't imagine."

His mask slipped for an instant and I caught a look of guilt. There one moment, gone the next. Lingering vulnerability from his recent ordeal. Universe, I hated that.

Delta's self-satisfied smirk was not helping my graciousness, however.

"Despite my better judgement, I do apologize, Delta. I wouldn't do it differently, but I've been the focus of Morven's hot pokers before and wouldn't wish them on my enemies."

Well, maybe one. Or two.

She nodded an acceptance.

"Where are we off to this morning?" Tarn asked.

"To see said torturer, the lovely Morven. I need her to schedule a meeting with council, then arrange for a tutorial with Gwen's scientist on the nature of DNA."

"She is scheduled to oversee updated mapping of the garden terrain," Delta said, packing away her mandolin, her pout disappeared.

As the garden tended to rearrange itself semi-regularly, a constant survey team was needed to keep track of important changes to prevent residents of Eden's Court from becoming lost.

We left to find her. Walking through my private wing, the vines twisting up the corridor walls usually brought that sweet 'I'm home' sensation. Was it my imagination or did they seem fragile this morning, thinner, with more broken strands among the tenacious green? The scent of crushed mint wove out from their leaves to tickle my nose.

We turned the bend in the hallway.

"Rachel, stop," Gabriel barked.

The straight shot of this last stretch of hall gave a clear picture of approaching guests. Guests that were not supposed to be here in my private wing. Nine of them. Walking toward us in a vee, like birds in formation if those birds moved like a gaggle of gunman from a television western. Slow, steady, and in synchronized step.

I whispered to Artemis, materializing her out of my sling and sending her bounding on little legs down the corridor to find and retrieve Morven. I worried sending her out on her own for the first time, but Morven needed to know about these guests. Artemis hadn't learned to speak human words, but Jack would be able to understand her.

Gabriel's celestial sword materialized as Tarn pulled his own weapon, and Delta reached for her gun. Gabriel stepped in front of me, joined by the other two. The sword hummed through the air as they put on their game face for the threat.

The group approached. All male. None familiar. My power scanned them in a wave and noted the unique disturbance to magic. Familiar. As much as their vertically slit pupils.

Kyn. All nine of them.

Ripples of unease tripped over my skin.

Aside from my brother, and my father before that, dragons hadn't visited Eden's Court in two thousand years. The Kyn had pulled out of all Kesayim realms but their own about the time they'd pulled out of the Achra world.

The nine halted in front of us, though my guard blocked my clear sight of them. I let out an impatient huff.

They had no visible weapons and made no sudden moves as they waited.

"What do you do here? This area is restricted," Gabriel challenged.

I sent a silent call out to Qest through our telepathic connection. He was my number one advisor for all things Kyn.

"We will speak with the Mother Heir," the frontmost of the Kyn visitors replied.

"You may schedule a meeting with her through proper channels," my lover said.

"The Mother Heir battles our leader to determine the survival of our race in a few short days. Scheduling an appointment is unnecessary."

This was getting ridiculous. "Gabriel, out of the way." I pushed through their bodies. "You want to speak with me, here I am. Though you have me at a disadvantage since I don't know your names."

The dragon blinked his copper eyes. He bowed his head with a regal gesture. The rest of the group copied the move.

"My lady, greetings. You may call me Roq. The proper name is not pronounceable with your vocal cords."

Really? Try me. I let the superior attitude pass.

"Set," came the next name.

"Kreeth."

"Meer."

"Sol."

"Jist."

"Brith."

"Ford."

"Zor."

The shortened names were all pronounced with a calm, flat intonation. Where was the fiery passion I saw in Qest?

"Hello, Roq. What prompted this visit may I ask?"

"We come with questions before you try to kill the Eemah. We doubt you will be able to do so on your own, and wanted to offer assistance."

Their pessimism triggered red flags. She was that strong. It didn't help that I'd spent so little time in dragon form. "A single female needs to defeat her for leadership. I have to do this myself."

"No, my lady. The female only needs to be part of the battle, although just she will be able to cut the pearl from the Eemah to assume rule."

I would not put others at risk in this fight, but I filed the information away. "Does this assistance depend on my answers to your questions?"

"Yes."

"You sound very unemotional about the whole thing. Is she not a beloved leader?"

"As you said during your last visit, our world is dying. And our people along with it as we have so few females and none any longer of breeding age. Yet you insist on thwarting the Eemah's will. What hope do you give us, Mother Heir, to cause us to care one way or another?"

It was a valid question. The only valid question and the entire point of all of my thrashing about these months.

"I intend to save our planet. Call it a work in progress."

"And will you save the Kyn from the Eemah's intentions only to have us die out from lack of reproduction? If you intend to save us, then offer your fertility as well." His eyes flared and a wisp of smoke escaped his nostrils. "That is our proposal."

My own dragon twitched, suddenly awake and very interested. Virile Kyn males. She stretched and rubbed against my insides. Paying attention.

Gabriel stepped forward again. "Watch yourself, lizard."

As a group, the Kyn shifted to readiness in their stance.

I grabbed Gabriel's arm in restraint.

Roq watched my lover carefully, eyes squared to him even as he continued to address me. "We nine are all of fertile age. Offer us a chance to breed with you and we will fight the Eemah by your side to assure her death."

Gabriel growled. His sword sung louder as it pulsed in his fist.

The dragon tilted his head, eyes flaring at the challenge threading the air. "You do not want to share, Janii?"

Gabriel flinched at the term. I hadn't heard anyone refer to him that way before, although in truth, that's what he was. The only living Janii in existence with both his demon and angel blood reunited to create the original race.

I kept my grip firmly around Gabriel's arm. This Kyn was correct. What sort of future did I offer his people? Another problem I had to consider.

"Gabriel is not your issue, Roq," I said. "My body, so my rules. I do not plan to be pregnant for the rest of my life."

"With thousands of years ahead of you, my lady, that is unlikely no matter your willingness to breed with us. We are not interested in fathering your official heir, although I have yet to hear that this Janii has been chosen your consort."

"I will be," Gabriel added, threat in his voice.

Roq nodded. "So you say. Although Kyn lovers may give even an incubus quite a competition in the bedroom."

My dragon purred at the implication and stretched further. My body responded to her interest, nipples taut, skin flushing. This was so not the time. "While I appreciate the offer, Roq, it would be unfair of me to commit to something this significant without thinking over the matter."

Gabriel sent me a scathing look. My calm and even-tempered Mr. Diplomacy had all but disappeared in some primal male testosterone ritual.

"Do not think too long, my lady," the Kyn representative warned. "The deadline for this battle approaches." His eyes skimmed my body. "We are a practical people, but your beauty and natural sexuality is an added allure, encouraging our proposal. I promise that you would not regret the opportunity to enjoy Kyn talents."

"Enough," Gabriel barked, shaking off my hand and stepping toward Roq with his Celestial sword raised. "Leave."

Quicker than I could track, Roq sidestepped the approach and managed to grab Gabriel's wrist above his grip, twisting.

The curtain of a Kyn dampening magic enveloped my bones even as I was still able to pull up energy from the earth ready to strike.

Gabriel's grunt of surprise and the dimming of his sword under the influence of Kyn's natural immunities against magic distracted me.

He shook off Roq's hold as his sword disappeared. Gabriel lunged at the man and they crashed into the nearest wall, leaves shaking down over them. They punched and grappled with one another, fairly matched in strength.

Tarn and Delta stepped forward to engage. The rest of the Kyn males as well.

My dragon roared. "Enough." The painful shattering noise kept all but Roq and Gabriel frozen in place. The meaty thud of contact between them continued.

I scooped my power up, weaving a netting with a little extra oomph of Kyn flavor to counteract Kyn immunity, and threw it over the grappling men. Caught, they fell apart, clawing at the invisible strands.

"Rachel, remove it!" Gabriel said.

"Will you behave if I do?"

"I am not a child."

"Then stop acting like one."

He gave up the struggle against the netting. A calm balance settled over him again. "I promise."

Roq's vertical pupils expanded and contracted with his ire, that fiery Kyn passion finally unveiled. "I was provoked."

"Stop complaining," I replied.

The Kyn representative quieted. His breath blew out with a tinge of smoke. "I, too, promise."

"Fine." I dissolved the magic and the men brushed themselves off and stood with as much dignity as two scuffling boys from the playground could muster.

Finally, Qest jogged up the corridor. *"Rachel?"* he asked through our minds. He exchanged an enigmatic look with Gabriel who nodded back. Men!

"Under control more or less," I answered.

"Roq, what do you do here?" My brother asked out loud.

"These gentlemen came with a proposal. Help with defeating the Eemah in battle in exchange for breeding rights with me."

Qest raised an eyebrow at Roq. "My sister is not a commodity."

"We will die, Qest. One way or another. Sacrifice by our leader is not too much to ask."

"She will not accept," Qest answered.

"Qest!!!" I reacted privately. *"Overstepping your bounds."*

"You want to do it?"

"No!"

"Then what? I'm your big brother. I protect you."

"I speak for myself." I had just finished fighting this battle with Gabriel.

Roq shifted his weight between his feet, tired of waiting for us I imagined. "Has your brother mentioned when you battle the Eemah you will have no access to your other magics? Dragon form will cut you off from everything but the power of your beast."

He sounded very sure of that.

He continued. "Do you value your life so little that you foolishly risk it without all available allies?"

"She won't be without allies. I fly with her," Qest said.

My gut twisted with a single lurch. "What?! No!"

But my brother ignored me.

"And you consider yourself more powerful than me, or any of my brethren?" Roq challenged.

"Powerful enough."

The answering silence deepened. The withering vines bore witness to the pause between these two. I held my breath in the space. The air in the hall grew heavy. A powerful force grew out from around my brother and Roq, as if a huge mass expanded into the space. As if their magic had a body of its own.

Neither of them shifted into dragon form, but the equivalent mass ballooned around us. Pushing. Crushing my skin and bone into my core. Invisible dragons testing their powers against one another.

Gabriel, Tarn, and Delta fell back toward the walls, displaced by the press. I heard the inner growl of Qest and Roq's beasts, the expansion of the power as they fought a silent duel of energy. My lungs constricted and I could not breathe in this battle.

"Rachel," Gabriel called a warning, his voice winded from the pressure.

I held my place. They would not push me away from my home in their personal confrontation.

The magic grew and I reached through it to combat the mass and effectively burst the balloon. My own dragon crowed with excitement. I ignored her and exerted pressure of my own.

I stepped closer to them, battling the invisible tide. Sweat beaded my forehead.

My concentration was so intense it took me long moments to realize the ground had begun to shake. A grating screech tore at my ears. The floor tilted and I lost my footing. All of us did as we were tossed to the ground. Earthquake!

The Kyn power inside me flickered, died, and Qest and Roq deflated, too.

A void opened up around me, a long stutter empty of any iota of magic. Every molecule of it blinked out of existence. I was surprised Eden's Court continued existing. It was happening! Magic was drying up, leaving Earth. And the effect was finally filtering into Eden's Court from the mundane world.

I heard a ragged gasp from Delta, several shocked coughs of discomfort from the other men. Tarn cried out in pain. The fae were mostly woven of magic. My gut spasmed.

And then it was back, as if the lights had been cut but suddenly returned in a flood. My ears popped.

I dragged in a breath.

"What was that?" Roq demanded, getting to his feet.

Get up off your butt, Rachel. You have too much to do to stay on the floor.

I stood and rolled my shoulders to work the knots. "That was the buzzer going off on our alarm." Our time was up. Shit! My thoughts hit high gear. "Roq, I decline your offer. But when I show up to battle the Eemah, will you or your friends get in my way?"

The power disruption had thrown him, although he dragged his attention back to me. His look was less than friendly, but he answered. "Do you mean will we fight you as well?"

"Yes, will you fight me, too?"

"It depends upon our best interests. Otherwise, we leave the battle to you and the Eemah." He sneered in Qest's direction, but added no comment.

Those interests seemed impossible to calculate given the circumstance, but it was the best I would get from him.

"Good. Then you'll see me in a few days, gentlemen. Please leave." The panic only now set in. My heart started beating a road race but I kept up the noble, in-control leader mask.

The Kyn glanced among themselves, perhaps communicating with their own silent telepathy. Roq finally nodded and they turned back toward the garden with no goodbye. What was the purpose of pleasantries when we faced the ultimate end. Everyone in the hallway understood the threat with certainty.

"Let's find Morven." I grabbed Gabriel's fingers, still blessedly nearby, and squeezed.

Gabriel watched them go then squeezed my fingers back. A show of support as he noted my anxiety. "There is still time."

"Thank you for the lie, but my plan is to keep on keeping on. The agenda is the same. Morven may have thoughts about how the rest of the Kesayim will make sense of that temporary loss of cabin pressure." I turned to my brother. "Was that chest beating with Roq necessary?"

"Yes."

"You will not be part of the battle with Grandmother," I said.

"Now who is being bossy?"

"I am your supreme leader."

"You are my younger sister who happens to have a title. Get over yourself. Plus, these are my people and this is my world as much as your own."

My necklace pulsed fiercely in agreement with him. Dammit, I hated when he was right. But the subject was not yet closed. Qest was simply unaware of that fact.

"Let's go," I said.

We went.

Chapter Nineteen

Slow count, Rachel. No one, including you, wants to be at this table, but you need to do this. Counting kept me from scowling back at the bitter faces of council.

Universe, I already had a headache. *Deep breath.*

And you're on in one, two, three... "Thank you ladies and gentlemen for coming this afternoon. I appreciate your response to Morven's last minute request to meet, because we are facing a crisis."

Kemuel's wings fanned out from his backless chair. "Why are Gabriel and Morven sitting around this table? Or Christian for that matter. Frederick is now the vampire representative."

Kemuel's presence at the meeting was my latest shock. He had never joined council in person, always choosing to send his angel representative. But Celendine was missing.

"I could ask the same of your presence, Kemuel. Is Celendine ill?"

"He is temporarily suspended pending an investigation."

Shit! I plastered on a confused expression. "Investigation?"

"For inappropriate relations with a demoness."

Satan, sitting as far away at the table from his angel nemesis as possible, rolled his eyes. "Prude."

Since angels in sexual relationships with demons tended to be executed for such behavior, Satan's response was a complete under-reaction. I'd ignore Kemuel's bad news and deal with it outside of council.

Gabriel, positioned on my right, expanded and contracted his own wings at Kemuel's statement. His parents had been executed for this reason. 'Inappropriate relations'. Or at least his angel mother. His father's execution was due less to firm demon policy on the matter and more from Satan's one-upmanship and impulsive whim. The fact my lover chose to unfurl his wings for this meeting was likely strategic. It left everyone on edge, an explicit power play although no one was quite sure of his purpose. Yet.

Knowing Gabriel, he had a purpose. Or I hoped he did. He never went public with his wings since he'd gained them fighting a magic duel. If this behavior was a remnant of Solinthe's abuse of him, I'd kill her dead ten thousand times more than I'd planned. Gabriel's eyes also glowed demon red instead of his usual green, making a point of his blended origins.

My temples kept up their pounding. "To answer your question, Kemuel, Morven is here to provide us with an update on the crisis. Christian has additional information to add to the issue. As you know, Eden's Court experienced an earthquake late this morning and a temporarily loss of all magic."

"And Gabriel?" the angels' leader persisted.

Sweet Universe, didn't he care what had happened? Talk about misaligned priorities.

"We will discuss that later," I intoned, trying not to crack my teeth as I ground them with my answer. "Morven, if you would please give us your report."

"Certainly, my lady."

I loved her unruffled nature in the face of this group of troublemakers.

"All sectors of Eden's Court felt effects from the unusual power void which lasted for approximately two minutes. The garden suffered severe withering and there were witnesses reporting at least seven magical beasts melted away in front of their eyes. Upkeep spells across all three sectors of the court, including the outer promenade, went down causing three deaths in the medical ward, fifty-seven structural collapses within the building, a small battle in the containment cells to restrain attempted escapees when their cells broke open, and another thirty-three minor injuries around the facilities as of current reports. Twenty-six people are missing. Disappeared."

Satan harrumphed. "Not to mention the quake inconvenienced my bocci game. I was a hair's breadth from a win." He turned toward me. "I assume you will insure this does not happen again."

I ignored him and gestured Morven to continue.

"The actual earthquake led to breakage of thousands of smaller items and furnishings. Crews are engaged in sorting through debris and discarding everything beyond repair. I estimate this will take most of this week."

Aubrey, his blue eyes sparking, shapeshifter energy barely contained, cut off the rest of the report. "Cut to the chase, Rachel. You want to tell us what caused this event?"

"The same thing that is causing the natural disasters across the mortal world." I pointed to the map from my room, transported to the meeting and set up on an easel behind me. "Earth's magic resources are dwindling. The core is depleted. It's crumbling the planet. Lillith warns me we have less than a month left before the mantle will be so destabilized that life will no longer be possible. We are running out of magic and it is killing us."

"Ridiculous!" Kemuel snorted. "We would have heard of this before."

"Not unless you've been privy to Lillith's secrets. She commanded me to stay quiet on the matter. The only thing she shared with me was the need to unite the Kesayim to solve the problem, without a lot of inconvenient instruction about how 'uniting' such a naturally divisive bunch would help. But I have done my research and I have most of the answer."

The room burst into competing noise, generally flavored by insulting scoffs of my pronouncement.

Gwen slammed her palm to the table. "Listen, you bunch of pigheaded fools. The witch community is fully convinced of Rachel's information. Did you not hear Morven's report? Did you sleep through the shake? I saw my own spells dissolve in front of my eyes. That has never happened. Aubrey, the shifters are just as much part of the Achra world as witches. Are you not concerned with the natural disasters there?"

Satan sat forward, his red eyes keenly focused on me. Sly. "So, where is the proof of our doom?"

"Colin, the witch who gave his life during the battle with the vampire hunters was a scientist. He left his journals and research with me before he died."

I looked toward Gwen and she nodded giving me permission to break the witches' secrets. "Witches are experiencing an alarming fall in their birth rate. The pattern is related to the problem with magic. I suspect if you kept your own statistics, you'd find similar trends among all Kesayim."

I explained Colin's findings and went on to discuss my father's conclusions from his journals. "The map behind us of natural disasters in the mortal world this past few months supports the conclusion. Christian is here because he has helped me with research about additional effects of the nulls on magic."

I shared more description of the null filter of magic and the ways it distilled the energy and made it more powerful. "The null DNA has a role in a single genetic code we are all meant to share. The evolution of our people all into one. An evolution which I believe will stop us from draining the magic resource, and instead, naturally refill the reservoir. My understanding of the need to merge DNA of Kesayim, null, and mortal species of human is supported by Christian's work."

I had their attention now. A singular quiet covered the room, but the faces remained pinched in suspicion. My pause was calculated to give me more sense of their reaction.

"Solinthe has plans to assassinate an identified list of nulls. I need court support to send guards to protect them. We need their DNA."

Frederick's vampire power flicked through his aura in murky swirls. "Christian's research is worthless. Based on his own sexual interests as I understand he has been fucking the null. The fact she is free and has access to the compound is offensive to all of my people. There is no way her DNA will be joined with our people. She is a killer and needs to be locked up again in the cells and executed as planned. The rest should be assassinated, so I say let Solinthe do her work. We do not reward genocide, and your proposal, my lady, is morally offensive. This entire hypothesis is ridiculous as Kemuel said."

Christian's power surged alive at the suggestion. "We are trying to save everyone's ungrateful hide, Frederick. I haven't had a chance to update Natalya due to circumstances our Mother Heir has outlined of Lillith's secrecy."

"My lady," Aubrey spoke, "while your ideas are fascinating, I think you overlook the obvious. The simplest explanations are usually the true ones. At the time of the earthquake and magic disturbance, there were ten Kyn in the same vicinity of the court. There haven't been Kyn here aside from one at a time in thousands of years. There were probably never that many congregated here in all of history. Kyn are naturally immune to magic. My guess is that their power overloaded our system. Not like the null, but enough to wreak havoc." He sat back and crossed his arms with a satisfied nod. "Since the group of them left, we've had no problems."

Qest interrupted. "Kyn presence would never affect magic or the court in that way."

I waved him quiet. The Kyn suggestion was a distractor and I wouldn't walk down that path and give Aubrey what he wanted. Tempers were on edge. My own included.

The shapeshifter leader continued. "I think the rest of your ideas are some wish to see patterns where none exist. Well intentioned, but too complicated to be anything but fantasy. A new leader wants to leave her mark. I understand that, but in your frantic attempts to make a statement, you are creating unnecessary drama."

I created drama? My anger perked its head more resolutely. I shoved it down. "I am putting you on notice. I am choosing Gabriel as my official consort, which is why he is seated next to me today to answer your question, Kemuel. With or without your belief in this crisis, I am going to continue my experiments, and save this place and my people. They matter and I won't let your shortsightedness destroy us."

Satan's quick acid response startled me. "This stinks of a conspiracy, my lady. Perhaps we should be worried about *your* motivations."

My spine straightened and a cold tingling feeling emanated through my limbs as my necklace pulsed. Raphael's warning in jest filtered back through my mind. "What are you saying, Satan?"

"From day one you have been herding us. You challenge our traditions, insisting shifters change their funeral customs. You decide to take over leadership of one of our races, the Kyn. You expelled the fae from Eden's Court which rids you of an inconvenient rival in Solinthe. You insist Kesayim be friends when there are good reasons we are not. Sitting in this room are two of your brothers, both holding quite a lot of power in your court. Qest has obviously seduced the witch leadership over to your position. You shove Gabriel in our face when we do not want him here. And you threatened punishment of my and Kemuel's people if we did not play your teamwork games. You are our Mother Heir, but that position has had limits for all of time. How come you want more power than all who came before you? Either you are power hungry or delusional. I doubt Lillith has given you any particular warnings."

My mouth stuck shut as the simmering anger crept higher in my pot. I'd forgotten the danger of a Morte Noire demon. His smile and humor hid destructive intentions. Satan was motivated by and fed off violence. The chaos of the crisis on Earth filled him with power. It was delicious to him.

"Prove my point, Rachel," he continued. "I feel your magic pushing at you. It's potent, belying your claim magic is disappearing. Even now you want to lash out and drop us to the floor as you did that night we met to watch Colin's progress. You want to force us to your way. That is the mark of a tyrant, dear lady."

The slimy bastard wouldn't twist my actions and words. He'd plotted this for some time. I knew it.

Satan stood and tugged down his shirt with regal affront. "I call for a vote. A resolution whereas if you take control of the Kyn, you are to be removed from office. If you choose Gabriel as consort, you are to be removed from office. If you pursue genetic manipulations, you are to be removed from office. Who seconds it?"

"I will vote first" Satan continued. "I vote yes to this resolution."

"Yes," came Kemuel.

"Yes," from Frederick.

"Yes," called Aubrey.

Gwen swore and sent her scathing regard across the table. "No, you pack of imbeciles."

"Never," added my brother.

Satan smirked, twisting his lips. "Majority rules, my lady. Make your choice. In the meantime, the demons are quitting the partnership program with the angels. Punish us as you will." He turned and strolled from the room. Asshole.

Morven, quiet until now, lost her usual calm. "Despite Satan's conspiracy theories, we are not a democracy. The Mother Heir cannot be voted in or out. Lillith's decrees are not optional."

Aubrey scowled. "According to Rachel, Lillith may not have our best interests at heart."

I sighed. "Morven, don't bother with the lecture. I have heard your opinions, gentlemen. I cannot convince you if you wish not to believe."

Less reaction was better at this point. The game would go underground now. An elephant bowed my shoulders, grinding me down even as I fought both it and the molten anger at my core. "I understand my choices. Make sure you understand your own. Open your eyes to energy fluctuations at the least. Ask questions. This is more than the normal variations in geological disturbances on Earth."

I pushed back my chair and stood. Gabriel's wings flared out as he took my side. Morven joined him along with Christian, Gwen, and Qest. Delta, Sebastian, and Tarn took their posts behind us.

I started to leave when Gabriel rested his hand on my shoulder to stop me. "A moment."

He turned back to the table and his celestial sword materialized as his fist opened to grasp its handle. His gaze found its target. "Kemuel, as someone who shares the angelic mandate to protect Achra, I ask you to listen. It may be easy to be persuaded by Satan, as ironic as that sounds. But for what it's worth and from what you know of my honor, I swear by this sword that what Rachel has told you is truth. You may fear a new future, and hate that I am part of it, but it is better than none at all. Please consider carefully. We are all worth it."

I loved this man. If there were ever a reason to survive this mess, he was it.

"Frederick," he continued, "remember who fought to save your people from the hunters. Aubrey, Rachel is just as committed to the survival of the shifters against Samuel's attempted coup, risking her life to save even two of your own people imprisoned in Faerie. If she is different from other Mother Heirs, perhaps it is her heart that is the difference."

His sword disappeared and he dipped his head at the silent council members. Then he took my hand and laid a gentle and very public kiss upon it. "I walk by your side, my lady. Always."

If only I was worthy of his praise. Right now, my only choice was to pretend. If I pretended hard enough, maybe we'd make it through alive.

* * * * *

Again, there I was trudging down the hall toward Mother's Rest to look for answers. Well, not so much answers as an understanding of the Freil Sorcha process. The countdown was on to the battle with the Eemah and I needed to study the ritual in order to pull it off. In order to save the Kyn, in order to save humanity, in order to save magic, in order to save the world. The confrontation with my grandmother was one cog in a bigger cascading pattern. I preferred thinking of her as a cog. A cog was impersonal. I didn't need to care about a cog.

My guards followed, blessedly quiet. The recent reaction from council dampened everyone's mood. Enthusiasm for saving the world was hard to come by when a portion of said world refused to believe it needed saving, and announced their intention to do everything in their power to keep you from saving it.

Walking head down, preoccupied with figuring out how to get Kesayim leadership's head out of their collective backsides and faced toward reality, I didn't see my newest visitor sitting in front of the door to Mother's Rest until I was on top of him.

Jack, his cream-colored poodle coat looking dapper, waited patiently for my approach.

"Hey Rache," he said by way of greeting. "You're looking bedraggled. I recommend pizza. It fixes virtually all of what ails ya."

"Jack. Did Morven send you? What now? More disaster?"

"Can't a dog just stop by to say hello and shoot the bull? Which reminds me, I haven't had a good steak in ages. I'm second guessing the pizza. Prime rib with a freshly baked potato, loaded. Sour cream, cheese, bacon." He licked his chops and let out a soft whine. "Oh, I wish I never got myself started."

"So, you're here for a chat?"

"Yup."

"About what? I was going to head down to do some research." I gestured toward the door to Mother's Rest.

"Oh, if you're busy..."

I knew that tone and that doggy expression of pained drama.

"Why don't you come down with me and we'll talk."

"To Mother's Rest?" The look of shock with his brown eyes widening, snout twitching, and a quick sneeze would be comical if I were in the mood to laugh.

"Yes. I have the magic to bring in one-time guests. And I couldn't think of anyone else I'd rather invite."

Tarn and Sebastian frowned and Delta's eyes sparkled with her grin. "I think the boys are insulted, my lady."

Jack circled his tail in excitement and settled down on his haunches. "Even Gabriel's not been inside Mother's Rest. Morven's been twice. Now me." He sneezed again and let out a yip.

I threw together the spell and waved it at the doorway. It was nice to see someone happy, and Jack deserved it. Although he relished attention and theatrics, he did do a lot of drudge work for Morven, and sometimes me. If I hadn't known how much he and

Morven loved one another, I'd question their
arrangement.

We entered Mother's Rest and descended the spiral
staircase, Jack's head turning from side to side taking in
the eerie speckled stone walls and otherworldly
atmosphere. When we got down to the map area, table
roiling with dark mist, his tail had stopped wagging.

"Boy, this place needs redecorating even more than
your original apartment. Kind of on the Addams family
macabre end of the spectrum. No wonder you look
stressed out having to spend so much time here."

I sighed. "I know, right?"

He examined my bookshelves and the couches
underneath and jumped onto the most comfortable. "I
owe you a big thanks, Rache, for the other day in the
desert part of the garden. Ya know, with Lillith and all.
The healing."

"Since I was the one that got the goddess mad to
begin with, leading to her temper tantrum, I think it's
me that owes you an apology, Jack. My fault she lashed
out and hurt you to start."

His tail thumped the couch. "Maybe we'll call it even,
then. If it makes you feel better."

There was no *even* in this situation. There was get the
job done or lose everything.

Jack stood up on the couch and circled his tail several
times before settling back down on the cushions and
putting his paws over his snout. "It's just seeing Lillith
in person got me thinking. Back to that day I came to
find you in Boston and convinced you to come back with
me to Eden's Court. I kinda wanted to ask if you regret
it? Meeting me? If you hadn't agreed, then maybe none

of this would be happening. Sure, being hit by Lillith's magic whammy sucked, but you've been dealing with a lot more since you came here. And I feel responsible, ya know? For this mess."

He felt responsible?

"Jack, the world didn't start falling apart because I came to Eden's Court. It was on its way whether I showed or not."

Oh! Right. Magic wasn't dying because of me. So why did it feel that way?

The pup continued to look doubtful. I walked to the couch and sat next to him, resting a hand on the lovely tight curl of his fur. "You gave me everything bringing me here. Family, identity. You helped me find love. I should be kissing your wet nose and bringing you doggy treats every last day of your life."

His paws left his nose and he sat higher. "I'm partial to beef, in case, ya know, you do want to drop by with those snacks. Maybe we could hang out together sometime. Catch a couple of Bewitched episodes."

My snort brought his tail to full wag, thumping harder and faster against the pillows.

He raised a paw and rested it on top of my thigh. "I'm sorry you have to carry such a load, Rache. I'm sorry you have to even do research about killing your grandmother. But remember how you said I'm not responsible for the world falling apart? You're not either. And although I hope you can save it, no matter what you're the best thing that's happened to Eden's Court ever. Everyone who's anyone knows it."

Dammit, I would not cry.

"All the important people?" I asked.

"The A list. Every last one. If they gave Oscars for Best Supreme Ruler in the Drama of Life category, you'd go home with a golden statue. And you'd kill the Red Carpet."

"If Artemis turns into half the familiar that you are, Jack, I'll be the luckiest Supreme Ruler in the world."

"Don't I know it," he said, and let out another snuffling sneeze.

Then, Jack waited patiently on the sofa, snoozing and then waking to occasionally groom himself, while I curled up next to him, opening myself to my inner dragon to take time getting to know her. Her power, her desires, her wisdom. She liked the attention, and curled up in contentment as much as Jack.

Making peace with her wild drives, I finally started searching for answers regarding my upcoming battle within the Mother Heirs' library, pulling down volume after volume.

Trouble was, there were no answers. Only endless questions.

* * * * *

I half-drowsed to the sound of the soft, small inhalations of Artemis asleep curled next to my thigh. The hypnotic strokes of the brush pulling through my hair brought my first peace in hours. We perched on the foot of my mattress, the semi-darkened room a relief to my jumbled senses.

"Thank you for making Gabriel go with them," I said, my defenses down around my ankles with the intimacy of this moment.

"You needed quiet time," Morven answered, tugging my hair with another long stroke.

Jack was curled in a corner asleep again, hind legs giving an occasional jerk in his doggy dreams.

The pull against my scalp brought tears to my eyes. The bristles shushed running through my hair, their sound lulling. "He's worried about me."

"Understandable."

Not much to say to that. I was worried too.

My hand drifted to the fine, smooth hairs on Artemis's tiny head, petting her in time to the movement of the brush. "This afternoon was helpful. I can almost grasp the concepts around DNA structure and replication. I feel like I'm back in high school biology with pressure on to cram for the final."

"Tomorrow is soon enough to apply the learning."

"What if..."

She cut me off. "Tonight Tarn, Sebastian, and Delta needed time with each other. Gabriel will be fine with your brothers. He is part of your family after all. You, my dear, need time without responsibility. To any of them. To anyone at all."

"But..."

She cut me off again. "You know I used to do this for your mother when we were girls together."

Artemis whimpered in her sleep as I caught myself pressing too hard at the rough of her neck. I lightened the pressure.

"I miss her," Morven said. "But having you here makes it easier."

"Really?"

"Really."

More quiet. I craved the quiet. But still, if I wanted to say what I needed, I was running out of time.

So...

"I need to thank you, Morven."

"Brushing your hair is nothing."

"Not for this. For supporting me these months. Your steadiness helped me survive."

"It is my job."

Was that all it was to her? I'd wanted to read more into it, but maybe that wasn't fair to her.

After another silent minute, she stopped brushing and moved around on the bed so that I could see her face. "Your mother would have been proud of you, Rachel. I know because I am proud of you. I have given you little these months. Your success has come from in here." Her fingers brushed the top of my ribs.

My cheeks heated under her gaze. "I wouldn't call it success. More like disaster management."

"Stop denigrating yourself. Watching you has brought me a peace I never thought to have again after my failure with your mother."

I started to protest that ridiculous interpretation when she quieted me. "In all her long lifetime of struggle to find a path here, your mother never found what you have in four months. Personal courage and a deep love for our people. Unshakeable purpose. Gabriel was right when he called it heart. You are gifted with a beautiful one."

My throat tightened. Damn wetness started leaking down my cheeks and I scrubbed it away. "Are you sure no one slipped anything into your cereal this morning? You are way too sappy to be the Morven I know."

She smiled and winked at me. That smile made *her* so beautiful.

"Last time you accused me of taking a hit of something. I assure you I am completely sober. My natural reserve is not all of me, my dear. It has a place, but with you, now, I do not wish it." She touched my hair, pushing back a piece that had fallen in my eyes.

"Tomorrow, when you try to blend your DNA with Gabriel's, I will protect you. With every last bit of myself."

"I know we have to experiment, but if I hurt him doing this—"

"I have never liked mixing business with personal lives, but Gabriel is meant to be part of this with you. From the first moment you two met. The bond you share must be related to the process."

"You sound like you believe in fate."

"Not on the whole. I believe in free will. But I find it curious that as we face this crisis that your closest connections are finding connections of their own."

"Christian and Leslie. Qest and Gwen. Tarn, Sebastian, and Delta."

"And ironically, Celendine and Morrea, although that connection may lead to tragedy. We are being driven together, and perhaps that is what will allow us to survive," Morven said.

The clearest example was Leslie and her null power. I knew that the key to situations when she strengthened magic instead of canceling it were her emotions about Christian and her proximity to him. In short, their relationship was the difference. In a smaller way Anna, her daughter, also activated her power as she quickly experienced companionship with Peter and Gregor.

I needed to risk the DNA blending process with Gabriel. Universe, I was scared out of my mind.

Morven stilled her brush and placed it on the bed. "Would you allow me to weave a protection spell over you? I know you have your own defenses, but you might look at this as a blessing. Our people do not have religion in the same way as Achra, since Lillith never required prayer or worship, but even if she is a creature from beyond our experience in this universe, there is still the miracle of the universe and the power of its connection."

"I would like that."

Morven's wrists, hands and fingers began to undulate and weave the most gorgeous spell. Witches' spells are like tapestries in the air made of color and shape. Hers sang with magenta and burnt orange, mint green and lavender, chocolate brown, canary yellow and purple dusk. Eggshell blues with darker, inky varieties. The shapes were delicate strands ballooning out to wide ribbons. Dashes and curves, miniature circles and sharp corners. An ocean of waves and the hint of both roots and branches grounding the spell and expanding it into the heavens.

With a last stroke, she finished the spell and blew on it to activate it. The tapestry swirled in place and moved from the air above us towards me, landing on my skin and wrapping it with tingly, vital power. The spell left sparkles where it touched.

I sighed with the feeling and turned to thank Morven, words half out of my mouth when everything changed.

Instead, a new voice snapped my head toward the far wall, in the direction of the large circular mirror from where the voice emanated.

Artemis woke and began small yipping barks, her warning lifting the hairs on my arms.

"Brava, Brava, Morven. You are quite talented," came languid feminine words, accompanied by the slow clap of the speaker's hands in sardonic appreciation.

In the center of the mirror was the face I least wanted to see in the world. Solinthe, the faerie queen.

"Your spells are potent," she said. "It is a shame that your protection will be insufficient," the fae queen continued. "Rachel, you seem to think you may act with impunity, trespassing on my property and stealing what is not yours. And I was growing so fond of you, too. Ah well."

All of my old rage surfaced, warring with my fear. I dragged in air and stood from the bed, walking closer to the mirror despite my feet's insistence I run far and fast. "People do not belong to you."

"Yet you think they belong to you. Banishing my folk from Eden's Court at a whim of temper. Arrogant. But you are afraid to really take what you want. You are a coward." She eyed me pointedly. "You want to save the world so badly, Rachel, but in the end, you will accomplish nothing because you do not have the balls to strike when you must. It is not evil to take what you want. There is no good or evil. There is only will. And I have a prodigious one."

"You are a twisted bitch, Solinthe. Crazy beyond belief since you refuse to see the crash of our world coming. You're bright enough I imagine, but your madness is a liability to us all."

Her face clouded to outrage. "I will kill you. I will harvest all of the nulls and gain the power needed to rebuild my soul. And Gabriel will return to me and sit by my side, chained if need be, because I wish it." Her face broke from its anger, softened, and her brow furrowed with doubt and longing. "I sacrificed myself to keep his people from killing one another with their civil war, so I deserve a prize from them. I deserve my soul."

"Not at the expense of everyone else, Solinthe. If you want my help retrieving your soul, I will do what I can and find other means."

Her head tilted and she stared at me, softness and confusion lingering. Consideration. But after a minute, the mirror grew sharp in its clarity of picture, her face contorting. "No," she barked. "There is no other way."

With no warning, she swiped her hand with a sharp motion. Cut through the air with power flung at the mirror from her side. Mere seconds of impulse.

Shit!

Inhale.

The mirror glass exploded.

Torpedoing shards, like arrows, tunneled toward me.

No time for shields.

Pain. Then, black.

* * * * *

My body floated awake with no discomfort. I blinked hard to get my bearings. A metal creak and the feel of wood against my back confused the freak out of me. I shifted in place and gazed out over a panorama of small lights in the distance and below. My hands gripped a bar in front of me. I blinked again.

I was on a ferris wheel! Hundreds of feet up. Not spinning, but stuck at the top of rotation. Carnival music drifted up from the base of the machine. A cool breeze blew over my skin. The smell of popcorn drifted up to the seat.

The city lights fanning out beneath me belonged to a major city.

Where was I?

"Paris."

My head jerked to the side. Lillith!

The goddess sat next to me in the car. Her glossy black hair glinted from the lights strung along the amusement park ride. "I love ferris wheels," she purred and rocked back and forth, tilting our car with her movement.

My stomach lurched. "Why am I here?"

"I took the liberty of arranging a visit with your unconscious essence while Morven and Gabriel and your other playmates heal you from those wicked glass shards rammed into your body."

"Solinthe attacked me."

"Indeed. She will kill you. You do not stand a chance, daughter."

"I am fighting with everything I've got."

She sighed, looking damned right depressed in a quick-change flash of mood. "You will fail. My world will die. All my beautiful Achra children are already dying."

"I will blend our DNA. That's the key, right? The world can only stabilize if we all become one species. It's what you couldn't finish on your own."

"You are so clever and so shortsighted at the same time. Even I ran out of power to finish the creation. I told you to grow your power, but instead, you resisted."

"So Solinthe will win."

"Unless you kill her first. But you don't want to kill her."

"I do."

Her raised brows told me she didn't believe me. "None of your plans will work unless all of the Kesayim participate. Solinthe will never allow her fae to participate, and she is more powerful than you. As fast as your magic has grown, she easily surprised you with the mirror. And that was from a distance."

"After I kill her, the fae will participate."

"Yet you still don't have enough magic to blend the DNA across the planet. Unless..."

She trailed off the word and instead started swinging the ferris wheel car again.

"Unless what?"

"Absorb her magic when you kill her. If you can kill her. That might give you enough ooomph. Or perhaps not." She frowned. "I suppose I can start again. Create a new world."

She couldn't give up on us. If only I could get this quixotic entity on board actually helping me. I'd call her nuts like Solinthe, but that attributed human values and characteristics to her. She was so far from operating on our plain, the comparisons were *ridiculous. I wanted to hate her like I did the fae queen, but as the end came closer I couldn't. She believed she experienced the human emotion of love for her mortals, although the closest equivalent if I did risk anthropomorphizing her was obsession.*

"Magic from death? That isn't how Kesayim power works."

"Death is part of the cycle. Why should it be excluded? Pay attention, daughter, when you destroy. You may learn something."

I squeezed the bar in front of me. "The finish line is coming up on us fast. I understand your rules and I've broken them. That last visit in the garden let me know how little you've appreciated it. But I need help convincing the Kesayim leadership this is real. I need them on board, as you said so yourself about the fae."

"I did so like this planet," she said while ignoring my request.

I kicked the side of the car and the thing went swinging again. "If you like it then help it to survive."

"You know I am forbidden."

"What's the worst that happens? Your people destroy it? That's pretty much happening as it is. Can't you interpret their limitations creatively?"

"They watch us carefully. Their interest peaks." Her form shimmered and the air waved with lines of color and disturbing movement before they solidified again into my mother's form. "You are the most difficult of Mother Heirs."

"I'm the one you're stuck with now, and now is all that counts."

Deep breath, Rachel. You can't lose it. My heartbeat slowed. I reached out then and placed a gentle hand on top of hers. Whoa! Did I do that? I prayed she wouldn't bite. "I'm sorry you're stuck with me. I know you want the Achra to survive. Just think of me managing these last steps of evolution in tribute to you. You set the stage." *I reached deep down for the next bit.* "And our debt to you for our existence is beyond repayment."

She pursed her lips as if tasting something sour and harrumphed. "I am sure the rest of the Kesayim leadership will come around. Once Earth begins to crumble faster, they will have no choice. Solinthe and the Eemah, of course, will have to die. Satan, maybe, but as long as he knows his food source of violence and chaos will disappear after enough destruction occurs, I think you can convince him."

"What happens if I can blend everyone's DNA? Will the damage stop immediately?" *The first question set off a cacophony of similar thoughts in my head.*

"I suppose you will have to see," she said.

Totally inadequate, but what did I expect?

"Now, hurry back to your body and wake up. Your lover is concerned. Have some extra sex. Maybe it will help with your power." She winked at me. "I have a fond spot for Gabriel."

Gwen had said Lillith fancied herself his patroness. Between Solinthe and Lillith's "fondness" for him, he could easily end up dead.

"You do remember almost killing him earlier this season? If you want to assist me in any way, try not to obliterate the people helping me with this project."

"Your insolence and disregard for my rules earns you consequences. But you will probably be dead soon enough. Sufficient punishment for your defiance I believe."

And on that cheery note...

I woke lunging up in my bed, gasping for breath, body screaming with pain.

"Hush," Gabriel whispered, gently pushing me back down and brushing my forehead with his lips. "The pain will pass. Morven just finished healing spells. We got to you in time."

The sheets around me were stained red. Lots of red. I'd lost a lot of blood. Morven sat on my other side. Above me, the last wisps of her spells dissolved in the air and a pile of glass shards littered the bed.

Artemis was pressing at my side, her warm body lending comfort.

Still weak, I reached down into the earth for my power, scooping up what I needed to balm the rest of my injuries. The pain eased into nothing, although tremors still shook my limbs. Solinthe came close this time, and with a simple attack.

Guilt rang through me like the strike of a tuning fork, vibrating in perfect pitch with my doubt. As much as I knew I replenished most of what I took with my brand of magic, any dip into the reservoir right now felt wrong.

"Tarn, Sebastian, and Delta are back outside your door," Gabriel said. "More guards will be posted at either end of your private wing. Your brothers arrive shortly to remain in the outer room."

"That's unnecessary and puts them at risk. If Solinthe tries for me here, they stand little chance." I thought about Lillith's warnings. My banishment spell wouldn't keep the fae queen out of Eden's Court. She was too strong. "We have to protect the nulls. If she kills them before I figure out how to blend everyone, nothing will matter."

"We can talk about this tomorrow," Gabriel said.

"Tomorrow you and I are busy doing our science experiment."

He blew out an exasperated breath. "You almost died, but I see even that will not keep you from your mission. Fine. Gwen is sending witches to protect as many on the null list as she can. She's working on Aubrey to sway his stance, and with some progress so we might have shifters helping soon. Kemuel has thawed a bit."

"Who spoke with him?"

"I did."

"He thawed? Talking to you?"

"A bit."

"Miracles, miracles."

"He cannot tolerate dead Achra."

"He believes us?"

"No. But he is paying attention."

I told Gabriel and Morven about Lillith's ferris wheel visitation and Gabriel's frown darkened until he caught me watching him and he tried to put on one of his masks. What had he and Lillith discussed when he visited her and received her "guidance?"

Morven stood. "You both need rest. And privacy. Tomorrow is soon enough for next steps. Goodnight, Rachel, Gabriel. I will tell your brothers not to disturb you when they arrive."

After Morven left and I convinced Gabriel I was back to full strength, he helped me change my bed linen. He snapped the top sheet straight with a crisp motion, and we worked in silence and tucked in the corners while I watched more of his frowns. Again. And again.

"What's wrong?" I asked finally.

"Simply tired."

"Uh, huh."

"You do not believe me."

"Let's just say, my Gabriel meter has become finely tuned."

He frowned again. Yep, definitely something up.

He grabbed a pillow and case from the pile of fresh sheets. "Do you ever wonder what will happen when we achieve our goal? Who we will become? The dragon called me Janii, which is difficult enough for me to hear, although true. And tomorrow, I may be more. Lillith is not the goddess I grew up imagining and our creation seems little more than a whim of some strange extraterrestrial race."

"Are you asking about what you and I will become or the Kesayim?"

"Both."

"What brought on this existential crisis?"

He paused and continued to work the pillow into the case, but would not meet my eyes. "Dreams of our children. A future for them I cannot predict."

My heart sped a bit faster like a sudden torrent of rain drops in a storm. "Do you really want my answer?" I balled up the old bloody sheets and threw them into a corner to be washed later by the invisible magical cleaning minions of this place, whomever they were.

Gabriel winced. "No."

"Too bad." I stuck my tongue out at him.

I crawled onto the bed and patted the mattress next to me. He hesitated, threw down the last pillow, and climbed over to me. I nudged him until he opened his arms so I could settle between them.

Waves of fatigue lapped over me, but I fought them. Sleep soon, but Gabriel needed my answer whether he thought so or not. "I spent my whole life until this past May not having an identity. Orphans are like nomadic plants, always searching for a place to sink roots into the ground, but having no clue in which kind of soil they'd thrive."

He brushed his fingertips over my wrist. "You do seem to have a green tinge to your skin."

I elbowed him for his wise crack. "What I meant was that I am used to unanswered questions about my identity. I've loved finding answers at Eden's Court, but part of me assumes I will never completely settle. Never be sure of my identity or purpose. It's my baseline, so the fact we may all change or evolve soon doesn't feel different."

The pit in my gut tried to argue otherwise. Never mind I might screw us five ways to Sunday and we would die in a fiery inferno of planetary destruction. *You better not mess this up, Rachel.*

His finger kept stroking my wrist while he listened. "You are at home in Eden."

"Home is changing, but it changes for everyone all of the time. I realize that now. It's more unsettling for you and the rest of the Kesayim. Lillith is brand new to me so I came at her with no assumptions. This reality was far from my wildest dreams. My goal is for all of us to survive. That's the deepest truth for me. If we can stay alive, I know the rest will sort itself."

If I said this forcefully enough, I might believe myself.

His arms squeezed tighter around me as he digested my words.

"You are an optimist, my love. Even when you are afraid you fail."

"Really? I never thought that of myself. I don't feel so optimistic after Solinthe."

"It is one of your most endearing qualities. I wish you would remember it more often when you doubt yourself."

I squirmed around in his arms to watch his face. "Whether I believed my original assumption growing up that our creation and evolution were simply physics and science at work, or the work of some god of the mortal religions, or of Mother Earth, or of Lillith and her alien species, it all sifts out the same. We have to keep moving. Keep living our lives putting one foot in front of the other and building in the face of chaos."

He landed a soft kiss on the tip of my nose. "Although I agree, I would argue that many times we need to stop and savor the stillness just as much. To be, not to build. That you do not do as well, my love."

I laughed. "Well, I have my personal Buddha here to remind me to slow down. If I rub your tummy, will you grant me a wish?"

"You are mixing all of your references. I am no Djinn and they are not Buddhist. Nor have you even freed me from a bottle to make me your slave."

I shrugged. "Sure, but why worry about details when I simply want to have hot sex with you. I'm all about reveling in being alive in the moment. Plus, that's Lillith's orders." My hand snaked down to rub against his groin through his pants.

His hips shifted and he hardened against my palm. "You are incorrigible."

"I hope so. For an incubus, you need way too much prodding." My fingers stroked again.

He groaned. "I suspect you of trying to distract me from my existential worries, as you call them."

"Guilty as charged." My fist closed around him through the fabric. "I love you. I want you."

He pressed himself up into my grip. "Anything you wish."

I released my fist and worked at the clasp of his pants, freeing him from the annoying clothing before I stripped mine.

He flipped me then and pinned me to the bed, his wings flaring out behind him. His lips were hot fierce pressure all over my body, suction at my nipples, thighs, neck, hips. Until he found my center and suckled there while I cried out for more, hips bucking.

I grabbed his hair, pulled until he climbed up my body and met my lips. I was wet and ready and desperate for him. Universe, I wanted this. Wanted to be joined with him forever.

"Mine," I bit out between the kisses. "Don't ever leave again."

He grabbed my hips, spreading my thighs and thrust inside me. Yes!

Gabriel pumped deep and hard, responding with a brutal answer to my demand with his own possession.

The magic responded, flowing up into our bodies, changing his eyes to demon red while song and color, beastly shapes and sounds, a rainbow of my powers, bounced around our bodies. Knitting us tighter, braiding us from two into one. The energy pulsed thicker, meatier than I'd ever tasted. Impossibly potent in the face of our dwindling resource. It grabbed onto our skin, weaving in and out of us.

Pressure building, until—

Orgasm. Hot, pulsing, forever bliss.

Floating, then bam!

I was gone.

Vision clouded away the room. But this time, it was different. This time, I was really elsewhere. Substantial. At least it felt that way, although as I looked down, my hand was invisible and my body ghostly.

I stood in the garden underneath the tree of the merkaz. There lounged two children, a boy and a girl, laughing while they ate a picnic in the shade of the branches. Raven locks. Sparkling emerald eyes. Faces covered in chocolate as they gobbled fruit dipped in that sweet, dark confection. Precious faces shaped like mine and Gabriel's.

The unicorn approached their tree. My unicorn. She stopped and turned her head, as if seeing the essence that was myself watching this scene. Drawn to where she looked, the children also turned their heads.

With their examination, I appeared, my body now visible, standing yards from them in the merkaz.

The little boy smiled, the little girl laughed harder and licked her fingers.

"Mother," the boy called.

I tried to speak and had to clear my throat, the sound rusty and creaking. I started again. "Are you real?" I said.

"Maybe." He stuck out his tongue at his sister who'd grabbed a strawberry from his hand.

The girl stuffed her mouth with the strawberry and chewed with relish.

"I'm dreaming," I said.

"Nah. You are dream walking in the future," the boy answered.

"So, you are real."

The girl finished her mouthful and spoke. "Nothing is real yet in future time."

"But at least you're a possibility." How I wanted them. The children Gabriel and I saw in our vision the first time we'd made love together. Our children. And in a world that survived the coming cataclysm.

The girl shrugged. "We are just as likely to be your sacrifice. Your price."

My legs wobbled. No! "I don't want to sacrifice you."

The boy stood and leaned against my unicorn, brushing her sides with the palm of his hand. "We are your joy. There's never joy without pain. We are born from choice. We are one possibility, and not existing from your choice alone. Others must decide too. We are an accumulation of choices of many pathseekers."

I stepped closer, wanting more than anything to scoop up my son, steal my daughter and run like hell. To make sure they were safe and became real. No one else had the right to make the decisions affecting their lives aside from me and Gabriel.

"You can't make choices for the others," my daughter chided.

As if she'd heard my thoughts. Maybe she had.

"Only your choices are your own," she said.

"Which ones make this future real? To see you born?"

"Not sure," the boy said with another shrug.

His sister got up and joined him at the unicorn. She rubbed her cheek against the beast's side, eliciting a soft whicker.

"Love. Acceptance. Letting go," my daughter answered. That is the start.

But I did love. I loved them. I loved their father. I loved so many here in Eden it kindled a fierce ache behind my ribcage. What else could I do? Acceptance and letting go sounded dandy, but what was it they wanted me to accept and let go of?

The unicorn faced me, tilting her regal head.

A swirling pull tugged at my arms and legs. Calling me back to my bedroom. No, I wasn't ready yet.

"Keep them safe," I said, the desperation building and clogging my throat.

She nodded and whickered again.

The world of the merkaz caved into blackness.

I woke, still draped with Gabriel's warm weight. His post-coital panting breaths buzzed my ear. I pushed him off me, uncomfortable with the panicked sourness in my gut.

He rolled to his side. "What's wrong, love?" His turn to ask.

Only seconds had passed for him. He never knew I'd gone. "Nothing."

He frowned, seeing through my lie. But for whatever reason, probably chalking my untruth up to my usual catalogue of worries, he pulled me close to nuzzle against my body. He settled us into the comforter and pillows in a warm nest.

"Sleep," he ordered, his voice soft in the command as he kissed the top of my head.

I murmured a non-committal response and lie still, feeling the press of his skin against mine, the rise and fall of his chest as he drifted into sleep, the tickle of his hair against my neck.

Sacrifice. Love. Acceptance. Letting go. My children. My future. Loss.

Numb confusion made a precious blank in my mind, and eventually, I fell into zombie sleep.

Chapter Twenty

A soft knock woke me. Although with my nerves wound tighter than a clockwork automaton with his key up his ass, a gentle breeze would have been enough to wake me.

Before I could untangle myself from Gabriel and the sheets, the door opened and Delta's head popped through. "Good morning, my lady. May I speak with you for a moment?" The demoness entered faster than my fuzzy mind could frame any response. She walked over to the corner of the bed, sauntered actually, and sat.

What freaking time was it? I rubbed sleep from my eyes and finished the struggle upright. "Clearly your request was a polite formality. We're having this discussion now I take it? Thank you for cushioning my tender supreme ruler sensibilities by pretending I was in charge."

I kept the sheet pulled up over my chest. Naked might not bother demons, but call me old fashioned.

Gabriel, awake by this time, had no problem climbing naked and irate out of the bed to stand glowering over Delta's perch. "You have plucked my last nerve, Delta. Rachel runs an informal court, but your actions border on insolence. Leave us now." He pointed at the door.

She smiled at him. "Someone woke on the wrong side of the bed."

Gabriel froze, dropped his arm, and his muscles loosened to alert but supple readiness. His voice lowered to a dangerous purr. "Are you defying me?"

Delta laughed. "Your sexy I'd-kill-you-as-easily-as-I'd-fuck-you incubus allure won't work on me."

Wow, I'd never heard it stated that way, but now that she'd said it, that was a great description of Gabriel's vibe in his most dangerous state.

I yanked my sheet higher as it began to slip. "Sweetie, why don't you get us a coffee while I check in with Delta?"

His muscle tension returned as he shifted from his truly deadly state, and his fist clenched and unclenched at his side. "Your guardswoman," he bit out, "should allow you to dress and wait until you join her in your anteroom to speak with her."

"Her anteroom," Delta said, "is standing room only. Tarn, Sebastian, Christian, Leslie, Anna—"

"What are Leslie and Anna doing here?" I asked. "I thought Christian was here alone."

As Delta mentioned them, I felt for my magic and noticed a stuttering here and gone quality to it, present in weak dribs and drabs at best. My anteroom would turn into a magic dead zone soon.

"Qest, Gwen, Jasper, Peter—" she continued.

"Jasper's here? When did he get back?" Of course he would come for his son given the absolute chaos of our world.

"Sebastian's brother, sister-in-law, nephew Gregor, Morven, and Jack," she finished the list.

Maybe it was good the nulls were outside my bedroom door. So many powerful Kesayim in such a small space led to uncomfortable pressure.

My sheet slipped again. "Delta, shut it! We can talk in here, but I need space to dress first."

With a flourish, she gestured me in the direction of my bathroom. Brat!

I pulled the sheet loose from the bed, wrapped it around me, and grabbed clothes on the way to the bathroom. Artemis yawned in the corner where she slept, ignoring the latest twist of events.

Before I entered, I blew Gabriel a kiss and told him to scram. I closed the door behind me, overhearing a few more zingers exchanged between Delta and my lover. Then, the door to my bedroom shut with a controlled slam.

I crawled into jeans and a tee and ran a brush through my hair. The mirror showed me a pale, drained face with dark circles under my eyes. I dug my fingertips into my temples, rubbing them for relief. Memories of the little girl and boy and my unicorn flashed. Of the mirror shattering. Of Eden shaking with the earthquake. Of angry faces of council.

No, Rachel. First things first. Delta. Then your full anteroom.

I brushed my teeth, splashed cold water over my face, and went out to see my newest guard.

The demoness stood at the bank of windows that looked out into the garden, more pensive than I'd ever seen her. All evidence of her saucy spark quiet.

"You wanted to talk?" I sat down on the bed, wishing more than anything I could crawl back under the comforter and sleep.

She turned away from the glass. "I am fucking up the situation with Tarn and Sebastian."

"Not one for small talk, are we?"

"I need your advice, my lady. It may not be the time, but there never seems to be a quiet moment in this place."

"It's Rachel. Any conversation involving the word fuck does not call for formality."

"Here's the bottom line, Rachel. I love the two fools."

"We're still talking Tarn and Sebastian, yes?"

"Keep up, please."

"Sorry."

Delta pursed her lips. "I love them. And I believe that they believe they love me."

"Dost the demoness doubt her worth?"

"I haven't gotten to the problem yet, Shakespeare."

"Okay," I said. I guess anyone else would consider her tone insolent, but I had no time to be sidetracked by small details.

"You know the two loved each other before I arrived," she said. "A true love that has great depth. My presence opened the door faster to finding a way for them to share that love, but without me, they would have come to it in their own time."

She shook her head at herself. "What I share with them is not the same. Our love, even if it is genuine on their end, came fast. It is a shallow thing in comparison and I shouldn't play games in light of their deep bond."

"Are you playing a game with them?" Her words inched up my hackles.

"No. I love them. But I am better at hijinks and troublemaking than anything steady. Perhaps my cute, sexy nature fooled them into believing they love me. And the mandolin. Who doesn't love a chick who can rock out?"

She was one of a kind, this demoness. She had a genuine quality about her and I could see how Tarn and Sebastian would fall for her, a breath of fresh air and joy. Tarn had exuded the same quality, but recent events had dimmed some of his light.

"Love can arrive fast," I said. "Like being hit by a semi. Gabriel and I found ours in a whirlwind, and it's plenty deep."

"I'd heard that of you two, together in a matter of days. But your natures aren't like mine. Yours are loyal, intense, driven, and geared toward leadership. You are healers at your core, and need to be together to do what you're meant." Delta gripped the handle of her dagger in its sheathe. "I should leave them. Bow out to let their relationship be the way it's meant."

My throat tightened with reminders. "Don't do it. You think you know what's best for them, but it's a trap. I learned the hard way to respect the choices made by the people I loved. Even if they're not mine."

Gabriel's stubborn, sweet face floated in my mind. Followed by the memory of his battered body when Lillith first threatened him in our dreamscape. Again, when we rescued him from Faerie. "If you love them, and they want you, respect that. Maybe they would have walked a different path without you, but that's not what happened. They're grown-ups and deserve a choice."

She sighed. "Point taken. Just promise that if I'm not around you'll shove them back on their path together. I don't want them derailed from some stupid reaction to my absence."

My necklace pulsed a cold warning and my gut roiled. *Gone like Jet.* I shook it off.

"Any reason you would leave?" I asked.

"Satan's recalled me since his tantrum with you at council."

"You're going?"

"No way. The glutton is drunk on the chaos of the world's condition or else he'd never suggest it. All demons are a bit tipsy with the situation. He's ruled his people well for so long by letting them do their own thing. He's not a micromanager, but given his current intemperance, I am ready for him to have me killed as punishment for refusing."

"Not on my watch!"

"Guarding your own guard. Sweet. I trust your power, but Satan is quite lethal when he puts his mind to it. And you cannot be everywhere despite how you insist on trying."

"I repeat my statement. Not on my watch."

She snorted. "Have it your way, but promise me you will help my boys nonetheless."

My shoulders fell, my anger ebbing back into its hiding place, nudged out by my exhaustion. "I'm not that powerful. All I can do is love them and be their friend. If anything helps, that's what will."

If anything happened to her, they couldn't fall apart. They deserved a happily ever after. Maybe there was something more I could do. *Stop it, Rachel! Let it go.*

Finally, Delta's impish smile returned. "Or maybe this point is moot and we'll all burn up in a fiery ball. The world ending does have a way of re-prioritizing one's fears. Or if we survive, I can plan the princess wedding of my dreams. Will you walk me down the aisle and give me away, Rachel?"

Her lips quirked with her next thought. "No, you should walk the boys down the aisle. I'll ask Gabriel to give me away. He'd love that."

"I don't know what his problem is with you, although your button pushing doesn't help. Maybe he's jealous that you are part of my guard and he isn't one of my official protectors any longer."

She shook her head. "At first maybe, but now he's jealous over Tarn and Sebastian."

"What?"

"They've been his close friends for a long time. Not that he's ever wanted to jump in the sack with them, but his self-imposed exile deprived him of their company. Now he returns and their time is spent with me. He has few friends and they're precious to him. Of course, I'm not taking them from him, but the heart is an irrational organ."

Delta's endless insights made me pause. Wisdom wrapped in an unlikely package.

A sharp rap at the door made me jump. "Rachel," Gabriel's voice interrupted, "we need you out here."

I stood, sudden jitters firing through my body. "We good?"

"Yes." She laughed, a refreshing sun shower. "I'll keep banging the two fools with a clear conscience."

I called to Artemis and folded her back into the magical sling. "You are full of poetry. Now, on to the madhouse in my anteroom."

* * * * *

Christian's voice, angry and determined, greeted me as I exited the bedroom. "I got them here with seconds to spare. They came to bring her and Anna to the confinement cells again. Or execute them as they stood. Only a warning from one of my friends on Frederick's staff saved us."

Gabriel faced my vampire brother as he stood next to the oversized stuffed chair where Leslie and her daughter sat, huddled more like it. Anna looked as if she'd been crying. Leslie stroked her hair, glaring at Gabriel as he spoke with Christian.

"Yet you cannot mean to take them back to the Achra realm," Gabriel said. "We need Leslie here for the genetic blending." My lover was clearly mid-argument with my brother.

"I won't put them at risk. Natalya wants them dead. We are leaving."

Jasper, sparing me a quick glance as I entered, tried to intervene in the argument. "Christian, she'll be no safer there. Thousands of Achra die daily. I've been Gwen's liaison, eyes and ears on the ground, and putting out fires. Literally."

"The threat is more direct here and it's unacceptable," Christian said. "Will you help us through the portal or not?"

"No," Gabriel answered, clear and calm. "The consequences to losing her are too serious."

Christian paused, stepped closer still to Leslie's chair.

The atmosphere in the room shifted, his pulsing energy flaring around him and Leslie. Energy he wielded while everyone else was drained by her presence. The brief flares when she kindled my power were few and far between. Only Christian seemed to benefit now without break. Positive emotion for the recipient seemed to be the key. And Leslie was far from feeling positive regard for much of anyone in this room. Except Christian.

I gasped at his concentrated power, fighting to walk through the thickness of the magic to get to Christian's side. To stop this.

The rest of my crew watched on with worried glances, just as unsure what to do with their own power missing in Leslie's presence. The lack of their magic left everyone looking pallid, like gasping fish floundering out of water. Only Qest seemed unaffected.

I caught his eyes as I moved closer to Christian and sent a private message through our Kyn bond. *"Stay put. Stay under Christian's radar."*

Qest nodded.

My vampire brother began speaking again. "You will help us through the portal. All of you if needed. You do see my position."

Oh, Christian! He was using a vampire mind trick, cajoling with the sensual allure of his species. And everyone was damn vulnerable to it without their magic.

Gabriel shook his head as if to clear it of confusion. Tarn, Sebastian, and even Gwen's eyes lost focus, pulled into my brother's will as it wormed its way into their minds and seduced them to his position. Their natural defenses were gone as Leslie's null abilities short circuited them. Somehow, her link to Christian allowed her to enhance his magic while draining everyone else's. A potent magnifying glass trained only on my brother.

He took them over with finesse, but with all the power of a waterfall, liquid crashing over sharp rocks to destroy everything in its path.

Qest remained steady, waiting as I asked, though unaffected. The strain in his eyes told me the fight he faced remaining still.

Jasper and Morven swayed on their feet under the vampire trance. Jack whimpered where he rested in the corner. Delta nodded at Christian's words, agreeing to them with his spell.

"Christian," I called, drawing his attention to me. Whether it was my own Kyn heritage or the fact I'd guarded myself well from vampire mind tricks since a previous encounter in council, I avoided my brother's persuasion with effort, teeth grit. The rest stood frozen at best, unable to move or respond.

My other magics sputtered in the face of Leslie's effect, but I kept walking toward Christian.

"Stop it. Now," I said. "Don't you see what you are doing?"

The gleam in his eyes reminded me of Natalya's madness when she learned her mortal lover had been killed. The Achra lovers to which vampires were drawn might be their greatest weakness, their need for them and to protect them subverting rational thought.

"He's trying to keep me and my daughter alive," Leslie said. "No one else is willing."

I didn't look her way. My gaze focused on Christian. "This is wrong. You know I will do everything in my power to protect her and Anna, but we need them. You understand that. Think of the research you've done. You are scared. I get it. I'm scared, too. We'll do this together."

By his side finally, I wrapped his arm with my hand, wanting to touch him, reassure him, convince him.

"You cannot be everywhere protecting everyone, no matter how you try," he said.

Delta had just said something similar to me, dammit.

"Help me or stay out of my way, Rachel. You can find another null for the blending. You have Solinthe's list."

"Let me relocate them to the merkaz. No one can enter there without my magic allowing it," I argued.

"What if her null effect messes up that protection, too?"

"Yet you think you can get her safely through a portal to mortal Earth?"

"She's agreed to let herself and Anna be placed unconscious for the portal trip. Like she was when she first arrived. But they cannot stay unconscious permanently in the merkaz."

"Let me try placing them there, Christian. We only have a few days left."

He shook his head. "No. I cannot risk it."

My anger flitted alive with his last refusal. With my contact at his arm, I started to siphon magic not from the earth, but from him. Storing it. "I have worked too damn hard, brother, for your panicked thrashings to sink us all. Quit this manipulation or I'll quit it for you."

"I don't want to hurt you, Rachel."

"Don't worry. You won't."

I stepped away from Christian. *"Now Qest!"* I called silently and used the store of siphoned power to momentarily restrain this heartbreaking betrayer.

Blurring motion, and my dragon brother broke his possum pose and sped at Christian. Slam. With a thud, Qest rammed his older brother, knocking him to the floor and pinning him as Christian, stunned, lost his magic hold on the room.

Confused motion. Leslie leapt from the chair at us, but Sebastian caught her, holding her with simple physical strength. When Anna ran at Sebastian to protect her mom, Delta caught the daughter and held her back.

Gabriel unholstered his gun, running to fall to his knees, joining Qest and Christian on the floor. Christian struggled, but my lover shoved the point of the pistol at Christian's temple.

My vampire brother went still under the press of the barrel.

"If you ever threaten Rachel again, I will kill you. I do not care if you are her brother. Try your magic now and let us see if I can pull the trigger faster than your spell."

"Gabriel, don't!" I barked.

Tarn was at Gabriel's side. "Easy, man. No harm has been done. Rachel is fine."

"We are still without power near the nulls. He is still a danger," my lover replied.

"Gabriel, let me talk to him," I said.

He paused, considering. "The gun remains for now."

I wouldn't win an argument over this with my lover's killing edge riding him heavy. I nodded agreement and lowered myself to Christian's other side.

It was awkward with Qest still pinning him and Gabriel holding the gun to his head, but I loved my brother and we had to get past this. "Christian, you need to convince me that you won't start this again. I can knock Leslie and Anna unconscious, but I know you and they would not want that."

He grimaced as I expected.

I continued. "I will if I have to, but find me another way. You love Leslie. She comes first for you at this point, but I need you to understand my position. I have billions of souls depending on my crazy plan to blend our DNA. Whether I'm a fool is unclear, but I've got nothing else in my back pocket so I need to try.

"If I can pull it off, Leslie and Anna have a future. If I can't, it doesn't matter how far and fast you run with them because we are all lost."

He spoke carefully to avoid jostling the gun. "If they die here before you even try your plan, my life is over. It will not matter to me if Earth crumbles."

It was the same attitude that had led Jet to betray his people. The powerhouse of despair destroyed many lives.

"I know, so it means taking a risk," I said. "You love more than Leslie even if she's your priority now. You love me, our brothers, your people. If you want a future with Leslie it means living in a world with all of these others."

His gaze flicked to Gabriel and back to me, all the movement he was free to make. "I do love you, although this has turned into a mess."

"Then we clean up the mess. Come with me to the merkaz. I have an idea how to shore up the entrance if Leslie or Anna affect the barrier."

He sighed. "Let me go and I promise to behave."

"Swear on it," Gabriel said.

"I swear. By the memory of our mother, whom I loved to the core." His eyes swerved back to Qest. "I am sorry."

"For a big brother, your role-modeling sucked today, Christian." Qest's voice shook in the admonishment.

"Let him go," I told Gabriel and Qest.

Gabriel exchanged a long look with Christian, weighing some quality. Then, he pulled away the gun and stood.

Qest rose and his face spoke the steep cost of his actions moving against Christian and of how close we'd come to needing to end our brother's life.

Christian took a few moments to stand. He turned to Sebastian and Delta. "Can you release them?"

I nodded permission and my guards let them go.

Anna ran to Leslie who backed them as far from the crowd as possible. Christian went to them, embracing Leslie and whispering reassurances. When he turned again to the rest of the gathering, his eyes landed on Peter standing in Jasper's arms. The boy's cheeks were wet from his own tears.

Three kids had witnessed this. Suffer the little children. Shit. I should have seen this coming. Why didn't I see this coming? There were too many details to track. Too many affected by this crisis.

"Peter, I'm sorry," Christian said. Remorse colored his face and words as he woke to the trauma he'd inflicted on the room.

Jasper rubbed his son's shoulders and sent his brother a warning look.

Peter stood a bit straighter. "That's okay, Uncle. You freaked me out, but I know you didn't mean it. When the magic is really big and full, it's hard to resist."

Christian left Leslie and came closer to his nephew. Peter flinched and Christian stopped his approach, a shadow of pain passing over his face until he smoothed his expression. "I appreciate your understanding. You are right. Big magic is tempting. I am sorry."

"Apologies only go so far," Jasper said. "Don't forget who your real enemies are, or who you count on to defend you in the end. You cannot afford to lose us, but you've sure tried hard this morning."

"Enough, Jasper," Gwen chastised. "We've lived too long not to learn the lesson of forgiveness. Especially for those we love."

My mind fumbled for a direction. Facing Satan, Solinthe or Lillith was far easier than crashing against my brother. The tension in the room shrunk its size further. Seventeen of us in one space meant for far fewer. Now that this crisis had passed, my nervous energy returned. If I didn't start moving, I'd shake apart. Or run away.

Universe bless Morven as she marched over. "Now that we have had a healthy dose of drama for the morning, my lady, I suggest we prepare for the first genetic blending attempt."

Her no-nonsense command let me draw in a needed deep breath. "Yes."

Her soldiering tone continued. "Everyone in the room has been updated about Solinthe's recent attack. Gathering your full support team to guard you during the experiment seemed prudent." As she examined the room it became clear she regretted that choice, but would make the best of it.

Pull yourself together, Rachel.

Gabriel moved to my side. "We will relocate to the merkaz?" he asked me.

I drew on his strength and the invisible cord that stretched between us. His question provided the life raft I needed to refocus.

"It's safer and with more room," I agreed. "I'm not worried about our group drawing attention as we relocate. All the troublemakers got their invitation and the party has already started. If the likely suspects want to dance, I'm ready."

Gwen laughed. "You sound Dirty Harryesque, Rachel."

"Yeah," I answered. "You've all signed on for the gunslingers-r-us crew. Welcome to the showdown." Laugh, don't cry.

My palms itched. Needing something. Needing all this to be over. Needing to do better. I couldn't undo the pain in the room. And that pain was only the start.

Chapter Twenty-one

The merkaz represented the most concentrated source of magic in Eden. I'd need every bit of it. The heart of the garden.

We'd escaped from my suite after our morning drama with no one in pursuit. Small miracle given the stream of steady crisis in my life. We were officially going underground. The council knew they couldn't arrest me. Where would they put me? The threat was more basic than that.

Many of the Kesayim remained loyal to me, but the complicated knot of politics and power among the council, its staff, and pathways of intel, complicated my plans. Even now I imagined different contingents and their search parties "concerned" about the whereabouts of the Mother Heir and, of course, the "escaped null".

As our crowd approached the merkaz, I waved a hand and the entrance to the nucleus of the garden opened for me, even with Leslie and Anna present. It was keyed solely to the Mother Heir, unable to be accessed by others. Or so everyone believed.

I stepped inside, breathing easier in this refuge where the garden's vibrancy notched one level higher, sliding over my senses like smooth potent whiskey. The merkaz was the garden on steroids, with the colors of its leaves, grass and flowers dialed up to ridiculous dripping richness. In some ways, it struck me as a distant cousin of Solinthe's Dr. Seuss realm with its high calorie startling design. But while Solinthe's landscape left a viewer with a headache, the merkaz left its guests weeping from its beauty. Touched in their souls.

Around me, shoulders dropped in similar relief, like a long, lovely sigh at journey's end. Too bad it was only a temporary reprieve.

I walked further into the refuge, grabbed Christian's arm, and tapped into the magic load Leslie enabled in him. I ignored his look of guilt as I again used him as a channel. The flow entered my bloodstream, and my muscles loosened. The power eased through me, filling me up and helping me find my center. I glanced over at Christian and my anger at him from this morning stuttered. In our connection, I tasted his confusion and regret, his own anger at his behavior. And his fear. But also, his love for Leslie and her daughter.

Nothing for it but to go to work.

In seconds, I used the rich source of his energy to create a magic-proof barrier woven from my Kyn powers. I coated the regular entryway to the merkaz with this force and released my brother. It worked. The barrier remained free of the null drain. We'd be safe.

I then snaked a more sophisticated and invisible tether between my middle brother and me. The link would keep a good pool of power accessible to me during the experiment. As Christian tapped into the potent earth of the merkaz with Leslie's magnifying influence, I'd be a secondary recipient of these goods through the line.

Christian started to comment at our tether, but thought better of it when he saw my face. "What now?" he asked.

The others gathered round and I felt suspiciously like a football coach in a huddle. "No one can get in here as far as I know. Gabriel and I will do our thing. The rest of you..." I shrugged. I had no ideas for them.

Gwen pulled her hair into a pony tail and stretched arms over head, arching her back like a cat. "I for one intend to enjoy a respite." She winked at me. "While protecting you and Gabriel to the end, of course, Rachel."

"Of course," I said. "You need your rest. This constant diet of emergency and threat of death ruins a girl's complexion. As long as everyone plays nice while we test out the DNA acrobatics, do what you like. Take naps, practice tai chi, set up croquet. Go crazy."

I appreciated Gwen's attempt at lightening the mood and was determined to contribute, especially to distract the swarm of bees vibrating in my stomach at the thought of the next few hours.

"We'll keep entertained," Gwen said.

Sweat pooled at the base of my spine at the thought of an audience for my experiment. I understood the need for guards when I went under with Gabriel, but this felt akin to taking off my clothes in front of everyone. At least the merkaz provided safety to my nearest and dearest while the rest of the Kesayim leadership targeted us.

My wood-carved throne in the center of the merkaz stood empty and majestic, but I preferred the bench under the Japanese maple. The tree drew me every time.

Gabriel followed as I walked over to run fingers against its rough trunk, the scrape of my palm almost a relief. I leaned against the wood, feeling the small dig of bark through my shirt.

Delta, Tarn, and Sebastian followed us.

I closed my eyes and soaked in the warmth of the day, valiant rays fighting the cold of uncertainty and doubt. I opened them to the view of four of the people I trusted most.

My foot tapped the ground. "Under the tree will do for our experiment. The grass is lush and comfy here."

"I have always found it such," Gabriel answered, a sexy grin reminding me of the times we'd made love on this spot. A moment of sweet memory in the middle of our crazy race.

"I'm tethering the three of you to Christian and to me," I told my guard. "You'll need his power if a threat arises."

"With Leslie around, the tether to Christian makes sense, my lady," Delta said. "But why to you?"

"Something tells me I could use your support." My hand grabbed Sebastian's and I squeezed his large fingers, a lifeline when my own started to tremor. "You love me, you love Gabriel. Tarn feels the same. And as Delta's wise enough to fall for the two of you, and you seem to have decided to jump on the same train with her, nothing is better for this project than the love you three share. It's the secret ingredient and special sauce."

Sebastian blushed red, but his free hand snaked over to Tarn's and the tip of his finger brushed the other man's palm for a fleeting second.

Tarn's face flicked slight pleasure before refocusing on me. "You need more power for the attempt than Christian can supply?"

"She is worried I will die," Gabriel answered with annoying certainty. "She has crammed every free moment with studying genetic information and processes."

Gut spasming, I stuck out my tongue at him, dared myself to laugh in the face of my black worry. "If this goes well, I'll drop the Mother Heir gig and go back to medical school. Lucky I was good in biology."

"I will not die, Rachel."

"You better not."

"So, how does our tether help?" Sebastian asked, more to cut the thick pain out of the air between us if I knew my guardsman.

"I'm not sure, but when we go in I hope to get a look at the works." The entire experiment smacked of handing a scalpel to a first-year medical student and asking him to perform intricate brain surgery, blindfolded and handcuffed. No pressure there.

Despite my earlier comment about medical school, my current aspirations were less professional and more instinctual. Survive. Growl and claw and scratch at the future to make sure everyone I loved survived.

Tarn nodded. "Depend on us. Create the tether. We will be there for you."

"Such intimate arrangements between us." Delta's lips tilted up on one side. "Does the tether qualify as bondage? Always wanted to try kinky."

Sebastian rolled his eyes at her.

"Don't pretend prudishness, boy scout," the demoness chided her lover, following it up by a smack to his butt.

Tarn chuckled at the byplay.

"As much fun as this is, time is a commodity and I need a quick moment with Qest before we begin."

Gabriel raised a brow at my statement, but stayed quiet while I wandered away and grabbed my brother, drawing him farther into the merkaz and away from everyone. I kept walking to be sure we found the distance to keep the supernatural hearing of my friends from intruding. I could use our telepathy for complete privacy, but somehow, I wanted to have this conversation out loud.

Qest stopped me after ten minutes. Like any place in the garden, even the merkaz's borders were infinite. "Stop, Rachel. Far enough. What?"

I looked at the face that was so close to my own. The man I trusted most aside from Gabriel.

"I've keyed the entryway to the merkaz to you."

Qest squinted. "What? How?"

"Short-term magic. I can force the wards to recognize someone else for a limited time. If Gabriel and I don't make it, get them out. Go where you want to ride out the storm."

"You're crazy, sister. Of course you will survive. That's what you do."

"Maybe. But if Gabriel doesn't, I'm not sure I want to."

"You realize you insisted Christian reject just this feeling. Rachel, I have never met a single individual with a will as strong as yours. Being scared makes sense, but both you and Gabriel will come through this. Your to do list alone is so long you will make it just because it would mess up the schedule. Don't give the Eemah or Solinthe the satisfaction."

Shit, the man was stubborn. "Look, Qest, let me have this small moment. The darkness is real. The big bad may win. Fine, be the optimist. Universe, I keep a running soundtrack in my head trying to maintain a positive attitude. But I need to say goodbye. In case. I can't face that with everyone, but with you... And if the worst happens, I need to say I'm sorry. Sorry I couldn't do this job and make it alright."

Qest's eyes flashed with fire, a puff of smoke blew from his nostrils. "You want absolution? I am not your man. I have said goodbye to too many. Mother, father, my dwindling Kyn people. I don't need goodbyes. They bring little relief. It's living that brings anything of value."

I dug my feet into the fecund ground to avoid stepping back, away from his anger. It slammed head first into my grief and doubt and rolled it on its side, busting blood and metal parts to pieces and leaving my mouth gaping open.

Qest continued. "Cancel the trip to pityville and get busy, sister. One sibling freak out per day is my limit."

He growled again at what must be my blank look and grabbed me in a blink, enclosing me in a brief, fierce hug before turning tail and marching back to the rest of the group.

I walked back, slow step after slow step.

Gabriel took a look at me and shook his head. "Qest is as stubborn as you, love."

"Apparently."

"Come." He held out his hand to me.

I took it and settled down on the grass under our tree, my head leaning on his shoulder, his arms wrapped around my body. No special position for magical DNA exploratory surgery. Just the comfort of one another.

My sigh drew a chuckle from him and I closed my eyes. Focusing inward, I milked the power from the tether and sought for the chaos magic of dream walking, twisting the process with a step to the left to aim it down into my body; dropping into a walking, waking dream. Next to me, the heat of Gabriel's form cooled a fraction as I pulled him into the journey.

Not a dream. More a 3D transport inside my body, shrinking our essence into miniatures to travel my bloodstream.

Swirling, pulsing liquid rushed around us. My senses tumbled in confusion with what passed for eyesight a hazy field ahead as I tried to steer, and magic the only force keeping me focused on reaching the goal. I aimed for stem cells within my bone marrow, the source of the repair system to the body and the place where changes to the DNA could be the launchpad to be replicated through the entire body.

The dark jet stream pulse of my blood hypnotized me on the journey and my hand squeezed tightly around Gabriel's, keeping him close.

His voice echoed in my ears. "What is that?" A bumpy white ball floated ahead, larger than us by a multiple of hundreds.

"White blood cell. The attack dog of the immune system."

It sped toward us and several more joined its flanks to gear up to destroy the invaders, namely us. I guess my body didn't find my magical miniaturized presence welcoming. Or maybe Gabriel registered as the foreign substance. Either way, we needed to dodge these suckers. Lurching to one side, the white globe grazed me and we went careening into the side of the blood vessel, the spongy surface scraping my skin and bouncing us back into the middle of the channel. Gabriel cursed as a second passed close by him and hit his arm as he jerked away. A dozen more sped toward us from farther down the vessel.

We needed away from them. As we were closer to the jackpot, I re-envisioned the area we targeted and grabbed more of Christian's energy, jumping us directly into the bone and through the barriers into the marrow, imagining us down to an even smaller size to penetrate the cell membranes of the stem cells.

We pushed through the goo of the membranes and into a cell as I shrunk us smaller again, swimming to its center and into the nucleus.

And there they were. My ladders. DNA; those twisting staircases from my recent dream. Funny how the answers tried to find me while I slept long before I understood the question. Score one for the unconscious mind. Although, part of me wondered if Lillith had tried to cheat those rules set down by her people and nudge me along with a nocturnal suggestion.

A sense of pause; a pregnant second settled around me as I took a breath. We floated next to this wondrous design. If Lillith created all of this, she must be greater than what I'd seen of her. The beauty choked in my throat. And for a few more moments, I felt the cords binding me to everything, everyone. The scale of it quieted my words. Nothing to say while gobsmacked by life. This wasn't Lillith alone. No single being could create to this scale. She was as much a cog as any of us. Linked together by spirit, the divine, the essence of creation. The label didn't matter. Who was I in this story? Talk about humbled. But neither could I stop my little part in this play. Otherwise, why stage the play to begin with?

"What now?" Gabriel asked, eyes wide, with even his immutable calm challenged by the overwhelming environment.

His question settled me back in the moment. My precious man.

He blinked and his hand fisted at his side. Close. Open. Close. Enzymes and amino acids floated by us as I backed us away from impact.

"We need to unzip this puppy and take a look."

The problem was that strands of DNA were enormous, and only select sections unzipped at one time to replicate. However, we needed an overview, with a way to look at the pattern of my DNA in order to figure out the next steps.

I swam us to the nearest staircase and we grabbed onto a rung, hand over hand traveling up the strand while I waited for inspiration. *The answer's not going to bite your ass for attention, Rachel. Just figure it out.*

"We climb."

Each rung consisted of two nucleotides joined seamlessly together. Even inside a living cell, my mind painted the picture in ways I could understand, the different nucleotides gradations of color.

Around us, what I guessed were enzymes darted back and forth, going about their business.

"Incoming," Gabriel warned as a barrage of structures torpedoed towards us.

"Damn." I imagined a barrier around us and called magic just as the first new biological slammed against us. The ladder vibrated from the impact against the shield. My grip loosened on the rungs with my relief after the danger passed.

So many shades of gray and globules of strange shapes. The rails of our ladder grew moist under my fingers. What did the shifting textures under my fingertips mean? All my hours of science study meant nothing as the full complexity of life inside a cell exploded around us. The perpetual movement distracted me.

"I can't figure this out, Gabriel. I need to see the blueprint and find the missing pieces."

Gabriel's calm returned, maybe in reaction to the panic even I heard in my voice. His pine eyes steadied on mine. "Stop trying to become a scientist, Rachel. Use who you are. What you are. Feel it. All around us. The magic. You can find a way, but it must be your way."

Tightening my grip, buffered by the magic shield I'd already called, I let myself breathe. In. Out. Let myself feel. Yes, the power flowed around me. Flowed through this cell and all of the countless others. The energy was in my lifeblood itself.

Next to me, my lover took his own deep breath. Gabriel's steady presence strengthened me, even as we hung in this impossible location, deep in our waking dream. My lovely angel-demon, my Janii.

"Demon. Yes. Demon magic," I mumbled my realization. Demons scanned patterns in order to figure out how to disrupt their order. I didn't need the disruption, but the scan would work to do the job.

Gabriel followed my disjointed words and nodded. The man seemed to intuitively know and understand my every thought. Scary. Wonderful.

"If you scan the blueprint, you will need a way to record the information. To create a set of directions to make the changes to the other DNA."

And by other, he meant his own. The genetic surgery I intended to practice on him scared me to death. There was a reason surgeons never cut into their own family members.

The rung scraped my skin as I tightened my fingers. A pulsing warmth beat from my necklace, giving me a solution for recording. The necklace. It was a fae instrument, after all. Solinthe described it as 'a tool for creation.' Why not use it for its purpose and lay down the pattern of the code in the woven strands? I explained the idea and he nodded.

"I have to get this right. One screw up and—"

Gabriel reached over from his place beside me on the ladder and pulled me towards him. Even in this dreamlike construct, his body heat melted me in all the right places. His lips pressed mine and shut down my spinning thoughts of failure.

After a forever, or maybe a few seconds, he released me.

"That was...wow. Nice."

His slow smile teased. "I hope better than nice."

I sighed. "Remind me why we're here and not getting busy in that oversized bed of mine."

"World. Dying. Last chance."

"Oh, right." My bubble burst, although Gabriel didn't give me any quarter.

"Here, where your fingers touch the rung, is as good a spot as any to scan for the pattern," he said, slapping the top of my hand with his own in punctuation. "Get to it."

"Pushy much?"

"Saving Eden, remember?"

"I thought you kissed me to stop all my worry."

"Stop the worry, start the action. The sooner you complete the project, the sooner I do get to perform countless nasty deeds with you in that gargantuan bed of yours back at court."

"Promises, promises."

"When have I not delivered?"

"You have a point," I answered.

"One that you seem to enjoy, if I remember."

I couldn't keep my barking laugh from escaping at the comment. "Laughter at my darkest hour. Imagine that. You really know how to show a gal a good time, sweetie."

"Pattern. Rung. Necklace," he reminded, tapping my hand again.

Did I imagine a tremble in his fingers?

"Okay, already."

I sighed and refocused on the spiral around us, the twisted ladder engulfing us as I set to work. The magic unfurled and observed the wickedly complex strands, sniffing along the surface and gulping down the flow of connections, forming a picture of the living code. The buzz of understanding grew stronger in my head, helping me "know" even without detailed appreciation for the science. It took forever. It took no time at all. Gorgeous. The synergy of the ladder was near perfect, with only the slightest sounds and pictures out of step.

"The pattern's amazing, but every now and again there are holes." Our words sounded half swallowed, as if absorbed by the giant cushion of organic material surrounding us.

"Gaps in the code?" Gabriel asked.

I nodded. Even my Mother Heir DNA wasn't the pinnacle of evolution, although I couldn't stop to figure out what was missing.

The scan continued as my magic 'read' the pattern. The buzzing sound grew louder and louder and I blinked as the magic reached the final section of the strand and the whirling combination of light and jarring pattern solidified into a shocking shape. Lillith. A final nub of the code mimicked the exact discordant form of the goddess as I experienced her in the portals and in my dream memories of her with her 'father'. Her essence was part of the DNA. She was like the final pair of nucleotides that signal an end to a sequence. The grand finale.

"What do you see?" Gabriel asked, maybe noting a change in my reaction as I scanned. Long moments passed before my breath returned.

"Lillith. Or something that looks like her natural form when I've met her in the gate void. She's part of my DNA, and the fact is monumentally disturbing. Thankfully, I have no real stomach in this waking dream or I might be emptying it about now. That bitch is inside me."

"Rachel, now is not the moment for philosophical consideration of what you found. Store the information in your necklace." His face held strain as he urged me to get on with business. What wasn't he telling me?

"Yeah. That." I pushed aside the sticky discomfort of Lillith with a shake of my head.

My fingers wrapped around the weave of my necklace, miniaturized along with the rest of me, and stroked the texture of the metal. I gathered the patterns and whispered them into the jewelry, laying them down into the molecules of the weave. The metal heated against my neck, so hot I imagined welts rising on my skin. It beat staccato patterns around my throat.

"Done. Now what?"

"We leave your glorious cell and jump next door," he said. His fist squeezed another quick pump.

The hairs on my arm stood at attention. The scrape of nerves like a porcupine rubbing up against my body, quills making friendly with my epidermis.

Gabriel's eyes glowed demon red as his magic prepared to lead us. An impatient bright orange tinged his aura.

"Do I swim us into the larger vessels in my body to get out?"

"I believe I can transport us along the dream ways without backtracking out of the marrow cell."

With an inward focus, his eyes closing, Gabriel reached up and out, calling a dreamscape version of vines down to us hanging above us as handholds.

He grabbed onto a solid tendril, wrapping it twice around his wrist. I followed his motion and tangled my own around my hand. Gabriel inhaled a word of power, grabbed to pull me to his side, and swung us. Almost to waking, but not quite.

Gray blur surrounded us with my body thrown into a swish of movement, as if we careened down a superhighway. Disoriented, I clung to Gabriel as I lost all sense of the familiar. A steady beat of sound, a new rhythmic susurration hit my ears as we transitioned. Not inside Rachel. Inside Gabriel. His body and its feel were an entirely new planet, as alien from mine as Mars from Earth. The warm bath of his bloodstream surrounded us as he maneuvered us, now at a slower pace, into one of his stem cells.

With a final pop, we nudged past a membrane and into a cell.

I wiped at my face, trying to push away the feeling that a layer of foreign ash coated my skin. Each breath was like inhaling through taffy, heavy and clogged, my inhalations more purposeful work than natural reflex. "Was it like this for you when we were inside me? Like your gut's screaming 'WRONG' at high decibels. The body does a good job sending go away signals to foreign invaders."

Gabriel smiled, a small bend of his lips. "Being inside of you is worth the discomfort."

"Cute, lover. But don't trouble yourself on my account."

"I suggest you proceed so we can end this project."

There was the hint of stress in his voice again. "Okay, Gabriel. What's wrong? There's something you're not telling me."

He blew out a whistling breath and his fists clenched yet again. "Satan is searching the dreamscape for me. I feel him walking the webs. So far, I have evaded his attempts to latch onto my dream essence, but it is a near thing. The sooner we're out, the sooner we are protected by the merkaz again."

"But our bodies are still protected there. We are still inside the merkaz."

"The dreamscape is just as real to demon-kind. You know attack is possible here. We lived it with Lillith when she found us there near the cliffs."

"The SOB. What is his problem? Why is he so hell bent, excuse the pun, on stopping me? The violent chaos on mortal Earth must taste delicious to him, but the enjoyment will be short lived if the place self-destructs."

"He is afraid."

"He should be. Our world is dying."

"His fear is more primal than that. The same fear as threatens us all in the darkest corner of our minds. The fear of losing ourselves, our identity. That we are not enough as we are. If he runs from the threat of Janii, how much worse is it to imagine the uniqueness of his species to be decimated as its recreated into more. Something foreign unrelated to who he understands himself to be."

"You feel the same way. You don't want this change for yourself."

Gabriel shook his head in denial. "It is only that I understand how he feels. Everything will change. Some would rather die than face such unknown."

"Not you."

"Not me. But I have something precious for which to face the black mystery of the future and my new identity. I have you. Satan is not so lucky to have such a fierce warrior in love with him and demanding he be strong and suck it up." His last words delivered with a crooked smile, he bent over to land a soft peck on my cheek. "The fear does not disappear even with my decision. Change happens, and I choose not to struggle against it. You do your work. I will convince Satan to desist if he finds us here."

"If by convince you mean shove a sword in his belly to stop his temper tantrum, then you have my blessing."

"Fierce indeed," he chuckled.

So, I did what I had no choice but do, breathe past the taffy and the layer of wrongness covering my skin and turn back to Gabriel's twisting DNA to face my task.

This end of the project was more time-consuming and detailed. Or maybe my anxiety over Gabriel's body was greater than over my own.

Tapping my pattern magic again, I sidled up to one of the DNA strands and began to unzip a piece, willing my fingers to stop their trembling. Comparing his strands to the pictures cradled inside my necklace, my power scanned first one then the other. I was the cook gathering her shopping list for the missing ingredients to prepare a feast, but also needing to adjust the recipe to mix them properly.

Gabriel's anatomy thrummed around me, the passing time counted by the swish of organelles and the tiniest particles of life bouncing about me doing their work.

My comparison list finished, Gabriel smiled encouragement. If the frenetic innards of his cell were tiny wild beasts answering to the call of their nature, I needed to cajole those beasts to come to me and fit into this new plan.

In some ways, this was like the shifter magic, reaching into the earth for the pattern of a beast and calling the elements of the earth to assemble into that pattern. But in others, it was like the angels' irresistible music, a symphony designed with elegant structure to mold together the forces of the universe into solid order. Call it hubris that I thought to perform this act of creation, even copycat creation as it was. Yeah, that's me, Rachel the would-be Lillith replacement. Oy! I wish I were anywhere but here, but it happened the flavors of my magics combined well to pull it off.

I focused the Mother-Heir magic and reached, humming a melody under my breath that came from thin air and disappeared as quickly out of my memory as it passed.

The building blocks of Gabriel's DNA swam toward the strand I'd unzipped and began to nudge up against the structure. I unhinged the places in his code on either side where they needed to join and knit the new particles into the existing strand. Sweat beaded on the dreamscaped version of my forehead.

Stop being such a wuss, Rachel. This isn't heavy labor. Maybe not, I argued with myself, but this is Gabriel's literal life I'm knitting, not a girl scout potholder project for a merit badge. I channeled my attention to the job, focusing every scrap of myself to the detail work. I couldn't afford any distraction, much like a juggler who was managing dozens of balls in the air, any slight threat to the work of balancing the feat meant disaster.

The last nucleotide snicked into place and the new piece of code hummed with tension, trying out this new existence so foreign from its previous. My magic stroked down its surface, smoothing everything in place and then re-zipping the strand.

Gabriel grunted at the gesture.

"You okay?"

He shrugged. "Yes, it only feels different. Unusual."

"You can feel the changes in just one of your cells? Impossible."

"Perhaps, but something jolted inside me."

"Does it hurt?"

"Not exactly."

"Now, if that doesn't fill me with confidence, nothing will," I groused.

"Let us see what happens when you replicate the cell. It is why you chose this type of cell, is it not? For its role in regeneration?"

"Fine." If my answer was more bitter than sweet, it was his own fault for rushing me headlong into this potential disaster.

The knots in my shoulders gained knots of their own, but I turned back to the new code and called magic again, this time, convincing the DNA to replicate and then get the cell busy dividing.

Bone marrow cells did this on a fairly regular basis, but the trick was to pull off what science had as yet failed to do, keep these cells regenerating for a full cellular DNA retrofit. I'd chosen a stem cell in specific within the bone marrow because they could differentiate into all other types of cells.

Energy poured out of my hands, igniting the spark to start the cascade of cell replication. I called, and called again, singing a song to drive the process toward my will. At first, there was no response. I sang louder, the melody and words rippling through the cell and its organelles and proteins, cajoling them to begin.

Dammit, it wasn't working. I jolted as Gabriel's fingers landed on my waist, resting along the curve, squeezing lightly. I inhaled against the heavy atmosphere and redoubled my song.

The cell stirred and I noticed a vital shift in energy as the busy innards of his cell shifted in their tracks and took up my call. Yes! I sung on to make sure the replication was in motion and undisturbed. My magic was firmly woven into supporting the process, all of my resources tied into the copying of the new code.

I risked diverting my attention back to Gabriel. "Staying in here isn't safe, it's going to get busy fast. I can power and monitor the progress outside of individual cells." I grabbed Gabriel's hand as he swung us out through the membranes and enlarged us as we hit the watery byways of space between cells in his tissue. Direct contact with his skin buffered me against his body's defense. His presence was the protective bubble I needed to keep my attention on feeding my magic to the process.

We'd barely moved far into his tissue, my magic still engaged in the orchestration process, when Gabriel grunted a warning. "Satan."

My attention skipped a beat and the pattern wavered. I clenched down again on the power and trusted Gabriel to do what needed doing. I let go of my hold on him, although it meant less protection from his body's defenses. He needed to be free to deal with his uncle.

A rippling of energy brushed against me as our guest arrived.

"My boy. Time to stop this foolishness," came the dark purr of his demon lordship.

I closed my eyes to keep distraction to a minimum. Watching Satan and Gabriel would only hurt my goal.

The smooth silk of my lover's voice responded. "We are saving our world, but you are drunk on the chaos of this upheaval. Wake up, Satan."

"You're meddling is unappreciated," the demon answered Gabriel. "You've been warned."

Then I felt Satan's attack. Chaos. Dark. Knife sharp. Movement, sliding and drunken. Gabriel's energy dodged and sliced back with slick purpose.

The battle magic knocked into the ordered progress of the dividing cells, making inroads of destruction on my nice cell replication. Thousands of cells broke apart with the impact. Shit.

I redoubled my efforts, singing strong angel power of order into the growing cells. My power flickered as I felt a drain. No! Not now. This magic took everything from me, the battle to craft life itself. Weakening, I called down the threads of connection to Tarn, Sebastian, and

Delta, and drew on the tethers to gather the needed energy. A surge of magic answered and I sang on.

I sang like my life depended on it. And it did. Everything was at risk.

Gabriel's energy both grew and shrank under the force of this internal cellular change and I felt him stumble again and again. Dammit. I needed to help him, but I needed to keep going with the cells more.

The panting breaths of both men were the backdrop to my work. They broke apart in a pause to their battle. "Even now, Solinthe plans to crush your little friends," Satan taunted. "As you foolishly play with this science experiment."

With Satan's words, a gear moved and clicked inside my mind. Solinthe. Satan was no one's puppet, but he sure seemed as if he played that role with her the last days. Wincing as I made my decision, I split off a tiny bit of my magic to send it scanning the demon.

There! She'd spelled Satan. I saw her web woven through him once I started looking. Sending Gabriel a silent message with my findings, I redoubled back on the cell work. The pace quickened, the multiplication a vortex that grew in presence. Soon. Soon I could let it go and let it take life of its own, the momentum enough to carry the process.

Swords clashed, but I couldn't do a damn thing more about the battle.

Gabriel's energy weakened, his body overwhelmed with the growing change inside him.

"Solinthe has cast magic on you, Satan," Gabriel said between the echo of ringing steel. "She sent you a gift recently, yes?"

"You need to die, boy."

"She has spelled you. Do you care to be your own man or not?"

Satan lunged and threw his power at Gabriel. Gabriel stumbled, fell to one knee, and threw himself left as the demon came at him with the sword. Narrow miss, but Gabriel was weakening. Much more of this, an assault both external from Satan and internal from his cellular reboot, and he'd be a collapsed and bleeding heap.

Almost. Almost. Yes! The cells had reached critical mass. I let my hold of the process go and spun to the fight while Gabriel yanked himself up and squared off again against his uncle.

Enough of this. "I'm getting pretty tired of these throw downs, Satan," I said. "How about we call it a night?" With a last surge, my magic reverberated up and out as I threw a hammer at Solinthe's web of energy snaking its way around Satan's skin.

Shatter. Direct hit. I exhaled in relief.

The low echo of Gabriel's beating heart throbbed in my eardrums.

The lord of demons faltered, eyes widening. He coughed and pulled himself taller. I had to give him credit, he took no longer than thirty seconds to shake himself like a wet dog, throw off the remaining cobwebs of the faerie queen's spell, and regain himself. "Damn that plotting soulless bitch. She sent me this fucking lapel pin for my collection." Satan slapped the small metal circle pinned to his chest. "She thought to enslave me? I will rend her in two and slowly burn the pieces over a bonfire."

I smiled back at his loving expression. "Well, she does have a sweet side like that." I leaned in to read the disc. "Demons are easy?" I tried to hold in my snort. "Clearly."

Satan glared in my direction.

"But if you're planning on making your displeasure known through creative torture, you can stand in line," I continued.

Gabriel struggled his way to my side as the slide of his tissues and viscous liquids swooshed around us. "Priorities, Rachel," he croaked. "Can we leave the dreamscape first and discuss Solinthe from outside my body?"

He gripped my arm, but more to keep himself upright. Universe, he was in pain. I saw it reflected out of his eyes, the red of chaos battle had faded back to his beautiful green. The changes to his body were breaking him apart. What had I done? Oily sludge rocked around my stomach, a sick wave of it running inside me to remind me of all I still might lose.

"Now, please," Gabriel whispered, and collapsed against me.

I grasped him to me and whisked us through our waking dream into the wide and brutally real world.

Chapter Twenty-two

Gabriel's body seized again, jerking against the ground in a rhythm of pain as I and Morven and Tarn, and anyone with a wisp of healing power, tried to stop Gabriel from rejecting the cellular changes, stop the battle he fought within himself rending him apart. I'd tethered all of them to Christian to use their power, but it wasn't healing that he needed. There was nothing to heal. He wasn't sick, only changing. Changing too fast.

His heart stopped, started again, switching on and off every few minutes.

Don't do this to me, Gabriel. The panic screamed from my pores, every rigid inch of me pushing back as my own heart raced to explode. How could I stop this? I had to stop it.

"It's not working," I shouted and barely noticed the others through the blur of tears. Shoving them away, I crawled on top of him and pressed him into the ground. Please. Please. Please. The chant poured from me with no control.

The ground shook around us. Earthquake, the third since we'd emerged from the dreamscape. I tented my body over Gabriel's to keep debris off him. The shaking stopped.

I dragged in a breath and grabbed for any control, any way to think through the problem. Okay. Something. There must be something.

One more deep breath and I let out a shaky note, started singing again as I had sung to his cells for replication. I sang through my half sob, limping cracking notes warbling out, finally straightening as I gained volume, gained purpose.

I sang my love. I sang my heart. Insisting. Within the notes all of my yearning. All of my hope. All of the connection and the picture of our future. Sang with my face pressed into his neck as I squeezed him at every point our bodies met. Into this love song I sang both messy chaos and precision order. Simple angel songs of order wouldn't work. Not enough. He was both angel and demon. His body was building and breaking down, becoming something more and losing what it had been.

I sang until my voice broke, sobbing and straining, riding his kicking body. Until the kicking slowed. Until finally, the seizing stopped. Until the whispered threads of my song caressed into the quiet hollow of his neck. His heartbeat pulsed weak but steady under his breastbone where it lay against mine. Alive, but too quiet. Universe. Please.

"Rachel." Strong hands pulled me away from him. I clung harder.

"Rachel," the steady voice demanded. "Give him space. He's alive. We need to move him to someplace better to recover."

Tarn. Yes. I recognized the speaker. He was still here? I'd lost track of the others. Yes. They were here.

I let Tarn move me. Although, as our bodies separated, I grasped Gabriel's hand. "That's far enough."

My eyes were all for Gabriel, and only the hard squeeze of a hand on my shoulder told me Gwen was squatting by my side as I kept my grip on his hand, as much a lifeline for me as him.

"I know it's not the time, Rachel, but Satan and Kemuel are outside the entry of the merkaz wishing to speak with you. They intend to listen to your proposal."

"They're together? On purpose?" Jasper asked from somewhere behind us.

For the life of me, I didn't care. Their purposeful cooperation might be one of the greater miracles of our time, but not the miracle I needed. "Tell them to go away."

"They're offering protection and escort back to your rooms. Including for Leslie and her daughter. Satan says, and I quote, 'inform the Mother Heir we'll keep the other Kesayim imbeciles in lock down until we can straighten out this crap,'" Gwen said.

Tarn's fingers checked the pulse at Gabriel's neck. "He will rest better in your bed."

"Yes. Okay." Panic still fought with numb unreality.

Sebastian knelt down on Gabriel's other side. "We can carry him, Rachel, but you'll have to let go for a moment." He kept his voice gentle, as if trying not to spook a skittish horse. Yeah, I kind of felt like one at the moment. As if all of my nerve endings had flipped to the outside of my skin and the merest brush of air set fire to my body.

Letting go of his hand took more effort than any of the magic I'd performed today.

"He'll be okay, Rachel," Sebastian assured.

But death already stood next to me, gaunt face leaning in with interest, his scythe by his side, waiting for the worst. If it came, I'd gladly accompany him anywhere he beckoned. Yes, I understood what Christian felt with the threat to Leslie.

Another tremor hit and I braced myself, hands to the earth, as our friends protected Gabriel's unmoving form. It stopped and I swallowed back my sob.

"Come, sweetie," Gwen said. "Let's get out of here."

Around me, the garden of the merkaz, with its potent simmering life, shuddered with my fear.

* * * * *

The shadows wrapping us, I kept my watch in the dark of my bedroom, my breath rising and falling in time with Gabriel's as he slept next to me. No, not sleep. Coma. His body still fought the changes, the process gone horribly wrong.

Morven had insisted I rest, sending everyone not vital to nearby rooms of their own now that we had the demons and angels on our side to act as defense. Leslie and her daughter were separated in particular to remove any barriers to Gabriel's healing. But he wasn't getting better and I wasn't resting. How could I?

The guards had removed any objects in the bedroom threatening to topple from the quakes. Their intensity and frequency had weakened since returning to my suite, but more with a sense of pause before the new onslaught of destruction began.

Artemis crawled from the back of my neck where she'd perched underneath my hair. She placed her paws gingerly as she walked from me over to Gabriel, nestling next to his head and delivering several tentative licks to his cheek.

"I want him to wake, too," I told her as she looked back at me with question in her puppy gaze.

A random wave of magic ruffled my skin and one of the throw pillows on the other side of the bed lifted up and floated a few feet before dropping to the ground. Another pillow followed its lead. A third. Gabriel? His face became blurry, and for a moment, I caught a glimpse of hair and snout and teeth, before the wave of energy subsided and his face returned to normal. Even in the coma, his body tried to use his new forms of magic. How would I protect him from himself?

A knock on the door was followed by Gwen's head peeking into the room. "No change?" she asked.

"He's doing new magic while unconscious, but he's still unconscious."

She sighed. "We've calculated the increased onslaught of earthquakes. They're even more pronounced in the Achra realm than here. At best, we have four days before humanity cannot come back from the destruction. It's worse than even Lillith's prediction."

I heard her, but Gabriel's inert form held my attention. His chiseled cheekbones. His braid, the fraying hairs escaping their weave, lying against a precious cheek.

"Did you hear me, my lady? You need to speak with Satan and Kemuel. They're parked outside the door of your suite, waiting."

"I'm busy."

"You are the Mother Heir. You need to talk to them and make plans."

"Why? So I can kill everyone on this planet in one fell swoop instead of letting the crumbling geology do it in pieces?"

"He's not dead, Rachel. You want to kill him off early to cut out the angst? Eliminates the anxiety, surely, but I'm not sure Gabriel would appreciate losing his life to save your difficult feelings."

"Don't fuck with me, Gwen."

"Or what? You'll kill me?"

The prickling energy that had started to build inside me drained away in a sudden rush and I slumped on the bed.

"I can't pretend to care when I don't."

"You *can* pretend. That's exactly the point. If walking through the motions are all you've got, then do that. Your 'pretend' is the only hope for all of us."

Gabriel stirred on the bed for the shortest of moments, then quieted back to the still nothing of the previous hours. Not even long enough for hope to catch. I kissed my fingertips and brushed them to his forehead.

"Get Tarn and Sebastian in here to watch him while I meet with Satan and Kemuel. But if you want anything to come of it, you and my brothers may want to attend. It will be difficult to 'pretend' to think through a plan when my mind has gone lost in space."

Gwen nodded and went to get the guys. I looked down at my grungy clothing, the same I'd worn for over a day. Good enough. There was no appropriate way to dress for the end of the world.

* * * * *

"We have found and saved one hundred nulls from your list," the angel intoned, sitting upright around the council table with our group of seven. "Solinthe has already killed over a thousand, but five hundred are unaccounted for and we remain hopeful."

"My people killed roughly twenty of Solinthe's spies here at court since yesterday," Satan added.

"The fae are banished. How could she have people here still?"

Satan rolled his eyes at Jasper's question. "Not fae spies, fool. Solinthe's wiles enwrap those from all the Kesayim species. If she can enscroll me, she can trap anyone. Except maybe these cursed nulls we are saving." He glanced at Qest. "And maybe Kyn."

Gwen grimaced. "Witches rescued one hundred nulls before the angels and demons put their force into the effort. That makes two hundred. Is it enough?"

"How should I know?"

Satan scowled at the conversation. "Mixing the DNA of billions is ambitious, my lady. Especially if your one experiment has left Gabriel comatose."

"I agree," I answered.

Christian jumped into the conversation, likely nervous I'd predict more disaster. "We have several more days to strategize for the group spell needed to reach across the planet. What we do know is we will need enough DNA from all of the species in order to spread the effect."

"So, we march blindly forward with no idea how to work the magic we need," the demon snarked.

Gwen interrupted. "Rachel will find a way. Our part is to make sure that all the Kesayim participate. That means keeping the Kyn from suicide, the nulls alive, and finding a way for the fae to participate without Solinthe's interference."

Satan tapped his foot under the table. "In other words, killing Solinthe. Nothing short of her death will allow the fae to join the effort."

I shrugged. "Guess so."

"Pffft. That's more of a trick than the whole DNA spell debacle," Satan added. "The fact she's yet to attack you since her last attempt on your life is suspicious. I expected it by now. Especially as you broke her spell over me. The mess is likely to explode in our face."

Satan's attitude was predictable, but pointless. He wouldn't be here if he wasn't ready to throw in with me regardless of his doubts. There were no other sane options now that I'd unclouded his mind.

"Morven is out collecting any intelligence she can about the fae queen's activity," Gwen added. "We need to prepare."

"Good luck with that," Satan scoffed.

Satan, I understood, but Kemuel's presence at this meeting surprised me. He was the type to die for his principles rather than make compromises. Why cooperate with me now?

Nothing to lose, I asked him to explain himself.

Kemuel straightened on his stool, his wings unfolding majestically and fanning behind him. "I have spent my entire life protecting Achra and the truth of the threat has become apparent. I will not stop now because I must cooperate with vermin to get the job done."

Universe, I would not lie to these men. "No need to cooperate Kemuel. As Satan pointed out, Gabriel is near death. My magic failed. Christian's optimism is misplaced."

Satan eyed me up and down, frowning. "They tell me he's not dead yet, my lady. And if you get your head out of your ass, you might be able to make something of this situation."

I wanted out of here. To escape back to Gabriel's bedside. The weighty fog kept at me and I needed to curl beside him and drift away. That's all. Sleep. Hopefully for eternity. I didn't have it in me to give more.

I refused to respond to Satan.

After a long stretch of quiet, he sneered in my direction. "Coward."

Qest, unspeaking through the meeting, couldn't contain himself longer. Smoke curled from his nostrils. "Rachel, I hate to agree with Satan, but you need to wake up to reality!"

He opened his mouth to continue, but instead, the room exploded in icy chill. Bright, painful light and form surrounded us. I wrenched to my feet, pushing from the table.

I knew that light.

Lillith.

My eyes watered, and my throat hurt from the burning cold as I inhaled.

Her voice pounded into the air and we found ourselves instinctually covering our ears as she screeched a warning. "How dare you waste my gift?" she howled.

Kemuel slid off his seat and knelt to our lunatic creator. Several beats later the other members of the group followed, even those who knew better. Leaving only me standing, trying to prepare for whatever came next from our mad progenitor.

"My Goddess. We are honored by your presence. I am humbled to be able to meet you," Kemuel insisted.

The form of the goddess hovered, floating nearest to me where her icicle chill invaded my bones. I shivered, but a deeper cold had already set itself into my soul. A chill leaving Lillith's threat of deep freeze was nothing in comparison.

"At peril of breaking my people's rules, I send you a null as a gift and you waste her?"

"Your gift? I'm sorry. You forgot to include a card, Lillith. I had no way of knowing or I would have sent a thank you note."

"Why haven't you fixed this?" she screeched.

By this, I assumed she meant the dying world. She should make up her mind. Did she really care if Earth died or not? Back on the ferris wheel she'd seemed willing to shrug off the failure and move on. Damn her alien crazy making. There was no way out from this maze.

The hours of dead void, gray and endless, wrapping my heart, fell away. The anger, so long a fiery and tenacious core of me, flared up to burn through the fog. It flamed into the room before I could draw my next breath.

My own screech rivaled even this cursed goddess. "I TRIED TO FIX IT!" I could barely speak with the rage. "Kill us now, Lillith. If you care for your humans, end it quickly so they don't linger in the cataclysm. I hate your games. I hate your twisted version of love. I hate you. Kill us and be done. I'm ready."

The anger burst and my magic spiraled out uncontrolled, breaking apart wooden chairs and flinging the bric a brac of the conference room into the walls. Coffee cups, a clock, wooden chairs. I hadn't lost control like this since my early days arriving at Eden's Court. My body trembled as it demanded destruction and pain in this endless moment.

More items flew through the air, splintering apart as winds howled around me. Wood and metal, plastic and paper. Whipping. Scouring our bodies. Creating a pocket of destruction.

Until...

Time unfroze. My body tired.

The storm subsided. I was left standing in a sea of debris, my family and associates covering their heads where they huddled on the floor. My fists couldn't stop clenching and unclenching. My breath came in short, shallow gasps. I wanted it over. I'd had enough.

Lillith's outrageous, zig zag form of light hovered in a pause. Waiting. As if I shocked her into silence. Finally, she spoke. "I would kill you now if I did not need you still, daughter. Though to kill you would end your suffering too quick. Look to the null," she said. "Kill Solinthe. You need her power." She winked out of the room, leaving a shocked emptiness behind as our group lurched to their feet in a daze.

The fire inside me dampened, although not extinguishing all together. The group turned to me with confused eyes.

Jasper stepped forward. "I don't want to die, Rachel. If you love me or Christian or Qest or Peter, don't consign us to nothingness out of your own grief. Death comes soon enough. If you have to suffer longer to delay its visit, then live with that suffering."

The surviving spark of my anger provided just enough heat to feed the stirrings of guilt.

Satan brushed off small splinters of wood from his clothing. It was a miracle no one had been injured in my temper tantrum.

"Apparently Lillith agrees nulls are important," he said. "I will continue to provide demon support to save them. However, I will be sending you the dry-cleaning bill for this suit once the difficulties are resolved. I find it amazing that I can be counted as a more level head than yourself. I will also forward you the name of a good therapist. You obviously need one."

At that, he walked out of the room.

Kemuel shook his head at my behavior and unfurled his wings with condescension before refolding them. "You insult the Goddess. We are lucky she did not end us all this instant. I will honor my commitment to you because Lillith clearly wants you to save us." With a disdainful scowl, he followed his new found demonic partner out into the halls.

Gwen tsked after they left. "I will coordinate with those two so we don't undermine each other's efforts. If you will excuse me." She exchanged a glance with Qest and left my family to our privacy.

"Sit!" Qest barked at me, gesturing to the few remaining usable chairs in the room.

I sat.

All three of my brothers found places to perch.

My fiery youngest brother got to work. "Chastising you is a luxury we can't afford and wasted breath. What do you think Lillith means about Leslie?" he asked me, although he glanced over at our middle brother.

Christian looked down at his hands upon the table. "Rachel must include Leslie's DNA in her genetic surgery. To add in the pieces unique to the nulls."

The fog lifted, a last exodus of confusion from my mind leaving me tired, but amazingly clear headed. Still determined, however. "I won't experiment on Gabriel again. My own code had incomplete spaces. If I do the surgery, I'll insert Leslie's missing pieces into myself and see what happens when I regenerate my cells."

Christian looked up at me, brow furrowed. "Will it place her in danger?"

I understood his worry. Even more so after what had happened with Gabriel. "I don't know how. I won't touch her code. She'll be the template, at least until the final show when everyone on this imploding planet gets the surgery."

Qest appeared unsettled. "You risk yourself going through that change at a time we need you more than anyone on this team. Eemah and Solinthe need your attention or this fails. And no one else can do the final spell."

"I won't risk anyone else until I know this process works," I answered.

"I volunteer," Christian interrupted. "Blend the complete code, including Leslie's, inside me."

I knew what he was doing. Penance. I wanted to argue, but maybe he needed it more than I needed to keep him safe. And in a strange way, the blend joined him with Leslie with an intimacy he desired.

I met his gaze and nodded to acknowledge that I saw his purpose. All of it. And loved him for both parts. "Okay. First I check on Gabriel, then we try for a blend. Leslie will agree?"

"She'll agree," he answered. "I'll get her from her rooms and meet you back at your suite."

I nodded, and remembered hearing the thudding swoosh inside arteries and veins while I'd been inside mine and Gabriel's bodies. I remembered feeling the liquid pulsing of blood and smaller structures swimming around me, busy with the mysterious purpose of life. And I imagined a red pool of this life force dripping from the broken form of Solinthe. Giving me the power through death to save life, or so Lillith suggested.

The picture both intrigued and repulsed me. But not repulsed enough to run away. Death was to be my friend. But was he going to be the last one I ever made?

* * * * *

I split up from my brothers before I reentered my rooms; Christian off to retrieve Leslie, Qest to help Gwen, and Jasper to check on Peter who was staying with Sebastian's family. Leaving me alone again with my fear.

A glorious sight greeted me as I dragged into my suite; Gabriel, walking out of the bedroom with Sebastian by his side, the two of them conferring closely. Sebastian appeared to be hovering by Gabriel to catch him if he fell. Gabriel's occasional amused but tired glances at his friend let me know he was well aware of the shifter's intent and tolerated it for the sake of their long relationship.

Gabriel moved slowly, but deliberately. I, on the other hand, had to slam down hard on my brakes to keep myself from running over to my demon lover and swallowing him whole. Although my own sense of dignity was non-existent, I knew Gabriel might prefer a less public display of my exuberant enthusiasm.

Gabriel's smile at my entrance delivered a warm slide of love and enveloped me in my first moment of peace since he'd collapsed in our dream walk. "You are just in time, my lady," he said in welcome, with an affected bow in my direction.

"On time for what?" My voice stuttered. I made it to his side and reached for his hand, my thumb tracing a pattern over his skin again and again to reassure myself he was real and alive. "You're okay?" I asked.

"I will be." He frowned, inspecting me closely. "You have not taken care of yourself." He sent a silent glare of censure to Sebastian, Tarn, and Delta. Finally, it landed accusingly on me.

"You try convincing her to eat or sleep when she's set her mind toward a single obsession," Tarn complained where he and Delta lounged with pleased looks on their faces. "Namely your impending death. You had the easy part being unconscious."

His lips twisted in calculation. "You are probably right. My apologies for leaving you all with her like this. I will not do so again."

Leaving them to suffer me? "Jerk," I answered, squeezing his captured hand with a firm pulse, but not too firm. Universe, who cared if he teased me. He was awake and walking. I hadn't killed him.

"We have to talk, but only if you're up to it," I said, wishing I could push him back into my bedroom and forget about the outside world, but this time, through the magic of his arms.

"Do we have a moment before the next crisis?" he asked.

"Maybe one."

He smiled at my answer and captured the thumb that had been obsessively rubbing his skin. He brought my hand to his lips and pressed a kiss, his eyes closed. Only his shaky breath near my fingers let me know the depth of feeling coursing through him.

"Sebastian has something important to...say," Gabriel announced, lowering my hand but keeping it clasped.

My shifter guard blinked and cleared his throat, turning to Tarn and Delta who stood across the room with quizzical gazes. "Tarn, Delta, I need you two to sit there." Sebastian pointed to the couch and began to move the coffee table in front of it over to the side of the room.

"And we shall sit here," Gabriel said, gesturing to the kitty corner love seat and moving me to sit, our thighs pressed together.

Okay, something smelled funny in the state of Denmark. This was strange behavior from Gabriel and Sebastian even for these strange times.

My shifter guard stood center on the now cleared rug facing Tarn and Delta on the couch while he fidgeted in place. "Oh, wait." He jogged back to the breakfront by the bedroom door and took something out of the right-side drawer. A cell phone.

He marched back to the rug with the device, scrolling through the screen on the phone before looking up at his audience. "Since this may be the last quiet moment before the storm, I needed to do something about a bunch of stuff spinning around my head." Sebastian took a deep and loud breath, hit another button on his phone, tossed it to the nearest side table, and took a dramatic pose with his arms out from his side and his legs spread.

A second later, the soulful and perky sounds of Marvin Gaye and Tammi Terrell came out of the phone singing about how there 'ain't no mountain high enough'.

At the same time, my shifter friend and coffee distributor started lip synching the duo's sentiments, shaking his hips and performing a sweet and saucy rendition, both male and female vocals, of the song. He threw arms out imploring Tarn and Delta as they sat with shit eating grins on the couch, watching his exploits.

After another moment, Gabriel's hand released mine and he raised both of them to begin to weave the knot of a spell. Witch magic.

Universe! He could consciously do new magic.

In the space behind Sebastian, the air filled with vivid pictures of majestic, blue topped mountains, valleys with wide rivers running beneath and between the peaks. The room smelled of a crisp pine scent, and fecund earth.

Sebastian sang to this backdrop about how 'if you need me, call me no matter where you are', and 'no matter how far'. He looked pointedly at Tarn and sang 'on the day I set you free I told you you could always count on me, darling' and 'how from that day on, I made a vow, I'll be there when you want me, someway, somehow'.

He sang the lyrics through to the end while the view of those mountains hung in the air. He sang with all of the repetitions of the chorus, with wild gestures and even a few line kicks with his legs. 'Ain't no mountain high enough to keep me from getting to you babe.' A large warrior of a man; loyal, gentle, dangerous, unafraid to make a fool of himself.

He finished with a dramatic fall to his knees, arms out wide toward Tarn and Delta, a little breathless from his swinging moves as the music from the phone faded. We all clapped like mad, hooting and hollering. Gabriel dropped his arms, the spell picture fading along with the music.

"Amazing," Tarn extolled. "Broadway material. You need an agent, man."

Sebastian was close enough to the couch for Delta to lean over and kiss him on the cheek. "The Rockettes have nothing on your kicks, sweetness."

"Wait, I'm not done," Sebastian said, pushing her back to her position on the cushions. He straightened on his knees and snaked out both hands, each grabbing one of Tarn and Delta's. "This may be the most insane moment to do this, but I need to. The two of you bring me more joy and love than anyone I know. You take me for all I am and make that feel damn precious. And wanted. And at times, I've been an idiot not to understand this. An idiot to refuse to listen to what my heart knows." He looked at Tarn with those last words.

"If we survive the next few days, and if you agree, I want to marry you. Both of you. Although I suppose that means you'd also have to agree to marry each other. I'm not sure how these three-way proposals are supposed to work because I couldn't find a manual anywhere in the court library."

The fae and demoness sat stunned on the couch. It took a few moments for my own eyes to un-pop. *Yes!*

But it wasn't my answer Sebastian wanted.

Delta's features slowly morphed into a sly grin. She said nothing, but turned toward Tarn. She knew as well as anyone in the room it was his to answer. He had waited so long.

"Are you sure, Seb?" he whispered.

"Yes. Completely."

Tarn was blinking hard, a sheen of wet at the corner of his eyes. "Then I suppose it would be ungallant of me to refuse. Especially after you worked up an act and all."

They both turned to Delta. She tilted her head in Tarn's direction. "What he said."

Sebastian beamed at them. He grabbed Delta behind the head and smashed her lips with his, pulling away before grabbing for Tarn. But once he'd caught Tarn, the fae pressed his own hand behind Sebastian's skull, trapping them in the kiss, making it linger. The kiss transformed into a slower, sensual exchange. All of the desire and love denied for so long unleashed and accepted. Raw. Honest. Sexy. Full of need. Overfull with love.

Delta looked on with no sense of jealousy, observing their deep love. Instead, with an expression of satisfaction and such happiness.

Beside me, Gabriel grunted his own satisfaction, and clasped my hand again, squeezing tight. He loved these men, too.

I leaned over to whisper in his ear. "Your spell was lovely. You helped make this moment perfect. I love you."

He turned to me with an unwavering gaze. "Never forget that I will always come for you. How did you doubt me?"

"I was afraid. Alone."

He ran a caress down my cheek and I shivered. His voice shook overfull with intensity. "There is no mountain high enough, valley low enough, river wide enough, dessert vast enough, forest large enough, sea immense enough, chasm deep enough to keep me from you. Ever. Even if this planet crumbles. Death is not enough to keep me away, Rachel. Do not forget it."

I swallowed past the lump in my throat while my chest filled with heat and light. "I won't." The chain connecting us quivered, solidifying more.

"How much magic can you access?" I asked, looking down at his strong, spell weaving hands. The DNA blending had changed him, but I didn't know how much.

"Some. It feels...rusty. Choppy."

"It hurts?"

He didn't answer.

"You need to tell me. We went to a whole lot of trouble with you almost dying and all. At least be honest so we know what we've got."

"It hurts, but not enough to keep me from using it. Not if it is needed to win our battle."

"My lady," Tarn interrupted. We looked up to see Delta and the boys holding hands. I guess we missed the end of the snog fest.

"I'm so happy for you guys." I stood and delivered hugs and sloppy kisses to all three.

Gabriel and the boys exchanged manly hugs. He even managed a quick peck on Delta's cheek.

"I promise to take good care of them," she said to Gabriel as he leaned back after the kiss.

"I will hold you to that."

"Thank you for loving them as you have these years. Your friendship helped make them the men I fell for."

Gabriel paused, deliberating, then nodded, accepting her offering. Peace between them at last.

"Best man and maid of honor?" the demoness asked us.

"I thought we were walking you down the aisle?"

"That too," she agreed. "Multi-tasking is what you do best, my lady."

Tarn laughed. "And just think of the deals we can find now for the honeymoon. Worldwide natural disasters drive airline and hotel prices down like nothing else. Sebastian's timing was impeccable."

"My timing was an indulgence on all our parts. Now back to work. What's next, my lady?" Sebastian asked.

The magic of my door chimed permission for others to enter and after waving my hands to allow access, Qest was charging in, Gwen, Christian, and Leslie behind him. I experienced the immediate dampening effect of Leslie's presence now that I'd removed the tether from

Christian. As she came near us, Gabriel grimaced with pain. Coincidence?

"She's done it," Qest growled. "Grandmother called for the fade. She didn't wait the full week. I feel her calling. It's strong. She's trying to avoid your challenge. We have to go now."

"Dammit. I counted on a few days to get the blending right with Leslie's DNA and apply it to myself. I need that boost to fight her."

Christian interrupted. "Take me and Leslie with you to the Kyn realm. Tether yourself to me again for extra energy. Leslie increases my power twenty-fold. I can feed some of that to you."

"The tether only counters the effect of her null dampening when she's near me. The total gain is zero."

Gabriel caught the situation quickly despite our lack of time to share my latest plan. "But if you are in your Kyn form, you will not be touched by her drain," he said. "Kyn immunity. And so Christian's tether may deliver extra magic as he said."

Time for the Freil Sorcha. I either battled her and took the pearl to become the new matriarch, or my fight for the planet was over before it begun with no Kyn left to merge their DNA. "I'd have to put her to sleep for the portal trip to the Kyn realm," I said.

Leslie blanched, but straightened taller. She grabbed Christian's hand as she jerked her head in agreement. When she touched his hand, a pulse shimmered over me, over all in the room. Gabriel stood up straighter, losing the hunched posture of pain he'd acquired after she entered the suite.

My lover's eyes widened. "Amazing. When she entered, the pain increased, but now that she touched Christian it is less. Less than before she entered."

"So, it's gone?"

"Not completely, but much better," Gabriel answered me.

"You need to come with us," I said to Leslie. "But you go under at
the portal until we're through."

"I already agreed. I'll do my part. You're not the only one who cares if we live."

"We need to leave, now!" Qest repeated.

"Get your weapons, guys. I need my dagger." The fae dagger would only act as a normal dagger against the Eemah as she cancelled out its magic. But I would need it to cut the pearl from her dead body.

I'd faced the idea of killing Solinthe, and the eager part of me settled into the idea despite my self-disgust. But I'd resisted picturing killing my grandmother. She was my blood. She was not evil or crazy, only stubborn and short-sighted and hopeless. Yes, she'd take down a hundred dragons, and potentially a planet due to her beliefs, but I knew the power of grief. Mere moments ago, I'd been ready to let the world fall apart consumed as I was with Gabriel, my failure and my loss. I refused to pass judgement on her, but the deed needed doing for the greater good. The good of the many over the one. I wasn't sure if that idea was the first step toward wisdom, or the first step toward damnation.

Guess it was time to find out.

Chapter Twenty-three

The wind cut to the bone as I stepped into the Kyn realm from the portal. Qest, having gone first through the portal, stood facing the mountainside where jewel-encrusted caverns sparkled in welcome, each faceted archway an entrance to a dragon's home. Thousands of these caverns decorated the mountainside, although only one-hundred were occupied as Kyn numbers dwindled and their race teetered on the edge of extinction.

The look of longing on Qest's face triggered the same hunger inside my Kyn heart. The hunger to let our dragons burst forth and ride the winds. The only physical desire that came close was the one I felt for the man by my side.

Gabriel raised an arm to block the gusts as he focused on the dragons congregated ahead of us. It appeared that the remaining hundred had answered the Eemah's call, encircling their leader as she perched on a large rock to speak to her people.

The rest of our group; Tarn, Sebastian, Delta, and Gwen, braced their feet on the rocky outcropping, taking stock of the situation. Christian appeared last from the gateway, cradling Leslie's sleeping body. I sent a small pulse of magic her way to rouse her and called to my Kyn brother.

"You still want to do this with me?"

"I have to, Rache. These are my people, even after spending so much time in human form. I remember flying these skies with Rom, wings stretched and ecstasy-drunk. I remember the songs the Kyn sang in slow-building glorious sound, and the nights perched high among the caves, peering out into the dark endless black and smelling its wildness."

My eyes watered, as much from the beauty in his voice as the stinging wind whipping my face.

Acceptance. Acceptance. Acceptance. Damn mantra. Just when I thought I'd made personal growth, I find out I still have to face the same battles inside myself every day. He would fight with me, because that was his choice.

"Okay," I said. "Let's do this."

I grabbed Gabriel's hand for a tight squeeze, quickly snaked magic tethers between myself and Christian to pipeline his energy, and walked toward the Eemah by Qest's side. I practiced my trick of shielding my thoughts as she was more than capable of reading my mind.

Around us, the ground shook with another tremor and Qest and I tumbled to the dirt and stone, riding out the wave as Earth tore itself apart. After over a minute, the quake subsided, and we stood and kept going. Toward the Eemah. Toward my grandmother. Her copper, gold, and pewter scales glistened even in the overcast day. Those silver reptilian eyes with black vertical pupils focused sharply on those gathered as her tail swung back and forth, the several dozen long golden spikes decorating it a reminder to those gathered of her power.

"My people," the Eemah was saying as we approached her perch over the crowd of dragons. "Even now, Earth crumbles. Even now, this planet dies. I do not choose for us to die slowly. There is no nobility in facing suffering and destruction in slow measures. No virtue in lingering. We will destroy the mother pearl and fly into the wind to let it eat us. A death befitting the Kyn."

"Grandmother," I called. A hundred sets of eyes turned toward me.

Yeah, I'd acknowledge our relationship if it reminded the Kyn that I shared their blood and specifically the blood of their ruler. "I am here to claim the right to the Freil Sorcha. To claim the right to battle you for the pearl and take leadership of the Kyn." My necklace pulsed an electric spark, transmitting excited hunger with the mention of the pearl.

The Eemah coughed a stream of smoke and fire, a disdainful sound emanating out of her nostrils where all of her speech originated. "You know nothing of our traditions except a few fancy words you have studied in your books. You come with flashy intent and noble sounding demands, but you are nothing to the longstanding history and connection of my children."

"I am my father's daughter," I answered. "With as much right to challenge you as any other."

I raised my fae dagger and the silver blade shone with its own magic. "This knife will cut out the pearl from your breast, Grandmother. You will not be leading the Kyn to death this day."

"Interloper," she accused.

"But I am not," Qest answered. "I grew by your side, flew at your wing. And if experience of our traditions is the standard, then I will rule along with Rachel and share that experience."

"You are male. You cannot rule."

"First, the pearl will choose. When it's cut from your chest, it will acknowledge who it deems the successor. That's how it has happened for millennia. Times necessitate change, and the pearl will decide. The difference between you and us is our ability to see a new future and understand the possibilities. You are stuck in the past and only see limitations."

The Eemah screeched a response, an eardrum shattering call of anger. "What I see is your death. Come and battle me, grandchildren, and I will lead you to early death as a gift."

She spread her large wings above her and launched herself skyward.

It was time.

From the distance, Gabriel and Gwen stood side by side in front of our group, lips moving quickly back and forth in conversation with intense concentration.

Qest ran some way from me and let his dragon take him over, his copper and emerald green scales breathtakingly beautiful, the obsidian razor spikes decorating his tail a wicked threat.

I closed my eyes and my beast rumbled, coughed out a roar, and joyously unfolded. Reaching. Growing and transforming me into what she considered my truest self. I spared a moment to worry for Artemis as the magic of my invisible sling tucked her away beyond this miracle into a holding location. If I died, what happened to my puppy?

No more time to worry. My wings stretched to their full spread, the biting wind now feeling like a gentle caress over the leathery skin. Free at last. I launched, chasing the battle. Qest hung back as he took to the air, understanding I needed to engage the Eemah for sake of the ritual, agreeing as we exchanged silent speech in our minds that he would join only if I needed the help.

Swimming up miles and miles into the gray blue of the day. Free and furious. My people would live.

The Eemah swirled through air currents, waiting with pause as I flew closer. Higher. Closer.

Dive. She swooped under me as I reached her height and a band of flame shot toward my underbelly. I twisted mid-air to dodge the fire, escaping the brunt, but hit in one large swath.

My dragon raged, the pain licking along the more delicate skin.

As the Eemah glided ahead, I sped faster. Faster. Caught her. Ram! My spikes tore into her side, tearing a long line of raw flesh. She roared in pain.

Heat blossomed inside of me, demanding exit. I shoved down my primal drive to burn her and exhaled smoke without the flame. If she incinerated, the pearl went with her. And so would the Kyn.

Screeching revenge, she turned back on me, our bodies flipping back and forth in the smoky air, teeth rending, score and stab with tails lashing out. Pain blossoming. We pulled apart.

Then, clashed together.

Again.

And again.

Impasse.

We battled like that for what felt like hours, but was likely a fraction of that. I wouldn't last much longer. Fatigue built in my bones, and I reached down the tethers to funnel energy. Nothing. Damn. Christian's power couldn't overcome Kyn proof against magic.

We tumbled and she raked my side with copper talons as I cried out denial.

"Rachel! Move!" Qest sent the words through our mind contact. Moments after, he rammed the Eemah from above, using the force of his weight and claws to punch holes through the top of her hide as she was shoved downward by a mile. She caught herself, stabilized and climbed toward us. Faster than before, flame constant, bathing me and then my brother with steady, blue-orange wrath.

With a millennia to grow her strength and fighting prowess, my grandmother barraged us again and again. Her hide was covered with our marks as black-red liquid dripped from her, but her strength lasted.

My dragon lagged, the pain of wounds and burns eating my focus. Qest swung out to my left, knocking his tail at the Eemah's neck. Hit!

She fell through the air before catching herself again.

I dove before she gained height and aimed for a wing. Claws out to grab. They caught and I tore them upward. Her wing shredded. Finally, she flagged, limped further ahead of us in the sky.

Maybe we could do this.

"Rachel!" called a familiar voice in my head. Gabriel. *"Nine more Kyn just launched. They fly your way!"*

The new Kyn power in Gabriel's blood had settled enough to let him reach my thoughts. *"I've tried to force a change to dragon shape to join you. I can't do it."* Panic and frustration tinged his voice.

I sent the information to Qest. Guess the nine decided they'd rather die the quick fade the Eemah promised than believe I could turn the tide of Earth's destruction. They were breaking the rules of the Freil Sorcha to rebalance their matriarch's odds, maybe realizing none of those rules mattered anymore.

My brother swung sideways as the first of the nine reached us, turning back on him with a quick push of wing and latching onto the attacker's neck to bite.

We needed more. If the tether wouldn't work, we needed another burst of power from Leslie.

The bite!

"Gabriel," I sent to his mind. *"Tell Christian to bite Leslie and drink from her."*

Provoking and sexual and intense, the emotion from a bite might throw her flaky effect into overdrive.

Nine were too many for Qest and me, and even now, the Eemah was turning back from her race away from us and returning to join them. I turned tail, literally, and ran through the skies.

Please work. Please, Universe.

Qest followed my lead as we bought time on the run. The winds whistled a sharp complaint at our flight. I couldn't keep this going. Not much longer. *Stay with it, girl. Don't fuck this up now.*

The air tasted of ozone-charged storm. Heavy. Expectant.

We circled in a wide arch back toward the side of the mountain where the rest of the Kyn and our friends huddled to watch this battle; tiny specks watching for the final result.

I waited for their help. Christian's help. Leslie's help. I needed them. We needed each other.

Finally—- Explosion of force rocketed up from the ground and buffeted me, tossing me through the air as magic poured into my body. So much that it bowled through Kyn immunity and lit up my power.

Wrapping me, healing me, joining my dragon with all of the innate magics of the Kesayim I contained even though I'd been told this was impossible. I sent healing magic at my brother, mending his wounds and burn marks, strengthening bones and skin to shield him in this fight.

Then, we turned in mid-air and raced head-on to the Eemah and the nine.

Engaged.

I tore at them again with teeth, talon and spikes, able to release my flame when it was directed at one of the nine. Their fiery deaths were no threat, although I didn't want them dead. Time disappeared as Qest and I wove between the clutch of Kyn. The Eemah did not hesitate to engage despite her additional warriors. I'd give her that. She fought her own battles.

I tilted on wing and banked right, watching as a new dragon flew toward our clash. Black as night. All obsidian except for pine green spikes protruding from his long tail.

Universe! Gabriel. Leslie's burst had allowed him to shift.

His innate grace transferred to this Kyn form. My dragon growled a welcome, recognizing a mate and fiercely possessive. I understood the sentiment, but sent her a coldly practical rebuff and swept back into battle.

We fought this way, the three of us, startled when minutes later another dragon appeared beside us. Cerulean blue with blood red spikes. Her punch was as hard as any other, but she smelled funny when I swooped close enough to watch her attack one of the nine. Actually, she didn't smell at all. Nothing. As if she wasn't there. I watched her flicker, her entire body disappearing and then reappearing within a breath's time.

"Gwen!" Qest sent.

Impossible, but somehow true.

Our new battle team improved the odds, but this needed to end or we'd all weaken with time.

The nine changed tactics, bunching together and flying closer to the Eemah. In coordination, they began to let loose toretts of flame at their leader. No! They were trying to burn her themselves to accomplish her goal.

Gwen, Qest, and Gabriel flew directly into the group of Kyn, knocking them away and turning back around to disrupt them again each time they tried to regroup. My friends swooped quickly and avoided engagement to focus on knocking the nine out of burning range.

This was my chance. I zoomed in on the Eemah and dug into my magic, pulling out the chaos of demon energy. The magic arrowed toward her as I chased after it, swinging the spikes of my tail as she stuttered from the disruption to her pattern. I swung the magic and the strength of my dragon again. And again. I battered her with chaos and brute force. I punched her skin with so many holes there were more gaps than intact hide.

She bled. She growled back protest, swinging her tail and talon at me. But my new tool was something another Kyn had never faced. Potent magic not their own, with her usual proof against it subsumed by the null gift. Power distilled and multiplied a hundred-fold. I rolled her senses with vampire allure. A song of power flowed out of my nostrils and I struck again.

She dropped. One mile, two miles, three miles down. I dove after her and swept my tail into her neck. Blood pumped out in a torrent and bubbled from her nostrils. Her wings faltered.

I flapped hard, pulling back to hover before launching toward her with talons outstretched and digging them into her neck at the same location, twisting with my Kyn strength. She careened her neck around despite the puncture, gazing at me with silver eyes, lids closing with a slow blink. Her head moved in the slightest nod. An acknowledgement. The faint echo of her voice in my head. *"Granddaughter."* Until I heard the low rending snap of bone.

"Grandmother." I let go and she plummeted down. Her body sped toward the ground.

Contact. It hit and skidded against other stone outcroppings, rolling until it settled still against a ledge. A broken, quiet bulk. Dead.

Silence swallowed me. The world disappeared for several long inhales of breath, until the sound of dragon wings pulled me back.

Above me, the battle had stopped. The nine pulled away from Qest, Gabriel, and Gwen, who willingly ended their fight.

The nine flew solemnly down to the Eemah's form, landing. Their stillness, the whistling wind the only accompaniment, hung over the group as they gazed at her unmoving form.

Surrounding her, they raised their heads to the skies and began to sing a rough lament. Bass low. Shaking the ground with its reverberation. Haunting, beautiful, full of grief. The other watching Kyn came to the call and settled around their fallen leader, joining in the mourning, singing her to rest.

My dragon fluttered with unease as she hung in the air. I needed to go down and face them. To face the next distasteful task and my newest responsibility. Hovering over the mourning Kyn, an emptiness hollowed my insides. I'd killed my grandmother. And part of me wondered whether she'd fought with less than full heart, allowing me this victory. Either way, she was dead by my doing.

'Out, damn'd spot! Out I say!' Although I hoped not to share Lady MacBeth's madness, the creeping stain of guilt painted my skin just as surely.

In the nearby sky, Gabriel, Qest, and Gwen watched the scene below. Gwen separated from them and began to fly downward, the cerulean outline of her form fading until she blinked out of existence, providing the answer to her power. She'd battled as a phantom Kyn formed from a witch spell. Never real but somehow able to do damage. Leslie's effect had been powerful to let Gwen pull this off.

I waited, hanging in the skies until the song below died down, ending in more silence.

Wings leaden, I drifted down to land beside the group. They parted to let my dragon enter their circle and rest next to the fallen Eemah. Gabriel and Qest landed outside the ring, and begrudgingly the crowd parted again to allow them access. Wings pulled back to allow the passage. Tails lifted, although swinging with a tight threat, spikes glistening under the pale sun.

Behind the gathering, the rest of my friends and family were jogging over to the location. To my surprise, their number had grown to include Satan, Kemuel, Aubrey, and, shockingly, Natalya, the vampire queen. I hadn't seen her since the coronation.

"Allow them through," I ordered the Kyn who followed the command with low growls and puffs of smoke.

Another tremor hit and the group braced through the shocks, falling into one another and losing their feet. When it ended, we rose again and settled, with many muttering anxious words.

In Kyn form, I spread my wings up and out until their voices quieted. "Today, we have lost a great individual. Your matriarch. My grandmother. I have ended her life through the Frail Sorcha in order to preserve yours. Most of you worry that our planet is tearing itself apart and death will come in awful spasms. I understand your fear. I am here to tell you that we will save ourselves. I am here to lead you to that moment.

"I am your Mother Heir. The Kyn are my people as much as the angels and demons, shifter and vampires, fae and witches." I looked at Leslie, huddled against the wind by Christian's side, looking glassy-eyed but with a new peace to her. "Nulls and Achra, too."

I crooned to my dragon and thanked her as I folded her away and let myself morph back to human form. The rumblings of the Kyn grew louder again. They were less pleased with my human form. Qest and Gabriel followed my lead with transformation.

With solid ground under my two feet, I turned to Gwen who'd made her way to Qest's now human side. "How do you feel about my brother?" I asked. "Make it formal between you two and your part of the alliance can be the X-chromosome preference behind Qest's Kyn heritage, with you both leading this dragon crew while I take care of a few other small details."

She turned to Qest who'd overheard my speech and gave him a considering look. He blushed in response. Her sly smile was punctuated by a subtle lick of her lips. His blush turned a deeper shade.

"A wise plan for an otherwise busy leader, Rachel. The merging of DNA may change the game among the species, but for now, I accept your proposal if the gentleman involved agrees. I know the Kyn like to marinate for at least one thousand years before they mate, but perhaps we can average our ages and qualify for the minimum age requirement." She swiped a lascivious look over his body. "He looks like a grown-up ready for prime time."

"Qest?" I asked.

"A cold way to form an alliance," he said.

Peeking at his aura, the colors throbbed in indecision, running hot and cold. He wanted it, but was afraid.

"I have every confidence in your heart, brother dear. And Gwen's. I've been watching and taken the measure of things. But Gwen and I are practical women and the ticking clock makes romantic interludes less optimal. Will you do this?"

Qest dropped his head, his eyes squeezed shut. After a moment, he opened them and squared his gaze on Gwen. He moved close to the witch leader's side and wrapped his hand behind her head, bunching her fire red hair in his fingers and dragging her in for a kiss.

He released her, licked his own lips, and smiled. "Sounds like a plan. Practical can be a turn on."

I tried to smile back, happy for my brother, although a numb grief smothered some of that joy. I gestured Tarn over to retrieve the fae dagger I'd given him to hold for me.

Facing the still form of the Eemah, my stomach clenched. Nothing for it but to get it done. My hand strayed to touch her hindquarter. The reptilian skin was cold to my touch, but I wanted the contact to my past. I'd craved it for so many years and even now, the pieces crumbled too soon. *Rom. Father. Grandmother. I'm so sorry.*

I forced my weighted arms and legs to climb over her limbs and positioned myself near her breastbone, thankful that she'd settled with that body area accessible. I closed my eyes and raised the dagger, willing the fae blade to cut through the tough layers of muscle and bone. Solinthe had confirmed that a fae tool did not need to make contact to do the work for which it was crafted. Only the magical intent of the wielder was needed. Leslie had unlocked and heightened my magic for this brief period even surrounded by the Kyn.

I opened my eyes and my grip on the dagger tightened as the Eemah's skin and bone parted under my gaze, revealing an opalescent sphere embedded in her body. Roughly the size of a softball, the pearl glowed even while covered in the red-blue liquid of the matriarch's blood. I leaned in and grasped the pearl, merging my energy with the gem and welcoming it into my hand. It recognized the female taste to my call and hummed at my Kyn identity, the dragon inside me purring back in ecstasy to be touching the thing. My necklace started a ruckus at the contact.

I backed away, pulling, and the pearl came with me.

The Kyn snorted in amazement and delight. Despite killing her, I don't think they'd believed I had a legitimate claim to the pearl. The pearl's acquiescence was proof enough.

I turned to the crowd and used magic to raise the level of my voice to be heard over the wind now that I'd lost the extra oomph of dragon form. "As your new matriarch, I pledge to keep you from harm to the best of my ability. My business is to save our world and my people. For now, I leave you in the care of my brother, Qest and his mate, Gwen of the witches, ruling as my proxies. We are about to change everything, but I promise that even while I do it that no one forgets the strength and story of the Kyn. No one forgets the joy of the dragon riding the winds, singing the song of life. Dragons will return to the world. I promise you this."

With my final words, the pearl began to glow between my fingers. Hot. Vibrating. I feared dropping the sphere, but it had other plans.

I gasped as tendrils shot out of the pearl and wrapped my hand, burrowed into my skin and snaked inside my body and bloodstream. The pain was at least as intense as the crazy pleasure, my nerves twisted into confusion in their response.

"Rachel," Gabriel called in panic. I felt him grab my arms and support my weight, but my vision had gone gray, my only focus point was the sensation of the pearl intruding into my body. Soon, my hand was empty as the entire mass of the gem was inside my skin.

The material dissolved into my blood and my cells gobbled it up, exploding with the contact. Coated with the last of Leslie's null energy, they changed. My DNA shifted, grew, and all of the gaps and minute irregularities smoothed into fullness as code from the pearl integrated into my own. Letting me become more. All of myself. Lillith's intended being.

My breath came out in a long hard exhale and I collapsed fully into Gabriel. Universe, amazing!

This entire time the pearl contained the complete code. All Kesayim. All mortal. All null. Waiting for this moment. The Kyn had guarded our future since the beginning.

Gabriel pushed me far enough away from him to look in my eyes. "What is wrong?"

I shook my head, blowing out with a whistle. "Nothing. For the first time, something is right."

Declining to expand on the subject, I asked Qest and Gwen to stay behind and help the Kyn plan. Gwen's bemused expression, combined with Qest's stunned one kept me chuckling on the inside. They'd need privacy to process their future, but privacy would be hard to come by riding the express train to final countdown.

"We need to speak," Natalya said, making her way next to me and ignoring Tarn and Sebastian's ominous glowers of protective instinct.

Despite the vampire queen's tall, dark and striking image, she remained stick thin. Her previous expression of devoted loyalty and her endless thanks to me at my coronation had gone AWOL, replaced by a sour pinching of her lips.

"You broke the oath you made to the Kesayim at the coronation," she said. "Interfering with internal matters of the Kesayim peoples."

"I broke one to keep another, Natalya. If you want to take issue with me then do it back at Eden's Court."

"You owe us explanations," Aubrey insisted.

Satan rolled his eyes. "Kemuel and I gave you the highlights. Bad timing that you were with us when we heard of the Kyn melodrama and whined about coming here. Don't let the killing of one Kesayim leader by our Mother Heir get your panties in a bunch. If you waste all of your temper tantruming now, what will you do when she has to kill another of us later? The whole thing will be boring beyond belief."

I suppressed a growl. "Satan, please stop helping."

"Of course, supreme leader," he said with a smile and half bow.

"I promise I will answer your questions, but can we go back to the garden first?"

Aubrey and Natalya grudgingly agreed. The rest of my party looked relieved. Too many negotiations while huddled around the corpse of a dragon as biting winds and groups of living Kyn keened their grief did not make for a relaxed atmosphere.

Unfinished business and plenty of it awaited, but my step skipped lighter. Hope stirred from her drugged sleep. I did not understand the changes the pearl brought, but I was ready to find out.

Chapter Twenty-four

We began our walk to the portal, Natalya shooting undecipherable looks at Christian's back as he walked ahead with Leslie. I didn't trust the vampire queen. Memories intruded of her madness during my visit to her realm.

Three quarters of the way to the gateway, Tarn stumbled. He stopped us. "Leslie's null effect has returned."

Nothing seemed out of place with my magic. "Gabriel, is she effecting your power?"

"Yes."

"I'd heard you sap the virility from a man, null," Satan complained. "If I wasn't quite certain of my skills, I'd weep."

Leslie's face scrunched in anger. Christian placed a restraining hand on her arm. "Do not let him goad you. It only feeds his out of control ego."

"I'm to be everyone's punching bag. Funny how Lillith believes I'm crucial, but her damn people want to drop me in the ocean with weights on my feet."

"A pretty picture," Natalya added with a hiss.

I chose to ignore Natalya's comment, although she deserved careful watching.

My power was on-line, full force. The changes from the pearl worked fast. "Leslie, you are a valuable part of our team now. You saved my butt when I was up in the air. I would not have succeeded without you."

Leslie's hand rose to cover her neck. I hadn't noticed a bite mark, but what I knew of vampire feedings could fit on the head of my toothbrush.

"Thank you," she said. She glanced at Christian, opened her mouth to say something more, and closed it, perhaps thinking better of it.

I started walking again. "We have portals to traverse, ladies and gentlemen. Time to work on the next part of the to do list."

* * * * *

We emerged from the portal into the garden, Christian carrying a sleeping Leslie now that her null effect was back.

The garden chirped me a welcome. It was my own personal love fest, always eager to greet me or send me cheery tidings of disaster at Eden's Court. Maybe the greetings distracted me, but next I knew, a blur of motion passed my side.

Natalya.

The vampire queen had knocked Christian down, wrenched Leslie from his arms, and pinned her to the ground, hands tight around her neck.

My magic punched out to blast Natalya away from the woman, throwing the vampire queen against the arborvitae bushes to our side.

The garden screeched in reaction.

Christian ran to Leslie as I used my magic to wake her. She didn't wake, but she was alive. Natalya's strangulation had sent the null unconscious directly from her sleep state.

Natalya rose snarling and launched herself at Christian, this time pinning my brother to the grass. Gabriel trained his gun to the queen's head, but waited to see what the hell this crazy lady would do.

"How dare you take Kevin's killer for a lover," she shouted, mouth ugly with hate. "I am your queen and you harbor this criminal in defiance of me. Sharing a son between us will not save you, Christian."

With Leslie out cold, Christian's power was nothing to his queen's. Mine, on the other hand, was a damn bit stronger. I raised my hands toward the vampiress.

"Rachel, no!" Christian yelled from the ground. "Don't hurt her."

Dammit. Gabriel frowned and looked to me. I gestured him to hold.

"Punish me if you will, Natalya, but hear me first," Christian shouted mere inches from her face to get her attention.

She hissed but made no further move. The glow of her eyes narrowed on him as she waited, overfull with power.

"Will you let me up?" He lay still under her grasp showing no fight. Waiting on her decision.

A long minute passed. My fingers twitched with the need to throw a spell. Now that my code was complete, the magic almost demanded use.

With a ragged breath, Natalya lifted off of Christian, backing up a step, but standing as if ready to leap at him; a branch ready to snap. He rose and glanced

Leslie's way where Tarn, Delta, and Sebastian guarded his love, Tarn working fae healing.

The yearning on Christian's face made it clear he wanted to rush to her side, but instead, he focused on Natalya. I'd give him credit for his self-control because I wanted nothing more than to blast her to the other side of the garden, not just to the arborvitae.

"Christian," I warned.

He lifted a hand to gesture me to wait and turned back to Natalya. "You mourn Kevin and I understand," he said. "I am sorry for it. Leslie's role with the vampire hunters was terrible. I lost my father to them. But now she is helping save us. She made choices because she believed vampires had killed her family. More and more it seems the fae were responsible for their death, namely Solinthe. Only Kesayim understand vampires could not have killed them. There was no way for her to know."

Natalya's expression remained unmoved. Universe, Christian. She wasn't caring.

"And now, I love her as you loved Kevin," he said. "And I ask the most difficult thing of you. Not to forgive her. Not to excuse her. Not to forget. But to let her live because we all need a future. Even you, my queen. I want you to have a future as much as I want one for myself."

Her eyes narrowed. "So I am to forget vengeance."

"Vengeance will not bring you relief from the pain, Natalya. Killing does not heal pain. Jet discovered that." Christian spared a glance my way. "He tried looking to death to answer his pain. In the end, he saw it for a mistake. Or so I've been told."

My heart constricted a painful jag and I forced myself to breathe, picturing my lost guard, my lost friend.

"Once Rachel has joined the DNA strands across the world, the vampires will be able to love whomever they wish. Even one another. Think of the gift this is, my queen. That is the miracle on which we should focus. We do not need more death. We need more love."

He looked at her with such clear belief on his face. With hope.

Natalya shut her eyes, a look of struggle fighting across her face. "My love is dead."

He reached to catch her hand and she let him. "You love your people, you always have. And they love you. It will be good, Natalya. Watch over us as we figure out our new future. I need your support. Give me what I need. Let me find happiness in this strange morphing future."

The vampire queen's shoulders slumped as I saw the fight leave her. A tear trailed down her face, but she didn't bother to wipe it away. "For you, Christian. And your foolish vision." She shook her head, forcing words out between teeth. "I do not know what comes. Maybe it is more pain. But I will give you the null's life. I find I cannot stand any of this longer."

"Thank you, Natalya." He leaned closer to her and kissed her bony cheek. He genuinely loved his queen, although I couldn't see the attraction.

She turned back toward me. "My pledge to you stands, Rachel. Do not cause me to regret it."

Christian finally risked moving to where Leslie roused on the ground, whispering encouragement to her. My guard made way for him and crowded closer to me, completing the wall between me and Natalya that Gabriel began after begrudgingly re-holstering his gun.

The peace was short-lived. The garden wailed again. "It comes, it comes. Save us now." The wail grew louder. With Leslie awake, and her null effect back on-line, the grass around her prone body started to wither.

What now? The garden was better than any home security system. Shriller in alarm, too. Artemis popped out of her sling at the same time, barking madly, running over my shoulders back and forth and nudging me with her cold nose.

From her mouth, a sound emerged between her yips. I struggled to make out the pattern. She was trying to speak months earlier than I'd been led to believe was possible.

"Fay. Fay. Fay." She barked more and repeated the sound. "Fay. Fay. Fay."

A word. Her first word. Months early.

"What's wrong?" Gabriel asked.

"I don't know. Artemis is telling me something and the garden is screaming in my head about an attack."

Tarn came closer. "Fae. She's saying fae."

At that moment, another louder bark sounded behind us and we turned to watch Jack come galloping across the fields toward our group. The standard poodle looked to have been running flat out for some time. "Attack," he called between tongue lolling breaths as he skidded to us. "A portal has opened in the gymnasium of your wing and is dumping fae and shifters. The nearest guards engaged them, but it's not good. Morven's called up everyone else to meet the assault."

"Impossible," Aubrey huffed. "My people wouldn't attack."

I started running and left everyone to follow. Shit. "Samuel's followers not yours," I yelled to Aubrey behind me.

But how did Solinthe break my spell and allow fae back into Eden's Court? And the bitch could create portals. I should have realized. Gabriel ran by my side.

With a thought, my power bubbled up swifter and smoother than ever and my body blurred into a four-footed canine predator, an African wild dog. My speed skyrocketed, a new gait shooting me ahead. Fast and good for distance. That's what I needed.

"Rachel," Gabriel called as he fell behind this faster form.

"Meet me there." I kept going. My people were dying. The kids were in my wing of the complex and Jasper along with Gregor's parents were their only protection.

I sped over the grass and undergrowth through the garden. *'Death'* the garden wailed between my ears. *'Protect us'* it insisted. The scent of copper blood flooded my nostrils. It must be my imagination. I was miles away from the battle.

In a moment, a greyhound joined my side. Aubrey. A moment later, a second, this one jet black. Gabriel. Next, a third animal. Gazelle. Sebastian. They'd left Leslie far enough behind to be able to shift.

"Rachel, you need a plan before running into battle," Gabriel spoke into my mind as he sped beside me, dodging obstacles in our path.

"Stop Solinthe. That's the plan."

He sighed in my mind. *"You have no weapons."*

"I have my dagger and my magic, which the pearl expanded to full force. I don't need to merge Leslie's DNA with mine. I have it now, and I'm immune to her null power."

I leaped over a fallen tree trunk in my path. I needed to be at the complex yesterday. Even my canine feet were too slow. The garden chanted non-stop at me, burning the message of urgency in my head. Although I knew it was helping me along, shrinking the distance to the complex as much as it sometimes magically expanded the garden in its vicissitudes.

"I stopped the last fight between shifters and fae using demon magic. I drained them then and I can do it now."

I remembered the maelstrom of force coursing out of me those months ago and the awful feeling as I sucked all of the magic out of the brawling crowd and onlookers and absorbed it into my own body.

My control and strength had grown since then, so maybe I could do it without blacking out. My magic hadn't resulted in a physical price the last few days. I couldn't afford to black out and lose my strength if Solinthe still lived. She'd only take advantage and redouble her effort.

"Then do it. Shut it down." Gabriel's agreement helped shore up my uncertainty.

Finally, there was the archway entrance to my wing. Outside it stood Morven with a half dozen guards. I shifted back to human mid-stride, almost stumbling with the fast transition. Gabriel, Aubrey, and Sebastian did the same behind me.

"Why aren't they defending the complex?" I asked, running to my seneschal and gesturing to the guards. "Forget that, what's the status?"

Morven was throwing up hands, weaving a spell of burnt orange and green, knots twisting over one another. She tied it with a flourish and set it free causing a streak of bright light bursting toward the arch and into the hallway.

"They portaled into the gymnasium. Two hundred in the first wave and more flowing through in bursts. We've lost track of the count. We've contained them to your wing with everyone available, but it has been difficult fighting the fae's glamour. My witches are spitting out truth spells that sniff out the glamour and unravel it, although it takes the fae little time to rebuild them."

Damn. At most, Eden's Court had two hundred guards after the fae ones were banished. The civilian population here was around three hundred non-fae in addition.

"Is the portal still open?" I asked.

"Yes."

"Is Solinthe with them?"

"No one reports seeing her. Samuel is here. Still at the gymnasium."

"I'll take care of him," Aubrey said.

Sebastian's fists flashed a brief shift to claws then back again to human skin. "I was to be your champion. Let me fight."

Aubrey scowled back, ready to respond, but Gabriel interrupted with a hand to Seb's arm. "You guard Rachel. It's your job and she needs you. Her magic is strong, but there will be many bodies with weapons and she needs to concentrate."

"Tarn, Delta, Kemuel, Satan, and Natalya are behind us. Christian and Leslie too. Send them to follow and make sure Leslie is protected. She's going to disrupt the magic in bursts. We can use that. I have to close down that portal and then I plan to drain the whole damn complex of whatever power is left."

Morven jerked her head. "Good."

"Let's go," I said, running into my wing.

Aubrey and Sebastian kept pace, also staying in human form until we could assess the situation. Gabriel kept up a spate of dialogue in my head as we trucked it down the corridor, passing bodies lying lifeless along the vine covered halls.

"Weave an invisibility spell around us for shielding," he said.

I wove the air to hide our group, remembering the first time I'd tapped this Kyn power outside council chambers my first full day at court. I trusted him to think clearly about all the pieces of my magic. Remembering the smorgasbord of choices still overwhelmed me after several months of sifting through them by trial and error.

"How do we close the portal?" Gabriel asked.

"Explode it, unhook it, shrink it. I have no idea. I have to take a closer look. I've never worried about them after I've created one or survived walking through avoiding Lillith."

We rounded a bend and ran into two men in battle, a fae had cornered a witch now on his knees, weaving defensive and shield spells frantically.

I dropped our shields and we attacked. Gabriel went for the fae with his celestial sword blazing while I threw my own shield over the witch.

Two more fae and a shifter ran down the corridor at us. Sebastian and Aubrey shifted forms and their animals plowed into the group. The fae enchantments around the enemy made Seb and Aubrey's attacks jerky, bodies off-balance and claws hesitating, but I evened the field, throwing chaos magic at Solinthe's warriors, draining off their magic after their movements faltered. In moments, the fae and Samuel's shifter were on the ground.

We ran on, almost at the gym, passing more downed warriors, some of them fae, but mostly my people. I would not let this happen.

My healing magic fanned behind me in a cloud of pale mint fog as we passed unconscious guards, trying to help any who still lived.

The fighting spilled out of the gymnasium. My power slammed into the crowd, parting it as Gabriel and Sebastian launched into the melee with swords raised and I had to lower my shields to let them go. Aubrey shifted to bear form and forged into the crowd with the brute killing strength of his new body.

The blur of energy mixed with savage physical attack, blood and cries of pain, claws and teeth, spells and snarls of rage, the flap of angel wings bunched in powerful strokes, songs of power, licking chaos magic, swam across my senses, disorienting me.

I kept throwing power to push aside the warriors and wade closer to the gym. My Kyn energy stirred and my dragon protected me as fae enchantments flew across the hall. I needed inside the room, although bodies blocked the entryway, the wooden doors thrown off their frames and in splinters to either side of the entrance.

"Follow her," I heard Gabriel scream at Sebastian as the men fought their way closer to me.

A vampire lifted and hurled a shifter in hyena form into the closest group of fighters, temporarily knocking away a knot blocking the entryway.

I ran for it and into the gymnasium, ducking as a slew of metal weapons came flying at me. Gabriel called up power and knocked aside the projectiles.

Chaos around me. Hundreds of bodies in combat. The room was huge, but somehow, the frantic movements shrunk it to one writhing undifferentiated mass. Blood and feces scented the air. Battle wasn't pretty. Magic only accounted for some of it. Physical carnage the rest. I spotted the hulk of Aubrey's Kodiak farther into the room, battling another bear in bloodthirsty combat. He'd found Samuel.

Across the room, Celendine battled back to back with Morrea. So much change in short order.

Focus, Rachel.

"Fight. Fight. Fight," called rising voices inside my mind. The murals depicting hundreds of animals of Eden painted the gymnasium walls. The creatures were calling to me, their eyes hungry as ever. The paintings shifted, the walls bulging as the baku and spider monster and griffins and harpies and unicorns and phoenix clamored to be let out.

Universe, they were real inside those walls. Not paintings, but a part of the fabric of Eden. And they wanted to join the fight.

The portal pulsed in the far-right corner, the torn edges of it a roiling fog surrounding the black hole of a center. Rougher than the gates I'd created or those already existing throughout the garden, this portal was also smaller. Still, it spewed new warriors into the room, one or two per minute.

A familiar but disembodied voice sliced out into the room along with them from the opening of the portal. *Hello, Rachel.*

Solinthe!

I hope you are enjoying my people's visit. Your banishment spell snapped easily. This wasn't in my head. Her voice filled the entire gym. Solinthe could not speak to me telepathically or read thoughts, but she commanded every fae in the room and saw through their eyes. Apparently, the portal was able to transport more than physical form.

Around me, the forces fought on, a few stumbling with distraction when the faerie queen's voice echoed above the sounds of the clashing warriors.

I refused to respond. She wanted me squirming. I wanted to gut open her belly and watch the light die in her eyes. None of the damn ambivalence Lillith predicted remained in my attitude toward Solinthe's death.

Watch your loyal retainers die. You think to save the world when you cannot even save the folk of Eden's Court. Pathetic.

I'd drawn my knife entering the gym, although Sebastian and Gabriel covered my sides and ruthlessly took down the enemy coming too close. My hand began to ache as it clenched tighter around the dagger.

I needed to close that portal now.

The voices from the mural clamored louder. Demanding. My angel song spiraled up from inside of me, answering the creatures' calls and coating the walls of the gymnasium, brushing the leaves, branches, and bark of the embedded pieces of garden, stirring a scent of fir and eucalyptus through the air, burrowing under the paint and enticing the beasts out, lending order to their natural forms to make them real.

A grey unicorn the color of storm clouds broke free first, rearing up and into the room, hooves crashing down on the nearest fae warrior. Her horn swiped to either side, cutting and puncturing other fae and Samuel's shifters.

The other creatures charged behind her, hundreds spilling into the room and attacking the nearest of Solinthe's forces.

My magic flowed strong, more like natural instinct than ever. Now for the portal. Energy spiraled up from the earth and gathered between my fingers, itching for release as I focused on the tendrils of the gateway.

A trumpet of sound distracted me and the unicorn charged toward me. Her horn dripped red as she parted the crowds. I stepped back and my stomach hollowed as the blood-covered tip pointed in my direction. She stopped short before she could impale me, snorted and dropped her head to brush my shoulder with her horn.

The room disappeared as a vision descended. I stood inside the portal, tendrils twining around me connecting the gateway with the potential of the universe. Writhing. The hum of the portal filled my ears. I spread out my hands, fingers wide, toward the walls. Magic whipped out of my fingertips, sending a jag of power into the portal to destroy. But in the moment of connection, everything exploded, billowing out. Out of the portal, out through Eden's Court, out through all of the gateways attaching Eden to Kesayim realms and mortal Earth. Out to spread destruction and a wave of fiery death. Until nothing was left but ash and the black unknown of the universe.

My eyes snapped open as the unicorn pulled back her horn and sent me a censuring look. I stumbled as the vision left me, limbs shaking. Shit! If I tried to destroy the portal, I destroyed the world. And still, new fae and some shifters popped out of Solinthe's gate joining the fight.

Gabriel stood against me with one arm supporting me, celestial sword raised in the other, although he'd also raised a dragon shield of his own to make us invisible in the battle. "Rachel?"

I unclenched my teeth and argued back at the wobbles in my limbs. "I'm fine. I can't destroy the portal or it will cause a chain reaction exploding everything."

"What do you need?"

Always getting to the heart of the matter, was Gabriel.

If I drained everyone not only did our folks go down along with our adversaries, but with the portal still open, more fae would come through with our people vulnerable while unconscious. And if Solinthe herself came through....

"I need to close it temporarily, not destroy it. Put it to sleep."

Sebastian battled near our hiding place and we both turned hearing Tarn's shout across the room. He and Delta had arrived and were engaged with four fae. Tarn's glowing scrollwork sword shone with his skin as he cut down opponents. Delta's short sword blurred with her quick and willowy movements, in for a cut, dancing back out of reach. Her eyes glowed wicked and she laughed in between strokes. So much life amid destruction.

Satan had full snarl on behind them, his dagger out and throwing chaos and drain magic at one fae after another. Kemuel's sword sung not far from Satan's side. Tag teaming.

Natalya was full fanged, levitating and throwing bodies beyond them.

Christian and Leslie wouldn't be far behind. Leslie's null force might affect the portal, but would it destroy the gateway or cause the slumber I wanted? I needed to test it out before she came barging into the area. "We need to find Leslie before she reaches us."

Gabriel raised an eyebrow in question. "She would not come here. She would go to Anna."

Her daughter. Leslie's first priority was to keep her kid safe.

"Then we find Christian and Leslie. He wouldn't leave her undefended," I said.

Too many bodies littered the floor. I swallowed down burning acid. If we left to find her, how many more would die before I got back? And I needed to make sure I understood how Leslie's effect would hit the portal. If I couldn't drain everyone yet, I could find a way to minimize damage while I figured out the 'sleep' situation. "I can't leave. I think I can slow down the action with a spell to make everyone fight in slow motion. Find Leslie and get her here. Don't bring Christian because I need her with her null power on-line."

"He will not leave her side."

"Convince him." And by that, Gabriel understood that I meant do whatever needed doing. "You might be able to access Kyn magic even with her power active. Weave a shield around her when you bring her to dampen her effect until we have her in place."

"This means leaving you unprotected."

"Watch my eyes roll, Gabriel. I trust you. You trust me. And I seem to have some big magic. Besides, Tarn, Sebastian, and Delta are still here."

He frowned but agreed once I promised to keep up my shield and drop it only when ready to throw my time slowing mojo spell. He dropped his, long enough to charge out into the crowd and fight to Tarn's side where he yelled unintelligible instructions to my fae guard, probably about watching my ass. I didn't want to die. I knew my limits. I was no warrior, but my magic was our only hope.

* * * * *

My necklace sat heated around my neck, humming pleasure as I raised my hands for the spell. With a deep breath, I connected back to my body in the first moment I had to feel my changes since I'd swallowed the pearl.

My blood ran free, smooth and full. I felt pretty damn good. Connected. Yeah, that was the best word for it. Everything inside me felt connected to everything else.

As I wove strings of witch colors in the air, I infused them with my will, my fae power taking the usually sparkling patterns and sharpening them to focused purpose, faerie enchantment mixed with the witchy spell. I dropped my shield and threw the knotted colors into the room, sending it spiraling into the gymnasium crowd and the overflow in the hall.

Hit! The effect rippled out and everything slowed. My people and Solinthe's fell into a slow warp, limbs moving in the smallest increments. Even my guard's dance was sluggish, catching Tarn, Delta, and Sebastian with sword strokes mid clash. They moved, but it took one hundred times longer to accomplish even part of a stroke.

The spell gave me too much time to watch the destruction. Part of me wanted to run through the crowd and push away the weapons, knock down their bodies, and trip up their magic. However, I needed to both keep my spell active, which meant retaining my focus, and examine the portal again to be ready. So instead, I sang out an angel melody to stabilize the magic, creating an order to the spell that would continue its cascading effect.

Solinthe's warriors continued to exit the gateway, but were swallowed into the time warp as they stepped through.

The mist surrounding the outside edge of the portal swirled as fast as ever and looked almost like the eddies that covered the large map table in Mother's Rest. The creep factor was definitely similar.

Keeping my shields, I moved closer to the opening. My sight expanded to watch the patterns of the portal. My necklace heated further and the damn gate began calling to me, a siren effect. My feet stopped following my commands as I moved closer and closer. I was being sucked inside.

The whicker of the unicorn sounded behind me, followed by her snort. She considered the situation ridiculous as well.

In front of the entrance, the mist sucked me the last step into the opening. I hated these portals and this was shaping up to be my least favorite experience with them.

Inside, I was surrounded by its grey nothing balanced over an endless abyss. The tiny licking tendrils of alien awareness cascaded over my skin. My limbs remained free, unlike the times Lillith bound me inside the portals. She said I'd float away into the nothingness without the restraint. It wasn't happening. My magical sight refused to focus on any pattern to this gap in the universe, although I was just proud I tried to observe instead of running. My slow and even breaths allowed me to resist the scream of panic that wanted out.

A mass began to grow in front of me, radiating the familiar dazzling light of a white-and-black void. My eyes swam and nausea forced me to close them. Any moment Lillith would speak. Her visits were way too frequent for my liking.

"Curious," came a different voice, lower in tone and less grating than Lillith's. "She has done what she claimed. A whole specimen."

The shock made me open my eyes, but I closed them quickly against the intensity of the jarring shape and light that sent a stampede of pain through my brain.

"Who are you?" I asked, blind and fighting the jagged fear squeezing my chest.

"And you hear me. Lovely."

"Are you related to Lillith?"

A shock of its laughter scraped my skin. I bit my lip to hold in the groan.

"I am one of her kind," it...he said. I decided the voice sounded male. If Lillith could pretend to be female, I'd do my own anthropomorphizing.

"Have I passed your test?" I tried my best to keep the anger out of my voice. I failed. *Watch it, Rachel. This never goes well with Lillith.* Nasty habits die hard.

"It was never your test. Only...You call her Lillith?"

I nodded from my blind state.

"Only Lillith's doomed project," he said.

"I'd object to the doomed descriptor, but there have been moments. Although I'm kind of on to a solution for a happy ending. Assuming I solve one or two little problems first. You wouldn't want to help? Now that I'm a whole specimen and all."

"We do not interfere."

"So I've heard. But then why come to check me out? That is interfering."

"This is my home. You came to me."

"The portal is your home?"

"Portal is the incorrect word. We live in-between."

"In-between what?"

"In-between your matter."

If I tried to figure this one out, I'd drive myself mad. "I didn't come to you. I was pulled into the...into your home."

"I did not do such."

"Maybe Lillith?"

"No."

Then Solinthe.

Time hadn't slowed for her. Any moment she would come looking for me.

"So, if this is in-between how can it open into the matter of my universe? For us it's like a hole between two places of our world. Why can I create those holes?"

Not to mention Solinthe.

"You do it by pushing aside your matter."

"And if I shove it together again?"

"You are inquisitive." He added nothing more.

My vision already showed me disaster if I tried to destroy the portal. Maybe it wasn't sleep the portal needed as much as a sort of plug between the matter to shut out the in-between space. Like some expandable spray foam insulation.

Leslie's power wouldn't help with this. I needed this done now. "Will you let us live if we save ourselves?"

The voice hummed in consideration. I squinted my eyes open a sliver and his light shifted in circles. "Lillith has not convinced us of the value your world adds. She created out of empty desire to possess. She is broken."

"If I convince you?"

Another long pause. The meat of my speeding pulse was heavy in my throat. The misty tendrils lapped in endless caresses.

"Save yourselves and we will listen to your words."

"Thank you. If I can ask you to return me to where I entered."

"I look forward to your arguments."

And a breath later I was outside the portal, the slow-motion battle raged on, my spell holding.

The drip of Solinthe's voice intruded in my head again. *I'm coming, Rachel. You will not stymie my people.*

To plug the in-between space, I needed material. Magic didn't allow me to create something out of nothing. I sifted through my plans, changing their order.

My friends battled in their sloth-like speed, Satan dripping in blood although I suspected little was his. Natalya's fangs were extended and she was levitating and slinging her telekinetic power to throw more bodies through the air. Aubrey and Samuel continued their fierce animalistic battle, with Samuel on the defensive in his shifter form.

If I dropped my shields and drained everyone's energy, I could transform that magic into my foam filler, and pray I plugged the gaps before Solinthe's warriors came through to do more harm to my unconscious people. I lowered my shields, disassembling the motion spell to focus on the drain.

"*Rachel,*" Gabriel's voice rang in my head. "*I have Leslie, but my shield is not blocking her effect.*"

I turned, distracted by the sight of Gabriel carrying Leslie into the gym. Her face was an unlovely frown of pissed-off.

They were part-way into the room and around her the combatants, now at normal speed, stumbled, losing magic. Shifters fell out of their animal shapes. Spells died mid-toss and weapons were fumbled. A roar of frustration bellowed across the space as Aubrey and Samuel transformed back into human form, grimaces of hate marring both their faces. Samuel lunged for an abandoned sword and ran at Aubrey.

"Aubrey, I have him," Sebastian yelled, intercepting Samuel. Just as he planned. He was the better warrior in human form. He was Aubrey's champion.

One-on-one Sebastian was more than enough to challenge Samuel. Until a knot of fae, regaining their footing, broke from their battles and attacked Sebastian as he fought Samuel. He pivoted to protect his side from their blows.

No! But I had seconds before Solinthe would arrive. I gathered the magic, building the spiral I needed to drain the crowd. I sucked up power from the earth, what little remained.

Gabriel dropped Leslie to her feet, wrapped her in another shield, and ran for Sebastian, celestial sword gleaning bright.

Closer, Delta broke off from her own fight and swung over to Sebastian's side. A fae sword clanged a metallic clash against Sebastian's, who'd blocked him easily. Another fae raised his weapon to bring it down on Sebastian's unprotected back. Delta danced into his sight and raised her weapon to block.

I screamed a warning as Samuel slipped in at her shoulder while she raised her blade to protect Sebastian. He thrust. His sword pierced up from below her ribcage into her body. Her eyes circled in surprise. Samuel smiled as blood gushed when he disengaged.

"Delta," Tarn yelled, cutting down his opponent and barreling to her side as Gabriel arrived and attacked the remaining fae.

Sebastian roared an ugly pain and swung back to Samuel. He pushed the shifter back, battering his blade again and again. Samuel stumbled. Sebastian sunk his sword deep into the traitor's body. Samuel coughed, fell, blood frothing from his lips.

Tarn cradled Delta against him. Shit, he had no healing power with Leslie nearby. But I was locked in to my spell, powerless to do anything but watch as I collected the magic.

Rachel, Solinthe's voice teased.

My power draw hit full level, ready. My necklace burned at my throat.

Magic funneled up and out, blasting the room, whistling through the halls of the entire complex of Eden's Court, with me powerless to change this throw of dice, committed to the drain.

"Gabriel," I screamed, as the magic drenched the gymnasium.

He threw up a Kyn shield around himself, Tarn, and Delta. The maelstrom hit. It sped across the room, chaos magic draining every bit of power from the crowd. They fell like marionettes cut from their strings, toppling to the ground.

I braced myself against the rush of energy as it collected into a cloud storm and sped toward me. All color, all texture, all taste, a stew of life force streaming to hit my body. Desperate, I reached to catch and deflect it, tapping my will and craft to batter it across the room, away from me and toward the portal opening.

My sight focused in on the portal opening and I looked for the gaps between the matter. All matter had space between it. I'd learned that in science years ago. But these empty places were larger now that I knew what to look for. I hit the energy molecules I'd drained with my will, forming my tool, morphing them into the filler between the matter. The power tasted molten as it changed and slid into the gaps. More. More. The in-between sucked in the energy with an almost endless need.

Rachel, what do you do, girl? Solinthe screamed. A large object hit the doorway of the portal, distending the air where the opening was partially blocked.

Solinthe!

The silent room held me in a numb limbo as I worked like crazy. Only the queen's shrieks of rage broke the eerie silence. Solinthe needed to stay the hell away from my people.

She hit it again and again as I stuffed the gateway. Endless seconds passing, Solinthe's punching force finally lessening. Soon, the air lay flat with no distention, only her hideous voice still in the room whispering vulgar threats. The in-between was filled; the last of the drain energy gone.

Later, Rachel. You will face me. You will die, along with those you love. And then her voice stopped.

Unconscious bodies were strewn across the room, but I only searched for a handful. I ran to where Tarn was bent over Delta, clinging to her, ragged sobs wracking his entire body. Gabriel knelt behind his friend, shaking his head at me as I caught his gaze. Too late for healing.

Nearby, Sebastian's unconscious body was collapsed near Samuel's lifeless and bloody corpse.

No fucking way. No fucking foreshadowing allowed with some automatic doom for my guards like a Grimm fairytale curse. This was meant to be a Shakespearian comedy. To end in a wedding, not in death. Not a fucking tragedy, a wedding.

I bit my lip hard to keep back my sobs. What do I do? Universe, I knew the first thing I had to do.

I stumbled over to Sebastian and laid trembling hands on his shoulder. He deserved to be awake. I tapped into what resources I had left inside my own body and siphoned power into Sebastian. His eyes opened, unfocused and blinking confusion. Until he latched onto my face and what I knew to be the wet streaks painting it. I watched comprehension snap onto his features.

He pushed up from the floor, knocking me back as he scrambled upright and over to Tarn. He slid to the ground next to the fae and wrenched him off of Delta.

"NO!" he howled. "NO. Delta." He collapsed over the demoness, a copy of Tarn's previous pose. Tarn grabbed him around the shoulders and bent over them both, a vise grip on the people he loved. One living, one dead.

I couldn't move watching their grief. I was a husk with my palms propped against the gritty gym floor to keep myself from falling. The magic had taken everything. I'd prepared for my own loss of Gabriel, but not for my friends to lose. Death must be laughing in my face with this surprise. Why was I surprised each time he visited?

Leslie nudged my side. She was awake as her power had been proof against my magic. "Let me help you."

Gabriel was there. "I'll take her." He lifted me into his arms and we returned to my guardsmen. To huddle around them, to offer them our touch, to cry with them.

There was nothing else to do.

Chapter Twenty-five

The sweet perfume of the roses saturated my nose, almost dizzying in intensity. I wrapped my arms around my knees, squeezing them to my chest, and focused on the prickle of grass against my skin. I rocked back and forth on the ground, trying to auto-induce my own lullaby state. Wasn't working so well.

The sun rose, a portrait of shifting oranges and yellows, over the wild roses. They had chosen to arrange themselves in geometric designs, appearing in a series of concentric circles linked together in chains. You never knew with this part of the garden. The flowers had minds of their own.

I knew he was there before he'd rounded the bend of the hedge, but it was always like that with Gabriel. Our link had only grown with the additions to both our DNA.

He'd been supervising the waking of Morven and a select team who restrained the sleeping fae and traitorous shifters, putting them in a makeshift prison. Our facility's restraining cells had never been built for these numbers.

And then there was clean-up after the battle. Three hundred dead counting theirs and ours. Three hundred.

Gabriel settled to the ground beside me, a grimace playing over his face as he bent. He still suffered from his changed genetics, although there was no point commenting. His side brushed my arm as I watched a lazy bumble bee land and dip into the interior of a blooming bud.

"Resting?" he asked.

"Something like that."

We sat for a time, letting the buzz of the industrious insect drift over us. The bee knew its purpose, was sure in itself. Lucky bee.

A restless tingle played inside my limbs, although I forced myself to stay seated. "Jet used to come here. Or he did at least once. To pray. He must have needed it badly."

Gabriel's warm hand landed on my knee and stopped my rocking. "Tarn and Sebastian are quiet, numb, but together. They will survive this. Stop blaming yourself."

"I'm not."

He snorted a puff of air, not deigning to answer, but clear in his lack of belief.

Why did I even try to lie to him? "I have to go to Faerie."

"I am coming with you," he said.

"I know. Solinthe must have used a lot of her power forming the portal. That's why she took so long to try coming through and why she's not back here yet. I need to take advantage of the weakness before she's full strength again."

"You were drained as well."

"I'm back to normal, the effect of the total DNA package."

We sat again in silence. The bee finished his work and flew away, clear in his next objective.

"She needs killing," Gabriel said.

"Yes, she does."

"I wish I could do this for you."

"I wish *you* could do this for *you*," I answered.

Gabriel turned his head away from my words. He still needed that escape. Neither of us were without regret.

I let go of my knees and straightened them, legs flat against the earth. "We go in tonight."

Gabriel took my hand, layering it between the two of his. Squeezing.

What sort of prayer had Jet spoken weeks ago in this rose garden? Did it bring him respite? I suspected not. Only at the end had I seen relief on his face. Only after doing what needed doing.

I would go to Faerie. I would bring my dagger. I would take Solinthe's life. It was what needed doing.

* * * * *

"Going in alone makes no sense," Qest complained and shoved fingers through his hair, spiky black strands standing upright from the rough treatment.

The last day coping with the Kyn had clearly left him on edge. I couldn't blame him.

"She will not be alone," Gabriel answered.

"Yes, but this is Solinthe. The more power ranged against her the better."

We stood in front of one of the portals to Faerie. The one that led to the fields outside of her main power base. Gwen stood beside Qest, wisely quiet. Morven rounded out our group.

"Trust your sister, Qest," Morven said. "She has reasons."

"Those being?"

There were disturbing reasons, and I didn't want to make any of them more real by speaking their names.

I opened my mouth to answer, but Gabriel interrupted. "The more bodies attacking, the more likely Solinthe will be to involve her warriors. We seek fewer deaths, not more. And frankly, between Rachel's expanded power from the pearl and my additions, if we cannot kill the faerie queen, nothing else will touch her. You would be a liability to Rachel. Cannon fodder to distract her in the fight."

Qest's face remained a red of determination. "The only way she's gotten this far is through a team effort, accepting others' help."

"I know, and I'm damned glad I learned that lesson, brother mine." I wanted to stop Qest's head from exploding. It was not the image I hoped to bring with me to Faerie.

Gwen laid a hand on her fiancée's shoulder. "She's already accepted our help. Some battles we go alone, love. She's trusting us to do our part as it comes. I expect there's more road to travel even after Solinthe's death."

"So, I'm the only one uncomfortable sending you into that bitch's clutches with paltry back-up?"

Gabriel raised an eyebrow and his body tightened so infinitesimally I doubted anyone else saw it.

With no other ideas, I lunged into Qest to squeeze the air from him with a hug, erasing his scowl better than any answer. Everyone, including me, was uncomfortable with the plan. My brother simply acted as the mouthpiece for all of us. The clenching fist in my gut was constant.

"Keep my people here safe," I said to him, pulling back from the hug. "Help me by making them ready. Give them hope. After the attack in the gym, and the more frequent quakes, everyone is scared."

He looked lost, my brother. That I hated.

"You told me in the merkaz before the genetic surgery that I would survive because that is what I do. You hate goodbyes, well you're not making one now. I'm getting busy living. It's only I have a few messy moments ahead before throwing the party of a lifetime. While I go and share a few sweet nothings with Solinthe, I need you picking the music play list. Gwen looks like a party girl, so she can help. And I hate to admit that Satan probably keeps a wicked dance queue. You can hook him up for advice."

Qest laughed. Good.

I turned to my seneschal. "When I get back, I'd like to hold a memorial service for the dead."

"That is an indulgence, my lady. One we may not have time for," Morven said.

"It will be brief. But...we need it. And I need to speak to the people of Eden's Court."

"Yes, my lady."

I pivoted away, but spun back on a whim and gave Morven the same tight embrace I'd given Qest. When I released her, she couldn't hide the hint of a smile. Victory. Hopefully only the first of the evening.

I turned to Gabriel. "Let's go."

* * * * *

The fields brimmed with black poppies as we stepped into Faerie. Gabriel materialized his sword. Solinthe would know of our presence the moment we came through the portal, so hiding was a waste.

Gabriel gestured toward the grouping of buildings in the distance. "She's on the other side of the main buildings, in the Hall of Mirrors." His time here as her 'employee' and later captive left him with his own ability to sense Solinthe.

The nausea and headaches caused by her realm were missing. Perhaps Rachel 2.0 came without the vulnerability to the dizzying effect of Faerie. Or was I on version 3.0? Depends when you started counting.

The night sky shone bright with the full moon, the beams erasing all chance of hiding our presence. Despite that, the landscape was empty. No guards stood at attention outside Solinthe's main buildings. The tiniest flying faeries usually buzzed along the winds. Dark troll-like figures often loped along hillsides on fae business. But even they were missing. I held no illusions we were sneaking up on the faerie queen. She knew we were coming. The question was more a matter of our welcome.

The sprawling concrete bunker of the Hall of Mirrors was an eyesore on the otherwise Doctor Seuss landscape of Faerie. We approached the doors, partially sunken to ground level.

Gabriel stopped me before the steps, several leading up and then several immediately down to the entrance, leaving the impression the building was sunken instead of level to the earth.

"If I enter first, I can play distraction," he said. "My Kyn shield will buy time with her as its proof against even fae magic. You need the minutes to gather your magic. If we wait here too long she might come out before you finish."

"No. She'll attack you."

"Not before she gloats. Solinthe's weakness is her self-importance. And for whatever strange reason, she likes me alive. Give me five minutes before you enter. Then you make your dramatic entrance and go after her."

"This is a stupid plan."

"There is no reliable plan with a creature so erratic, and I have new tricks she will not expect."

"Five minutes."

He nodded and landed a quick kiss on my lips, fire and purpose in the press. Then I let him go into Solinthe's bunker of bonkers with its thousands of mirrors letting her perv on all of her people. How could I let him go? I was an idiot. This trust thing really sucked.

Each mirror was a visual through one of her fae, letting her see out of their eyes and hear out of their ears. This spy tool had been her first foot into my life through Tarn. After I made her blow up Tarn's mirror, she'd relied on his connection to the magic book Tarn and I had recovered together. Now that I'd cut that tie between her and Tarn, she had to rely on other sources to know my steps. Of course, her spy network was no longer an issue. It was time. She knew it was time and would be ready.

I got to work gathering up and storing magic from the earth, using the idea of a pack like I used for Artemis to create a waiting place for the power. A little fold in reality to tuck the force away for safekeeping and immediate access. I'd left Artemis behind with Morven. The pup had been irate and her newest word was 'no', yapped with great frequency and agitation.

There was no place for her here. There was no place for Gabriel. I accepted his presence, but would have left him home if I'd had any chance of his agreement. However, if this didn't work, I admit I preferred to shuck my mortal coil with him by my side. There was no plan B.

I patted the satchel at my waist one more time to make sure I had what I needed and finished filling my pack with the little magic left inside Earth's core. It slid up faster than before the pearl, but would it be enough?

Time's up.

I stepped down up then down the few steps and opened the bunker's doors. The inside was as dark and narrow as I remembered, with the long corridor stretching ahead of me until it turned a bend out of sight. This first stretch was empty. No Gabriel. No Solinthe.

The mirrors, of mismatched sizes in mismatched frames, hung along the walls dark and inactive. No pictures at all. Not even throwing a normal reflection as I passed. As if I wasn't there. Creepy crawlies rappelled up my spine, climbing in panic away from the residue of terror that coated the hallway.

My dagger out, a gun strapped to my thigh where Gabriel had insisted I place it despite my lack of firearm knowhow, I walked cautiously down the corridor and turned the bend, almost tripping over the first body.

Bound hand and foot, gagged, my heart clogged my throat as I noticed hundreds of men and women, even children, tied this way and stacked on either side of the halls. Universe!

I blinked back tears and had to look carefully to confirm that they lived. Or at least most. The bodies closest to me started twisting, grunts of protest erupting from behind their gags. These hostages had a purpose. They weren't fae. A sick knot in my gut developed with my suspicion.

There were so many. If I stopped to untie them, I knew Solinthe would use the delay. Where was Gabriel?

I tried to avoid stepping on anyone as I proceeded forward, silently asking their forgiveness. But if I didn't kill Solinthe, freeing them was pointless.

I stopped before the next twist in the hall, hearing a faint tinkling laughter ahead. With a deep breath, I kept going, passing the empty mirrors and the piles of bodies, around three more bends, the laughter staying in front of my progress. The handle of the dagger grew wet with perspiration. A slippery grip could cost me at the wrong moment. I switched it to the other fist and wiped my palm on my jeans.

Rounding the next corner, I found Gabriel. And Solinthe.

Gabriel lay on the floor, tied and gagged like the rest of the hostages, with the faerie queen standing over him, a sick grin on her face, running her fingertips over the flat end of her dagger with slow strokes. She'd bound him again.

"Hello, Rachel. Do you like my presents? All tied up with bows for your enjoyment. You love nulls so much, I couldn't resist collecting them for you."

Now that my magic wasn't blocked by nulls, I hadn't been sure of their identities. Suspected, but hadn't known for fact. One of the few benefits in this situation was the fact Solinthe knew nothing about my expanded DNA and new immunity to the null effect. Gabriel wasn't immune, which explained how she got him.

But how was she able to use her magic with their presence? I sensed it brimming inside of her, a bright flame in no danger of expulsion.

I shoved down my near panic at seeing him bound and concentrated on Solinthe. "Almost two hundred of your people died attacking Eden's Court."

"Necessary casualties," she said. Her voice beat against my skin, raising the throat stuffing terror I often felt in her presence. Granted, Solinthe scared me out of my underwear, but I didn't remember feeling this way when she spoke to me in the gymnasium.

And then the forehead slapping moment. She was using a glamour to spread terror. It was subtly done, spreading out from her pores in such minute amounts it was hard to trace the magic. As much as I wanted to throw up my shields to shut out the terror, if I did I'd broadcast my null immunity. I needed her believing I was helpless.

I had one shot at this. No luxury to use my magic store on anything but what I planned.

Universe, Gabriel. Hold on. Had she injured him already?

"I believe I will kill your lover and make you watch. Then, I will kill you."

She kicked him in the side, forcing a grunt from his gagged mouth. His eyes spoke volumes to me, urging me to wait. Urging me to stay steady. They insisted his pain was nothing to our purpose. I wanted to argue back. My eyes were clogged with the tears that I knew must not fall. Not here. Not now.

Figure it out, Rachel. How is she powerful with these nulls all over the place?

I took my time and looked her over. There, at her neck, hung a pendant, and she never wore necklaces. The piece was complex, many small precious jewels with fine gold latticework wrapping the faceted stones. A fae tool she'd crafted, somehow blocking the effects of the nulls and allowing her to use her magic.

I needed to get close to remove the pendant. My free hand rested against my hip near the lip of the bag hanging over my shoulder. *Deep breath, Rachel.*

Solinthe squatted next to Gabriel and lifted her dagger. With a lightning move, she sliced a red line on the skin of his arm. Laughed. Then raised the point back to stab.

"Wait!" I lunged forward, throwing my body into hers. We fell back. Too easy. She let me push her away and I kept my power to myself, using mundane strength.

She grabbed my neck, still laughing, her fae will constricting the muscle and withering the skin of my neck. She squeezed. It hurt. The choking and the terror made my sight dim. Her face so close to mine. No shields, I watched the open glee in her eyes.

My hands wanted to grab onto Solinthe's and pull them away. Instead, I kept my grip on my own knife and used the other and fumbled by my side, fingers digging for the bag. Feeling open the pouch. Fighting to stay conscious. Where was it?

Cold steel. Thin cylinder. Hollow; one edge with a pointed lip. My tap. The fae tool I'd crafted.

Solinthe's face was eager, anticipatory.

In one disjointed move, I stabbed the tap into her side and opened up my magic store.

She screamed as I began my drain, siphoning her power, sending it not into me, but down into the core of the earth. Her grip loosened around my neck as she threw her magic at me, the Kyn shields I barely raised in time taking the brunt of her attack. I'd kept ahold of my dagger. Barely.

I drank in ragged breaths of air, coughing.

She fell back from me, reaching for the cylinder, trying to pull it out. The barbs I'd implanted to pop out after impact did their work keeping it caught. Plus, this was a fae tool. My will delivered it to act on its purpose. My throat burned, my skin burned, all of the cells in my body burned with the force of my power.

Solinthe snarled and vaulted back at me, her dagger in her grip aimed to do damage. I dodged to the side. I still needed to kill her, not simply drain her magic.

Instead of attacking again, she scurried back in a crouch, considering me. Noticing and cataloging.

More dangerous.

I coughed again and watched her carefully. "You've been jealous since the moment we met. I have what you don't. Two things. A soul and Gabriel's love. All you have is your madness. Lonely, perverted madness."

Her lip twisted and she tried to shake the magic drain. I saw her throw her power at the tap. She slowed it. Damn. The power draining to the earth became a trickle.

"You want my soul, come and get it," I said. I threw up a spell, weaving a quick knotted pattern.

My aura flared, the brightness a temporary blind before it settled into pulsing colors. Enticing. Even I was dazzled by my own glow. I needed her closer and while her power was reduced by some of the drain.

"Cut it from me," I taunted.

She waited. And waited. Shit, it wasn't working.

"You want to be loved, Solinthe. No one will ever love you without a soul. Because without a soul, you can't love back. Eternal loneliness is your doom."

She leapt.

Slammed my body.

I grabbed her wrist as she tried to sink the dagger, my other hand pushing her chest off of mine while I gripped my own blade. It scraped us both, blood welling in my palm.

Dammit, more Rachel!

Grabbing.

Almost. Shit, she was strong.

Universe, the tip of her knife was close. My fingers tangled in the chain around her neck. One good yank. The pendant broke from her neck. I stole more precious energy from my store and sent a flare of Kyn fire blasting into the jewels.

We burned together. My dragon unfurled inside. Roared fierce pleasure, wanting her death.

Solinthe screamed as her fae pendant burnt to ashes. As her magic died with the bodies and bodies of nulls stacked in the halls, and her with no protection.

Her strength faded in a sudden rush and I flipped her off of me, to her back. The blood of my palm made my hold on my dagger slippery. The cylinder tapping her magic rocked back into full force, draining her power in a torrent.

Her eyes widened with fear. Fear as she saw her death.

I repositioned my dagger, pushed her face to the side with my palm, and stabbed her neck behind the ear, pulling the blade down and forward until it ripped into the carotid. Severing.

My will cut her life. Blood gushed up and covered me as she frothed and jerked in her draining blood. Her eyes opened wide with a look of shock.

She died. Beneath my red, dripping hands.

The power of her life force erupted up and out, too much for the tap, overflowing and rushing at me. It rolled over my body in a crashing wave, throwing me back.

I slammed into the mirrored wall, the shattering shards of glass biting into my back. The magic ate into my cells, force feeding them to the point of bursting. I was pain, nothing more. Raw. Molten. Eternal. Wishing for death just to stop it.

Then black.

Chapter Twenty-six

"You don't have to do this." Qest's frowning brow mirrored the concerned insistence in his words.

"Of course I do. My people need it and more importantly, they deserve it. Too much is about to go down in too short a time."

"You're still in pain."

"I'll be in pain until I work the spell. There's no getting around that."

Since killing Solinthe, my body was on excruciating overload, the energy from her death shoved inside all of my cells until they felt they would burst. Lillith's suggestion had a purpose after all, giving me the boost I'd need for my plans.

But despite the pain, the dumbfounded expressions on the crowd in front of me meant I needed to speak. I stood at the foot of my throne in the merkaz, surrounded by the hundreds and hundreds of residents of Eden's Court. Those still alive at least.

Gabriel was at my side, quiet. He knew. And to my right, Morven, who also understood. My youngest brother, however, wore his heart on his sleeve, and his protective brotherly instincts were on full throttle and aimed at me.

All of the Kesayim leadership were present. Satan, Kemuel, Gwen, Natalya, Aubrey, and, ironically, Ivryind, standing as the highest ranking surviving fae. He looked more stupefied than almost anyone else present.

I had woke after my battle with Solinthe ringed by fae warriors. Every fae in existence felt their queen's death. Maybe the entire planet felt her death. She'd been alive since Lillith created the first Kesayim at the dawn of humanity. So their numb confusion made them easy to lead in my first conscious moments. They walked as virtual zombies, following my orders to untie Gabriel and the nulls with no protest. After that, Gabriel took one look at me and began issuing the commands. Then he got me home.

And here I was with my people. Tarn and Sebastian stood at the front of the masses. Sebastian's eyes were rimmed with red. Tarn's delicate face was turned to granite, a cut jagged grimness. They stood rigid not quite next to one another, and the distance they'd put between one another started another round of clenching in my gut.

I stepped up onto the dais high enough for the crowds to see me, and knotted out the spell for my voice to be broadcast to everyone. "Friends," I began. "Yesterday, our community faced a tragedy unlike any other. The divides that have plagued our peoples came to a head and we were attacked from within. Kesayim died. Many good people sacrificed themselves to protect the vision of Eden's Court, a place where we're meant to come together. In the end, we won. I am glad. And I'll be glad again when we save our world. We will save it.

"You have been told the reasons for why the Earth's core is disintegrating. We've found a solution in the form of a spell, but it means change for each and every one of you. Change to your bodies, your way of life, your magic. Everything will change."

I watched the crowds shift in place, murmuring their discomfort, whispering questions. But I couldn't lie to them. Not when so much lay ahead. "We will become a single species. All of the Kesayim and all of mortal humanity who you call Achra. We can face this and remake our world. Our alternative is destruction, and there's been enough death. The old ways have nourished you for millennia. None of us will ever forget. But they are not enough for us to survive any longer."

A voice called from the crowd. "Is the faerie queen really dead?"

"Yes." The picture of her covered in red with her eyes wide with protest, shock and desperation flooded through my vision.

"You are sure?"

"I killed her. I am sure."

Then Tarn's ragged voice erupted, edged with anger. "Did she suffer?"

Universe, Tarn. This was not the place. But he needed something. So did the others who'd lost loved ones to her attack.

"I believe so," I answered quietly.

I wanted to say more, hesitating because there were no good words really.

Instead, a rumbling, tearing sound echoed through my ears. I started to lose my balance, the entire dais undulating as the leaves and limbs of nearby trees toppled to the ground. A quake. We were so close to the end.

The crowds called out in surprise and fear, bodies falling into one another as they tried to grab onto any security. The garden screeched and Gabriel grabbed me off the dais before I fell, throwing us to the grass to wait out the tremor, sheltering me under his body.

After a long five minutes, the earthquake ended.

I stood, scanning the area, brushing off dirt. The new scrapes at my hands and knees were nothing to the abuse I'd recently survived. My gaze hit the Japanese maple. It had split, its trunk leaning over to touch the ground virtually severed from its base.

No! My tree.

"Are you alright?" Gabriel asked.

Words choked my throat.

He followed my gaze and sighed. "I am sorry, love."

I nodded, dragged in a breath, and headed out among my people to help them, promising myself to finish my plans and try the damn spell tomorrow. Life's usually a bunch of grey, but this was all or nothing, black or white, life or death.

* * * * *

The table map in Mother's Rest was black. All black. The roiling mist bubbled darkly dense on its surface. The walls enclosed me, bearing down, raising my pulse as it throbbed strong and fast in my throat.

The presence of this place was just like the portals; a link to the alien beings that had orchestrated the entire mess of our existence. I hated them. I loved them.

Without them, I would never have existed and never had to face the impossible task tomorrow.

Fuck the bunch of them. I couldn't stay here longer. I'd reached a decision about my plan and my exhaustion was a lead weight pressing each square inch of skin. I clamored up the spiral staircase and slammed out of the wooden door.

Gabriel, I expected to find waiting, calmly leaning against the wall of the hallway. But not Tarn and Seb, although there they were. My fae guard stood with arms crossed over his chest, still grim granite. Sebastian, next to him, was anything but.

He stormed up to me, a hands-length away, face contorting with anger. "You weren't planning on bringing us tomorrow?"

My cheeks went hot. "No."

Tarn snorted. "I told you."

Sebastian rounded on him. "Shut up!"

My shifter guard turned back to me. I owed him an explanation. "You've been through a lot. I thought you'd do better with space."

"That's the problem with everyone. They think they fucking know what's best."

The accusation slammed my chest. "Seb, I don't know."

Tarn stalked closer to Sebastian, controlled fury in the clench of his fist resting at the hilt of his sword. "Leave her alone. You do not have to be a hero in every scenario and fight the good fight, or do what is noble. If Rachel does not want us at the spell site, suck it up. She can save the planet without you."

"And do what? Stay back to savor the joys of being ignored by you?"

"I am not ignoring you."

"Of course you fucking are. You've checked out," he yelled.

"You might use this opportunity to re-evaluate what you want, Sebastian," Tarn accused.

The shifter's growl set my skin standing as Sebastian pushed into Tarn, chest to chest. "You think I only decided to marry you because of Del-, Delta." He stumbled over her name and inhaled a long shuddering breathe. "You Prick. You don't think much of me, do you?"

"Ridiculous. And untrue. But I know you too well. Better than you know yourself. Give it time, because after the freshness of our grief, you will leave me. I do not care for my heart to be sliced from my chest twice. I am giving you what you want whether you realize it or not."

The air trembled with a tight rage pausing around Sebastian. Then, the storm broke.

"Fucking asshole." Sebastian raised his fist and slammed it into Tarn's face, the fae falling back as Seb charged into him and hit him again as they fell to the floor.

Dammit! The two of them went at it, slamming punches. Elbows. Fists. Grunting contact. I backed up and turned to Gabriel who still watched saying nothing, his brow furrowed as our friends beat the shit out of each other.

"Stop them," I said.

"Not yet."

"Why the hell not?" I barked.

"They need this."

Screw that, this was a time for healing not more destruction. They loved each other.

"Stop it," I screamed, and waded over to separate them. They rolled again in their battle and I stumbled, the fall jarring my hip. An elbow got me in the stomach and I doubled over lacking the ability to breathe.

Energy spun active around me and Gabriel was there. "ENOUGH!" his dragon roared. My own dragon stirred inside me, intrigued.

Damn, love, you'll end it now that I got whacked?

Between my sucking back oxygen, Gabriel grabbed Sebastian's vest and pulled him off of Tarn. He shoved my guard feet away and glared at both men. "I would let the two of you go several more rounds, but I need to keep Rachel intact and she will only get hurt more or drain her needed magic trying to break up the battle."

Their ragged inhales punctuated the new silence of the hallway, the sound raw against their throats.

I sat up and rubbed my temple with a squeeze. Universe, I needed sleep. Or a massage. Yep, a massage would do it. Oh yeah, Rachel, can't schedule one of those until after tomorrow.

Gabriel continued, staring at his friends with an intense look of love and frustration. "You are angry. Of course you are and you are entitled to it. Delta is dead. She died doing her job, but that is no salve. There is nothing to say or do that changes the loss. Nothing to make it better. Tomorrow, Rachel will save us and we will help her as we can, but even with my confidence in her success, there is still a chance we die. Is this how you want to spend your last night together? The anger will keep. Do yourselves a favor, honor Delta and hold each other instead of tearing each other apart."

He bent over to me and wrapped his large hand around my bicep, helping me stand. "You are fine?"

"Yes," I nodded.

Everything hurt. My body, my cells, my heart.

"Please, guys," I said to my guard. "Join me tomorrow, but just be kind to each other tonight."

Tarn's eyes were squeezed shut while tears leaked down Sebastian's face. I went over to my fae friend and kissed his cheek. Then did the same to Sebastian's. "I love you both."

There was nothing more I could do for them. I gestured Gabriel to me and we began to move down the hall toward my suite. I turned back and saw Tarn rising, walking to Sebastian. I saw him brush Seb's cheek with his fingertips, lean in, and whisper, resting his skull against his lover's.

I sighed out and pressed my hip against Gabriel's as we walked, the connection steadying me as I placed one foot in front of the other.

Tomorrow.

Chapter Twenty-seven

"Take breaks. Lots of breaks."

Morven raised an eyebrow, silently accusing me of stating the obvious and questioning my sanity all at once. Her underwhelming response to my insistence kept my muscles rigid as planks. My seneschal was one of dozens of volunteers who would trade off amongst themselves to keep the portals open between Eden, all seven Kesayim realms, and mortal Earth. That meant each standing inside the abyss of portal blackness for a good chunk of time. If my plan worked and I distributed the magical virus mortal-side to evolve the DNA of the planet's population, then the open portals would allow the airborne virus to filter back to infect the Kesayim. I hoped.

If I could have guaranteed successful release of the virus twice, I'd infect the Kesayim directly in Eden. I couldn't. Even the first time around might crash and burn. In case the virus didn't filter through the portals, I'd send the infected Kesayim I was toting with me today back to their respective realms to infect their fellow species.

We stood by an unfamiliar portal with a direct link to the continent of Africa. Pungent herbs grew around us in clusters, half wilted. Dying. The garden purred with excitement even as the magic of the earth evaporated, browning tracks of previously verdant green. I wanted to cry. The tears wouldn't come. No time.

The garden crumbled into a brittle husk as a few hundred other volunteers from all the Kesayim stood in queue waiting to accompany me through the gateway. The dozens of mortal shifter kids ran around swinging sticks at one another and generally fomenting chaos. Aubrey and his helpers would have their hands full. The kids and their shifter minders would travel through the gateway almost last, to be proceeded and followed by the angels and demons as their extra guard.

"You look like you've swallowed a rancid morsel," Satan said, bedecked in his best Armani suit, today's button reading *Welcome to the End of the World.*

Figures.

"You do realize that a suit may not be appropriate fashion for a rift valley with erupting volcanos?" I answered.

"If I'm going to go out, I intend to do it with panache."

"Your people are ready?"

"My demons are all prepared to protect the poor little tykes so they can make your magic cleaner and smoother. And we will act as table food for you to grow more super-creature DNA."

"Not table food." Geez, he insisted on provocation to the very last. "I need to have Kesayim on hand with blended DNA to culture some of it into more virus and bring it back here to spread to the rest of the Kesayim in case the cloud doesn't make it through the portals well."

"I stand corrected. Not table food. Lab rats. Or growth medium, however you insist on stating the facts."

"Just get them ready to move. Once I go through, each Kesayim group will enter the portal one by one."

"Ignore Satan, my lady," Kemuel added. "We will do our jobs." His wings unfurled and he gave a single flap for emphasis. The competition never ended between he and Satan. I suspected they insisted on staying near one another on this journey simply because they refused to let the other out of their vision as the gene therapy magic overtook them.

Everyone was present. Jasper and his wife were overseeing the witch contingent as Gwen was busy helping Qest with the Kyn. I'd asked each of the six remaining Kesayim peoples to offer twenty-five or so volunteers of the level headed, stable type. Aside from the mortal shifter kids, the only other kids were Peter, Anna, and Gregor. But any children on this mission made me uneasy.

Okay, girl. You do know every single kid on this planet is in just as much risk. I did not make myself feel better with that pep talk.

Qest pushed his way through the crowds to me from where he'd gathered all two hundred of the remaining Kyn. "How far outside Addis Ababa do we need to get before we shift to dragon form?"

"Far enough not to break any buildings or cause traffic accidents. Head north to get out of the city. It's the closest border. We'll be flying Northeast towards the Rift Valley. Don't worry about avoiding notice. Dragon sightings are the least of our problems. But don't go so far out of the city that the Kesayim you'll be transporting have to make a long trek. The whole point is making the three hundred plus mile trip to the volcano feasible."

He glanced back at the waiting group of Kyn, the lot of them pacing or stretching or sweating in their unfamiliar mortal forms. Every last one had come. "We need to send them through first after you. The sooner they change back into dragons the better. This form is an acquired taste they've yet to acquire."

"Qest, thank you for getting them ready so quickly. Whatever oratory feats you pulled off, they must be amazing. I needed them to make this work."

A sheepish grin met my thanks. "Gwen's to thank. Her ability to simultaneously charm and brow beat even a fish to walk on land is impressive." He paused and flushed a deep red. "But I owe you thanks for your push with Gwen. I'm not sure how it happened. She's...." He shook his head.

"You both needed each other. And she's too wise a woman not to see the gift you are, brother."

His embarrassment dropped away and he rested his hands on my shoulders. "If it had to take the loss of our parents and the twenty-five years we lost you to deliver us the extraordinary person you are, I don't regret it."

Satan rolled his eyes at us. "How sickeningly sweet."

When Qest let go, I kicked the demon in the shin. Not too hard, but hard enough. He snorted in response.

I turned back to my brother. "Tell me that again tomorrow and I'll bask in the praise."

He leaned in to kiss my forehead. "Let's go do this thing."

Walking toward the portal, I glanced at the quietest bunch of the queue standing near Leslie and Anna. The nulls captured by Solinthe had barely recovered from the trauma, not to mention the shock of their identities and role in the new world order. The rest of the nulls my people had collected for protection looked less glassy-eyed, but still stiff and pale. I would leave them behind if I saw any way around their participation. I didn't. Only my enhanced power had allowed me a quick jury-rig of fae crafted devices to be worn around their necks, suppressing their effects on the garden and Kesayim. Solinthe's pendant had given me the idea, although I used it in reverse to suppress the null power instead of protect the Kesayim magic. Each of the nulls wore a small pendant of an enhanced piece of geode I'd grabbed and adapted from Mother Heir stores. Who knew what goodies were stacked in storage.

I joined Gabriel, Tarn, and Sebastian who waited with somber faces. Their Save the world or else faces. It was now or never. Deep breath, and we stepped through into Addis Mercato, the largest open-air marketplace of Addis Ababa, Ethiopia.

Mortal Earth. My feet sank down into the ground, connected in a way they hadn't been for a long time. At ten in the morning, the sky was the dark of twilight, the ash from the multiple erupting volcanoes farther east blocking the sunlight. This plain old Earth may not have the vibrant colors of Kesayim realms, but it brought comfort in its weight. The ash muted color had taste, tangy and tart, sweet and sour.

A light rain filtered down on the surrounding markets. I caught my footing on the churned soil after almost slipping and beginning an auspicious day with my ass in the mud. Gabriel caught my arm and saved my dignity, although dignity was a casualty I'd gladly accept in this battle.

I hadn't expected the crowds of people milling through the markets examining tables, large blankets and booths spread out with goods. Booths were make-shift and pulled away from the buildings they typically abutted with those structures in various stages of destruction. Walls crumbled, fallen into mounds of jagged cement, metal, plastic.

Men sifted through the remains, lugging debris, searching, removing. A small bulldozer rumbled across the road, moving toward a dump truck already filled to overflowing with earthquake damage. Catch as catch can recovery whirred around us with market wares offered for sale between the piles of rubble moved into heaps to make way for life.

Even in the face of cataclysms, folks needed food and necessities. Men, women and children walked with a quick tightness to their stride, calling between each other, helping one another. Voices rumbled up and down. Some women wore hijabs, others straw hats to keep off the rain. Vegetables and spices exchanged hands. Bottled water. Shoes and head garb. Batteries.

It took a moment to register, but most of the vendors distributed goods without money. Some looked official, maybe part of a government effort. I wanted to go over to the tables and ask what was happening.

A warm burning radiated from my chest watching people come together. Saving each other's butts with the chaos of natural disaster literally exploding around them. How did they do it? My legs barely held me up anymore.

"Rachel, the spell." Gabriel called me back from my almost hypnosis.

"Sorry. Yeah." I breathed out and twisted the green and brown spell pattern of the homing beacon in front of the portal even as the first of the Kyn made their way through.

The spell was designed to show each member of our group the directions to the plateau near the volcano, like a personal GPS but without the annoying voice in their ears telling them to take the next exit.

We caught curious stares from the crowds around us as person after person from our group arrived and exited out from around the edge of a nearby cement building, half in ruin. The citizens of Addis Ababa flowed around the Kesayim, too distracted by the necessity of staying alive to bother with strangers as long as those strangers didn't disrupt their purpose.

We sent the Kyn off toward the city's edge and began the long process of supervising the rest of the arrivals. The overfull feeling kept sliding around inside me. If I couldn't release the virus soon, I would explode as surely as our planet.

Next came the witches, followed by the fae, then vampires, then angels, then the shifter contingent with their mortal offspring. I wasn't exactly sure how their presence would assist, but they had a role. Magic flowed cleaner in their presence, and I needed all the clean I could get. After them trailed the demons.

Once we'd set them on their way out of the city, the nulls arrived. Gabriel went to Leslie and began providing the half-dazed people with rough directions. My homing beacons floated over the group, their suppressed null effects allowing it life. But this crew were equally freaked by the evidence of the magic and needed to rely on some traditional directions in case their confusion muddied their ability to rely on the glowing GPS. The plan was to make our way alongside this group to where the rest of the Kesayim waited outside the city, with Kyn transformed to dragon form and ready to fly us west.

With a last direction to Christian who helped herd these disoriented nulls, I turned to reconnect with Sebastian and give the signal to head out. Until I saw a flash in the corner of my eyesight.

Two short dark heads jogged across the far side of the market, fifty yards from me, their bubbling laughter floating over the crowd. Cotton candy light, playing hide and seek on the air. Behind them strode Lillith, wrapped in a robe to blend with the local population, calling to the children with a lower caw to slow their pace.

The children. Our children. Gabriel's and mine. The boy and girl from my visions. I stepped toward their direction.

"Rachel, we need to leave," Gabriel said.

"Did you see them?" I asked.

"Who?"

"Our children."

"Rachel." His voice dropped an octave, both question and centering anchor in my name.

Did I tell him? What was the point? Lillith's purpose and the impossibility of their presence were nothing I could understand. *Keep your focus, Rachel.*

Everything hurt, and we needed to get to the volcano. "It doesn't matter. Let's go."

"I do not believe you."

"I promise to share if it means something. Right now, I need to focus on our goal, otherwise I fall apart. Literally."

Gabriel stared me down for another long minute, then turned to send the nod to Sebastian and Leslie.

We started out of the city.

* * * * *

On the outskirts of Addis Ababa, we began the job of mounting skittish Kesayim, nulls and human shifter children onto the backs of equally skittish dragons. Released from human form, the Kyn exulted in a return to their natural shape. But that didn't keep them from hunching with displeasure and retreating a step as Qest, Gwen, and I divided the remaining group and cajoled them toward the lizards, hoisting each up on the backs of the reluctantly participating dragons.

Gwen, not actually able to carry anyone in her shadow dragon form, accompanied the nulls to supervise along with Christian and Leslie.

Aubrey and Sebastian chaperoned the shifter children, who whooped it up when they realized they'd be flying through the air on the backs of the Kyn. Qest had volunteered to carry them himself. At least someone was happy with our plan.

Satan, however, refused to fly with his demons, insisting he was entitled to ride on my back once I changed into my dragon form. "Status has its privileges," he said with a ridiculous smile.

This, of course, meant that Kemuel was coming with us as well. Fuck it that Gabriel had to ride between the two men who were ultimately responsible for his horrendous treatment most of his life. Gabriel rested a hand on my shoulder to keep me from throttling Satan.

He laid a gentle kiss on my cheek and directed me a distance away to complete my own transformation. I wished Gabriel could fly as his own dragon, but without the influence of Leslie's explosion of power, he couldn't make the change into his Kyn form. Not without the full code.

Like everyone else, he would soon be exposed to the viral load I carried in my body. Gene therapy. The virus, once released and airborne, would enter the world's population, magic woven into the virus to suppress immune systems so that the DNA could work its way replicating inside everyone's code. Last night had been spent growing the virus. Now I had to get to the delivery system portion of the program and pray the thing worked.

I jogged far enough away to find room to let out my dragon. Turning inward, I stroked her and called my welcome. Already interested in the many Kyn around her, and always wanting to come play, she purred a response and leapt to her freedom.

My body changed, stretched into the full and beautiful form that brought such pleasure. Scales and claws and fire slid into being and both she and I celebrated. In the past, I'd lost myself to my dragon, but I'd practiced retaining control. After a few moments of glee, I gave a firm command and returned to Satan and Gabriel to begin the journey.

Gabriel jumped atop me with a single leap, which sounds more illicit than it actually was. Satan made a typical comment with, "My, what big teeth you have, Grandma." Although he did have an admiring gleam in his expression as he said it. I only wished I could make a snack of him in one bite to give him his just fairytale desserts. But the demon limited his comments to the one and leapt up after Gabriel, Kemuel following.

The dark, soot-filled sky beckoned and I gave into the call. Dragon after dragon took to the skies after me, flying east. Launching with their passengers clinging to their scales in amazement or terror or both, I listened to the Kyns' telepathic exchange. They spoke of their relief reconnecting to mortal Earth, reminiscing over their long-ago practice of dwelling in solitary splendor in the mundane world.

Even though we flew over mostly non-habitable terrain, the Kyn felt the world around us, touching the four corners of Earth, alive with a curiosity none of them had felt in thousands of years. They mourned the chaos and destruction plaguing the villages and cities, killing people, rending the earth.

Through our telepathic link, I tasted the desolation they now found. Cataclysm. Fear. Death. A bitter, metallic burning taste of grit and toxin. The images were mine for the taking, but the choice I'd made to block them out and to stay focused on my goal was subverted by the stream of information overflowing from my fellow dragons. Their grief woke the basic nature of their beasts. One of empathy and love; the Goddess's mandate alive in their species. Perhaps a love stronger than any of the other Kesayim felt for Achra, dwarfing that of vampire and angel.

From my right, I heard Roq's demand as he glided beside me. "What you plan will save them?" His desperation was jagged and astringent.

I flew faster. "I hope."

After dozens of calls of dismay poured into my mind from the other Kyn, I'd had enough and erected a shield.

Although this was the first time my body felt at ease since I'd filled it with virus, the substantial size increase finally giving me room to breathe, it was time to take advantage of that space. My wings caressed the airwaves, heading ever eastward as I focused within and flicked power at the virus, stirring it into replication, filling my now larger to the brim.

"Rachel?" Gabriel sent me mind to mind when he felt me reinitiate the replication.

"I need more."

"You are draining yourself too low."

"Sing to me. That will help."

He stopped speaking. Knowing him, processing my favor. And then, because he is the man I love beyond all others; the man who knows just how much to push and how much to let me be; how much to reach out and touch my soul with the lightest of brushes; he sang. An angel's lullaby, the lyrical language soothing, lightening the pain, like being wrapped in the softest down. The soft notes brought me back to the first time Gabriel had sung them to me. My first night in Eden when I'd seen the vision of his childhood and woke crying from the pain of it in his arms, his hands stroking my hair.

"Rest softly my dearest, my wings will wrap you, Rest safe in my arms."

He repeated the beautiful verse over and over as we flew. Not only within my mind, but aloud as well. Satan said nothing, perhaps listening as intently as I. Kemuel as well. When angels sing, the world weeps with the beauty. It holds its collective breath, listening. If Satan ever mourned the demons' severing from their angelic heritage, here was more than enough reason.

As the virus multiplied and filled this larger body to its limits, as the pain set in once more pushing against my skin, the song soothed me and kept me flying. Soothed my fear. Soothed the sick knots of an unknown future.

Again, I thought of that first night in Eden when I was just as scared, just as unaware of what the future might bring. I'd survived and found friendship, belonging, and purpose. Not for a moment did I regret Jack's fateful visit to me in my Watertown home.

Everything from that day forward had led to this morning's destination, the Rift Valley of East Africa. Filled with volcanos, the entire area was one gigantic center for seismic activity even before we'd hit a crisis of world destruction. And to boot it was a crucial site for human evolution with many well-preserved human and animal fossils found throughout the valley with ideal conditions for proliferation of life. A cradle of humanity, bearing witness to the whole human evolution in the last million years, ever since Lillith wove her creations. But was it to be the key to the future of humanity?

Below me, the volcanoes of the Rift Valley were small dots against the ground. With a nod to my fellow Kyn, I dove into the passing downdraft, pulling up against the force to level as we approached our target, 353 miles from Addis Ababa.

There it was. Dalafilla; a perfect cone-shape volcano almost 2000 feet at its highest point. Prior to now, it had last erupted in 2008, the biggest eruption ever recorded in Ethiopia. The Sulphur Dioxide plume had extended over the Arabian Peninsula, Pakistan, Northern India, and had reached even Japan's Marshall Islands half way around the world. Highly active and constantly erupting these last few months, I counted on its power to help me in my plan.

I stuck the landing with a small jolt as my four clawed feet touched the warmed earth. Passengers dismounted, Gabriel moving to gather the other groups to direct them in the next steps.

Qest, Jasper, Christian, Sebastian, and Tarn gathered near. I couldn't change back to regular Rachel shape. The amount of virus I now carried was too large to fit my body. Qest was still in dragon form. I'd need every last dragon to fly the skies soon enough.

The men each reached out to lay a hand on my scaled hide. Qest snaked his tail to brush it against me in comfort. The rain and the distant rumbling roar of the eruptions made it difficult to hear.

"We love you," Christian called over the noise.

If dragons could shed tears, I'd be drowning the crew of them about now. Instead, I tilted my head in a nod.

"They know you feel the same without needing a response," Qest spoke mind to mind.

Gabriel joined us and calmly sent them on their way with last instructions. He turned to me and leaned in to place a kiss against my scaled haunches. *"Soon, love,"* he sent to me.

The Kesayim, mortals and nulls spread out into a large circle on the plain to the side of Dalafilla, placed in the exact configuration we had planned. The Kyn perched directly behind the ring, a second circle mirroring the first. We were all distant enough from the peak to keep from burning up from the heat or being washed by the lava flow and ash.

Gabriel joined me at the center of the circle. Even this far from the volcano, the rain mixed with soot to cover everyone, the crowd a dingy brown and soaked to the skin.

The group stood still in the moment, even the children, pressed into immobility by the weight of terrible possibility. The last minutes of existence, or the first. The strain of it left eyes squinting and faces taut as they waited for me.

Closing my eyes, I beckoned the stores of virus in my body to migrate, using will and intent to activate the RNA and give them purpose. The magic was dying. I drew down on the earth, skimming every bit of energy possible to push it toward my goal. The planet's crust was shattering, the reserves drained away. My dragon stirred the fire inside her and drew in a deep breath.

She exhaled, fire rushing to my nostrils. At the last moment, I transfigured the fire into cool mist, folding a small bit of the virus into the spaces between the droplets.

I blew out with one target in mind.

Gabriel. Positioned barely three feet from my snout, he was enveloped in the cloud. He inhaled the vapor with a deep expansion and contraction of his chest and belly. His eyes closed, his body quivered as he struggled to remain still.

I watched carefully, praying for success. He opened his pine green eyes, glazed with whatever effect coursed through him, and nodded. Universe, I wanted to know if it had worked. But the minimum I hoped for was knowing he survived.

Gabriel kept standing. Alive. Next test passed.

Damn, Rachel, no time girl. Just do it. In the end, it wouldn't matter. There was no alternative.

I inhaled another deep breath, and this time, blew with a billowing force, folding in large amounts of the virus. For a shaky moment, the magic stuttered, weakened. Finally, the virus swirled out in a cloud of vapor and engulfed the circle of our waiting group.

Gabriel straightened and flagged a signal to Aubrey and Leslie. As a whole, the crowd of nulls ripped off the geode pendants blocking their power and threw them behind and away from the circle. The flare of their effect shone bright as it bounced off of the mortal shifter children positioned strategically among them by Aubrey. I counted on the emotion of the moment to trigger the nulls.

The cloud of virus met the flare and sparkled, invigorating the potency of the concoction as my people inhaled, coughing and sputtering. Some fell to their knees on the muddy ground while many simply swayed, hanging onto one another as the virus infiltrated and wrought its changes.

My body used its newfound space to start making more virus. The flutter of internal activity stretched out against my skin, distracting. Universe, focus.

Through the rain, I examined our folk. Had it taken? Were they stable? We'd cautioned everyone to wait before testing the changes. Gabriel gestured again and Tarn stepped forward into the circle.

Sebastian moved next to him and bent to speak into his ear. The fae nodded in acknowledgement. Sebastian stepped back. Tarn paused, sent an irreverent gesture Seb's way, then Tarn's body blurred. Shifted.

In its place sat a gorgeous white wolf who sneezed twice, tested out his four pawed legs, and sending a glance up to Seb, leapt farther into the circle. Up into the air, and up, and up, galloping above the ground by ten feet with vampiric levitation. Opening his toothy, incisor jaws as he flew, he sang; an angelic tune of order and beauty. Nothing that was meant to come out of a wolf's mouth.

He raced through the air over to Gabriel and me and landed. His form blurred again. Tarn, in his normal fae body, knelt before us, head bowed. After a pregnant moment, he looked up at us, a wide grin painting his face.

Tarn yelled over the rain and eruption, the wet causing his white gold locks to hang limp around his shoulders, although the devil was still as handsome as ever. "I think it worked, my lady. Still, I have yet to work witch magic, stir demon chaos, or shift to Kyn form. A bit of a gut churning sensation, but the fizzy bubble feeling within my bloodstream is well worth the new power. Seb's been keeping shifter fun to himself, the lout."

I tried to smile back a dragon smile. Not sure it translated, but Tarn seemed to get the point.

"Gabriel, cue Gwen for her part," I sent my lover.

Another waving gesture by Gabriel at the witch, and she was running in our direction, her body growing mid-stride. Expanding. Expanding. Into a dragon, the change complete as she met us.

Her cerulean blue-skinned dragon with blood red spikes was no longer a shadow form. She was Kyn in fact. And now I knew the rest of the gathering could return to the Kesayim realms, access this shape, and spread the virus among those peoples just as I had.

My senses shot down through the earth's crust to feel out the magic. Still weak, almost gone. I'd hoped even with this first modest change... But expecting several hundred evolved people to replenish a world full of magic was a fool's fantasy.

Fine, next step, Rachel. Another barely accessible twist of fae magic and I sent a shock wave of intent over everyone including myself, starting the creation of virus inside their bodies from their newly whole DNA structure. Worried that the virus would form diluted, I'd planned for an added layer of spell, using their existing genetic codes to each strengthen the components of the corresponding sections of evolved code. Healthy code from Kyn, witches, faeries, vampires, angels, demons, shifters, nulls, and mortal shifter children. Then the energy twisted the forming viral RNA, adjusting its expression to add a sleeper element to the change. Six months. Full powers would slowly emerge over six months' time, giving everyone a chance to adjust to a new reality. This original group with immediate powers could assist everyone in the transition. The same sleeper delay would now be true of the virus delivered to mortal humanity.

A few of the crowd jolted with this second change. Universe, this was a lot to ask of them. There was no alternative.

"It is growing," Gabriel confirmed over the roar for me when the virus started forming under his own skin. He turned to our friend. "Take them home, Tarn." Then my lover and best friend, wet and weary himself, rested his hand against my haunches. "You and I have work to do, my love."

Chapter Twenty-eight

Gabriel's dragon form thrilled me all over again. Obsidian with pine green spikes. My mate. The humming appreciation woke me up, much needed with my tank empty and the soil crying.

The original Kyn, impatient to fly, waited for us in the circle after Gabriel's change. Qest included. They wouldn't be returning to Addis Ababa with everyone else. I needed their millennia of experience to help me guarantee delivery of the virus worldwide. I needed them to fly to the four corners, dump the virus, and pray that it was enough along with my volcano plan.

Qest waited for my word, impatient. Whether to end this interminable wait of not knowing or to begin life fresh, I didn't bother to ask. I wasn't sure myself which I craved anymore.

"I love you," I said to him.

"I love you back, sister."

"Stay away from knights with dragon-slaying swords."

"They're busy running from impending doom. Too busy to worry about little 'ole me."

"Maybe. I just need you back soon because we're going to start our own band. I'm inspired by Gwen's brother. I'm lead vocals. You can play sax or base or ukulele. Maybe didgeridoo."

"Musical. Like our father."

"Like our father."

He blew a whiff of smoke at me, thumped me with his tail, and called to the rest of the Kyn to fly. Lift off. Spreading in all directions. Wings beating until the small dots of their mass winked out of sight.

Gabriel and I turned to Dalafilla and launched into the air.

Kyn tolerated heat and ash well enough, although on our first approach, the visibility sucked. Whispering a small spell in my mind, I cleared our view on ascent. Closer. Closer. We needed to drop our spray of virus into the volcano to make use of the plume.

Closer. We tilted into a bank of air to position ourselves over the cone. Almost there. We'd position ourselves over the opening and blow out the viral load.

Then, Gabriel broke ranks in one confusing moment and circled back. *"Rachel, wait. Look, on the edge of the cone."*

Oh, Universe. There they were. The three of them. Lillith and our children, bodies buffeted by the spray of gas and molten ash. Little hands pushed hair away from their faces where it kept blowing forward with the wind.

Lillith's familiar grating singsong voice filled our heads. *"Your price, dearest daughter. My people decided. Sacrifice these children and they will allow this world to continue if your part of the plan works."*

Knifing disbelief. No!

Fight back. She was bluffing to cause trouble. Had to be. *"We are already saving it."*

"You are setting circumstances which would allow it to survive if you had enough time. Even now it is

unclear whether the new genetic code will take root in time. The magic is almost gone, and you still need it until your seed is spread. But even the mutated genes well planted in all of humanity will not replenish the magic before my precious Earth falls apart. Take their deal and save it. You've solved the puzzle, but you need their cooperation."

"Fuck you."

"I don't believe that offer is on the table, dearest. But I have waited too long to see my vision bear fruit. These children are not even real. They are only possibility. I will not lose an entire world due to your squeamish sensibilities."

"Why this price? What good comes of it?" Gabriel demanded, pulling hard to the side and circling to stay close enough to our children, as if there was some move he might make to sweep them to safety. If you listened carefully, you heard the slight fray to his voice.

Impossibly, it was our dark-haired dimpled daughter who answered, and I swallowed her smooth, clear voice. *"How else are they to know that you surrender to the true unknown of future? Humanity, even with this evolution, is not a perfect and completed story."*

Our son leaned over and pecked her cheek. *"Besides, all choice comes with consequence. A price to pay does not always diminish. Sometimes it enlarges."*

Give up a future to guarantee some future. With no damn way to know what that future meant or even if it would work. Although, apparently, it meant no children. My dragon's fire burned hotter in my belly, sputtering and flaring back and forth around the store of virus. The virus that needed out so we might live. A bargain of death for life.

"Rachel," Gabriel called. *"I cannot make this choice. It is yours."* Tears beaded his voice.

So I was to believe that the sacrifice was noble and made the survival of our world that much more valuable. Fuck that. It was loss plain and simple. No bows to dress it up. Just a permanent hole in my chest where joyful hope was to be cut away. My wings flapped sluggish against the wind. My heart shriveled and expanded and shriveled again, shifting in my chest in a chaotic dance of pain, and love.

Love, acceptance, letting go. Here again the lesson. I hated this damn lesson. The dark heads of my maybe children looked up at my dragon. They smiled at me and nodded.

Wings keeping me hovering in indecision. Pause. And pause again. The magic leached from me, making it harder to stay airborne. No. No. No. Pause. Fuck. There was no choice after all.

So I answered. *"Okay, Lillith,"* I said.

The goddess tilted her head.

My children stretched up arms to wave. "Bye, Mother, Father."

They turned in unison. And jumped into the cone.

Gabriel's cry was the snap of a tree branch, sudden and wrenching. Then silent.

Our never children.

My wings faltered again.

The cone smoked constantly, steady discharge, the viscous magma spurting out the top, gas and ash erupting into the air.

I dragged the virus through my body toward its exit. *"Gabriel, we need to do this now."*

"Yes," he said. If his voice was tight I couldn't focus on it now. His obsidian body flew next to mine and we made our descent.

"Now!"

We dumped the virus, the steam blowing out from Gabriel and me over the center of the activity, letting the force propel it upward along with the columns of gas and ash. Almost drained, I focused my will on the plume and Gabriel joined his magic with mine, forcing the clouds of material to travel further, higher into the atmosphere, to extend their travel to spread over the entire globe.

Again and again we expelled the virus.

Until nothing remained. Empty.

The magic stuttered again. I grabbed for enough to stay in Kyn form and keep airborne. Nothing.

"Gabriel, land!"

We dove away and down, back toward the plateau. I was losing my dragon, my bones shrunk, falling.

The solid ground rushed up and gleefully called out to me in welcome. I kept my wings long enough to lighten impact. Thunk! I slammed shoulder and arm down after rolling the last yards to avoid my head. Pain, hot and screaming, lanced through me, breath absent from my lungs the only thing keeping me from yelling in agony.

Tick. Tick. Tick. Unable to count time passing. Finally, my brain woke. Something was cradling my head. Skin. Hands. Oh, and there were words. A visual blur.

"Rachel?"

Then the blurry mass bobbing in my vision cleared.

Gabriel.

"Hey," I think I said.

His face was covered in mud. "Can you move your body? Go slow."

"Landing hurt."

"Yes, love."

"How are you upright?"

"I had enough power left for my other wings."

"Angel. Damn, I forgot. Or I could have shifted to some bird. I'm awful at this." I got to work wiggling my limbs and ruling out spinal damage to his satisfaction, and even sat up without blacking out, although it was close.

With no more magic for self-healing, I fought back nausea, hoping for a simple concussion and not skull fractures. "Will it work?" I asked. The damage from the fall didn't matter if the virus failed.

"I do not know."

Of course. How would he?

"You are here with me, that is all that matters," he said, and ran fingertips over my jaw, tenderness that I needed more than anything with glass for my soul. His kiss brought relief, a slow, sweet healing that soothed the layers of pain, chaos and heartbreak. Well, at least enough to be almost bearable.

My fingers rested on his breastbone, taking in the steady thump of his heart, so loud and clear.

Nothing blocked the sound. No beat of rain, no rumbling of volcano. I blinked into the distance. Dalafilla had fallen quiet. The clouds hung low and grey, but no longer spit drops.

Something...

"What's happening at the cone?"

A new rumbling began. What the hell?

White foam poured out of the top of Dalafilla, running down the sides in all directions. A buzzing carbonation frissoned through my bones. Expectant. Potent. I squinted to make out the foam.

My fingers dug into Gabriel and I must have jerked forward because he adjusted his hands to steady me.

"Uh...." My attempt at getting out the word failed spectacularly.

"Unicorns," he said.

Unicorns. Hundreds. Thousands. No, innumerable. The herd galloped over the ground, bodies dense as iron with their number, packing the soil with fleet hooves. Graceful and brutal both. Unending. Sculpted, beautiful bodies racing towards us. About to trample. Death by unicorn, although with the shock came acceptance.

Wet streamed my cheeks even as they met us. My breath stilled with quiet, full expectation, as they parted around the place we knelt, leaping over or to the side to race onward.

My pain melted back, and without realizing I had started drawing magic from the earth again, healing. With each moment of this flood the power reservoir of the world filled more. The passing of the unicorns planted health and vitality at every point of contact. Healing.

"Thank you, thank you," the only words I found, repeating them with mantra-like devotion.

In watching the beasts, I hit a hypnotic trance, unclear of how much time passed, and trembling with relief and awe. I came to as the mass of unicorns trickled to a halt, Dalafilla empty. My fingers ached with the vise grip I'd made of Gabriel's hand.

We stood alone on the plain. Although not quite. Stepping towards us, one solitary specimen. His horn was black dusted gold, his coat dark midnight.

Part of me wanted to bow, as if the unicorn waited for recognition of his royalty. Instead, I struggled to stand, Gabriel giving me a hand so I managed some grace. This was not my unicorn.

When the beast spoke, I knew its voice. "My kind will reserve judgment on the value of your world."

Oh. This was Lillith's peer, or father or whatever. The being from the portal back at the gymnasium battle. "If indeed it is redeemable, we will avoid the irrevocable error of destroying the planet. That may always come later."

"How kind," I answered, and dipped my head with all the cold condescension he deserved.

Gabriel nudged me to behave. Dammit, how did he expect me to control the attitude?

"It may be that your people kill themselves anyway in the chaos of mass transformation."

Cheery asshole.

"We'll manage." Screw him if I'd acknowledge having had the same thought.

"We will be watching."

"Counting on it," I said.

His horn dipped.

Then, he disappeared.

Just as well. There was nothing to do about Lillith and her folk. Our work remained despite them. Survive. Build. Grow.

My gaze drifted to Dalafilla's cone.

Love.

Gabriel drew me from my thoughts with a kiss at the back of my neck, and I shivered. "Come fly with me, Rachel. Let us see the world you have saved, and witness the unicorns' touch."

Our dragons flew. Cairo and Johannesburg, Paris, London, and Prague, Beijing, Mumbai, Montreal, New York, San Francisco, San Paulo, Buenos Ares, Lima. Even the tip of the Antarctic. Recovering all. The people stunned, but wearing expressions of relief, busy picking up mess, burying dead. No signs of physical changes from the virus, but that would be too soon to expect with my six-month sleeper spell. What we did spy were unicorns, bounding down streets and through crowds of shocked humans. With their passing came rebirth, green and solid land.

I should be thrilled. I'd fought for this for months now. Why couldn't I care?

Finally, Gabriel nudged me again toward the east coast of the United States and we glided over the Boston waterfront, turning then to Watertown where everything began months ago when I was just an unsuspecting gal making my way through mundane life on my own; everything changing that fateful April thirtieth on my twenty-fifth birthday when Jack pushed me out of the way of the speeding car near my two-family and introduced me to the wacky world of magic and Kesayim.

From the skies, I spied the same Armenian family restaurant I'd visit on a Sunday afternoon if my pennies added to something greater than nothing. The same drab laundromat I'd frequent once a week to do my laundry.

The yellow buses of the MBTA stood unmoving in the Watertown streets after the chaos. Soon, they'd chug to life to allow commuters to cut across the greater Boston area and get to work. I'd been one of those commuters.

Dragon form cut through the commuting hassles, and soon enough, all that humanity knew about the limits of their daily existence would shatter and reform. Universe, what would it bring?

Residents of the suburban streets gazed up seeing our approach. We landed in the nearest green park and melted back to our natural bodies. A child nearby pointed with a shout. "They were dragons. Where's their fire?" Others stood mouth-gaped. A cop pedaled toward us on a bicycle.

Out from behind the closest church, a unicorn sprung and raced across the green. Then another. Another. The policeman shifted paths and spoke into his radio as he pursued the beasts. People screamed out in fear and awe and glee seeing the unicorns.

"Come on," Gabriel said, grabbing my arm and pulling us into a run. Shifter power had us fleet of foot, and we outdistanced the witnesses to our transformation.

We galloped, Gabriel directing us down sidewalks and roadways. The race woke life in me the dragon flight hadn't. Or maybe it was the connection with a place I'd once called home. Excitement got my veins rushing a carbonated flood. My lips stretched upward and I laughed.

"Stop here, love," my companion called.

We braked and I realized our location. My old street, just feet from the front door of my apartment in the yellow two-family.

I turned to Gabriel. "How did you find it?"

"Morven," he said.

Of course.

He walked up to the door and turned the doorknob.

I grabbed his hand. "Wait, other people must live here now."

"No, they don't," he said.

"How do you know?"

"Morven."

Of course.

The door opened easily, unlocked.

"No key?" I asked.

"Magic. You may be familiar with it."

"Smartass."

"You have paid compliment many a time to my ass, although I never thought of it as smart."

"Let's go in." I was just about bouncing on my toes.

He winked. "That was the plan."

I pushed past him and into the front hall, into the kitchen with the outdated stove and fridge and peeling linoleum flooring. The place was empty, but I didn't care. I inhaled the smell of musty apartment. Universe, I was here.

Gabriel peeked around the corner into my living room. "In here, Rachel."

I followed. Why was he acting so strange?

He walked up to the bay window and turned back to me, a slow smile across his face.

"What?"

"Come here."

"You're very demanding, sir." I took a closer look at the sexy, green-eyed smirk of his. "You're glowing. And even more devastatingly gorgeous than before. Why hadn't I noticed? Your new fae genes give you an unfair advantage."

"You have always glowed. And always had an advantage over me."

"I have?"

He nodded and his hands snaked behind me and into my hair, the handhold bringing me close against him. "Do you know, legend says two lovers touched by a unicorn's horn simultaneously are destined for one another?"

"I know. Once upon a time a lovely man told me so while we strolled in the Garden of Eden."

"Intelligent man, that one."

"I think so myself."

His lips were whispering close to mine. Damn tempting. I wanted him.

"I distinctly remember our unicorn touching us in unison," he murmured. "And now I can attest to the truth of the legend, because you are destined for me."

"Sure of yourself, are you?"

"Rachel, I love you. I need you in my life. And after too long of a maddening delay, I need to ask if you will marry me? I don't want to be simply a consort."

Oh! My chest tightened and my pulse started going wild. Why surprise, girl? You assumed it yourself. And you've wanted it for forever.

I closed the gap between our lips and answered with my words vibrating against his mouth. "If I agree to marry you, will you agree to marry me? I'd hate to put us on unequal footing at the start."

"I accept."

"Me too."

And then there was no more talk.

Instead, there was Gabriel pushing me against a wall. Hands pulling fabric off and away. Ripping. Teeth and tongue at my lips and throat. He pinched my nipples as I ran nails down his pecs. He repositioned his hands to dig fingers into my hips. We adjusted bodies, panted, moaned, and gritted past the fast and unrelenting arousal until finally Gabriel wrapped my legs around his hips. He bumped his silk point against my clit and I moaned. With a sharp inhale, he sunk into my wet.

We left behind romance for simple lust. He was alive. I was alive. We needed to be here having glorious, primitive sex.

So full in me. The wet sucking sound of the in and out penetration built the pleasure. "Faster," I ordered.

He grunted back and I raked nails down his back and dug into his ass. Tight and perfect.

Universe, he was perfect. This was perfect.

While deep inside me, his wings materialized and brushed my sides, the soft feathers rubbed against me again and again. The hairs of my arms raised to standing.

I tangled fingers in his hair, pulling, crying with the painful pleasure of him.

"Please!" I said. He backed us away from the wall, knowing my mind. His strength carried us as my legs tightened further around him. And in that moment, with space behind me, I let angel wings fold out from my back and wrapped them around his own. Weaving them. Together.

The end built. Almost there. Close. Yes.

He thrust into me, harder.

Deep. One last time. And then, he cried out. I joined him. Pushing over the edge. Such joy. Shaking with completion.

"I love you, sweet," Gabriel said, cheek pressed to mine as he let my legs fall and we tumbled into the seat of the bay window. We laughed. And kissed. Here together and surviving. Thank you, Universe.

In each other's arms and celebrating life, long moments passed before I felt it. Shaking. The earth rumbled into movement again. The screaming voices starting up in my head deafened me.

"HOME! HOME! HOME!" repeated endlessly with the screeching tones of the garden. *"HOME! HOME! HOME!"* it sang with some lovesick cackling chant.

"RACHEL, WE'VE CRASHED! EDEN'S COURT CRASHED!" Qest's voice yelled over the garden's din. *"FIND US!"*

The shaking stopped with a last jarring reverberation. Our moment shattered, we gathered clothes and ran to find   our   home,   whatever   remained   of   it.

Chapter Twenty-nine

So damn hot. How many times did I have to push the wet mess of my hair out of my eyes before it stayed? *Okay, Rachel, focus.* "Is everybody out of the complex?"

Even Morven looked wilted in the afternoon heat, her suit jacket off and long discarded. The dirt streaks on her blouse and face attested to the long hours she'd put in coping with the catastrophe of Eden falling from the sky. Still, she answered with her stock calm. "As far as we can tell, but if not, the vines and erupting roots and vegetation will tear the rest of Eden's Court down within the half-hour and the question will be moot."

"So fast." My worry tightened the last few muscles it had previously missed as I glanced around at the crowds of Eden's Court refugees milling through the garden around me. At least our magic got most of the basic needs met as we figured out what came next.

Morven wiped at one of her dirt smudges, seemingly offended by its presence. "Earth wanted all of its parts reunited and apparently believes the Kesayim's realms and their structures needed immediate assimilation."

"What about the messengers sent to find the Kyn realm?"

"Just returned. It fell in central China. It took longer to find because no Kyn were residing to report, so we could not reach anyone by spell or psychic sending as we did the rest."

At that, Qest appeared from whatever crisis he'd been managing among the thousands available for choice. "My people won't care. All they want is to be free in the world again. My guess is most are well on their way to finding new lairs. Their psychic output is a bit like listening to children hyped on sugar, babbling and bouncing around about their new toys."

"Well, at least someone's happy." Aside from the garden which still sang away in my head with ecstatic joy. My headache had settled in for a nice visit and Universe I wanted to sleep. But what else was new. "And we have all seven realms aside from Eden accounted for now. Shifters in Western Canada, L'Etrange in Brazil, angels in Scandinavia, vampires in India, fae in Ireland, and witches in Australia."

From around my neck where Artemis perched, I heard another small voice. "I am happy."

I reached to stroke her fur and she let out a little nip. "I know, girl." The curl of her fur steadied me, fingertips sliding over the soft texture. I tried to remember it was enough.

The merkaz acted as our base of operations as we coordinated our new reality, the magical barrier separating it from the rest of the garden disappearing with the rest of the court's destruction.

Tarn sat on the steps of the throne dais to our left, lounging back on the stone as if he had not a care in the world. For some reason, the garden let the throne remain. "Sit, Rachel. You've been non-stop since you found us. You look like you're going to drop. Time for a water break or Gabriel will eviscerate me when he returns."

"Then bring me water. I won't die from this heat." At least not yet. Of course it was hot, it was heading toward winter in the subtropical part of South Africa. Apparently, that's where Eden intended to assimilate with the mundane planet.

Standing, not lounging, to Tarn's side, Sebastian also sent me a disapproving look. "What do we do if officials from Johannesburg show up? The whole world must have noticed eight landmasses crashing down from the sky. Satellites, GPS and everything."

Tarn reached over and slapped the back of Seb's calf. "Idiot, she needs fewer worries, not more."

I sighed. "Tarn, drop the overprotective schtick. Sebastian, we deal with that situation when it comes. I have no clue, so we'll do what I've done for months now. Improvise."

Gwen jogged over to us and I was ready for a break to the bickering. Even bickering was too much in this heat. With no logical explanation, Gwen looked fresh and perky in the heat, wearing a bright blue miniskirt and emerald green crop top. "The last of my spell messages returned." She handed me a list. "These are the witch households available to house other Kesayim. Aubrey added his shifter households onto the end. The vampires also have a few hundred hidey holes set up worldwide from when they needed to spend time with Achras to feed."

I remembered Christian's dazed amazement earlier when he'd whispered to me the vampires no longer required blood to survive, a side effect of the genetic blending, even among the Kesayim with the delayed activation of the DNA integration. I'd take the little celebrations where I could.

Relieved of her list, Gwen sidled over to Qest and pecked him on the cheek in greeting. My brother blushed. "Okay, then we divide up the remainder we know need shelter and get them transportation to these addresses," he said.

Children's screams came from the distance. Not the desperate kind. The exuberant kind as kids ran each other into the ground in play. The ache skimmed over my heart for a beat before I tucked it away for later.

Leslie and Christian joined us from their job, coordinating the needs of our littlest refugees. They'd been indulging in their own bickering from the way Leslie glared at my middle brother. "Leslie, leave it," Christian called as she stormed up to me.

"We need to find them," she said.

I recognized the panic in her face. "There's nothing we can do," I said, already knowing what this was about. Nulls.

"We were kidnapped and bound, and even after being released, we cooperated with your plans. Forty have disappeared after being changed into something we have no clue how to handle. There's been eight deaths already among us as powers activated and tempers flared. You need to help find them."

Fear I'd tried to keep at bay woke screaming in my mind, louder than even the garden's voices. This same problem would happen multiplied by infinity worldwide in six months when the sleeper spell on the DNA disintegrated.

The lines on Leslie's face had grown since I first met her. She'd suffered enough. The solid tangle in my stomach expanded. Okay, a plan. I could do this. "I've had people scanning, but they could be anywhere on the planet by now. Once we get everyone a place to sleep, I can organize a..."

Morven cut me off. "No. Leslie, those people are on their own. It may not seem just and I understand your concern, but Rachel cannot save everyone. Her role in history is considerable for she has guaranteed history itself will continue. That is enough. What happens next is not her story to write."

What?

Leslie's scowl told me what she thought of Morven's words. "What about the children? Don't they deserve someone to fight for them? Whose job is that? Some of those missing people are parents. Are you going to tell their kids why their mothers and fathers are gone?"

Gone.

I found myself leaning back from her barrage. I needed...

Morven caught my arm. "Rachel, sit. You are trembling."

Why had I thought it was hot earlier? Maybe Sebastian could locate a few blankets.

I found myself on the dais with a pair of arms around me. Tarn's. He was shaking. Oh, that was me. A tiny tongue licked my face. Artemis. Morven squatted in my line of vision. Even then she looked blurry. "Gwen and others will handle the list and organize quartering the Kesayim."

She popped out of sight and I heard more of her stern, seneschal voice. "You have inherited the same powers as everyone else. Find them yourself. Organize. We all make choices, Leslie. Difficult ones based on what we decide matters. But in the end, many things matter. Judging another's heart and soul is not yours to do."

I heard Christian's murmuring reassurance. "Come, sweetheart, let's check on Anna. We have decisions to make." Then louder words by him. "Rachel, do what Morven says. We will be fine."

Then I was shuffled from one pair of arms to another. Familiar, too. Qest's. I smelled the fire of him. Maybe if he blew on me it would melt the ice cubes. He hugged me tight, but nothing was tight enough. We sat like that awhile until voices intruded.

"What in that unholy fool's head does he think he's doing?" Gwen said, her brogue deepening. It did that when she became annoyed.

The words didn't quite register.

"He's flying above the garden with Kemuel," Qest answered, the rumble of his voice vibrated my bones as my head lay against his chest.

Who?

"And they're singing together," Gwen said. "I'd almost believe the world has ended. Is that a dirty song? Yes, the world has ended. Kemuel is singing about diddling bar maids with Satan."

The description was enough to chip through the cold fog, and I looked up. Saw Satan and Kemuel. Their angel wings extended and gliding with a lazy, chaotic weave, singing at the top of their lungs with deep, beautiful vulgar vigor.

The song finished and they laughed together. A few moments later, they landed next to the throne and Satan threw his arm around Kemuel's shoulders in camaraderie. The two could be twins except for their opposite coloring. I'd thought that before, right?

"Announcement, ladies and gentlemen," the demon said. "I am having a button special made for Kemuel. It is to read, 'Congratulate Me! I Finally got the Stick Removed from my Ass."

Kemuel shoved away his newfound friend, but kept his smile. "The one I make for you will read, 'Caution! Maturity Under Construction.'

Satan laughed loud and shoved back at the angel. "He's almost got the hang of it, eh?" he asked. Turning, Satan took in our huddled group. "What faces. Such sour puss expressions. And you, Rachel, you look pathetic. This is a moment of celebration. You've saved the world and we are all gloriously alive and reborn into amazing power."

I shrunk at his broad, joyous smile. Why was he happy?

"I see," he said. "Saving the world is not enough. You wish to singlehandedly kiss every survivor on the planet, make them a meal, do their dishes, and sing them to sleep. Not sufficient for you, girl?"

I forced out words from behind the tight barrier in my throat. "No, Satan. But it's hard to rejoice when so many have died."

They were dead. Gone. No children.

The damn demon smiled broader. "What did that lovely Achra philosopher, say? Hoobs? No, Hobbes. Cheery fellow. He said that outside of society, the life of man was solitary, poor, nasty, brutish and short. Catchy, yes? Well, you've given humanity a fighting chance at society again. And at the least, a life a fraction less short. That's something. More than I'd have done for the lot of us. Take a vacation, love. A beach in Fiji. Many Mai Tai's. Go get laid. I'm sure Gabriel's around here somewhere to accommodate."

And with the magic that was my lover, my now fiancée, Gabriel appeared and took me from my brother's arms. He stood me up, and walked us over to Satan. Oh, good. I could still walk.

"Thank you," he told the leader of the demons. "You are correct. She has done enough and it is time she rests." He lifted Artemis and deposited her into Satan's hands, leaving the demon with a look of shock plastered across his face. After which Gabriel walked us out into the forest away from everyone.

We walked and walked. One foot placed. Then another. I lost myself in the repetition and the firm ground catching each footfall, the snake of impact up my calves, knees, thighs and hips. My body finally warmed. Gabriel had let go of me a bit into the journey, and every once in a while, I'd feel the brush of his side against mine. A limb knocking into my hip. Present.

We reached a clearing, with a small stream running down from the tangled vegetation-brimmed hillside sloping into the area. Red bursts of tiny blooms dotted the fallen tree trunks crossing the small banks of the gurgling water. Insects buzzed around the surface, tasting the moisture.

I walked to the largest of the fallen wood and sat, branches cracking and spongy wood giving way, but holding in the end. Gabriel sat next to me. I listened to the running stream, the splashes of tumbling movement, the snatches of smooth, bright color. Light breeze against my skin. Calm. Picturesque. Heartbreakingly lovely.

And then I cried. Sobbed. For a long, long time. Gabriel cried with me, he held onto me.

I fell asleep in his arms.

* * * * *

We were married beside the hardwood throne, under the full moon of our next chapter. My wedding gift from the garden was a new Japanese maple sapling in the exact spot of the original tree destroyed by the earthquake. Scents of night-blooming flowers, pungent herbs, and moist earth brought back memories of Gabriel and my first night together in the garden. Our first lovemaking. The place where I had feared his reaction to my necessary but reluctant sharing of my life story and of my longing for him. The place where I inhaled the chocolate and cherries of his scent as magic overtook our bodies. The place I learned that vulnerability was not a burden, but the greatest gift of all.

The memories brought a deep, needful longing and joy to my soul. Not only because Gabriel stood by my side, but because we shared this moment with the other people I loved most in this world. And shared not only their company, but the wedding ceremony itself. Standing beside us to be bound in marriage were Qest and Gwen, Christian and Leslie, Tarn and Sebastian.

I admit I thrilled the most at Tarn and Sebastian's marriage. They had fought harder and lost the most to make their way to this moment.

As Gabriel had suggested they join us in the ceremony, Tarn had shrugged his shoulders. "Why not? I will make an honest man of Seb. Plus, I believe he would agree to more sex if we wed. He's still a bit of a prude."

Sebastian had rolled his eyes. "The rumor of fae romanticism is overrated." But then his eyes grew thoughtful. "Delta would want us to."

"Yes, she would like that," Tarn said. They wandered off holding hands. They were recovering. Grief never ends, it just becomes slightly bearable.

Leslie had surprised me the most when Gabriel approached her about the wedding. She simply glanced over at Christian and said yes. He had closed his eyes, whispered a thank you to the universe, and delivered a gentle kiss to the bend of her wrist.

Gwen had laughed when asked to join us, whispered something into Qest's ear that made him blush again, pinched his ass, and agreed with vigor. Qest really had no choice in the matter.

The crowds had been sent to homes around the world for refuge if they had no place on mortal Earth of their own to stay. Sent by wing or by hoof or by dragon flight since portals were a thing of the past. As they also were the gateway to the aliens' home, I hoped there would be no more visits from Lillith and her ilk. A gal can dream.

We had few witnesses for the event. Jasper, his wife, and Peter. Stuart, Jasper's father and my mother's first consort. Sebastian's brother, Felix, sister-in-law, Cindy, and their son, Gregor. Morven, Jack, Artemis. Leslie's daughter, Anna. Gwen's brother, Raphael and his wife, Jaida.

We wanted small. We wanted only love in attendance. No more need for majestic display of ritual for the Mother Heir. She was history. The new world of magic left no one supreme in power over another. We were all to be fully human together.

When Darwin wrote The Descent of Man, he mentioned survival of the fittest just twice. He mentioned love ninety-five times. After having spent weeks trying to figure out how to manipulate our DNA and join our species, I knew that genes existed to help us connect, not set us apart, against or above one another.

I told Morven of the plan for the wedding, worried she'd insist on pomp and circumstance. Instead, she pulled me in for a hug and kissed my cheek. "Finally," she said.

"I couldn't have done this without you," I said to her. Telling Morven made everything more real, although I did not simply mean the wedding. "Where do I go now?"

"That is for you and Gabriel to decide. You have options."

"But without you?"

"I am away to my daughters' homes. It has been overdue. I miss being near them."

"Yes, children are important," I said, swallowing hard and trying not to choke.

"We will watch the events of the reborn world unfold, each from our place. That will be enough. And from time to time, you will visit me."

"Me, too," Jack added from his place at her heels. "You always forget me. What am I, chopped liver?"

Morven glanced down at her familiar and her eyes softened further. "Bring Artemis. Jack would like that."

"Damn right. I'll miss her. And she'll need more guidance from a seasoned familiar. Not anyone can do the job, you know."

I kneeled down and wrapped Jack in my arms. "Thank you for finding me and bringing me home. You will always be the first in my heart."

"Don't let Gabriel hear you, Rache. I like my balls where they are, thank you very much." Gotta love a poodle with priorities. I kissed him and got a face full of wet dog tongue in return.

I stood. Morven pushed aside the most recent stray hairs falling into my eyes, grunted in satisfaction and kissed the tip of my nose this time. "I love you, child."

"I love you, too." If she kept this up, I'd end up drowning myself before the wedding.

"Go get ready," she commanded.

So I did.

* * * * *

It was Rafael who agreed to officiate. That's where Gabriel had gone earlier, to recruit him for the task. It turns out not only was Rafe a Justice of the Peace, but a shaman as well. Being alive so long enables one to collect a lot of interesting credentials.

The Kesayim didn't have a central religious authority, and there was no particular government to sanction our marriages. Like everything else about our new existence, this was virgin territory. Create as you go along. Write your own adventure.

Wedding finery was out. I had on the same jeans and tee I'd worn all day. I figured if they were good enough for saving the world, they were good enough for a wedding.

We stood barefoot on the ground. The full moon officiated along with Rafael, glowing bright and vivid with her generous curves low in the sky. So low and large that with one hop you could jump into her lap. Her light softened the meadow before the throne and painted everyone and everything with a silver glimmer and with peace.

No bouquets or adornments for the lot of us, or so I thought. We stood in a semi-circle ready to begin when the garden decided to participate. With a hissing sigh, vines rose from the earth and into the air, arching over our heads, weaving together into a layered canopy. Flowers of riotous colors budded open into full bloom along the vines. Reds, oranges, blues, yellows, purples. A rainbow. A promise. Deep fragrance erupted out of their petals. *"Merry, merry, love, love,"* the garden sang as the canopy grew to cover us under the night sky.

"Is this typical?" Leslie asked.

"Nothing is typical," I said.

After the vines grew still and solid in form, Rafael stepped to the front of us.

Gabriel took my hand and the garden sent one last jolt of magic, a single thin vine snaking up and twining our wrists together with a heart-shaped knot, tiny thorns at the places our skin touched. Loose enough not to prick. For now. The other couples, I noticed, received similar treatment. Apparently, the garden lived on romanticism. Or sadism.

Rafe chuckled, the colors of the peacock tattoo adorning the side of his face muted in the moonlight, and waited one last moment for any additions by the garden. He finally began to speak.

"Nelson Mandela once said that the greatest glory in living lies not in never falling, but in rising every time we fall. Today, you come together and commit to sharing your lives. You rise after the world has stumbled to confirm that love is the greatest of forces even in the face of pain and destruction and loss. You rise to choose a path together."

He paused and nodded at us to proceed.

Gabriel took a step into me and we rested our free hands on the other's upper arm to stand even closer. Almost an embrace.

As each couple did the same, Raphael twisted a golden knot spell in the air before him, the loops and twirls intricate and swooping. The sparkling motes of air absorbed the soft light of our moon and Rafe's last sharp movement released the spell into the night.

The motes leapt off the knots and flew to the places we stood. As they settled against my skin, with tingling hot-cold frissons, I repeated the words I'd practiced earlier. "I will marry you, I will love you, and we will journey. For all of time and through all pain and joy. You are my beloved and I am yours."

Gabriel smiled and repeated the same, his smoke and cinnamon voice making my blood leap in ecstatic welcome. "I will marry you, I will love you, and we will journey. For all of time and through all pain and joy. You are my beloved and I am yours."

As he finished, the motes of the spell constricted down my skin to one small area over my breastbone, and bore into the place directly over my heart.

Later, when we were alone we'd look for the tattoos that would appear in the same place over each of our hearts, visible only to one another, the design unique to us. No rings. We didn't need to prove our connection with each other to the world. The tattoos were to remind one another of our joining. That's who mattered.

In that moment, the vine around our wrists tightened and the thorns pressed into our skin, drawing blood. The red welled at the joined points, the same for Gabriel, and our blood mingled.

I looked down to see the ghostly chain running out from underneath our breastbones, attaching us together since the first moment we met, solidify for a brief second into true matter before fading back into transparency. I had imagined that the chain had formed at our months-ago introduction in the garden, but now I did not believe that.

The poet Rumi got it right. Lovers don't finally meet somewhere. They are in each other all along. Gabriel had been born inside of me and me inside him.

Before us, Rafael smiled. I blinked, because standing next to him watching our ceremony was my unicorn. All pale sea foam and pearl opalescent horn tipped with black. Gliding grace. She had come to witness our marriage.

The vine at our wrists released us and slithered back into the earth. I stood frozen as the unicorn moved toward me. I barely breathed. No one spoke, captive to her presence. She was raw magic.

Standing feet from me, she stopped and whickered a soft greeting. So, so carefully I reached out a hand and rested it on the bridge of her nose. A moment only, then removing it and rubbing the tips of my fingers together to memorize the feel.

She lowered her horn with a smooth dip and let it touch my abdomen. Sparks rippled through my body and I swayed as Gabriel grabbed me to hold me steady.

The unicorn raised her head and her eyes rested on mine. *"A new beginning,"* she whispered into my mind, caressing where the sound lingered.

Then, she turned and ambled out of the meadow into the forest. Gone.

With my gaze lingering after her, Gabriel's lips touched my cheek and I turned into him, joining the kiss. Beginning our lives together. A comedy, not a tragedy after all.

* * * * *

A month and a day, Gwen had promised, and here we were. The dinner dishes had been cleared and the group of us lingered in Rafael's living room in front of a fire, embers popping and sizzling as they escaped up the chimney.

Gwen and Qest, Tarn and Seb, me and Gabriel. Artemis was curled up asleep by the fire. Jaida was helping Rafael with clean-up in the kitchen.

Tarn lounged back in Sebastian's arms, feet up on the sofa, quietly strumming the mandolin, practicing notes and singing under his breath as he devotedly set to learning the instrument. Keeping a piece of Delta in their lives. Sebastian hummed along to the melody, eyes closed and relaxing in the moment.

Qest and Gwen focused on the chess board before them and Gwen laughed as she knocked another of Qest's pieces off the board.

"That is unfair," my brother said.

"You can enact revenge later in bed," she answered.

No blush from Qest this time. Apparently, he'd grown used to his new wife. "Well, that goes without saying, Gwen. Less foreplay and more game please, dear."

Gwen was good for his spirit. I swallowed back my laugh of pleasure. It would only distract Qest from his next move and I silently rooted for his victory.

A slippery surge of energy gurgled up inside me and I saw the ghostly image of a little chestnut haired boy with Qest's emerald green eyes dance over the couple. This was the same image Gwen and her witches had conjured in prediction months back as they tried to magic the answer to their fertility problem. At the time, Gwen insisted this was the image of my and Colin's son. Now, with all of humanity's genetics anyone's guess, the emerald eyes and coloring seemed to reflect her own future with my brother.

I opened my mouth to say something, until Gabriel laid a hand on my shoulder. "Let it be," he whispered. The man always knew.

Okay, Rachel. Stop with the interference. They'll find out soon enough.

My own hand dropped to my flat belly and once again, I imagined a stirring. The tiny, nothing of a movement heightened each nerve in my body. Maybe.

From in front of the fire Artemis yawned and stretched her paws, and in the sudden surge of puppy exuberance, bounded over to me. She jumped in my lap and started her never-ending ritual of rubbing her face in my own. You'd think she was a cat. Sometimes, I almost heard a purr as she greeted me in her excitement.

"Soon I have littermate to play with me," she said. "Nice strong girl. Growing in your belly." Her paw petted my cheek. "Good mother."

Gabriel sucked in a shocked noise. "Rachel?"

I shrugged my shoulders. "Maybe."

He grinned.

In life, we lose some things and we gain others. Hope. A new beginning. Never what we expected, but perhaps that's as it should be.

Gabriel rested his strong, lean fingers over my own atop my abdomen.

It was enough. More than enough.

"And every day, the world will drag you by the hand, yelling. 'This is important! And this is important! And this is important! You need to worry about this! And this! And this!' And each day, it's up to you to yank your hand back, put it on your heart and say, 'No. This is what's important.'" ~ Iain Thomas

THE END

About the author

Ever since she was a young girl and her fifth grade teacher read the class Peter S. Beagle's novel THE LAST UNICORN, Michelle has been fascinated with all things magical, mysterious and otherworldly. She wrote her first tragic fantasy novella in middle school, recruiting art-minded friends to draw pictures of the fantastical universes she created.

After taking the road frequently traveled (not quite as romantic as the less traveled variety) and getting a BA in political science and a Masters in social work, she settled in New England. Along the way she started a family, as well as a collection of cats.

Finally, Michelle grabbed the proverbial bull by its spiky protrustions and pursued her passion. She now writes fantasy, urban fantasy, and admits to a fascination with gateways and portals, which seem to crop up in any story she writes.

She can be contacted at michellepicardwrites@gmail.com or through her website at www.michellepicard.com.

www.ingramcontent.com/pod-product-compliance
Lightning Source LLC
Chambersburg PA
CBHW071002280626
47160CB00014B/10